WHERE
HOPE
PREVAILS

Books by Janette Oke

Return to Harmony★ • Another Homecoming★
Tomorrow's Dream★ • Dana's Valley★★

RETURN TO THE CANADIAN WEST★★
Where Courage Calls •Where Trust Lies •Where Hope Prevails

ACTS OF FAITH★
The Centurion's Wife • The Hidden Flame • The Damascus Way

CANADIAN WEST
When Calls the Heart • When Comes the Spring
When Breaks the Dawn •When Hope Springs New
Beyond the Gathering Storm
When Tomorrow Comes

LOVE COMES SOFTLY
Love Comes Softly • Love's Enduring Promise
Love's Long Journey • Love's Abiding Joy
Love's Unending Legacy • Love's Unfolding Dream
Love Takes Wing • Love Finds a Home

A PRAIRIE LEGACY
The Tender Years •A Searching Heart
A Quiet Strength • Like Gold Refined

SEASONS OF THE HEART
Once Upon a Summer • The Winds of Autumn
Winter Is Not Forever • Spring's Gentle Promise

SONG OF ACADIA★
The Meeting Place • The Sacred Shore • The Birthright
The Distant Beacon • The Beloved Land

WOMEN OF THE WEST
The Calling of Emily Evans • Julia's Last Hope
Roses for Mama • A Woman Named Damaris
They Called Her Mrs. Doc • The Measure of a Heart
A Bride for Donnigan • Heart of the Wilderness
Too Long a Stranger • The Bluebird and the Sparrow
A Gown of Spanish Lace • Drums of Change

Also look for *Janette Oke: A Heart for the Prairie* by Laurel Oke Logan

★with Davis Bunn   ★★with Laurel Oke Logan

RETURN *to the* CANADIAN WEST • BOOK 3

WHERE
HOPE
PREVAILS

JANETTE OKE
LAUREL OKE LOGAN

BETHANYHOUSE

a division of Baker Publishing Group
Minneapolis, Minnesota

© 2016 by Janette Oke and Laurel Oke Logan

Published by Bethany House Publishers
11400 Hampshire Avenue South
Bloomington, Minnesota 55438
www.bethanyhouse.com

Bethany House Publishers is a division of
Baker Publishing Group, Grand Rapids, Michigan

Printed in the United States of America

Library of Congress Cataloging-in-Publication Data

Names: Oke, Janette, author. | Logan, Laurel Oke, author.
Title: Where hope prevails / Janette Oke, Laurel Oke Logan.
Description: Minneapolis, Minnesota : Bethany House, a division of Baker Publishing Group, [2016] | Series: Return to the Canadian West ; book 3
Identifiers: LCCN 2016004388| ISBN 9780764217838 (cloth : alk. paper) | ISBN 9780764217685 (pbk.) | ISBN 9780764217845 (large-print pbk.)
Subjects: LCSH: Women pioneers--Fiction. | Canada, Western--Fiction. | GSAFD: Love stories. | Western stories. | Christian fiction.
Classification: LCC PR9199.3.O38 W543 2016 | DDC 813/.54--dc23
LC record available at http://lccn.loc.gov/2016004388

Scripture quotations are from the King James Version of the Bible.

Cover design by Dan Thornberg, Design Source Creative Services

16 17 18 19 20 21 22   7 6 5 4 3 2 1

List of Characters

The Thatcher Family

Beth—Elizabeth Thatcher
Mother—Priscilla Thatcher
Father—William Thatcher
Julie—Beth's younger sister
Margret, John, and JW Bryce—Beth's older, married sister and family

Others

Jarrick "Jack" Thornton—a Mountie and Beth's suitor
Molly McFarland Russo—owner of the boarding house
Frank Russo—retired miner who married Molly in *Where Trust Lies*
Teddy Boy and Marnie—orphaned teenagers adopted by Molly
Philip Davidson—pastor and longtime friend of Jarrick
Robert Harris Hughes—new schoolteacher

Prologue

Dearest Molly,

Today I purchased my ticket for the long train ride from Toronto, across the miles of open prairie, to Lethbridge, and then I'll endure once more the long hours by automobile to your welcome village—my heart's second home. I'm not afraid of the journey this time, I'm pleased to tell you. So much has changed in me since that original teaching assignment. The rather frail and inexperienced Elizabeth Thatcher who arrived over a year ago in Coal Valley is now a different woman altogether. I feel I've proven myself somewhat, and grown more courageous. At least, I do hope so.

Can it truly be only a long summer since I said good-bye to you, my students, and all my friends in Coal Valley? I find myself pacing the carpeted halls of Father's grand house with impatience, yearning instead for my simple life with all of you. I can almost hear your hearty laughter at me as you read such a thought. But you of all people know what I mean, Molly, since you have your own deep roots in our beautiful valley.

This time, though, I realize more fully how much I will miss my parents and my beloved sisters. Julie has begged Father time and again to join me for more than a visit, but so far he and Mother have not given in to her pleadings. She's still impetuous and strong-willed, as you know from meeting her, but we love her dearly for all her passions. Margret accepts the inevitability of my departure with solemn resignation. She and John will soon have their hands full with their second child. If only I could scoop up my little nephew, JW, and fit him in a suitcase! Nevertheless, I'm filled with joy at the thought of returning after this time away—and of seeing you, my dear friend, so much like a second mother to me. I feel I do not lack family there with you.

Molly, I know you've already heard reports that we had some very difficult days during the last part of the summer, when our lovely cruise came to a sudden and dreadful end. I so wished to talk with you during the awful time when we didn't know where our darling Julie was. You probably have not heard, though, that Nick, the young man who instigated her kidnapping, was someone we thought to be a friend. It was all carried out with the aid of two young women on board that Julie befriended. They seemed trustworthy enough. (I can feel my hand tremble as I write.) Our suffering during the days of Julie's disappearance was nearly unbearable. I must admit that my own faith was shaken. I'm not altogether proud of my responses, but I believe I've grown. Thank the good Lord she was found safe!

I have room only to mention how grateful I was to see Edward Montclair and Jack Thornton, our stalwart Mounties, coming swiftly to our aid. I'm full of thanksgiving to the Lord for the wisdom He gave them in discovering where Julie had been taken. Their services turned the tide, indeed.

Though I feel propriety requires I keep my comments here brief, no doubt you've long suspected my growing affinity for Jack. (Yes, I still address him in person by his given name, Jarrick—though perhaps his mother and I are the only ones who do!) How can I express the comfort I've gained from having his strong, protective presence during our crisis?

Sadly, I suppose we must remind ourselves there is danger everywhere—I haven't forgotten that it appeared even in Coal Valley with Davie Grant and his bootlegging crimes, touching many of my students, children whom I dearly love—even your Marnie and Teddy Boy. Thank the Lord again they are safe in your care, Molly. Oh yes! And now in Frank's also. I look forward to congratulating you both on your recent marriage. You and Frank, eloping at your age—like a pair of teenagers! I can't wait to share more with you when I arrive, on or about the 15th of the month.

Your devoted friend,
Beth

Chapter 1

It wasn't just that there were far fewer potholes—the road through the thick woods leading to Coal Valley had clearly been graded in Beth's absence over the summer—but something else seemed strange. The trip still was taking hours as the taxi driver headed west into the foothills and gradually up into the magnificent Rocky Mountains. And every turn in the road meant civilization with its conveniences was left farther behind—no telephones, no doctors, no plumbing or electricity.

But Beth felt no hesitation at the thought of coming back to Coal Valley. She could already picture Miss Molly standing on the porch of her large boarding house, weathered gray over the years but homey and inviting. Ample home-cooked meals, long conversations in the evenings after the dishes were done, and then up to the cozy room with a thick quilt to burrow under against the cold. Anticipation drew Beth forward, willing away the miles.

Still, there was something slightly puzzling this time as she looked out at the rugged scenery. Beth was hard-pressed to understand a small tingle of apprehension casting a shadow over her excitement at returning to western Canada.

She strained forward to grasp the back of the driver's seat and tentatively asked, "Excuse me, sir, I hate to suggest it, but are you certain this is the right road to Coal Valley?"

A snort. "Yes, miss. I been here plenty'a times. Couple more miles, we're there."

Beth fell back against the hard seat, pushed her hat more tightly against her dark hair, and adjusted the long hatpin holding it in place. She hoped she wouldn't seem too bedraggled by the time she arrived. *Will anyone be there to meet me? Miss Molly surely—no, she's Mrs. Russo now. And her Frank? Or Teddy and Marnie, the other schoolchildren, their mothers? I want to see everyone.*

Brushing at wrinkles in her skirt and adjusting her jacket, Beth scanned the shear mountain faces far above the tree line and the valley below with its meandering river. But neither offered signs of familiarity. The train track, ever present and steadily climbing higher with them, was the only recognizable feature in the scene. *Has it been so long that I don't remember the way any better than this?*

The journey from Toronto to the little mining village clinging to an eastern range of the Rockies had been anything but restful. Beth had grown rather accustomed to the difficulties of train travel—at least she now knew what to anticipate. So it was odd at journey's end, just as she expected to feel most connected to her western home, that she would feel such a sense of being lost.

And then as she stared through the dusty window, she noticed the trees . . . *they don't come right up to the road as I remember.* Beth cranked the window down partway and peered at the roadside scene flying by. Sure enough, she could make out telltale stumps scattered down in the ditch, their circular tops still creamy yellow after the recent amputation of everything above.

She leaned forward again. "Why have so many trees been cut down?"

"Eh?"

"The trees—so many are cleared away."

"They're gettin' ready to widen the road and gravel it." The man chuckled. "Your little town's growin' gangbusters, miss. Plenty'a change since you was here last, I guess."

Beth nodded and frowned. *Not too much, I hope!* she thought as she rolled the window up against the dust.

Already there'd been more than enough frustration and tumult during the last weeks of her summer. Back in Toronto after their cruise through the Maritimes was cut short by Julie's disappearance, Beth couldn't help but hope she might be able to share this trip west with Jarrick. *Jarrick.* Even thinking his name drew a secret smile and made Beth's face flush.

Her whole family had effectively fallen in love with him during his short stay with them— even Mother. He had been proudly introduced to their various social circles, paraded out at every opportunity in his bright red Mountie jacket. The flashing smile, copper-colored hair, and tidy mustache—along with those bright blue eyes and quick wit—won him wide approval. And it was more thrilling than Beth could have imagined standing next to him as he towered above her. She allowed herself a hand tucked through his arm and tried not to blush with joy that they were accepted by all as "a courting couple."

Only Mrs. Montclair could break the spell, overtly comparing him to Edward and mourning her son's recent departure. *"Well, he was needed in the West again, that's all. There just aren't many officers who can fill my Edward's shoes. They'd be lost without him."*

Jarrick had merely smiled at the woman, with a discreet wink down at Beth.

And then came the news that *"Miss Thatcher should postpone her return—the School Board is working through some issues regarding Coal Valley's current situation. We look forward to her return . . ."* etc. Beth tried not to imagine what the delay could mean, but it was clear that Jarrick would not be able to wait longer for her deferred departure. They had said a tearful good-bye, and she remained in Toronto without him.

Three more weeks passed before everything was finally in place for Beth to set out alone. She spent the journey west reading and looking forward to Jarrick meeting her train. However, almost as soon as they had been reunited on the weathered platform of the Lethbridge train station, he had received a handwritten message of an important assignment requiring his hasty departure. It was such a disappointment to them both, especially when they had anticipated a couple of days in the city at the home of friends before Beth continued out to Coal Valley.

She squinted away tears, thinking again about that long-awaited promised dinner—at their own special Lethbridge restaurant—postponed once again. *Life certainly has a way of stealing away precious moments—or at least undermining our plans for them! The very occasion when I was certain Jarrick would propose* . . . "Thank You, Father," she prayed against her frustrations, "that You always understand how I feel and are with me, even when I can't see Your purposes." She prayed for Jarrick too—sure that his disappointment with how things had turned out matched hers.

The car rolled around another curve too quickly for Beth's comfort. Her short legs made it difficult to keep her feet planted firmly on the floor. Instead she braced an arm against the door, forcing into silence the complaint she would like to have muttered aloud.

Suddenly a familiar bend in the road and then a path into the woods pulled her focus to the window. *We're close!* she exulted silently. *We're almost there!* The trees thinned quickly, and her small town came into view. *Coal Valley—finally.*

Beth hovered in the shelter of the taxi's open door while the driver unloaded her trunks and bags onto the short wooden sidewalk. *Where am I?* She didn't dare speak the thought aloud, but it was hard to believe this was Coal Valley! Beth's gaze moved first to a coat of bright white paint on the two broad walls to her left. The mining company hadn't bothered in the past to dress up its quickly constructed buildings. Now green trim boards traced the front doors and large windows. Even the company name had been spelled out in bold black letters across the front—as if they owned the town itself. Beth wondered to herself if perhaps, in a way, they did.

On the opposite side of the street, overgrown bushes had been pruned back and flowers planted along the path to what had been the Grants' saloon—and not so long ago, Beth's schoolhouse. The former establishment's sign had been replaced, and Beth smiled at *Abigail's Teahouse* in scrolling blue letters.

Good for you, Abigail. You've done it—begun your own business. Beth thought back to the welcome she'd received there a year before. The mothers, most newly widowed, had met in that very building to explain their offer of the teaching position. Clearly they were half expecting Beth to turn tail and run at the very notion of holding school in a pool hall. Yet somehow they had won her heart and her confidence that day. Abigail Stanton had been a strong leader among the women, a source of courage and comfort for them all.

The community garden next to the tea shop was lush with produce, filling what had been a vacant lot. *Perhaps this winter won't be as difficult as the last, with plenty of food for canning.* And next . . . next was Molly's large boarding house. *Home,* Beth breathed in relief. *At least that hasn't changed.*

But then she noticed more stumps. They seemed to spring up everywhere—all around. Just past each of the familiar buildings they were lurking, ugly and dead. The forest had been driven back farther from the town's tiny core. Her smile faded.

"Miss Thatcher! Miss Thatcher!"

Beth turned toward an avalanche of children tumbling from the company meeting hall. "Miss Thatcher, you're back. We missed ya so much."

Fourteen-year-old Marnie, almost a younger sister to Beth, was the first to reach her with a warm embrace. "Felt like you'd never get here."

The girl's slim form and narrow face seemed somehow more mature than Beth's memory of her. Her long brown hair was drawn back with bobby pins. *Why, she's not a child anymore, much more poised.* "Darling, I've missed you too."

Beth was passed from hug to hug, only vaguely aware that a crowd was gathering quickly. Neighbors hurried to join them from every direction as Beth reached for the shoulder or cheek of her students, smiling into each set of bright eyes.

"Oh my, you've all grown so much! What did you do all summer that added so many inches?" They laughed with her, calling over each other with their comments and questions.

"What did you do while you were gone, Miss Thatcher?"

"Miss Thatcher, we missed you."

"Summer's so long without you."

"It seemed like school would never get started!"

Beth laughed again. "Well, isn't that just the nicest compliment any teacher could hear!"

"We're awful glad yer back, anyhow."

Small Anna Kate blurted out, "We got a new schoolroom, Miss Thatcher."

"Really? Where . . . ?" But Beth was offered no further information with all the commotion.

"We got more kids too," Levi said, tugging at the shirt of another boy, dragging him closer. "This is Mikey. He's my new friend."

"Pleased to meet you, Michael." Beth looked around her and noticed several other children standing farther away whom she didn't recognize. "I'm so pleased to meet all of you," she said with a wave and smile.

"I'm sure we'll get to know one another very soon."

Anna Kate was pulling on her arm. "Come see our new classroom. The company gived us their building fer a school. 'Cause they builded a new one down at the river. Come see, Miss Thatcher."

Breathlessly, Beth followed the excited group toward the meeting hall, where they had already shared so many times for club meetings, school performances, and church. *A proper classroom this year! It doesn't sound much like the mine company I know. I'll have to make a point of thanking Mr. Gowan.*

Catching sight of Molly waiting at the fringe of the crowd, Beth almost ran toward her. The woman's plump arms spread wide, a smile crinkling the softened skin around her eyes. Her thinning hair had collected even more gray threads among the dark strands, but the faded and mended housedress was surely the same. Beth leaned into the embrace. *I should have thought to bring fabric for a new dress or two. I'll get some from Lethbridge for her the next time I'm there.*

"Welcome home, dearie." Molly patted her back affectionately. "Awful good ta see ya."

Pushing back and cocking her head, Beth said around a smile, "So good to see you too— *Mrs. Russo!*"

"Heaven help us, but we done it. We truly did."

"Molly, I'm so pleased for you both—for you and our dear Frank."

"Well, there's time enough fer all that later. If ya don't follow the small ones quick to see their surprise, I think they might just pick ya up and carry ya in."

Beth laughed, slipping an arm through Molly's and following the crowd into the wooden building. Inside were even more neighbors, along with simple paper decorations and a table spread with cookies and punch.

"Oh my," Beth whispered. "This is so lovely. You must have been the one to spread the news about when I would be back, but you all shouldn't have gone to all this work—"

"'Course we should." Molly leaned her head against Beth's. "We're terrible glad yer back with us, Beth. You're likely too tired from yer travels to enjoy a crowd much, though."

"Not too tired for *this*. I've been waiting for this moment for a long time."

Beth made the rounds, talking with the children and their mothers. She knew, as before, that the men—those who had gradually replaced the victims of the mine explosion—would be hard at work in the nearby mine. The familiar rhythmic throbbing of machinery near at hand felt rather comforting to Beth. It meant industry, work, and profit. It meant the needs of families being met.

But Frank Russo had long ago retired from the mine, though his missing right hand served as a constant reminder of all he had given the company—old Frank who had up and married Miss Molly during the summer. As Beth greeted those who pressed in around her, she watched for his familiar face. At last she spied him in a corner of the room. *How like Frank to wait quietly in the background until he's noticed.* Beth hurried over to settle her arms around his shoulders.

"Welcome'a back, Miss Beth."

"Oh, Frank, it's been so long. And seeing you is like coming home to my favorite uncle—my favorite *Italian* uncle."

He laughed, his barrel chest shaking as he drew Beth in again for a second hug. "You are'a too kind, Miss Beth. But we know I'm more like'a your *Grandpa* Frank."

"Any man spry enough to elope can't hold any claims on being *old.*"

His whiskered face spread into a wide grin as he winked. "My Mollina and I, we make'a each other happy, eh?"

"I'm sure you do. And I was so pleased to hear about it." Beth planted a light kiss on the stubbly cheek.

"Miss Thatcher, will you come with me?" Ruth Murphy tapped her on the shoulder, looking apologetic. "We're ready to bless the food—and we don't want to start without our guest of honor."

"Of course." Beth patted Frank's arm and turned to follow.

During the festivities, Beth was introduced to five new families who had joined the community. She heard about the row of new company houses that had been added, now accommodating even some of the single men who had spent the previous winter in a camp of makeshift shelters.

As Beth became acquainted with the newest additions to her little school, she wondered how she could possibly manage so many students. Five new families represented twelve new schoolchildren, she quickly calculated, ranging in age from six to fifteen.

But a number of families had also moved on. With their men the victims of the mine explosion, these widows had been forced to find livelihood elsewhere. Even more than a year after the fact, the terrible accident was still exerting its brutal impact on the community.

Seated on a wooden bench at last, Molly at her side, Beth's eyes swept the room. There was so much she wanted to discuss with her dear friend. "You've all been awfully busy getting this party together. It's such a lovely gift." She looked around the room. "But where's Frances?"

A sigh. "Oh, didn't ya hear about that? She's moved away too—ta be with her relatives in Vancouver. Weren't nothing for her here, now that she's a widow an' a grievin' mother both. But I sure am gonna miss her."

"I'm so sorry, Molly. She was your best friend."

"She was and is. But life's full'a hard choices. Family's gotta come first." She paused thoughtfully. "And maybe I'll just take the train out there fer a visit someday. Now, wouldn't that be an adventure?"

"It would be magnificent, I'm sure, Molly— but maybe a little scary too." Beth was imagining the rows of mountain ranges the tracks would cross between here and the western coast.

"Well, there's a whole lot more travelin' done now than years back when Bertram— God rest his soul—and me first come to these parts. People in and out'a here all the time now, and the road's only gettin' better. Wish ya could'a met the new man today. But he's already gone back out this week to see his fiancée. So many folks comin' an' goin'. I can't keep up."

"I'm sorry, who?"

"The new teacher."

Beth spun to fully face Molly. "The new what?"

Molly's lips puckered, and her forehead drew together in a frown. "Oh, ya didn't know?" She hurried on, reaching for Beth's hand. "Was sure you'd heard that bit. Don't fret. It's good news, dearie. The school board come, had a long look at our town, made a list of kids we got now, and decided it'll take *two* teachers to educate 'em all. So you'll only have ta teach *half* of 'em this year. And even that's plenty." She squeezed Beth's hand, giving her a comforting smile.

Unspoken questions tumbled around in Beth's mind. *Where will he . . . ? What will I . . . ? Which of my children . . . ?* It was too difficult to comprehend.

"The dividin' up ain't been done yet," Molly continued. "'Course, no decision on that till the both of ya are present. But I s'pose most is of the mind he'd take the older and you'd have the younger—a gentler, motherin' touch."

Beth's thoughts flew instantly to Teddy and his best friend, Addison, to Luela and James, Peter and Bonnie. She had expected to spend much of her time and focus preparing these older students for their end-of-year exams.

She had been looking forward to watching them graduate with so many more opportunities beyond the coal mine. *Just how many of my students is this new teacher taking?* Beth concealed a shudder by setting her coffee cup down. "Who is this man? What do you know about him?"

"We're lucky to have him," Molly answered, still holding Beth's hand. "Mr. Robert Harris Hughes he's called—two last names, if ya can imagine." But her chuckle sounded a bit forced. "He's real educated—from the East, like yerself."

"You've all met him?"

"Sure. Was here most'a last week. He stayed at my place."

"And where is he now?"

"Back in Calgary—went to visit his fiancée. 'Peers she don't care much ta come out so far. Then again, they ain't married yet either. So there's no point anyhow."

Beth processed the patchy information aloud. "He's engaged to a woman who doesn't live in the area—doesn't even want to visit. He's wealthy—and educated in the East. Then whatever would induce him to come *way out here?*"

Molly smiled wryly and snorted. "Well, dearie, *you did.*"

Chapter
2

By the time her welcome-home festivities
were concluding and people were drifting away, Beth was more than ready to head
over to Molly's in order to wash up and take
a nap.

Marnie approached with a warm smile.
"I come ta show you to yer place. Ya ready?"

"I surely am. Do you know where my luggage has gone?"

Marnie, who was already heading toward
the exit, called back confidently, "The boys
took everything over for ya."

Abigail hurried over from a final table she
had wiped clean, a gentle smile on her face.
"I'm so glad we'll be sharing space this year,
Miss Beth," she said. "We've cleaned and
scrubbed to get everything all ready. I hope
you'll like it."

Beth was caught off guard by the unexpected words. "I'm afraid I don't understand. Are you staying with Molly now too?"

"No. Oh, dear, I'm sorry." Abigail faltered, glancing around the nearly empty room and back to Beth. Her brown eyes searched Beth's face. "Well, I . . . I guess nobody told ya then. I know Molly meant to. S'pose she got too busy with catchin' up. It's just that her boarding house is so full up now—all those company men comin' and goin'—the family don't even eat in the dining room no more, just in the kitchen, where there's room. An' that Mr. Harris Hughes, he needed a room too. So we all put our heads together to figure out a way to give ya a home. Molly was sure you'd rather have yer own place . . . now that yer soon to be wed." Abigail, uncertain now, rubbed a hand across the back of her neck. "I'm surprised she didn't speak with ya about it. I hate to be the one . . ."

Beth forced away her disappointment, battling to conceal a tumult of thoughts. *Whoever said I was soon to be married? Why should that rumor put me out on my own? So the new teacher's even going to claim my room at Molly's! This is too much! I wish she'd asked me. I think I'd have slept in the bathtub if I could have just stayed there with them....* But Beth was also fully aware that there was no way they could have communicated these decisions efficiently over such a distance. She could only weather the storm and make the best of what had already been decided without her knowledge or participation.

Studying Beth's expression, Abigail hesitated again, finally clearing her throat. Her words came tenderly. "I'm so sorry no one told ya, Miss Beth. I'm sure this comes as a big surprise to ya." She forced a smile. "Guess it's the day fer those—fer surprises—the good ones and the troublin'." She glanced around the room again. "I don't see Molly no more. Do you wanna go find her now? She's likely already gone home—busy getting supper on the table for her boarders, I suppose. But I'll go with ya if you like. I don't know what's to be done. . . ."

"It's fine, Abigail." Beth reached out for a reassuring touch on the other woman's arm. "If you all feel you've found a good situation for me, I'm confident it'll work out fine. However, I admit I *am*—well, surprised. That's all. I just didn't expect that where I roomed would be in question."

"Would you like to come see for yerself, then?"

"Yes, of course. Thank you."

Marnie hurried out the door, a step or two ahead of Abigail and Beth. But the girl didn't turn to the left, as Beth presumed, toward Abigail's small home in the tidy row of company-housing duplicates. She was moving directly across the street.

Beth refused to betray her questions this time, forcing her facial muscles to hold a smile so they wouldn't reveal further objections. *Where are we going? Am I to stay in the teahouse? Is it possible that Abigail lives there now—saving money that way? Is there enough room to share? I don't remember anything off the main room but a small kitchen and a storage room.*

Taking a shortcut with a hop over the flowerbed, Marnie continued past the main door and rushed around the far end of the building. Beth could hear her footsteps skipping up the outdoor stairs.

Suddenly Beth couldn't breathe. *Not there! Anywhere but there!* The Grants' second-floor residence was the only place in Coal Valley Beth never wanted to set foot. Having had no cause to venture near, she managed to avoid the unpleasant couple who had lived above the school—who had owned the building in which she had taught the previous year.

The Grants were gone now from Coal Valley, but Beth's fears about them were unchanged. Merely the sound of Marnie's footsteps on their stairway had stirred memories of Davie's cruel threats and attempted attack,

of Helen's scowling demeanor, of the husband's eventual arrest and his wife's attempted
suicide. Beth could not at this moment recall
if she'd been told where that last incident had
occurred—here in Coal Valley or elsewhere.
The reality was she hadn't wanted to know
any details. Now her mind conjured up an
image of the despairing woman's blood on
the floor. . . . *Surely, surely, that's not what Abigail meant when she said they had "cleaned and
scrubbed."*

Obediently—in stunned silence—Beth
climbed up after Marnie and Abigail to the
landing. The woman reached into her pocket
for a key and hurried to unlock the door, then
placed the cold metal item into Beth's open
palm as Marnie disappeared inside. "This is
yours, dear." Abigail cleared her throat quietly,
drawing back her shoulders. She seemed to
comprehend at least some of Beth's thoughts
and was now empathetically dismayed at the
situation.

Beth dropped her gaze a moment and
struggled for a response that would be considered gracious. "I'm not sure how big it is
inside—but the more the merrier, eh? I'm
grateful you're willing to share."

Abigail's expression fell further. "I've
been livin' with Ruth Murphy—now that I'm
alone."

"A-alone?" Beth stuttered. "What about the children?"

Bewilderment spread to Abigail's face. "Why, Beth, I *lost* my son, my Peter. Don't you recall?"

They stared at one another, each unable to speak. At last Beth tipped her head to one side quizzically. "But Emily? And Miles and Gabe?"

Abigail's mouth fell open, and her eyes dropped. Soft tears were already forming in their corners. "Oh no, dear. They ain't mine. Didn't ya never know that?" She sighed deeply, as if a familiar pain pressed against her chest, making it hard to breathe. "No, they ain't mine. Just my niece and my nephews. They belonged ta my husband's brother." She cleared her throat before she seemed able to continue. "We lost 'em both— Noah and Cyrus—on the day of the accident. And their momma, Grace, it seemed she just couldn't bear it all. She took to bed an' solitude fer a long, long time." Again Abigail's eyes lowered. "Not one of us knew what to do—so I guess we did nothin' but wait and pray. Didn't even speak on it much. Just cared fer them kids best we could. But Grace's come through it now, and she's moved back with her own momma . . . and them kids went too."

From beyond the door, sounds echoed as Marnie moved about inside.

Abigail paused, then said, "When I said we'd be sharin', I meant we're sharin' the building—since I'll be running the tearoom downstairs and you'll be livin' right here above." She finished with a forced nod.

Beth drew in a deep breath, trying to summon the same stubborn courage etched across Abigail's face. "I'm so sorry. I—I'll be fine here. Thank you, Abigail."

With a solemn squeeze of Beth's shoulder, Abigail retreated down the stairs and Beth turned toward the looming doorway. *Oh, Father,* she cried out silently, *I thought I knew this place. I thought I knew these people. How could I have been blind to such sorrow? Help me now. Please, please give me strength.*

Forcing herself forward, Beth entered her new home. Marnie had drawn back the curtains of two small gabled windows facing north toward the top of the mountain, allowing a little additional light. The small lamp only dimly lit the room. Beth took one step at a time inside, her eyes darting in every direction quickly, ashamed of how much fear she was feeling. Further, she was shocked at how small the living area actually was, the low slope of the roof cutting away much of the usable space beneath.

"Yer trunks are against the short wall, Miss Thatcher," Marnie said with a wave of her hand. "They don't fit so good, since we already brung in some furniture for ya. See! Miss Molly gave ya a sofa she found in the city. Looks 'most as good as new. And you got a table and two chairs from some other ladies here. They don't match, but that don't matter. Mrs. Blane made yer curtains. She pieced 'em from scraps, and we all agreed they look real nice." Marnie paused. "Do you like 'em?"

Beth lifted her eyebrows as if doing so could drag the corners of her mouth into a smile. "They're very nice—like a patchwork quilt. I'll be sure to thank her."

"The bedroom's through here. I'll get the windows open, and you'll have a nice cross breeze if you use just the screen door fer now."

But Beth's feet felt fastened to the floor. She let her eyes scan around carefully for any telltale signs of previous trouble. *I will not cry. I will not cry—at least, not until after Marnie leaves.*

"Ya look tired," Marnie blurted. "Do you wanna lie down a spell?"

"Yes. Oh yes. I'd like that. Thank you, darling. I'll stop by at Molly's after a bit for a nice visit." She shook her head slightly to clear the dark cloud that had descended. "Thanks so much. I'm glad you came with me. I hope you come back often—anytime. You're such good company, Marnie. Anytime at all."

"I'd like that, Miss Thatcher. I'm so glad yer back." Marnie smiled warmly, and Beth was reminded of how much more mature she seemed. The girl turned at the door with a little wave, and Beth listened to the footsteps retreating down the staircase.

All Beth wanted at the moment was to fall onto a soft bed and cry through her turbulent emotions. But entering the dusky bedroom seemed impossible. She turned instead to the small sofa that Molly had graciously provided and curled up against an armrest, her feet tucked under her skirt. Tears rolled down her cheeks, and soon her breath was ragged and uneven. *I don't understand, Father. I thought You brought me back here. And now it seems everything, absolutely everything, is falling apart. I don't have a proper home—can't stay where I wanted with the people I love— and now I find I was oblivious to just how terrible the consequences of the mine tragedy truly were—especially for the children I thought I had come to know. Did I speak to them about their mother? Did I say anything that caused them more pain? I suppose I'll never know. I'll never even see the three of them again.* Beth tucked her face into the crook of her arm. *And now the town's gone and hired another teacher. And*

Jarrick is so busy elsewhere I might hardly see him at all.

⁂

Beth woke with a sharp ache in her neck. After a quick wash, touching as little in the apartment as possible, she was relieved to pull the door shut behind her and abandon the Grants' abode, even if it would be only for a short visit with her dear second family—Molly and Frank, Teddy and Marnie. She hoped she could convince Marnie to spend the night with her. It was entirely inconceivable that Beth could stay alone.

Seated at Molly's kitchen table, she chose her words carefully as her friend discussed the lodging arrangement.

"Dearie, I was pleased for ya that you could have some solitude this time. And soon you may well be carin' for a husband too. Ya haven't said, but we've all been wonderin'—guessin', I suppose—how soon there might be weddin' bells. So we figured it might be wise for ya to be on yer own."

No, Molly, Jarrick and I haven't even spoken of when that might occur. In fact, he hasn't even actually proposed to me yet. "That's kind of you, Molly. It's a generous gesture, since I'm certainly aware there's a shortage of housing here."

"Well, we didn't want the place ya lived to be any hindrance ta future plans." Molly smiled broadly and set the kettle on the table, lowering herself into the chair opposite Beth. She seemed to be moving more slowly than Beth remembered. "'Course, I'm sorry we didn't lay it all out fer ya ahead of time. It all seemed to come out in little shocks. Ya sure you're okay with everything now? You 'pear to be a mite low."

"I'm tired. It's been a long day." Beth quickly turned the conversation toward more pleasant topics. "But it was so nice to be able to talk with so many of the children and their mothers. Everyone here seems hale and happy. And they've grown. Not just taller, but older somehow."

"You're surprised, dearie?" Molly said playfully. "Didn't they teach ya in yer schoolin' that's what children do every time they close their eyes?"

Beth was relieved she was able to laugh along easily. "Yes, but it rather sneaks up on one during an absence. I suppose I just expected them to stay as they were in my memory."

"Nor did any of us expect all that'd come yer way while you were gone," Molly said, reaching across the table for Beth's hand. "I was so sorry to hear of yer troubles in the summer, during what was to be such a lovely time. Who can tell when strife will come? Reading yer last letter just broke my heart fer ya all, but I'm glad to have ya near enough to see fer myself that you're back to normal."

Beth shook her head and sat straighter in her chair. "Most of my visit with my family was very nice. We had some lovely weeks traveling together, then that truly dreadful week when Julie was missing. But we managed to cling to hope in God, and He was faithful."

Molly took a sip. "He always is. But it don't make the journey easy, anyhow."

"Oh no, it was not. It certainly was not." Again Beth searched for a way to direct the conversation to something more cheerful. She reached for a cookie and carefully broke it into two pieces. Dabbing up the crumbs with an index finger she said, "Jarrick wished he could have come out with me to see all of you today. He's awfully busy now. I think they're having him catch up on his duties all at once."

"No doubt they're glad to have him back. Such a blessin', though, that he could follow Edward out east to help."

"It truly was. Molly, I got to know him in new ways. His strength. His certainty. His gentleness." Beth flushed self-consciously. "He's such a wonderful man."

"I'm happy fer ya, dearie. I truly am."

"And you," Beth met the older woman's eyes. "How is it with you? Married now—to another wonderful man."

"Pshaw. I can't deny that he is. But I guess my blushin' days is over. We're good together, me an' Frank. I'll allow you that. And I'm mighty grateful fer him. I truly am."

"You're perfect for each other," Beth sighed. "And you both deserve love."

"Well, now, I'm not sure I want ta claim that I *deserve* it, but a gracious God seen fit to bless me anyway with a second husband, a pair of the best children to care fer that a woman could want, and a whole community to be part of. And a lovely young friend." Molly grasped Beth's hand. "The way I figure, I've got more'n my share of blessed."

⁕

Marnie was thrilled at Beth's invitation to spend the night, and Beth could not have been more relieved. The teenager appeared entirely at ease moving around the Grants' frightening little apartment, digging into the cupboard below the washbasin for a small bar of soap she said was left over from their cleaning. She pulled and pushed at the trunks until Beth identified the one that held things she needed immediately, and then climbed on a chair to fetch another lamp from the top of the wardrobe in the bedroom. Beth was rather ashamed of her own tentativeness in the dreary space. She reminded herself that Marnie had already been there often as she helped with cleaning and readying the two small rooms.

They chatted easily while preparing for bed. "What else is new, dear? Tell me something that might still be a surprise." Beth quickly amended, "A *good* surprise."

Marnie squinted reflectively from her seat on the edge of the bed. "Did'ja hear about the new church?"

"No, is there a plan for that too?"

"Got it halfways done already. Just up the hill. In the meadow along the back road 'cross from the miners' camp."

"That's wonderful. Have you seen Pastor Davidson lately? I'm sure he's glad to have something more permanent than the hall." Beth held her breath as she stepped behind the open wardrobe door to change into a nightgown. She wanted no more bad news today. *Please don't say that Philip's gone.*

"He sure is excited fer us! And what's more, he's the one who's gonna be pastor— every Sunday. Soon as it's done bein' built."

"Wonderful, Marnie! I'm delighted to hear that," Beth said from her makeshift dressing room.

"Yeah, he's got someone in trainin' now. Follows him around—learnin' names and places and stuff. Gonna take over them other churches once Pastor comes to stay with us." Marnie pulled off her stockings and dropped them in the corner where she had let her dress land in a pile, then stood to her feet in a thin white slip, old and neatly patched in several places. Beth went and reached automatically to gather the clothing and drape the items over the bedroom chair, the familiar action reminding her of her sister Julie's haphazard-looking bedroom at home. Though Marnie was several years younger than Julie, it was a comforting feeling. And Marnie seemed entirely at ease sharing the space as well. "Want to get in first—then I can blow out the light," Marnie offered.

Beth was grateful to comply. She would have preferred that it be left burning but knew better than to even consider such nonsense—a fire hazard just to appease her own silly fear of the dark. Sliding her feet gingerly under the sheets, she reminded herself that this was *not* the Grants' bed but one provided by Molly or the other generous townsfolk. It was still difficult not to give way to jitters. Beth was too conscious of how close to the Grants' faded wallpaper she was forced to lie, as if it might bear some lingering hints of evil and tragedy.

Instead Beth rolled onto her side and faced the center of the room, retreating as far from the wall as possible. She could just see the profile of Marnie's face in the darkness, the girl still chattering amiably.

At last I feel as if it's going to be fine. Oh my, what a day. Beth's mind retraced the highs and lows, half listening to Marnie as she thought back over the surprise disclosures. As the room grew quieter, she brought up some questions.

"Marnie, I suppose you've met the new teacher."

"Yes. 'Course."

"What do you think of him?"

"He's all right. Kinda straight and stiff. But seems nice enough. Real smart too. Knows all kinda big words." Marnie laughed and punched her pillow up, tucking her hands under her head. "I think sometimes folks agree with him just 'cause they don't understand what he's sayin'." She chuckled.

"Hmmm. Do you like him?"

There was a teasing tone in her answer. "Might be a hard teacher—but then, so are *you*. So either way, we still have ta get down to work, I guess."

Beth allowed herself a little snicker at Marnie's assessment. "Have you heard anyone say how the classes will be divided? Do the students have an opinion?"

"Well, of course we all want to be with you. But since we can't, I s'pose we think he's gonna take the olders, and you'll keep the littles." Marnie sighed. "Teddy Boy don't wanna come back ta school. Did ya know that?"

"Oh no, he doesn't?"

"Don't worry. Papa Frank'll talk him inta it."

Beth liked the sound of the girl's affectionate name for Frank. The early loss of their mother had been further intensified by their father's tragic death in the mine accident. Very soon afterward they'd come to live with Molly, and she had enfolded the pair into her arms and heart. Beth was even more pleased to know that their new stepfather would hold his ground on the issue of Teddy's education.

"But you know my brother. Thinks he's grown and ready to work in them mines. Thinks he's ready to start makin' money hand over fist like the other men—he an' Addie both. Good thing yer back so you can talk to 'em too. Leastwise, the Coolidges could really use the money Addie would make. He's gotta be the man of their family now, but Teddy Boy, he's got Papa Frank to care fer 'im. Maybe you could talk to Mrs. Coolidge—fer Addie's sake."

"I'll do what I can." Beth truly hoped to

influence Addison's mother to allow the boy one more school year, his last before graduation. "I think I read in a letter that they're living in Frank's old cabin. Is that true?"

"Yah. With seven, though, they really fill it up to overflowin'."

"Have they said anything—?"

Beth stopped midsentence as a sudden shiver ran through her body. She was certain she'd heard a faint noise in the next room. "Marnie," she whispered tersely, "did you hear that?"

"Hear what?"

The scratching sound came again, more distinctly. "That!"

"Prob'ly just mice."

"Mice! Where?"

Something thumped.

"Nope, that ain't mice," the girl said, rolling toward the door.

Beth could feel herself trembling already. "Could you . . . ? Do you think we should . . . could you check?"

Without hesitation Marnie threw back her covers, dropped her feet to the floor, and relit the lamp. Beth forced herself to follow as the circle of flickering glow moved ahead of Marnie into the main room. Shifting shadows all around made Beth press a hand to her lips to keep from crying out.

"Where d'ya hear it?"

"I—I'm not sure. But it sounded close."

They stood in silence for several long moments, Beth breathing in shallow puffs. However, no more sounds were heard.

"Guess it's gone."

"Gone? Gone where?"

"Just gone. Back where it come from."

Beth retreated after Marnie into the bedroom and crawled back into bed. The low ceiling seemed to crowd even closer now as the girl blew out the light.

"Marnie, what do you suppose . . . ?" She dared not finish the thought.

"Can't of been much. Maybe a bird or a squirrel."

"At night?"

"I s'pose that'd be odd. 'Less they was disturbed by people livin' here again." She chuckled.

Beth clutched the covers more snugly under her chin, hunching beneath them. Eyes wide, she looked around the room from one dark shadow to the next. She dreaded voicing her rising fear aloud. In fact, she fought against it desperately, her mind telling her the wild thought was utter nonsense. At last, the question tumbled out in a tremulous voice. "You don't suppose . . . it couldn't be something like . . . like a ghost, could it? Of Mrs. Grant, or her husband?"

Marnie was staring at Beth. "That what you're thinkin'?"

Beth attempted a feeble laugh, as if she'd been kidding. "No, well, I mean . . . it's not that I believe in ghosts, it's just, I just couldn't help but think . . . to wonder if . . ."

"I don't know much 'bout that, Miss Thatcher, but I just figure," said Marnie around a deep yawn, "I figure ya gotta be *dead* 'fore you could haunt somebody. An' old Davie, he ain't dead. Just stuck in some jail in Calgary. Nor his missus neither. Even if she tried to get herself dead."

"I see. Of course. I suppose you're right."

"If yer scared'a the dark, Miss Thatcher, maybe try countin' sheep."

Marnie's innocent suggestion did not feel at all helpful to Beth, though she said nothing further. It was rather humbling to be given such advice from someone who'd been her student—a mere teenager. Yet tired as Beth was, hours passed before she was able to ignore the many muted sounds she heard and surrender to sleep.

Chapter
3

After a long day of unpacking and orga-
nizing, along with contrived trips back
to Molly's for this and that, Beth was disappointed that Marnie would not be permitted
a second night with her. She knew at some
point she would have to face her fears, but
she had hoped to have at least a little longer
to acclimate herself to her new home.

That evening Beth first stashed away every
scrap of food Molly had sent back with her,
hoping to ward off any small creatures searching for a handout. She really didn't relish rely-
ing so heavily on Molly's generosity. But, in
truth, she'd had no opportunity to prepare for
setting up housekeeping on her own.

It was obvious she would need to return
to Lethbridge to purchase dishes, pots, and
other housekeeping items. Even though the

return trip would be time-consuming, the possibilities for setting up her own living quarters raised her spirits a little. As she wrote out her list, she allowed herself to imagine living there as Jarrick's wife. *Oh, if only things work out for us soon. And just maybe, Jarrick will be back in Lethbridge this weekend!*

But as the shadows lengthened, Beth's joyful contemplations could no longer put off the inevitable. She locked the exterior door carefully and checked each corner of the room for any intruders—real and imagined—even locking the unpacked trunks filled with clothes and school supplies and searching behind them. Then she forced herself into the bedroom. Once more she methodically examined the whole room, tiny as it was—beneath the bed, behind the overstuffed chair, and all around the wardrobe. Still she could feel prickles of anxiety over her body.

This is ridiculous! What would Julie say? Then she whispered aloud rather pitifully, "Oh, I wish Julie were here. I could use her fearlessness tonight."

Rather forcefully, Beth threw back the covers and plumped up her pillow. *Now stop it,* she scolded. *You're an adult. You're responsible for meeting the educational goals of children. You can spend the night by yourself in a place that has been empty for months, has been thoroughly cleaned, and is safe and secure.* She climbed in, pulled the covers up to her chin. *You can certainly manage to sleep here,* she continued. *And there are no such things as ghosts! Besides, as Marnie said, Davie and Helen are both alive, remember, and long gone from these rooms and from Coal Valley.*

Almost as soon as she blew out the lamp and settled her tired body against the rather lumpy mattress, the noises came again. Mentally she sorted them into categories. *Now, that was just the floorboards creaking . . . that one was from outdoors. I'm sure that was just the snap of dying embers in the woodstove—oh, I wonder if that flapping sound could be a bird? Do birds fly at night? I hope so.*

Beth prayed valiantly. *Father, I need courage. It's silly and I feel like a child again, but please have mercy and answer me anyway. What is the verse I learned in Sunday school? Oh yes, Psalm 4:8. "I will both lay me down in peace, and sleep: for thou, LORD, only makest me dwell in safety." I take that promise, God, as my own. I know I can trust You—only You.* She rolled to her side facing the center of the room and silently recited the verse over again several times.

But then . . . *What is that?* She sat up, blanket clutched tight against her chest. This sound seemed to come from somewhere on the roof, or worse, from the long attic space running under the peak of the roof. Beth's fears rolled over her, wave upon wave.

"A mighty fortress is our God," she sang aloud. "A bulwark never failing . . ." The song seemed to shore up Beth's confidence and likely drowned out whatever sounds might have come next. Unfortunately, though, it did little to induce sleep.

One more night, then back to Lethbridge. The escape could not come soon enough.

⁂

With bleary eyes, Beth greeted Alberto Giordano, the familiar miner who was the company driver for trips back and forth to the city. He held the car door open for Beth, and though his warm smile came easily, he spoke slowly with a thick accent. "I am glad you are back here, miss."

"Your English is coming along so nicely, *signore*. I'm very glad to see you again too," she told him as she settled into the back seat of the car. As much as she disliked the road before them, Beth was grateful for a ride on one of his frequent errands back out to the prairie, bringing supplies and mail along with the occasional passenger.

Almost instantly Beth fell asleep and woke only as she felt the vehicle slowing to a stop.

"Are we there already?" She reached quickly to check her hair and straighten her hat.

"Yes, miss," he answered with a twinkle in his eye.

Beth pushed open the door and stepped out onto the sidewalk.

"I meet you here at eight? Is good, yes?" he suggested.

"Yes, thank you. I'll be back right here at eight this evening."

Stepping away from the car, Beth looked carefully around, sorting through how to proceed next. Her thoughts centered first on Jarrick. She had worried about how best to contact him, not relishing the thought of showing up at his station unannounced. Instead, she hurried inside the nearest shop—a drugstore—and asked if she might be allowed to use their wall-mounted telephone. "It's a local call," she assured him. She was relieved that the man behind the counter agreed easily.

"Hello, operator, will you please connect me with the RCMP station? Thank you." She cleared her throat to steady her voice as she waited, leaning closer to the mouthpiece in hopes that this would give her added privacy. At last she heard a strong male voice answer, "RCMP, Lethbridge Station—how may I help you?"

"Yes, I'd like to speak with Constable Jack Thornton, if I may."

"You're in luck. He's in his office today. If you'll wait just a moment, ma'am, I'll fetch him."

Beth felt her heart flutter and pressed the receiver tighter against her ear. The moments spent waiting seemed like forever. Finally she heard the familiar voice. "This is Jack Thornton."

"Oh, Jarrick, it's Beth."

A pause. "Beth? Truly? Where are you?"

Quickly Beth explained why she was in town, and they made plans for dinner. "At five, then. Oh yes, Jarrick, I can't wait to see you either. Good-bye." She blushed as she set the receiver back in its cradle and smiled shyly at the man behind the counter. By his expression it was obvious he had heard everything.

"Thank you so much for the use of your telephone."

"My pleasure. Have a nice day, miss."

Beth allowed herself a deep breath only after she had closed the door to the drugstore. She paused on the busy sidewalk to collect herself. *Jarrick is here. We'll have a chance to visit after all!* In addition, this would be his first opportunity to introduce his colleagues to her—the woman he'd crossed a continent to help when her sister was kidnapped that summer. *Will they be sizing me up, wondering if I'm worth all the time and effort?* She quickly set such questions aside, then wondered if they now might have the dinner they'd had to postpone just a week ago after meeting briefly on the Lethbridge station platform. *How could he? He just found out I'm here. There's no time to make a reservation. But he'll find some place for us, I'm sure.*

Beth walked toward Kirkham Bros. with a spring in her step, ready now to take on her next objective. She hadn't arrived in Coal Valley with much spending money, but she hoped to find what she needed to equip a small kitchen and to make things feel fresh and homey. She would also need a modest supply of food, canned goods and dry ingredients mostly, as she was determined to prepare most of her own meals despite Molly's standing invitation. In truth, however, she was merely guessing on what she'd need. She had never actually stocked a kitchen before. *Since I don't know that much about cooking . . . yet,* she told herself. In the late afternoon Alberto would stop at each of the stores she'd listed to load her purchases into the car while she and Jarrick had dinner.

At last she hailed a taxicab for the ride to the RCMP headquarters, her heart beating with eagerness to see Jarrick. She'd already been in the building the first time she'd arrived in Lethbridge. She and poor Edward had reported the theft of all their luggage after he'd sent it off with a thief. The memory brought a smile. *All's well that ends well—so long as enough time has passed.* Her precious violin was now safely stored in a trunk in her little second-floor home, and Father's precious brass compass was back on his desk where it belonged.

Jarrick appeared in the hallway as soon as she paused at the reception desk. Beaming his welcome and lifting both hands toward her, he crossed the room in long strides. No uniform this time, he was dressed in a dark gray double-breasted suit. For a moment Beth wished she had selected a nicer dress for the occasion, but his genuine delight in seeing her drove away all doubts.

"Beth, you're here! What a pleasant surprise that you'd be able to visit this soon." He reached for her arm affectionately, seeming to tower above her. Beth felt herself blushing but did not move away. "Sweetheart, I can hardly wait to show you off. Are you ready?" he asked.

"Yes. I think so."

Jarrick began with the officer at the front desk. "Ollie, I'd like you to meet Miss Elizabeth Thatcher. Beth, this is Ollie Brannigan, affectionately known as the public face of this office."

"Hard to believe this is the schnozzle they want to represent the Force"—he gestured at his rather bulbous nose—"but we didn't get these jobs for our looks, except maybe Thornton here." Both men chuckled, and Ollie extended a hand. "So good to meet you, Miss Thatcher. Jack brags about you all the time."

"He's very kind. . . ."

The man behind the desk continued, "I'm glad to finally have a face to put with the name. Say, I hear he's taking you out for dinner."

From the corner of her eye, Beth noticed Jarrick make a small signal for silence, and he followed the gesture swiftly by saying, "Well, Ollie, I've got more introductions to make. We should keep moving."

"Nice to meet you, Miss Thatcher. Hope to see more of you. Say, my wife, Alice, would like to have you both over to dinner—whenever Jack's ready to share your time." He laughed and winked at Jarrick.

"So nice to meet you, Mr. Brannigan."

"Please, it's just Ollie."

The introductions that followed were mostly the same, and Beth was certain she'd never remember all the names and faces. For the most part she took her cues from Jarrick and smiled at each one. At last he was escorting her from the building and opening the door to a stylish police vehicle, a touring car complete with large whitewall tires and an alarm bell mounted on the hood.

"Your chariot awaits, my lady."

"Thank you, kind sir." Beth heard herself tittering like a schoolgirl as he took her hand and helped her into the passenger seat. "Only please don't ring that bell."

They talked about the happenings of the previous week as if there weren't great unspoken overtones to the evening. It was a lovely surprise when he eased the car into a parking spot next to "their" restaurant and the engine rattled to silence.

"Well, this seems like the best place in town. Shall we see if we can get in?" He winked, both of them aware of how long they had looked forward to such an evening.

Once inside, Beth was surprised to find that the establishment did not seem quite as elegant as she'd remembered—or perhaps she had grown accustomed once again to the beautiful restaurants in the East. The thought was a fleeting one, though, and Jarrick soon captured all her attention, beginning with the single rose across her plate on their corner table.

"Oh, Jarrick, how sweet of you."

"What? Me? How would I know anything about this?" he said with pretended nonchalance, running a finger over his mustache. "Maybe the maître d' just remembers how beautiful you are."

Beth blushed and sat down in the chair Jarrick held for her. She felt his warm pat on her shoulder before he signaled to the waiter and took the opposite seat. Looking across at him, she was struck once more by how handsome he was, especially when his blue eyes danced in the candlelight. She breathed in deeply, determined to treasure every moment of this meal.

Jarrick had ordered their food when he made the reservation, and the first course arrived shortly. His penetrating gaze and careful questions soon had Beth spilling out all that had transpired on her arrival. He listened just as carefully while she skirted around Molly's primary reason—a possible wedding—for housing her on her own, but the omission left him somewhat bewildered.

"There wasn't any *other* place you could have stayed? Not with one of the families? Not with . . . I don't know, with the Sanderses, or Ruth Murphy?"

"Abigail is living with Ruth now. You can't even imagine how crowded the town

is, Jarrick. It's not just the new miners.
They're having to accommodate builders,
too, for all the construction. I was told over
breakfast yesterday that some men crowd
in six to a two-bedroom house! And you
know how tiny they are. Soon they'll have
finished two floors of tenement housing in
the company's new building down by the
river. How long has it been since you were
there, Jarrick?"

"Mmm, it's been at least two or three
months. I haven't needed to go west as often—
particularly since you haven't been there,
Beth." He smiled and reached across to touch
her hand lightly. "I spend more time out on
the prairie now, hardly ever in one place for
long. But I'm aware the town's been growing
like a weed over the summer. I'm still surprised, though, there isn't room somewhere
for you to live more comfortably."

"I'll be fine," Beth assured him and hurried on to another subject.

Dessert arrived, and still Jarrick seemed in
no hurry to turn the conversation toward the
two of them, to their future. He was clearly
enjoying the suspense, and Beth refused to
be the one to speak first.

At last he cleared his throat and flashed a
boyish grin. "Well, I'm sure you know we are
not here at our special place just to catch up

on news from Coal Valley." He again reached across to stroke the back of her hand, then surrounded it with his.

Beth could feel her pulse racing. Warmth rushed into her cheeks, and her face turned down, only peeking up at him from under her hat brim.

"You know that I love you," he whispered. "More than I could ever have imagined. And that you're so much more—more precious, exciting, generous, and courageous a person than I had pictured I'd ever meet." He lifted her hand, leaning his head closer to hers. "It's so clear you're truly a gift of God in my life, and I'm so very grateful for the way He's brought us together. Even the strange and trying circumstances we've recently shared are seen more clearly in light of what God is doing in both our lives—no doubt to prepare us for the future." He paused. "I'd like that future to be together, sweetheart, if you're willing."

Beth watched him produce a small box from his pocket. He set it on the table in front of her. "You must know I'd like you to be my wife, Elizabeth Thatcher. I'd be so honored if you would."

Beth took a quick breath.

"Before you answer," he hurried on, "there are some details we should discuss."

Surprised, she drew her gaze away from the unopened box to meet his.

"I feel it's important that we begin in unity, Beth—that we're aligned with what we picture next in our future. And I don't think it's fair you should answer my proposal, hopefully with a 'yes,' and then afterwards we start a discussion about what you've just agreed to."

She nodded almost imperceptibly. "That's wise." The suggestion, however, felt somewhat dispiriting.

He cleared his throat again and pulled his chair forward, crossed his arms on the table. "The most obvious path would be that you'd at least finish the school year in Coal Valley— and that I'd go on working on my assignments here. At some point during the year we could marry, and I'd spend as much time with you in the mountains as possible. It isn't ideal, but I believe I know you well enough to know you wouldn't want to leave your students before the end of the school year." His tone deepened, and he frowned. "Of course, we could wait to marry until the term is over, but I'd rather not." This time he was the one to look away. "I guess I don't have the patience for that particular plan."

Beth didn't like the sound of a wait either. This time she was the one who reached across to tenderly lay her hand on his. "What is it . . . well, what do you see after that?" she asked.

"You mean, at the end of the school year?"

"Yes. Is there a way we could stay in Coal Valley so I could continue teaching after this year?"

His rubbed his chin. "I'm afraid I wouldn't be able to plan that far in advance. As a Mountie, I'm required to come and go wherever I'm assigned—wherever the Force sends me. I don't really have a say in my postings or in how long I'd stay in each one. It's a truly difficult arrangement for any bride to accept, and I'm painfully aware of that. But, Beth, I'm afraid it's unlikely I'd ever be posted near Coal Valley again." His hand grasped Beth's. His voice went even quieter. "There is another alternative, sweetheart."

Beth blinked, waited.

"Your father has offered me a position at his company."

She stared across the table, stunned with this revelation.

"He says he's ready to appoint a new head of security in Toronto and would like me to consider the job."

Beth drew away, dropping her hands to her lap. "But—but you just said you weren't allowed to choose your own placement." She bit her lip and stole another glance at him.

"It wouldn't be an RCMP position, Beth. I'd have to resign from the Force in order to work for your father." His brow furrowed deeply.

Beth felt her stomach tighten. *Leave the Force? How can he even consider such a thing? He's always spoken so assuredly about his role— of his calling.* Tears formed in the corners of her eyes, and she blinked them away.

"Beth, I only want to make the best choice possible for us. Maybe it *would* be best if we settled down somewhere—somewhere closer to family."

But I am . . . I am close to family, to my family here. But it was too difficult to speak the words aloud.

He persisted, saying, "And someday we'll want children of our own. It would be so much easier if we could count on staying in one place, not picking up and relocating every few years."

"But I thought Edward mentioned an obligation to a minimum period of time. Are you even *allowed* to leave the Force?"

He shifted in his chair before answering. "I haven't completed my contracted years. It would require that I buy myself out of the service."

"Isn't it costly? When he first came to the

West, Edward wasn't worried about that because his father is—wealthy, but . . ."

Jarrick's lips pressed together tightly before he answered, his voice low, "Your father said he'd be more than willing to pay the sum for me."

Beth was sure she could hear the sound of defeat. She whispered breathlessly, "Is that what you want, Jarrick? Is it?"

"Sweetheart," he pleaded, "I just want to take care of you in the best way I know how. I would give up anything on earth to be sure I was making the right decision for the two of us. You mean so much to me, Beth. I can't even describe it."

The strength of his love for her was at this moment breaking Beth's heart. *Is this what I'm giving back to him—the destruction of his own desires? But what can I say? It's his decision, his responsibility before God. But I thought I'd be the one to make a sacrifice. I was prepared for that. It's so much harder to watch him forfeit his dreams instead. But, truly, I'd hoped I'd never have to leave this place—that we could stay here together.*

"I love you too, Jarrick," Beth whispered. "I look to you to lead us, and whatever you decide, I know that I want to be with you—to be your wife."

Her smile was tremulous as she felt his

hands enfold hers, and tears were falling on the tablecloth by the time he slipped the ring over her finger and promised, "I'll take care of you, Beth. I'll love you as best I can—God helping me."

"I know you will, my darling. I trust you."

They were engaged. And Beth was determined to submit to her husband wherever he would lead. Along with her joy, though, her heart ached at the distressing possibility that he might be leaving so much of himself behind.

Chapter
4

Hello, Father, is Mother with you? I want to talk with you both, please." Beth squeezed the receiver against her ear and gazed at the new diamond ring on her finger, glittering in its white gold setting. Jarrick stood close behind her, his hands on her shoulders as she sat in front of the desktop telephone. Neither of them was concerned that others in the RCMP office might overhear. Everyone in the building had heard their announcement by now.

"Okay, she's here, Beth. Mother's standing right here," her father's voice crackled over the line. "What's your news?"

"Jarrick and I are engaged." A pause. "Can you hear me? I said we are engaged."

"Yes, yes, we hear you. We're thrilled for you both!"

Beth tipped her head to see Jarrick's reaction. "I guess it's not a very big surprise to anyone there, but I have a very lovely ring on my finger to prove it."

Another longer pause, and then Father answered, "Your mother is pleased as she can be. She wishes she could give you a great big hug." He added, "As do I, my dear."

"We're hoping to be married in the spring, Father. Do you think you all can come in April? We want to avoid as much of the winter as possible. There's always a good chance of a storm even then, but we don't want to put the wedding off any longer than that."

"Oh, I see. You're planning to marry in the West, then?" There was a small pause and muffled voices before Father spoke again. "Yes, we'll be certain to clear our calendars. Let us know as soon as you have a fixed date. We're so happy for you, Beth. Give Jack our love and best wishes." Before Beth could respond he said, "Your mother wants to tell you for herself. Here she is—here's Mother."

"Beth, Beth, can you hear me?"

"Yes, Mother. We're here, both of us."

"Father says you're to marry in the West. I thought you'd come home, perhaps in the summer? Our church is so lovely in late June."

Beth exchanged glances with Jarrick. "No, I think we're quite certain we'd like to have the ceremony here, where people know us as a couple."

"Oh . . . oh, I just never considered it. Well . . . oh, dear. Of course, I don't mind the travel, but it will greatly limit the guest list. Have you thought of that? We shall have to consider it carefully."

"It won't be a large wedding, Mother. It will be in Coal Valley, where we met. I can't wait for you to see the town, to meet our friends here."

Even through the miles of telephone line, Beth could hear her mother exhale her disappointment. "Yes, darling, we would be—we will be happy to come to you there."

Having conceded the point, her mother's happiness flowed over the telephone lines and buoyed Beth's spirit. Had Beth not known about Father's offer to Jarrick—his generous but problematic proposition—she would have been beside herself with delight at their acceptance of her beloved. But she didn't dare bring up the subject of the employment offer. She knew Jarrick and her parents would outnumber her in such a discussion.

During the ride home that night, the darkening sky filled with stars as Beth stared out from the back seat of Alberto's car. Her mind tumbled round and round with the question, *Is there any way to avoid moving back east? Any way to keep Jarrick where he belongs?*

She reminded herself that her role as his wife would be to let him know her thoughts, then support his decision. *O Lord God,* she prayed, *I've always felt that Mother's undue influence led to Father's leaving the sea he loved and taking a management position. But he continued to travel anyway, despite her objections. True, nobody ever told me outright, but I'm sure of it, just the same. And I will not follow her example, no matter what. I won't try to manipulate my husband.* She shook her head and twisted a strand of hair fallen from beneath her hat. *I just never thought the issue would be reversed—that I'd be struggling against Jarrick's taking a city job even though he'd be home every evening. I know if we stayed here it would be much more difficult in so many ways, involving frequent, long absences, but I really can't see him as anything but part of the Force. Am I wrong, Lord? If so, please give me peace about this. But it's got to be Jarrick's decision.*

Supper at Molly's on Sunday evening was an event. They crowded together at her kitchen table, their hostess scurrying back and forth to serve two rooms filled with people. Once the boarders had been fed and dispersed and just the family had gathered afterward in the parlor for dessert, Beth knew they anticipated she had returned with happy news to report. She looked around at their expectant faces and brought out the engagement ring she had kept hidden all day, glowing with pride and grateful to have her "other family" with which she could share her pleasure.

"It's so pretty!" Marnie exclaimed. "Shucks, Miss Thatcher! It's the prettiest thing I ever seen."

Molly patted Beth's knee as they sat together on the parlor sofa. "Ain't we glad now that we put ya in Abby's place?"

Yes, Beth thought to herself. *That's what I'll call it. Not the Grants' anymore, but Abigail's place.* She said, "I'm afraid I'll be alone there for some time yet. We don't plan to be married until the spring—probably in April. There are many details to be worked through."

"I could stay with ya, ta help," Marnie offered, rising from the footstool to stand in front of Molly, arms out in a beseeching fashion. "That'll make it easier here too, Miss Molly. Don't ya see? Then you can have my room for two of them other men. That'd help you all fit better, wouldn't it?"

Beth held her breath. *It would certainly be a relief to share the space, especially with someone as dear as Marnie.* Aloud she put in, "I wouldn't mind at all. In fact, I'd truly enjoy her company. If it's fine with you both, I feel it's a splendid idea."

Molly looked doubtful. "I still gotta have yer help here though, Marnie. With school and all, it don't leave ya much time. You'd hardly do more 'an sleep over there."

"It's a good idea anyways, and it gives ya my room to rent out."

"It would indeed." Molly looked back and forth between Marnie and Beth and shrugged.

The arrangement was settled and plans immediately made. Frank would move a straw mattress to Beth's bedroom to be positioned where the roofline sloped down so low that the area wasn't useable for much else. Beth would situate the smallest of her trunks for Marnie's nightstand and also some personal storage. The girl would join Beth each evening after her chores were done.

"An' it'll be so easy to get help with my homework. I'll be livin' with the teacher. I might even get the best grades ever!" Marnie exclaimed in triumph.

Beth smiled and said, "Yes, dear, I can help, but you'll need to do the actual work yourself, you know." They all laughed, and Marnie assured them she wouldn't take advantage of her housing situation.

Impatient to get things going, Marnie clutched at Frank's good hand and coaxed him out of his chair so they could get the mattress and her belongings to her new home. Molly and Beth followed, their arms filled with bedding and clothing.

Outside Abby's place, three boxes containing Beth's purchases were waiting at the foot of the stairs. Frank quickly announced that he'd come back to haul them up, "Soon as'a we get the mattress in'a place."

As Molly was helping Beth unpack the new supplies, she confessed quietly, "Frank's gettin' too old fer so much carryin' and the like, but there's no way to tell 'im."

"Helping others is so much a part of who he is. It would be very difficult for him to be told to cut back."

"To be sure."

Molly and Beth set to work making up Marnie's bed.

Later that night, in the darkness, Marnie whispered to Beth, "Ya think we'll hear them noises again?"

"I suppose so. I heard them again last night."

"Maybe we can figure it out. I'll listen."

However, the soft sounds of Marnie's even breathing came long before the scratching sounds returned. By then just the girl's presence was enough for Beth to relax and rest more easily.

⚜

Beth rose early Monday, though school would not actually begin until the other teacher returned from Calgary. She was determined to figure out how to use her stove and prepare a breakfast of pancakes and eggs without waking Marnie. But the fire was far more difficult to manage than she had anticipated. Each time she thought the little flames were licking high enough, she'd turn away only to find a moment later they had died again. When Marnie emerged, rubbing her eyes, Beth still hadn't produced enough fire to heat the pan.

"I'll do it," the teenager offered. "Won't take me but a few minutes." She set directly to work. "Now, I'll tell ya, it's best not to let them embers die. Keep 'em banked in the night so all ya have to do is stir 'em up in the mornin' and add fresh wood. Of course, coal will last ya longer. But it don't start so easy." The slender shoulders hunched close to the firebox as she gave her instructions, blowing periodically on the infant flame. Beth listened carefully and tried to watch over Marnie's shoulder to see exactly what she did. In no time Marnie pushed the frying pan in place. "You can fix the temperature fer now by moving the pan around on top here. But soon I'm sure you'll know by the looks of yer fire how hot it's gonna be." She hesitated. "Want me to cook while you get dressed? I heard ya tell Teddy Boy that you'd go fishin' with him this morning. I know he likes to get started 'fore sun's up too high."

"Yes, he's excited to show me around the new buildings. *'Around seven,'* he told me. There's still plenty of time for me to help with the cooking. I want to learn, Marnie. I truly do. How will I ever feed Jarrick if I can't even build a fire?" She kept her tone breezy, despite her genuine concerns about running a household for a husband. When Marnie wasn't looking, Beth held up her hand to admire the new ring.

The first few pancakes burned before Beth got the hang of testing the temperature. Only the last four were large and plump and evenly browned. She presented them to Marnie. "How's that?"

"Good as Miss Molly's."

"Oh, you little fibber." They both laughed. "But I suppose they're good enough to eat anyway. And that's what counts."

Teddy's knock came before Beth and Marnie had finished eating. When he had stepped inside and greeted them both, he looked a bit longingly at the last pancake. Beth smiled and invited him to finish it up while she got ready for their outing. She tied on a straw hat and pulled a light wrap over a simple housedress good enough for fishing.

Marnie insisted that she would wash up the breakfast dishes, repeating how thankful she was to be living with Beth.

"The fish're bitin' best near the foot-bridge," Teddy said over his shoulder. "But I want to take you 'round to the sawmill first. I thought you'd like to see where all this new lumber's comin' from." He grinned in the morning light, and Beth thought she could see a smattering of hairs growing above his lip. "I worked fer the company a little this summer. Got myself a little money tucked away now."

Beth tried to match his stride as they trudged down the road between the company houses. The only movement outdoors yet was a lone father chopping wood next to a pile of logs. They waved their greetings, and then Teddy turned off on a path Beth couldn't recall, wending their way downhill toward the river. The mine noise she'd heard from town was growing louder. The woods ended abruptly, opening to a wide expanse of barren hillside full of machinery and men. To Beth it seemed like a forest graveyard with the ugly stumps as markers. She felt a pang of sorrow. "They cleared all this in one summer?"

"You bet we did," declared Teddy, boyish pride pushing out his chest. "It ain't hard with the right equipment. An' we had almost two dozen men workin' at it most days, not countin' the ones in the mine."

"No wonder there's not enough room to house everyone in town." Beth's gaze traveled over the desolation of the hillside, sweeping down toward the frenzy of activity surrounding the enormous mill at the water's edge. For a moment she watched as men loaded straight, round tree carcasses into one end of an oblong building, while others removed long white boards to be added to mountainous stacks. Hidden somewhere under the long roof, the rattling machinery sliced the wood and spewed sawdust high into the air. Beth clutched her throat. "How much farther do they intend to clear the trees? Do you have any idea?"

"Naw, guess the plan is to keep cuttin'— soon's they're done buildin' what they need here they'll start shippin' lumber out too, along with the coal. Hear there's a good market for it all. Folks are callin' it a *building boom*. And the company men say that by havin' both businesses, they'll be makin' money hand over fist."

Beth sighed. Marnie had used the same phrase to describe Teddy's hopes. "I see" was all she could manage in response.

She looked over the landscape once more, now recognizing only an outcropping of limestone close to where she had often gathered wildflowers along the river. Rather abruptly turning her back on the devastation, she said, "We don't have much time. Let's go fishing. Are you ready?"

"Sure am," he agreed. "I already took the poles an' things to the spot and dug up some fresh bait."

"You must have been up before the sun."

His nose wrinkled. "Have ta be. Or I don't got time to do the things I *want* to do."

Soon Addison and Peter joined them, dropping their lines into the water near an overhanging tree. After Teddy got Beth set up with a pole, they sat in a row on the grassy bank and listened to the water gurgling its way over the rocky riverbed.

Five beautiful fish hung from a line in Teddy's hand by the time they were ready to leave. Soaked to the knees from wading and splashing one another, they started a ragged parade back to town, Beth trudging beside Teddy, and Peter and Addison ahead. She felt dwarfed by their tall, lean forms. Had they *all* grown so much over the summer? Her shoes squished water with every step, but she didn't mind. They were old and would soon dry out.

"Good morning, gentlemen," a male voice

greeted them. "How did you find the fishing today?"

Unable to see the man yet, Beth assumed he was one of their fathers.

"Hi," Addison returned as they approached him.

"Morning, Mr. Hughes—uh, I mean, Harris—uh, sir." Peter obviously was trying to remember the correct way to address the man.

Addison tacked on quickly, "We done pretty good, sir. We got five." He gestured back toward Teddy, who held the fish in the air, dangling them almost above Beth's head.

"We *did well*," corrected Mr. Robert Harris Hughes.

"Yes, sir," the boys answered in unison, suddenly shy.

They had shuffled to a halt, and Beth was able merely to peer between a jumble of bodies and arms at the man standing before them. He was rather young and neither particularly tall nor robust, yet the way he carried himself required respect, she knew immediately.

Beth flinched, wishing she could meet her fellow teacher under more appropriate circumstances, but she forced herself out from among the boys with as much confidence as she could muster. Though painfully aware of her wet shoes, the water marks on her modest frock, and her tangled mass of hair she had snagged on a branch, she managed, "Good morning. You must be Mr. Harris Hughes. I am Miss Elizabeth Thatcher." Deciding that the name probably meant nothing to him, she forced a wayward curl behind her ear, swallowed, and went on to explain with what she hoped was some dignity, "I'm the—the *other* teacher."

His dark eyebrows rose. "I'm pleased to meet you, Miss Thatcher. I had no idea I'd find you . . . here." His smile turned into something a little less cordial as he stood before her in clothing more appropriate for a horseback ride through a well-manicured field—brown tweed suit belted at the waist and pant legs tucked into tall leather boots. On his head was a flat wool cap tilted toward one ear. "You may imagine my surprise at finding you out fishing here with these boys."

"And spending time with my—with our students." Beth forced a weak smile and shrugged. "Where else?"

"Indeed."

For a long moment no one spoke. The boys seemed uncomfortable, and Beth could think of nothing further until she finally said, "Oh, yes, I was hoping that you and I could sit down together in order to plan for the school year. Do you suppose you'd have time today, Mr. Harris Hughes?" Her voice trailed off.

He nodded once, his eyes nearly closing contemplatively. "Yes, Miss Thatcher, I had hoped we could do so. How propitious that we came across one another so early in the day."

"Indeed. Is there, would there be a time that would suit you?" She inwardly berated herself for sounding so tentative.

"I am just setting off for a vigorous morning walk. If you are available at half past ten, I believe we would have the schoolhouse at our disposal."

"That would work nicely."

"Fine. Good day then, Miss Thatcher. I look forward to speaking with you shortly." He doffed his cap slightly and paused briefly to nod toward the boys. "Gentlemen." Then he pushed his way between them on the narrow path.

"Have a nice walk, sir." The boys stood staring after him until he had rounded the first bend.

Teddy let out a low whistle. "Ain't he just . . ."

"*Isn't* he," Beth muttered.

"Okay, yeah, *isn't* he just a humdinger! Did ya see them boots? Bet he even polishes 'em!"

"Oh, Teddy, please."

Beth hurried her entourage back into town, promising she'd stop by Addison's home after her meeting to share their catch for lunch, then rushed back to her modest residence. She left the shoes on the steps to dry. Beth wished fleetingly that she'd be able to bathe before her appointment, but there was not enough time. And it was going to take enough work to put her tangled hair back in order. Washing up well in the large basin would have to suffice. She scrubbed hard. It would be inexcusable if she still smelled the slightest bit like fish by ten thirty.

Chapter
5

Wearing a tea-length dress of smoky-gray georgette embroidered with pink roses, proper shoes, and her hair now pinned up in a neat and sensible fashion, Beth made her way across the rutted dirt street. Though she knew she was more than compensating for her earlier impression, she had found nothing else in her wardrobe that seemed quite appropriate to the moment. She could only hope she wouldn't cross paths with anyone. They would likely assume she was on her way to a funeral and would wonder whose.

She approached the door, pondering whether she should knock or boldly enter. She decided on the latter and pushed her way into the schoolhouse. To her surprise the large room was now littered with sawn boards and workmen's tools. "Hello? Mr. Harris Hughes?" she called.

He emerged immediately from a corner hidden behind the door. "Miss Thatcher, you're very punctual. I appreciate your respect of another's time."

"Of course." She stepped forward cautiously and looked around. "I had expected things to be ready for school. I was here just last week, and there wasn't any clutter then at all. Do you know what's happening?"

He held out a hand to escort her past the rubble, and Beth accepted it gingerly. He had laid aside jacket and hat, and she could now see his hair slicked straight back except for one tidy wave sculpted in the front. In collared shirt, suspenders, and full-cut trousers he brought to mind some of the gentlemen who had shared the summer cruise ship—a pretentious mixture of leisure and high style. *Stop it,* she admonished herself, *you don't even know him yet.*

His demeanor, however, was brashly confident and fully in charge. "Our space is being divided into two classrooms. I'm not certain why it wasn't completed sooner, but one can only assume the decision was confirmed over the weekend. I tried to encourage the construction two weeks ago while I was in town, but apparently they must have thought better of it back then."

"I see." He seemed to be rather sure of his own opinions. *Perhaps they wished to wait until my arrival. Shouldn't you assume I should be given a voice, Mr. Harris Hughes?* But then she silently acknowledged that no one had talked to her about much of anything related to the school, and certainly not this construction.

He motioned to a table in the only tidy corner of the space.

"We could meet at Abigail's," Beth suggested. "At least it would be clean and quiet."

"Oh?" He seemed surprised. "I thought you'd want to talk here about the design. I've thoroughly dusted off this table as you can see. I have my books in these boxes nearby." He gestured toward them. "And I've asked the workmen to take a break so we'll have some quiet for our discussion."

"Yes, if you like," Beth agreed.

He drew out a chair, wiped it with a handkerchief—"Just to be sure," he said with a little smile—and helped Beth settle on it. She laid the notebook she'd brought with her on the table and opened it to where she'd tucked a pencil. "I think we should begin with the students," she said. "I've listed them here, and I've been thinking—"

Beth's words were cut short by the sound of the man sucking air through his teeth. "Pardon me, Miss Thatcher, but I hoped we might begin with the building itself—the reason I've set up our meeting here. I do hope you don't mind very much. I've sketched out some design ideas, and there would still be time to change the work order if I were able to speak with the foreman today."

"There is a foreman?" *That seems odd, even unnecessary, just for adding a simple wall.*

"Well, I assume so."

"Who would that be?" Beth felt warmth rising in her cheeks. *Why am I being so disagreeable? I feel as if we're sparring rather than talking.* She cleared her throat and tried to relax her shoulders, to sit comfortably instead of poker straight.

The man checked the notes on the table in front of him. "I spoke with a Walter Deedles, who seems to be in charge."

Beth couldn't help but smile, calling to mind an image of the small, bespectacled mining supervisor. "Yes, he works for the company, that's true. I suppose Walter is as good as anyone to serve as liaison. Have they explained to you what they intend to build?"

"Not in detail," he said, "but if I could just show you these sketches, I think you'd agree with my design. And I'll pass the instructions along so we can all be in accord."

Beth held her tongue. *It's just a wall. They'll put it right down the middle of the space and call it a day.* But she leaned closer as he explained his proposal. The plan seemed equitable and very workable. She'd be content with either of the classrooms, and he had wisely added a small mudroom, which would be invaluable in this climate. "And in the center of the dividing wall," he said, "I've drawn a door to access the opposite room."

Beth cocked her head, trying to imagine the reason for his suggested door. "When would we use that?"

"Use what?"

"The door . . . between classrooms. Since we're dividing the students by age, at what point during the day would they need to pass from one to the other? Wouldn't it be sufficient to access the rooms from the shared entry?" She hurried to finish before he could interrupt again. "And don't you think, that is, I'm afraid it would make things a good deal noisier for both of us. The sound would carry between rooms much easier that way."

"Oh dear. Is that what you envisioned— that we would each teach half of the children?" He sat back in his chair.

"How else would we split the teaching?" she asked meekly.

"I thought, perhaps, that we would teach by subject. Most of my own studies have focused on the disciplines of science and art, though of course my graduate work was in the broader study of education itself. Since I've read extensively the various educational philosophies, I can assure you, Miss Thatcher, that the one-room schoolhouse model is rather passé, replaced now with specialized instruction based on subject matter."

Beth blinked, stared at him for a moment, then blinked again. *How can I . . . ? What can he . . . ? What is he talking about?* "Mr. Harris, uh, Harris Hughes," she said, stumbling over his name, "I don't think you understand our families here. If you could see the progress made last year, in just one year. We focus on reading, on writing and—"

"On 'rithmatic?" He chuckled mockingly. "Please, Miss Thatcher." He held up a hand, palm out. "Please don't expect me to believe you've surrendered to such archaic methods. There's so much more that modern children need to know if they're ever to rise above such backward communities."

How dare you! She took a quick breath and forced herself to remain calm, though her words sounded more stern than she intended. "I believe in teaching fundamental skills first and using other subjects to enrich the lessons. And I assure you, Mr. . . . Mr. . . . sir, that I received my teaching degree from the best women's college in Ontario."

"Ah," he countered. "Well, then . . . yes, I see."

Beth took a deep breath and stood to her feet.

"Please, please. Don't be upset, Miss Thatcher. I meant no disrespect." He gestured that she should take her seat again.

Beth stood firm, leaning forward with her hands braced on the table before her, ready to mount a defense.

"Miss Thatcher, I'm afraid that people often misunderstand my meaning. Perhaps I should have said simply that I believe there are superior methods now and that we can achieve more using a targeted approach to learning by specializing. I'm certain you'll agree if you'll just hear me out." He rose suddenly and drew a textbook from one of his boxes, laying it on top of Beth's notebook. "You see, I propose we set our sights higher, think of the classroom's impact on society as a whole, and educate with the intention of producing thinkers rather than just workers."

Beth sputtered, vainly trying to reply.

He hurried on, "I see we're getting nowhere. Let me make a suggestion. Let's lay aside this discussion and return to the building design. I think you'll find that my overall proposal works well with either teaching model. Yes?

And that's the first hurdle we can surmount together. Don't you agree?"

Beth forced herself to ease back onto her chair. She tucked trembling hands out of sight in her lap and fidgeted with her ring, spinning it round and round as he spoke.

"I'm sure you must be comfortable enough with what I've drawn that it can be given to Mr. Deedles today?"

"I really don't like the door."

"Oh my. We needn't make such a fuss about a door, need we? If you don't like it, I'm sure you can just ignore it."

On every point during the remaining discussion Robert Harris Hughes used the same tactic. He appeared to care nothing for Beth's ideas, the routines she had established, the calendar of school events she hoped would augment the daily lessons, the specific children with whom he'd be entrusted. It was all she could do to keep a carefully measured tone. Of one thing she was certain. She would hold her ground on his muddled division of students into different subjects. She would not leave the precious little ones in the hands of this stranger, no matter what he said to manipulate and intimidate her. It was difficult enough to imagine her older pupils being required to learn under his overbearing tutelage. But he certainly would not be allowed to direct his imperious mannerisms on little Anna Kate or any of the smallest ones from last year's class. She cringed to picture Jonah Sanders stuttering out an answer to a question posed by this overbearing schoolmaster, or poor little Levi Blane, so thin and frail.

Beth squared her shoulders. *If I learned anything over the summer, it's that I'm not going to ignore my instincts again, particularly when people I love are in jeopardy. I'm not the woman I was, Mr. Robert Harris Hughes. I think you'll find I'm quite capable of standing up to you now.*

But by the time Beth dragged herself back up the stairs she was worn out, body and soul. She knew she'd missed lunch with the boys. The one positive result of their meeting was that Beth had managed to retain sole guardianship of the younger half of the students. Heart-weary, she slipped off and folded away the silly dress and donned a comfortable blouse and skirt, then curled up and fell asleep, exhausted from the mental wrestling match she'd endured.

⁂

When Beth woke dark shadows had gathered in the corners of her bedroom. Dusk had fallen, and she had been asleep for hours. Ashamed, she splashed some water on her face and checked her fire. It had gone out. So the long process of nurturing the flames began again until Beth could warm up a simple meal of leftover roast beef and vegetables that Molly had sent home with her. Sitting alone at the table, she held out her left hand and studied the engagement ring in the candlelight, wishing with all her heart that Jarrick were sitting across from her. She would have given almost anything to hear his comforting words just then, to have him stand between the offensive man and herself, to defend her point of view. But Beth refused to cry. She would be able to face this infuriating stranger with the knowledge that he had not driven her to tears.

Sounding like it was just beside her chair, a too-familiar scratching sent shivers up her back. *That's it! That's what I've been hearing!*

Beth leaped up and bolted away. From a safe distance she scanned the corner where the table stood. There was nothing on the floor, nothing to be seen at all besides chair legs and table legs. However, there was a small wall next to her chair—a short partition that supported the rafters and created a tiny attic space just beyond it. *Whatever I heard is on the other side of that wall!*

Beth snatched up her wrap and rushed out. She desperately needed to feel safe again, to hear loving voices and see kind eyes. She hastened away to Molly's.

Chapter
6

Beth found herself avoiding the new teacher whenever possible. The school wall was quickly assembled, and she now was working to clean up the dust and debris left behind. Robert Harris Hughes, it seemed, had more important work elsewhere. It goaded Beth further that he'd been provided a room at Molly's guest house, though he typically chose not to eat there. He had voiced openly that he preferred Abigail's quiet dining room to Molly's bustling one. Still, his presence in the familiar home provided one more reason to eat on her own as often as possible rather than risk crossing paths with him at the boarding house. However, if it weren't for Molly's generous servings of leftovers sent over with Marnie, Beth was sure she'd be eating cold canned food morning, noon, and night. She had so little experience cooking, and there were few dishes she knew how to prepare. *How on earth will I feed a husband—a family?* she fretted.

But right now instead of worrying about such matters, Beth set her mind to being thankful. She could have grumbled about cleaning the schoolrooms alone but decided that in many ways she preferred to manage it on her own without her colleague. So she prayed as she swept and tidied both rooms that God would give her a heart to serve in whatever way she could.

The ample size of her designated classroom delighted Beth. And on Thursday there were new desks delivered by the school district—enough to seat twenty students in each room. Eighteen were actually enrolled in Beth's classroom from first to fifth grade, including nine of the new children. There would be a similar-sized group next door.

Near the front of her room, between the only window and a chalkboard that spanned most of the wall, Beth arranged the large table and chair meant for her own use. A modest potbellied stove was at the back next to a well-stocked hod of coal and a low row of hooks for the children's coats. As she thought back to teaching in the borrowed saloon, Beth reveled in the marvelous new bounty. And, best of all, at the end of each day she could simply pull the door closed without having to dismantle and store away her teaching items in preparation for the pool hall's evening customers.

One by one she hung the precious paintings her sister Julie had furnished, each holding special memories of their travels in the Maritime Provinces. Even on canvas, the vibrant ocean scenes managed to convey life and movement. Almost all of Coal Valley's children had been born and raised in the mountains or on the prairie. Beth was certain they'd enjoy these Canadian landscapes showing very different scenery from what they knew.

Next Beth tacked up the alphabet cards where they'd be easily seen from every desk. She hung the flag with a framed print of the king's photograph beside it. Then out came boxes of reading books and primers, an illustrated Bible story book, a globe and an atlas, the science and art and music supplies. *That silly man certainly cannot accuse me of not developing my students in all areas of their studies,* she told herself, then chuckled at the thought of giving a music lesson while he was trying to lecture on philosophy. *Well, it wouldn't be my fault!* She shook her head. *He's the one who insisted on his silly door.* In the haste to get the wall erected, the door construction had been rather haphazard, and a one-inch gap remained at the bottom. The doors into the mudroom at the entryway were just as inadequate, and Beth was certain both classes would be frustrated by the unnecessary opening between her classroom and his.

⸎

Most evenings found Beth lingering in Molly's kitchen, reluctant to return to whatever creature—or creatures—might be prowling behind the walls. When Frank learned about her distress, he went over to the apartment and found a small opening under the eaves into the attic space next to her dining table and patched it well. Beth was much relieved that he had found no access from the attic areas into her rooms. Hopefully the night visitations would stop altogether, but at least Frank's efforts assured Beth that whatever was making the noises should remain on the other side. Still, she often stayed with Molly's family until Marnie was finished with chores, and the two of them would walk back through the darkness together. Beth drew courage from the girl's nonchalant attitude toward the undefinable sounds. She could tell Marnie wasn't interested in discussing the problem further, simply shrugging off Beth's worries with youthful aplomb.

Twice when she was alone, Beth had plucked up the courage to explore for any evidence of an intruder, though she found nothing specific and could locate no additional openings into the attic areas. However, upon arriving home after school one day she was quite certain an oatmeal bowl she'd placed in the basin after breakfast had mysteriously been licked clean. *Surely it couldn't have dried out so quickly.* And as she inspected further in subsequent days, she was sure the trash bucket was being invaded, some choice scraps pilfered. But there was never enough evidence to be absolutely convinced she wasn't imagining things.

She was able to dismiss it all, though, when Monday morning arrived and school was set to commence. She was both thrilled to begin doing what she loved and also concerned that September was almost spent. There was much instruction time to be recovered somehow before the school year was on track.

"Please take your seats, children," Beth called out over the first-day hubbub. "It's time to begin. I'm so glad to see you again, and I'm looking forward to getting to know those of you who are new this year. You'll find a card with your name printed on it taped to the corner of your assigned desk." The sounds of similar shuffling could be easily heard from the neighboring classroom.

Beth helped the youngest ones find their seats in the front row. Big sister Anna Noonan, all of nine years old, was leading her younger sister, Dorothy, toward the front.

"This is Dotty," Anna said to Beth. "She can't read yet. But I been reading to her at home. We don't got that many books, but she really likes it, 'specially the fairy tales."

"I'm glad to hear it, Anna. And don't you worry, she's in the perfect place for learning now. And you can go on helping her at home." Beth knelt down to eye level and smiled at the timid child, her long brown hair tied back with a bright yellow bow. "Welcome, Dorothy. I'm glad you're here." Her words coaxed out a shy smile.

The last of the students found his name and scurried into his seat.

"We shall begin as we've done in the past, with the Lord's Prayer and the Pledge of Allegiance," Beth told them. "And, children, don't worry if this is new for you. We'll practice every day, and soon you'll be able to join in easily. Please stand quietly beside your desks, fold your hands, and close your eyes."

The long summer's absence seemed to evaporate from Beth's memory. She was fully alive, doing what she loved best.

"Marnie, I'm sorry, but the fire's gone out again. I'm afraid breakfast will have to be from the pantry. I think there's some cheese and a few biscuits left. Do you mind?" It was the third time in one week that Beth had been unable to cook anything for them before school.

"Can I eat that last piece of Miss Molly's pie?"

"For breakfast?"

"Why not? It tastes just as good cold, an' it's apple, so it's good fer me. You know, an apple a day . . ."

Beth sighed. "I suppose. Don't forget your assignment."

"Won't matter," Marnie mumbled. "He's just gonna make me do it over anyhow."

"You've done your best, darling. That's all any of us can do." Beth set the cold teapot back on its shelf with a sigh.

Marnie's face emerged from behind the door of the pantry cupboard. "The cheese is gone."

"What? I'm sure there was still—"

"Something must'a ate it—took bites out'a the biscuits too."

Beth hurried to look. "What on earth . . . ?"

"Ain't mice, then," Marnie declared. "Not 'less there's a whole passel of 'em."

"Oh dear! Do you think . . . is it possible

that something large, like maybe a raccoon, got in? I've been leaving the window open during the day for the fresh air, but there's a screen on it."

"We don't got no raccoons out here."

"Are you sure?"

Marnie stared back blankly. "Well, have ya seen any?"

"I guess not. I haven't thought about it, I suppose. Then what? A squirrel? A rat?" She could hardly contain her shudder.

"We don't got them neither, not rats, least-ways. Plenty'a squirrels though. But I don't think they could get inside the pantry cupboard. Door's too heavy."

Beth was losing patience. "I'm sure I have no idea what it might be. But let's keep things closed up now as a precaution." She pulled the dormer window shut and turned the handle tightly into place. Marnie checked that the pantry door was secure before they hurried off to the school together.

After the frantic start to her day, Beth enjoyed the quiet moments spent in early-morning preparation in her classroom. She wrote out the first reading assignments and the arithmetic questions on the chalkboard so her older students could begin work quietly while she taught lessons to her younger ones.

This morning it was Daniel Murphy's turn

to tend the fire. He greeted Beth and hurried to stir up the coals before adding more. The crackling blaze soon took the edge off the chilly room. Mr. Harris Hughes had composed a schedule so that each assigned boy was needed only once a week. Thankfully, this was one less thing for Beth to bother with, frustrated as she was from struggling to keep her fire at home lit. Somehow the boys managed to produce far less smoke than Beth. She wondered if she'd ever become proficient.

Despite the other teacher's tacit disapproval, Beth continued to stand at the front door and ring the school bell. True, it wasn't necessary, as the children and their mothers were well aware of the time, but she found it a pleasurable way to begin a day, and she looked forward to greeting each personally as they entered the shared foyer. In truth, it was also a rare opportunity to speak with the older students, with whom she still felt a connection.

"Good morning, Luela. My, that's a lovely necklace."

"I got it fer my birthday. Momma ordered it from the store."

"Well, happy birthday, dear! Does that mean you're sixteen now? Oh my."

"Yes, I am."

The girl's eyes sparkled until her brother piped in with, "Sweet sixteen an'—"

"You hush up, Addie!" Luela sputtered.

Beth clucked at the teenage boy who towered above her, shaking her head and rolling her eyes. "Addison, shame on you." He merely laughed, and Luela swatted his arm.

"Now, don't forget," Beth repeated often to each group who entered, "Bible club begins tonight. We're meeting here at the school. I hope you can come."

As the days progressed, a significant source of irritation for Beth was the volume of Robert Harris Hughes's voice. She doubted that her softly spoken lessons were nearly the imposition on him as were his commanding orations resonating through the gap at the bottom of the door. There were times she could even make out words, though thankfully it was more often the dull rumble of indistinguishable speech.

The most common complaint from his students to Beth's empathetic ear was that the new teacher simply talked far too much. Beth, from her position on the other side, could not agree more. Yet she knew there was really nothing this man would receive as a suggestion from her, and so she—and his captive audience—endured the droning throughout most of the day. Her young students seemed to tune him out just as easily as they did the racket of the lumber mill and mine.

Admittedly, Beth took some small satisfaction that he was also hearing the oral recitations of her class. She tried not to allow this thought to influence how often she worked with her students on repeating poetry, or Bible verses, or songs together. In moments of utter honesty, she was rather certain the tensions she felt toward her colleague were provoking her stubborn spirit more than a little.

When school was dismissed each day, a considerable amount of grading went home with her, though Beth found herself as grateful as the children to leave the classroom behind. Sometimes on a mild evening she would sit on Molly's porch, feet tucked under her in one of the rocking chairs, with papers stacked beneath a heavy book to keep them from blowing away. As she worked through each of the pages, she appreciated the activity of the children playing nearby, of the women calling out to one another, of the men returning to their families after a long day. If there was mending to be done, Molly would sometimes join Beth for a chat as they sat grading and sewing on patches.

"The church is 'most done. Ya been by to see it yet?"

"I haven't had time."

"Time? It ain't that far away, dearie."

Beth sighed. "I know. I should just decide

to walk over there one of these evenings. Do they keep it locked?"

"Why, no. Ain't nothin' there to steal."

Beth smiled. "I guess you're right. Maybe I'll go tomorrow."

"Any one'a yer kids would be proud to go along to show it off to ya. Maybe you should ask 'em."

"That's a good idea. I'm sure everyone's excited to see it completed and to have church in a building meant for that purpose. Not to mention having Pastor Davidson all to ourselves." A new thought brought a sigh. "When are Esther and Bardo getting married? Isn't that soon? I'll bet no one's more anxious than she."

"Oh, maybe so. Though since it ain't her first trip up the aisle, dearie, I don't s'pose she's as starry-eyed as you."

"Me? I'm starry-eyed?"

Molly lowered the sock she was mending and peered over her reading glasses. Her pursed lips and one cocked eyebrow revealed her amusement.

"All right," Beth conceded with a little smile. "Yes, I am rather excited. But I have a long time to wait until April. It feels like forever. And what's worse, I've hardly seen Jarrick at all."

"Well, I wish yer Jack was around more

myself. I'd grown accustomed to his wit." The sharp sound of a child's cry turned both their heads. "Oh dear, it's one'a the new girls." Molly stood for a better look. "The smallest Ruffinelli child. What's her name?"

"Pearl? Ah, that's too bad. She's so sweet. Can you see her, Molly? Is she in trouble?" Beth hurried to gather the pages and tuck them under a book.

Molly, with a hand over her eyes, said, "Her brother Henry's got her now, carryin' her home. Looks like she'll be fine. Probably a skinned knee."

"You know what, Molly? I wouldn't be at all surprised if she stumbled over one of these silly stumps," Beth muttered.

"The stumps? What makes ya say that?"

"They're everywhere. One can hardly take a step in this town without having to weave in and out among them."

Molly settled back and took up her work again. "Where ya been walkin' that's so thick with stumps?"

"Just . . . well, everywhere! They crowd in behind most of the buildings. Where the children are trying to play. Something should be done about them. They're such an eyesore, and—and dangerous."

"Ya don't say. What do ya figure should be done?"

"Oh, I don't know. Can't they be chopped out or dug up or something?"

"Well," Molly smiled, maybe a bit patronizingly, "why don't ya go try to dig one? See how that goes fer yerself."

"Not me, of course. But with all these men, and most of them fathers, plus so many machines, you'd think there'd be a little more concern about the well-being of the children."

"Hmm?" A thoughtful pause. "You're getting yerself all worked up like this on account'a the children, is it?"

Beth was growing more impatient by the minute. "You don't agree? I'm quite surprised."

"Dearie, I'm afraid ya don't have any way'a knowin' how powerful hard it is to get rid of a stump. They're mighty stubborn about bein' dug up." Molly removed her reading glasses and scrutinized Beth's face. "And what's more, ain't ya been watching these kids? Why, them stumps're the best playground they got. The girls are using 'em fer tea parties and playin' house round 'em. And the boys have rigged a board across one fer a teeter totter in the clearin' behind their homes. I hear 'em laughin' and playin' there whenever I go visitin'. Seems to me they're doin' just fine."

Beth pressed her lips together, unable to yield. "But in the winter the snow will cover them, and the children will trip and get hurt. I think they're dangerous. I really do."

Molly looked genuinely puzzled. "What're you truly saying, dearie? What's yer real complaint?" She rocked forward in her chair to be closer to Beth.

"I just don't like them. That's all."

"But *why?*"

With a long hesitation, trying to put into words her tumbling thoughts, Beth thought back to her feelings as she had first arrived back in town and when she saw the stubble on the hillside beyond the new mill. "I don't know. They're awfully ugly, I suppose—like scars on what was such a lovely landscape. Doesn't it make you sad to think about it, Molly? The trees were alive once—beautiful, living things that grew and gave shade and held birds in their branches." The more she voiced the rising bitterness aloud, the more Beth felt a hard lump rising in her throat. She hadn't realized how much the sight of them had been festering. "It's worse than barren now—worse than if there was simply a field instead. Down by the mill it's absolutely ghastly to behold."

Molly placed a comforting hand on Beth's knee. "Yes, dearie, but they stood in the way too. If our town was to continue to grow, them trees had ta come down, had to make room fer the new. And, what's more, now those self-same trees been turned into boards fer new homes, fer the blessings of a school wall and a fine church 'most done. Seems like a good trade to me."

"But I liked it the way it was." Beth rubbed at her ink-stained fingers, refusing to raise her eyes. She suspected it could be helpful to discuss her frustrations, but it was also humbling to feel so vulnerable and childlike.

"I see. It's the *changin'* that you don't like."

"What do you mean?"

"How different it all seems. That ya come back to find it don't even *look* right no more. Leastwise, not how ya hold this place in yer memories. Maybe sometimes it even feels ugly to ya now."

Beth whispered, "I suppose. Yes, that *is* how I feel."

For a moment Molly seemed to be contemplating Beth's reaction carefully, looking out at the view from her front porch. From this vantage point the missing trees revealed much more of the town than could be seen last spring. "Dearie, I've lived a long time. And I can tell ya that my own life's been full'a stumps—all kinds of 'em. From the pain of losing my first husband, my dearest Bertram, and long before that to working through every single change in our plans together. Leavin' friends and family, always movin' on whenever he got some new scheme in his head." Her throat seemed to constrict, and the words sounded more forced. "To comin' to understand we'd never have a baby all our own. All of it hard—all of it not the way I wanted things to be. An' as every one of 'em beautiful tall dreams come crashin' down like felled trees in a clearin', it felt like there weren't nothin' left fer me but an old field of stumps."

Beth took the woman's hand in hers, squeezing it tightly.

Molly continued, "I've found ya can't cling to what ain't gonna be—can't even build on the ruins till the wishin' for what ya wanted first dies away. But it takes *time* fer that to happen. Often time has ta pass 'fore you can see them old dead dreams fade to naught. And then, only then, somethin' else can spring up instead. Like, fer me, it's this town, my own new family with Frank an' Teddy Boy an' Marnie, an' all these children, these friends— and you." She wiped her cheek without apology, and her smile was a little wobbly. "I'm so sorry it ain't easy, but it's true nonetheless. Hard as it be, a body can't grow without having some growin' pains along the way. Can't reach ahead 'cept that you let go of what lies behind. Not just in lettin' the first dream get chopped away, but sometimes living beside the ugly old stumps'a the past till it wanes and somethin' new takes root. But we got hope through it all that the good Lord knows long before we do what's to come. And we can trust Him. Fer those of us with faith in our redeemin' God, there's always hope."

Beth tried to produce a smile. She wished she could wholly agree with Molly's sage words. They clearly contained powerful truth. But the far-reaching implication was more than Beth, at this moment, could accept. There were dreams in her heart she couldn't yet find the courage to give up. Instead she slid down to her knees beside the dear woman's rocking chair, folded her arms around Molly, and shared a long, consoling embrace.

Chapter 7

Just as Beth was gathering the last of her things for school, the scratching sound came as clear as day. Marnie had already skipped ahead down the stairs. Beth stood perfectly still, listening for a source—or at least a direction. And then a low rumble seemed to come from the kitchen window, already closed tight. As quietly as she could, Beth edged toward it, trying not to breathe. Slowly, ever so slowly, she moved closer to the glass, her eyes darting in every direction.

First she saw only a tail. A long scruff with thin stripes arched and then dipped out of view. *I think it is a raccoon!*

But when a whiskered, slant-eyed face with upright triangle ears emerged, Beth gasped. *Why, it's a cat! I think it's Mrs. Grant's old tabby cat, Penelope! So she's the source of all the racket!*

But how could she have gotten in before, and even more incredible, into the cupboard?

Seeing Beth in the window now, the tabby became more assertive, writhing back and forth, yowling to be allowed in. Telling herself she wouldn't be afraid of a silly old cat, Beth twisted the handle and pulled the pane open a little, intending to shoo the intruder away. Immediately it slipped under one corner of the screen and pounced to the floor in a wild leap. Beth fell back against the table, trying to catch her balance. *The screen is loose! Oh no, what have I done?*

Stalking and skulking around the room, Penelope actually *was* frightening to behold, as if the animal were searching high and low for her former owner. *If I feed it, perhaps it'll leave.* Beth rushed to the icebox and poured a saucer of milk, placing it on the floor as quickly as possible without spilling it. Even more quickly the cat dove to crouch beside the bowl, licking furiously. Its stomach looked pinched in at the sides, its fur tattered and thin.

Seeing its emaciated state, Beth removed a slice of chicken from the icebox and tossed it onto the floor beside the milk. The yowling dropped in pitch and became a fearsome warning tone. Beth backed away.

Now what? School would begin shortly, and there was a cat in her kitchen. She couldn't leave it inside, yet dared not touch it. So she waited, desperately wondering what on earth to do.

The chicken soon had disappeared, and the saucer was licked dry. Penelope began again to prowl around the room. She jumped up and hooked her front paws on the lip of the trash can, pushing her head deep inside. Beth was grateful that the old metal pail was so heavy. *How can I get rid of her now? She probably has fleas or ticks—or worse. I've got to get her out of here!*

Backing toward the door, Beth opened it wide. "Here, kitty-kitty. Come, puss, over here, Penelope." *What on earth does one say to a cat?* Mother had never allowed the family to own an indoor pet, so Beth had no idea how to coax it into obeying. The cat ignored every appeal and leaped in a single bound onto the counter.

"No!" Beth rushed forward, waving anxious hands. "Shoo! Get down! Shoo!" She was haughtily ignored.

Then Beth spotted the broom in a corner. She reached for it and held it out as a weapon and a shield. "Shoo!" she repeated, now with the added threat of the broom. "Get out, Penelope! Go away!"

For several minutes Beth played hide and seek with the bedraggled creature as it ducked under and around the furnishings, but it slowly edged closer and closer to the door. "Shoo! Scoot! Go!" *Almost there—almost—almost . . .* One last flip of the broom and Penelope slunk out the door. Beth slammed it and leaned against it, breathing in gasps.

It took several minutes to tidy her hair, gather her papers and books, and hurry out the door. Only then did it occur to her that she could have simply set the chicken out on the step. The thought made her laugh aloud. She felt it was perhaps a mercy no one had seen the battle of wills and wits she'd waged with the Grants' abandoned kitty.

As Beth dismissed class for the day she asked, "Who would like to walk over with me to see the new church? I haven't been there yet, and I'm looking forward to it."

"Aw, Miss Thatcher, I wanna go. But Mama says I gotta come right home," Anna Kate complained.

"Perhaps another time, darling. And besides, you'll have lots of opportunities to see it. Your mother and her fiancé will be married there soon."

"Uh-huh, next week." The little girl's eyes brightened. "An' I get to be flower girl. Levi's gonna pick me some down by the crick."

Beth smiled broadly while giving the child's braid a little tug. "That's lovely, darling. Anyone else want to show me to it?"

"I'll take ya," ten-year-old Ida Edwards volunteered. "My daddy's been helpin' build it. I go sometimes and take a snack over to him. So I know the way."

"Who cares," Georgie called from across the room. "Everybody knows the way. It ain't that far."

Beth raised a warning finger and answered the little girl, who was one of the new children. "Thank you, Ida. I'd be pleased to have a chance to chat with you a little on the way. We can get to know one another a little better." A wide grin revealing two missing teeth flashed in answer.

In the end a small group joined Beth and Ida for their walk past Molly's and up the hill toward Frank's former cabin. Instead of turning off the road onto the well-worn path through the woods, they continued on just over the crest of the hill and found themselves gazing at rows of bright new boards on the side of the new church building.

"It gots lots'a windows," Ida hurried to point out. "More 'an a dozen. And there's a little room at the end, past the one where our church'll meet, fer the pastor, Momma says. Not for livin' in—just for workin'."

She paused, having confused herself with the explanation. "Don't know what he does when he ain't preachin', but anyways, he gots a room for it."

Beth smiled affectionately. "I'm sure Pastor Davidson will find some good ways to stay busy."

"It's gonna have a bell too. Not yet, but someday. They built a place up top ta put it."

"It's rather a large building." Beth scanned up the walls of the front narthex to the tall spire far above and the vacant space in the simple belfry. "I hadn't pictured it quite so big. And the steeple so tall."

"Yeah, my daddy helped ta make it just like that—so high in the front. And he said it was a mercy nobody fell off it. They might'a died or somethin'." Ida's eyes grew large.

Georgie muttered, "He didn't do no more'n the rest of 'em. I know 'cause my momma does the washin' for Mr. Gowan's crew, and they talk about stuff like that waitin' at my house sometimes. Mr. Gowan said that maybe God will be good ta our town, on account'a we're buildin' Him such a nice house ta live in. You think so, Miss Thatcher?"

Beth drew a slow breath. "I think God is always good no matter what we do or don't do. And He loves each one of us very much too." She sat down on one of those hated stumps in order to be at eye level. "Do your mothers love you more if you behave but less if you don't?"

A momentary silence as the children grappled with the question.

"I don't th-th-think so," Jonah answered slowly. "Momma always s-says she loves me no m-matter what." He thought some more, screwed up his face. "But m-maybe she's *happier* when I'm g-good."

Beth smiled and nodded. "And that's the way God loves, even more so, no matter what. But like your mother, Jonah, we can *please* Him by doing things that are kind and good, by obeying what He tells us in the Bible, and by making a fine place for the people of our church to meet. This is a place where we can learn more about Him, pray, and sing hymns of praise. Doing it together is good for us, and it's something God likes a lot."

Their response was less than Beth had hoped. The children seemed to have lost interest. She prayed that the truth of this conversation over time would find its way into their hearts.

"Wanna go in?" Ida suggested.

"Yes, let's."

The interior of the building seemed even larger, particularly so because it was still empty. Beth hoped for the sake of Bardo and

Esther's wedding that finishing it up would be done in time. It seemed impossible that the room would be ready for a wedding in a week.

Beth was struck with the simplicity of the sanctuary's platform—a wood podium on a small riser with no ornamentation or pageantry at all. No banners, no piano, not even a cross. *I hadn't expected much,* she thought, *but it seems so humble, plain. Will it convey a proper sense of respect?* Almost instantly she heard a silent rebuke from deep within. *It's not the building, it's what God sees in the hearts of His people. I know that. I do.*

Still, she couldn't help but wish Esther would have a finer chamber in which to be married. And then she stopped abruptly as a mental image of her own wedding filled her mind, accompanied by a sharp intake of breath. Her eyes swept the room again. *It's so much* homier *than anything I had ever imagined. Homey is nice, but what will Mother think? What can be done to decorate it? Is there any amount of creativity that will be enough to soften this empty space?*

The only way for Beth to still her consternation was to begin immediately to plan how she might help Esther turn it into a wedding chapel.

Esther and Bardo's upcoming wedding brought a frenzy of activity. Extra men joined the builders to work long into the night to finish the church, and then the women took over. Beth turned a school art class into fashioning autumn finery out of leaves, dried grasses, and berries to attach on the ends of rows up the aisle, and the girls and some boys helped get them all in place. Beth also created a wreath for the front of the podium, and Frank made a small wooden cross to insert in the middle. *Maybe it can stay here for a while,* Beth thought as she surveyed the finished piece.

Even as she continued with dusting and polishing to put the new sanctuary in order, she mentally worked through options for her own ceremony. The floor was stained a dark walnut with the window and door moldings painted white, contrasting against the pale green of the walls. The wooden pews were dark, and the platform was covered with a thin brown carpet. Beth clung to the hope that with enough flourishes, the interior would be considered quaint rather than rustic, and charming rather than plain. She felt a bit guilty at her relief that only family would be coming, considering the two thousand–plus miles on a dusty train. *Particularly not Mrs. Montclair, who would never understand my decision to wed here . . . and, worst of all in her eyes, not to marry her Edward!* she thought with a small grin. But looking out the sparkling new window at the splendid mountain views, Beth sighed blissfully. *I don't care. I'd rather be here.*

She wrote to Mother that evening, explaining some of the ideas she was developing, and requested that she might wear the special wedding dress still carefully wrapped and preserved in the carved cedar chest upstairs—the dress from Europe that had been passed down from Grandmama. Margret had looked breathtaking when she was married in the gown. And even though Beth was fully aware of how much it would need to be altered for her much smaller form, she had always dreamed she might also be given the honor.

Margret, Beth sighed to herself as she finished up the missive, *I wish we weren't so far apart. I wish I could visit with you just now. You must be so anxious for this baby due in January. That's not so far away. Oh, and what I'd trade to spend another day playing with your sweet little boy.* She was more than certain Margret and family would not make such a daunting journey with a new baby.

Beginning a second letter, Beth asked Julie to be her maid of honor and requested that she and Mother shop for two matching dresses in Toronto—one for Julie and the other for

Marnie, whom Beth wanted for her second attendant. She had no doubt that the girl would readily accept. "Something tea-length in cornflower blue—but not too extravagant, nothing that would need to be fitted," Beth urged in her letter. "And I would very much like it to be something Marnie might be able to wear again on special occasions."

April seemed too far away to bear. Beth felt for the ring on her finger. *If only I knew when Jarrick might visit—if I could have a chance to talk with him about all the details, to tour the church with him and make plans.* She hoped she hadn't overstepped propriety in what she had arranged without him. And yet there seemed a thousand decisions still to be made.

Who's going to marry us? Surely Jarrick will choose Philip to be his best man, but then who would serve as minister? How many other groomsmen will he want? Will my own two attendants be enough? And if not, then who would I ask? Molly? Beth smiled affectionately at the thought.

Each night found Beth wishing into the darkness that Jarrick would make a surprise visit soon. She forced her mind not to worry about where they would live after the school year was over. And she often asked God if He would *please, please* move Jarrick's heart to stay in the West. But as she passed the tree stumps nearest to her stairs, she fought against troublesome worries that her persistent dream might be cut down like one of these evergreens.

***

Beth told Marnie about her discovery of Penelope, and the girl seemed impressed with Beth's fortitude. "Maybe we can make friends with her," Marnie suggested. "I bet Miss Molly'd be glad to let us take some scraps from the chicken bin," she said. So they began to leave bits of food at the foot of the stairs for Penelope. It took surprisingly few repetitions for the cat to regularly make her appearance just as Beth and Marnie were heading out the door in the morning.

"Here, kitty-kitty," they'd call. But Penelope would hunch in the bushes, waiting for them to leave. Each time one of them took a step toward her, the tabby would edge away with a low warning rumble in her chest. Another step, and with a whip of her tail she'd be gone altogether. Beth worried aloud that their offering might be rejected and that anything left would attract rodents from the nearby woods. But Marnie was certain the scraggly creature would always clean her plate, and she seemed to be correct.

One morning Beth spoke toward the bushes, "I'm going to win you over, you silly thing. We're going to be friends yet." At the very least, Beth was grateful that she was no longer overcome by fear whenever something would go bump in the night—and that Frank had fixed the loose window screen.

The fire in her wood stove was still a constant burden. Beth found the whole process easier now, but it was also easy to simply forget and neglect it. *What a nuisance! How do mothers manage with so much other work to do?* With Marnie's help, Beth had become rather proficient at making biscuits and pancakes, eggs and oatmeal, but she had yet to master anything more substantial. October was passing, and Beth had prepared only three or four evening meals on her own.

Marnie offered frequently to help with grading some of the papers after supper and to prepare materials Beth needed for the next day. A secret hope began to stir as Beth watched the girl throw herself into each of these activities. *Wouldn't Marnie make a wonderful teacher? Oh, how I'd love to see her get a teaching certificate. That would change everything for her future.*

Chapter
8

"Miss Thatcher, excuse me if you please. I have here a letter for you." A tall, dark-haired young man stood in the classroom doorway, the stream of students exiting around him.

"Why, Paolo," Beth exclaimed, "it's so good to see you! It's been far too long. What brings you to our valley?"

"Yes, ma'am," he answered with a wide grin and strode across the floor. "I have wanted to come here to greet you. But I have not found a right time. And then my papa, he let me come visit—and also to deliver this letter from the city to you." His explanation tumbled out quickly, as if he felt the need to apologize for his absence. "I am working still at my job in Lethbridge, but very soon it comes to the end. And with the rest of our family, I will join Papa here soon. He is hurrying to make ready the house and I will help him for a few days." His English had improved considerably since Beth had last spoken with him.

Beth accepted the letter with a quick look at the sender. *Jarrick!* Her heart soared, and she tucked it in with her papers to take home. She motioned for Paolo to take a seat in the front row. The desk chair was too small, of course, and his legs stretched out far into the aisle. "I'm sorry to hear about your job in Lethbridge ending, but I'm glad your family will be coming soon. You certainly are looking well."

He laughed. "Mama says I'm more giraffe than boy."

Beth smiled at his little joke. "I have to say, Paolo, I was hoping to hear you had registered for school. Have you at least had a chance to continue your English studies on your own?"

"A little," he answered hesitantly. "I read at night as late as I can. But I am so tired, having worked all day. I often fall asleep. In any way, I am too old to attend school."

"Aren't you still sixteen? Teddy and Addison are both older than you—they're seventeen."

"Yes, ma'am," he answered, "but I must help to provide for my family."

Beth knew that Heidi Coolidge, who was a widow, was certainly sacrificing to see that Addison was able to finish his education. "Maybe you could still write the exams by studying on your own. I could help you—"

"Thank you, Miss Thatcher," he put in quickly. "You are very kind."

By the way he shook his head Beth knew he had already dismissed the possibility. She would not pursue it, at least not now. "When does your family arrive?"

"We don't know yet. The plans keep changing. But my papa, he insists he will be ready for us as soon as we can come."

"I'm sure he just wants his family back together again. It's been too long—over a year for him, hasn't it?"

"Yes, it will soon be two years. But my papa, he's glad to drive for the company. He's glad he can be visiting my mama whenever he is in the city."

They chatted for several minutes more until Paolo stood suddenly and excused himself. "I am to return now. My papa, he not allow I should stay too long."

Beth walked the young man to the door. "Please come again whenever you're able, Paolo. It's so good to see you. And greet your father for me." She patted his arm. "I can't wait to meet your mother, your family. I'm so happy you can all be together again. I hope they come soon."

"Thank you, ma'am."

A new thought occurred and she said quickly, "You have younger siblings, don't you?"

"Yes, I do. A sister and two brothers."

"Then they'll be able to come to school here. I'll be happy to help them with English."

Paolo hesitated. "It could be so, Miss Thatcher. But as I have said, I don't know when . . ."

"Well, we'll have to wait and see, I suppose."

"Yes, ma'am," he answered, "we will wait and we will see."

With a tip of his hat he departed, and Beth hurried back to her desk—and the letter.

My darling Beth, it began, *I've just returned to Lethbridge, and I wanted to let you know I'm approved to pay a visit to you this weekend. I'll arrive on Friday afternoon with Edward. He's bringing his fiancée, Kate, who wanted to see the area. I also know that she wants to meet you. They'll drive straight back after dinner, but I can stay until Philip drives out Sunday. I can't wait to see you. It's been far too long. . . .*

Warm tears filled her eyes so she couldn't read more. *Oh yes, it's been far, far too long—almost a full month.* She blinked away the tears and tucked the letter back with her stack of papers to wait until she was alone. She was determined not to risk being caught crying by Mr. Robert Harris Hughes.

⁕

"Marnie," Beth began as they worked together cutting out paper shapes for geometry class. "I want to host a meal on Friday evening. Can you help me?"

The girl looked up. "Fer who?"

"Well, for Jarrick and—"

"Ya mean Jack Thornton?"

"Yes, and Constable Edward Montclair and his fiancée. And Pastor Philip, I suppose. He'll be here for the weekend too."

Marnie stared at Beth. "Ya only got two chairs."

Beth's musings hadn't solved that particular problem. "Perhaps I could borrow some."

"Where would ya put 'em all? Yer table ain't big enough, yer room neither." She gestured around the small quarters.

"Well, I don't know."

They went back to work again in silence. Finally Beth looked up once more. "We could have a picnic. It's still warm enough."

"Well . . ." Marnie, with her practical mind, seemed to be evaluating the idea. "The sun sets pretty early. Can ya get 'em fed so soon if ya eat outdoors?"

"You're right, it's dark early already. But they arrive in the afternoon. I think I can make that work. We'll have to eat at five." She hesitated. "It's just that, well, you know I haven't had a chance to cook very much."

Marnie kept her head tucked low over her work, but Beth could tell she was smiling as she continued to slice through the paper with the scissors. Without raising her eyes Marnie said, "I could help ya. It ain't hard."

"Would you? I'd appreciate that so much."

"Sure." She nodded. "I can *teach* ya." She let the word hang in the air between them.

Reaching out a hand, Beth gave the slender shoulder a playful squeeze. "Yes, darling, you can be *my* teacher for a change."

Plans fell into place rather quickly. Beth would serve a pot roast, which Marnie promised was simple to prepare—particularly important since Beth would be teaching during the day on Friday. She'd have as much as possible ready and waiting before that morning. However, her plan required that she rise even earlier Friday in order to peel vegetables, and it would mean dealing with the very temperamental fire. So much would depend on it not going out during the day. Beth hoped that there'd be opportunities during school to run across the street and check that all was well. *How on earth does Molly know for certain her meat will be cooked properly after church every week, and with so many extra mouths to feed? I had no idea how hard this is!*

By Wednesday Beth alternated between periods of great confidence and terrible doubt. Marnie had helped make two pies—one apple and one custard. These had turned out beautifully, though they'd left a terrible mess in the oven which required much scraping to clean and smelled awful as the residue burned away. On Thursday they worked together to make a pan of rolls. This time the cleanup was manageable.

Before school Friday morning, Marnie was exclaiming about the meal plans as she set a reading book on each desk. "Yer almost ready now. All the hard parts is done. Won't Constable Thornton be surprised—and proud! Ya got a great big pot roast, vegetables a'plenty, rolls and pies and lemonade. That's a meal fit fer a king. Leastways, it's fit for two officers and a pastor." She turned to smile, but then her gaze swept past Beth and her expression changed.

"Miss Thatcher." The authoritative voice came from the doorway between the classrooms. "May I speak with you please?" Robert Harris Hughes was standing in the opening, a large atlas in his hands. *How long has he been there? And why?*

"Of course." Beth laid down the chalk she'd been writing assignments with, dusted her hands together, and crossed the room, her mouth suddenly feeling dry. "How can I help you?"

The familiar smile came in answer. "As you can see, I was returning your book. Here it is. Thank you for allowing me to borrow it. I found it very helpful for my class."

"You're certainly welcome to it anytime." Beth received the atlas from his hands.

He cleared his throat. "I also wanted to give you a copy of the schedule for cleaning chalkboards that I've worked out for the girls. Since the young men are helping with the fire, I find it fitting that the young ladies also be given an assignment."

"Sir, I'm not sure that all of the girls will be able to do so. Most have chores at home—"

"Well, I don't believe there's any harm in setting the schedule to include them. If their parents feel it's unsatisfactory, I'm certain they'll be in touch."

Beth took a breath and struggled for a suitable response. "Well, I suppose I don't mind doing both the boards myself. It doesn't take long to wipe them—there are only two."

"You see," he insisted, "you're making

my own point. It won't take the girls long either, and they'll have a truly important sense of sharing the maintenance of our building together."

Beth rubbed at the binding of the large book, trying not to let her frustration show. "I'm sure you'll hear back from some of their mothers."

"That may well be. I look forward to speaking with them." He pushed the paper containing his schedule into Beth's hand and turned as if to leave, then swung back again. "Forgive me for eavesdropping, Miss Thatcher, but I gather you'll have visitors this weekend. How nice for you."

Beth attempted a smile. "Yes, my fiancé is coming—with some friends."

"And Pastor Davidson?"

"Yes, he's a friend."

"I see. Miss Thatcher, I find him a difficult man to intercept. I've sent several messages and still have received no response. Of course, he's frequently absent from town, but one might hope—"

"I'm sure he's just been busy. Philip is setting up his new church here while at the same time training a replacement for the other churches he's been pastoring."

"Philip? I see. Yes, you must be friends."

Her face growing warm, Beth hurried on,

"He's been an acquaintance of my fiancé's for many years. We—"

"Fine, fine." His eyebrows rose. Beth knew this change of expression would be followed by a particularly difficult request. "Miss Thatcher," he said deliberately, dragging out the words, "I wonder if you might be so kind as to arrange a meeting between myself and your friend Pastor Davidson."

For a moment Beth was at a total loss, finally stammering out that there probably wouldn't be time.

Marnie offered from across the room, "Miss Thatcher, you could invite the teacher fer supper. Ya got lots of food."

Beth froze in place. He watched, seeming amused at the uncomfortable predicament he had managed to create for Beth. Her shoulders rose as she fought against the desire to flatly deny him, her mind racing to sort through what would be considered congenial or whether she should take a stand. She felt her heart racing. "Yes," she heard her voice answering, "of course you may come to supper if you like. We plan to eat at five."

"Splendid." His eyebrows rose again. "I shall arrive promptly at five." And with a nod of his head he was gone. The door closed behind him.

Eyes wide in disbelief, Beth twisted her

head slowly toward the girl who stood smiling proudly. "Oh, Marnie," she groaned.

"What? What did I do?"

Immediately after school on Friday, Beth hurried across the street, past Abigail's entrance, and around the corner to the stairs. To her delight, there was Jarrick already sitting on a step waiting for her.

"Darling!" she cried, pulling him to his feet and throwing her arms around his waist.

He held her tightly and kissed the top of her head with a sigh. "Aren't you a sight for sore eyes?"

Just as quickly Beth remembered the meat she had placed in the oven. She grabbed Jarrick's hand and started to lead him upwards. "Come inside. I've got to check the pot roast."

He laughed and held his ground. "First things first, my Beth. I've missed you." He was reaching to draw her close again.

And then none of it mattered—not the meal or the responsibility of hosting guests. Beth returned his gaze, amazed that his familiar blue eyes could elicit such a strong response in her just by looking into her own. "I missed you," he repeated meaningfully.

Beth leaned forward on the stair step for a long embrace, a gentle kiss. "I missed you too," she whispered. "It's been a month since I've seen you."

"Really? To me it feels like at least two."

"Oh, Jarrick."

❧

Frank had managed to create a small table out of spare boards for the food, and it was set up in the clearing behind Beth's quarters. He suggested a close grouping of stumps for seating. Teddy lit a large bonfire to provide light when darkness fell and to keep mosquitoes away. She could imagine what her mother would say about her first dinner party, but there seemed to be no alternative.

Those stumps! she could almost hear her mother exclaim. *How will your poor guests manage their plates?* Beth didn't know whether to agree with her mother or defend the seating arrangement. *I sure hope Kate will wear a sensible dress for a visit to our mountains,* she thought as she checked on the roast.

Jarrick agreed that the lovely fall afternoon would be a wonderful setting for a meal. He carried load after load of plates, utensils, and food down the long stairs. To Beth's great relief, the pot roast seemed to have cooked to perfection, and everything else was soon dished up and ready.

Philip arrived with Edward and Kate just

as Jarrick stepped out on the landing, bringing the pitcher of lemonade to the table. Beth could hear the sound of their approaching laughter. She checked her hair, wiped perspiration from her face with a tea towel, and hurried down to join them.

"It's so good to see you all. I've been looking forward to this all week." The words were true, as far as they went. She'd been rather terrified too. "Edward, this must be Kate. It's so nice to meet you at last!"

The young woman was very pretty with a round face and smooth white skin set off by dark, perfectly bobbed hair. Surprisingly shy, Kate almost hid her beautiful brown eyes behind her long, full bangs, tipping her head down against Edward's shoulder.

"This is my gal!" Edward boasted. "Katherine Duncan, this is Elizabeth Thatcher. Elizabeth, this is my Kate."

"Hello, Elizabeth. I'm pleased to meet you," the young woman said, extending a hand but remaining close to Edward.

Beth caught the hand in both of her own, smiling warmly. Kate's skin was very soft and cool to the touch. *She doesn't fit here at all,* Beth worried. *Why on earth would this lovely creature want to come way out here to picnic in my backyard?* "I'm sorry we can't be indoors, Kate," she quickly said. "I'm afraid my place just isn't adequate for all of us. I hope you don't mind sitting by the fire."

"No, it's fine. It's lovely, actually."

"We like to be outdoors," Edward assured Beth as he slipped an arm around Kate. "You might not assume this by looking at her, but my Kate's ready for anything."

You're right, Edward, I wouldn't guess that. She appears in every way like a . . . like a china doll, and a timid one at that.

Beth took another look around, imagining how the setting probably seemed to the others, but she squared her shoulders and invited her guests to find seats, purposefully avoiding calling them stumps.

"We're going to take advantage of our remaining nice weather and the wonderful views." Philip agreed with a wink as Edward settled Kate on a stump and sat down on one nearby.

And then Beth heard the unmistakable sound of firm footsteps and a throat being cleared. Robert Harris Hughes had arrived. With as much poise as possible, she motioned toward him and announced, with appropriate enthusiasm, "Everyone, please may I present our second teacher. Yes, that's correct. This year Coal Valley has been assigned *two* teachers. This is Mr. Robert Harris Hughes. He's just come here from the East."

Jarrick stepped forward for a handshake. "It's good to meet you, Mr. Hughes. I'm Jack Thornton. Are you from Ontario?"

"Yes, from Hamilton. My family is in steel on the Hughes side and in education on the Harris side." He raised those dark eyebrows high. "My grandmother, actually, was the one who encouraged me to keep both surnames so as not to overlook either side of the family tree. So it's out of respect for her that I've chosen to honor her request, going by Harris Hughes. But please," he offered without a pause, "please just call me Robert."

He sure didn't make such an offer to me, Beth inwardly protested as she began to remove coverings from the dishes on the table. But the duties of serving her meal, which did smell delicious, soon had her full attention. She couldn't help but whisper when she couldn't be overheard, "Thank You, Lord, that everything's turned out all right." *And thanks to Marnie too.* She would tell the girl later how impossible it would have been without her help.

The conversation flowed easily. Edward and Robert led most of the discussion with Jarrick and Philip interjecting frequently. Kate was almost silent, though she often smiled at Edward. Somehow this young lady managed to maintain a feminine demeanor while sitting on a stump in the outdoors. *I have no idea if she's enjoying herself,* Beth thought as she watched Kate. *Or maybe she just likes being with Edward.* She found herself smiling a little as she thought, *I'm glad he's found someone who seems to hold him in as high esteem as his mother does.*

The sun was already disappearing behind the mountain peaks by the time most of the dishes had been carried back up the stairs by a procession of helpers and Beth had managed to serve pie and coffee. As the sunset faded, the flames from the bonfire seemed to come alive, casting glowing reflections on faces and hands.

Beth brought down a wrap for Kate and one for herself against the growing chill, and Jarrick rolled a cut log closer to Beth's stump to sit beside her. She tucked her hand through Jarrick's arm, and he slid his over it. She wondered if she could possibly feel happier, more at peace. *And they liked my meal,* she couldn't help but exult.

Robert produced a pipe, sending puffs of smoke wafting upward with sparks from the fire. The night sky filling with stars provided a backdrop for an outline of dark pine trees. And the enjoyable conversation continued.

"Have you been to Europe, Edward?" Robert asked around the stem of his pipe.

"Why no, but we hope to travel there for our honeymoon. Not right away—it'll have to be delayed, perhaps next summer. With the Force, you know, I can't plan quite so far ahead."

Robert shifted and leaned forward. "I've traveled rather extensively in Europe, and while there I met some interesting philosophers. I even attended a lecture on education by Bertrand Russell."

"Indeed," Edward acknowledged with a nod. "Logical Atomism and all that—I've read a little from his works during college. Not an assignment, mind you, simply what my peers were reading and discussing. It's all very lofty and intellectual. I'm afraid it's also a little heady and academic for me."

Robert rested his elbows on his knees, and he was off. "Perhaps," he countered, "but I feel he expounds upon many practical applications as well, particularly in light of modern educational theory. Our society is changing very quickly, not just in technological fields but also in the disciplines of philosophy and the humanities." And on he went about discarding the "old ways" and that those achieving a higher degree of education would lead in advancements of thought. "It's our duty as well as a privilege," he added, leaning back with another puff on his pipe.

"I suppose it is, in a way," Edward said, though he didn't sound very convinced.

"Wasn't he a pacifist—refused to fight during the Great War?" Philip interjected.

"He did, and he is."

"Then forgive me, Robert, but in what sense has he truly been willing to *defend* society?"

Robert shrugged off the question, his lofty tone unchanged. "A discussion of Russell's views on war and pacifism isn't necessary in a discussion relating to education. Mind you, I believe it's a worthy dialogue on its own. But if we're to adequately address his ideas on social reform through schooling, I believe he has a fascinating perspective that should be examined carefully."

Jarrick lowered his cup of coffee and smiled. "And you feel those perspectives apply even way out here, far away from, well, almost everything?"

"Of course. Here more than anywhere. You see, if his theories prove effective in a community as illiterate and underdeveloped as this, it fairly well substantiates their efficacy elsewhere."

Beth felt herself stiffen at the man's dismissive attitude about her beloved Coal Valley.

He went on. "That, in fact, is the primary reason I've traveled so far from my home. To test his model in the most extreme of environments."

Beth felt an involuntary shudder, and she took a deep breath. *He's here to experiment on our children? To somehow prove that his and Russell's ideas are the correct ones for all of us?*

"You see, Philip, that's precisely what I've been saying," Robert continued. "Without education we can't change the tenor of our society—can't help the common man to rise above his own expectations regarding his position and duties. And this is never more apparent than in conditions where little has been offered to uplift a man's dignity, where his sense of self is confined by the manual labor into which he's been thrust, as if he had no choice in the matter."

"Oh, I do agree that education is important, Robert," the pastor responded. "And I think you're absolutely correct about the assumptions often made. But I don't believe education alone brings the type of change you're suggesting without also engaging a person's heart. We weren't created to be one-dimensional people. There's so much more to the idea of personhood than just one's mind."

"Yes, yes. And Russell certainly accounted for that, but—"

"No, I don't think you understand what I'm saying," Philip persisted. "It's not that somehow we may discover something in how we view ourselves or our environment that we'll find suitably fulfilling, that will help us rise above the daily struggle for existence. I'm saying that everything in the natural world proclaims there's something infinitely more—some wisdom and reason behind everything we see. Just look around. It doesn't take a college degree to see it." Philip gestured in the darkness and up toward the stars hanging as if within reach. "We aren't the center of it all. But I do believe we're of inestimable value, because we were made in the image of a loving and creative God. That's where our sense of self and dignity comes from—from the marvelous Creator who filled the world with such incredible beauty and gave it to us for a time. It all underscores the value He places on us, His creation."

"I see. Well, of course this would be your point of view. You are, after all, a religious man by vocation. Though I will say, there's begun a movement within the most prestigious religious colleges to cast aside such antiquated—"

"I'm not just a religious man by vocation," Philip put in, "but it's the foundation of every facet of who I am. The fact that I know I have a Creator and a Savior changes every thought and action."

Beth was very grateful to hear Philip

speaking so directly with this man. She had sensed there was much more to Mr. Robert Harris Hughes's theories of education, and now she felt she understood better just what she was up against. *Who knows what all he's been teaching to his class? I'll have to actually listen from time to time. Perhaps I could counter those things for the older children during our Bible club.* She shuddered again and felt Jarrick's arm reach around to draw her close, as if she were simply cold. Beth nestled up against him, grateful to accept his warmth along with his unspoken support.

⁕

Jarrick bunked in the cottage Philip shared with two other men, coming over to the boarding house for meals. On Saturday the couple spent the morning with Frank and Molly. After lunch they walked outside for a while, ending at the church. Beth drew Jarrick into the sanctuary, hoping to make some decisions about their wedding. She called out, "Hello . . . Philip, are you here?"

He appeared quickly from the small door at the side of the platform. "Hello, Beth. Jack. I thought you might stop in. Maybe you've come to discuss your wedding?"

Jarrick laughed. "That would seem appropriate, I suppose. If you ask me, there's lots of time. But I doubt Beth sees things quite that way."

"Yes, I think she's probably ready to plan now."

Beth looked around, not certain how to begin. "I, um . . ." Her mind was suddenly overcome by what to mention first—the attendants, the decorations, the ceremony itself? *What does the pastor need to know, and what should wait till later?*

Jarrick broke the spell. "Let's start with you, Phil. Will you marry us?"

Beth blinked hard, unable to meet his eye. That had been one of her unanswered questions.

"Of course. I'd be honored to do it. And maybe then you'll be able to stop sleeping on my floor every time you come to town." He grinned and reached out to shake Jarrick's hand. "Seriously, though, I was hoping you would ask."

"Well, who else?" They laughed together.

Beth worked to gather her composure. "I have some notes—I don't have them with me now. But I had a few more questions regarding how the wedding—"

"Say," Philip announced, "I have a copy of a ceremony in the back. Let's go to my office and look through that."

She followed dutifully in line, frowning

downward toward the brown carpet. Several patched-together bookshelves, a rather scarred desk, and four mismatched chairs furnished the small office. "Sorry it's not very tidy yet," he said, motioning them to the chairs. "It's difficult to get everything put away, and I still have boxes of books. Some I haven't even brought from Lethbridge yet." He hurried on. "I received most of them from a pastor friend in Calgary, a mentor really, who retired. I can't tell you how grateful I am." Rustling through a stack of papers, he uncovered the wedding-ceremony booklet. "This is what I've got. You of course can modify things, but it gives you the basic format." He passed it to Jarrick. "Take it with you. I don't suppose I'll need it back anytime soon."

"Thanks."

They both turned toward Beth. "What else?" Philip wondered.

She felt her face flush. "I'm not sure. I . . ." Their attentive expressions made it difficult to collect her thoughts.

Philip chuckled, his eyes twinkling, and said, "Well, I can understand that. You've never done this before."

"So we'll try to get it right the first time," Jarrick shot back, to more laughter.

Their levity didn't help. *Oh, Jarrick, I wish we could have discussed this alone first.* At last

Beth managed quietly, "Well, I was thinking of using white tulle to decorate."

"White what?" Philip's brow furrowed.

"A tool?" Jarrick repeated.

"Tulle. It's a fabric. It's soft and makes nice bows. It drapes well. . . ." Beth's explanation trailed off as she realized both men were hopelessly bewildered by the topic. "All right, maybe we should look around for a bit, talk a little by ourselves, and sort out what needs to be decided now and what can wait." Beth didn't feel as confident as her words sounded, but the other two seemed relieved.

"Besides," Jarrick said as they stood, "I'm sure I'll be happy with whatever you decide to do for decorations, Beth. I can't imagine what I could suggest."

But I want to do this with *you, Jarrick,* she mourned silently.

"I know I wouldn't trust you any farther than I could throw you, Jack," Philip joked, and the men laughed again. "I'll be here most of the day if you want to take up wedding plans again."

<hr>

"It's a nice sanctuary," Jarrick said as they walked around. He seemed unaware that she was very quiet, withdrawn. He stepped onto the stage. "Do you think we'll have enough seating? How many are you expecting to travel from Toronto?"

"Only my family—not even all of them," she answered, her voice low. "Margret and John won't be able to come because of the new baby." She averted her eyes. "But Julie and my parents will probably take a train out a week or so early."

"I don't think I'll have many family members either. My parents will come, of course, and my two younger brothers and sister. But I think that'll be all. My other brother, the oldest of us, lives way out east in Halifax now, so he can't come." He cleared his throat and came down the aisle to take a seat near where Beth was standing. "Will you sit with me for a minute? There's something I want to try to say."

She lowered herself onto the pew next to him and waited, still feeling disappointed at how things had stalled and at Jarrick's lack of interest in the details.

"I feel I need to tell you about my mother, Beth. But I'm not sure how. And I don't want to sound . . . well, disrespectful."

"Oh?"

He winced and said slowly, "My mother can be rather . . . difficult. I do think she means well, but she's quite outspoken with opinions, ideas."

An image of Beth's own mother came to mind. "I understand."

"No, you probably don't, Beth, I'm afraid. But I suppose a wedding is one of those times when those with strong ideas can't keep from expressing them. I want you to know that my one strong idea is that I want to marry you. But I'm not worried about all the details. Actually, it's kind of a woman's thing anyway, isn't it?" He allowed himself a chuckle. "But I'll support you—with all of your decisions. I promise to do that."

You're not going to help?

He sighed. "The thing I *can* do for you is to delay my parents' arrival until the last possible moment. That way, there's not much time left for her to say anything."

Beth studied a seam on her skirt and tried to understand what exactly he meant.

"She likes to be in charge, Beth. And I don't want her to undermine all that you've done." Jarrick shook his head. "I don't know how my father manages. She questions almost everything he does, even farming decisions."

"She does?" Beth's eyes were wide as she stared at Jarrick.

"Yes." He shook his head. "I'm so glad you're not like that, sweetheart. I know you're my helpmate. You're so good about trusting me, letting me lead. It's a character trait in you that I deeply appreciate. But then again, you're so good at managing things too. I know you'll do a wonderful job with the wedding plans. I can't wait to see how you whip this room into shape." He reached for her hand.

Beth sat in shock. *I have to do it all? And your mother is going to hate it? Is that what you're saying?* She took a breath before trying to respond but then decided against saying anything at all.

It turned out that Philip needed to leave shortly after Sunday dinner, so Beth's weekend with Jarrick ended rather abruptly. Too soon they were loading his bag into the trunk of Philip's car.

"It was so wonderful to have you here." Beth's whisper sounded a bit shaky.

Jarrick placed a hand around her waist and stepped closer. "It won't be long until I'm back again. Maybe in a couple weeks or so, if I can manage it. I don't think my next assignment will be quite so far away."

"That would be . . . nice." She sniffed and looked into his eyes.

"I'm very glad to know Marnie's staying with you, Beth. When you told me you were living alone, especially there, I was afraid you wouldn't like it very much."

"Actually, I don't." She dropped her gaze, afraid she'd been too blunt.

"Well, it won't be much longer. I hope it helps to remember that."

Beth shook her head. "It does—and it doesn't. But I'll make do somehow."

"That's the courage and pluck I love about you." He bent down to kiss her forehead. "And, Beth," he added, "I want to say, I noticed how you reacted to Robert. I get the sense you don't like the man very much."

"You mean, *Mr. Robert Harris Hughes?*" She knew she was allowing pent-up emotions to fall rather unfairly on Robert's shoulders . . . and now on Jarrick's.

He ducked a bit to look into her face. "I hope he can spend some more time talking to Philip. I think they communicate pretty well with one another, with a shared respect that might be important for him in order to see faith in a new light."

"He doesn't grate on your nerves? I find him very irritating. His airs, his self-importance."

"That's what I was afraid of." Jarrick shook his head. "No, he doesn't bother me. He seems to be honestly looking for wisdom, but I was afraid you didn't see him like that."

"How can he not bother you? Who knows what he's saying to those students?"

"Pray about it, sweetheart. And I will too. You never know what God is saying to the man in ways we cannot see."

As Beth watched Philip's car pull away in a cloud of dust, she realized she and Jarrick hadn't even decided on the number of attendants. Surely he would have an opinion at least about that. Right now it felt to Beth as if Jarrick had no sooner arrived than his visit became just a memory.

I wish I knew when he'll be back again. I think it would have been so much easier to say good-bye if I could count down to when he'd return. But maybe . . . maybe that's what it's like to be in love with a Mountie.

Chapter
9

The week began with Beth's new daily rit-
ual. She walked with a handful of scraps
to the bottom step and attempted to summon the obstinate cat to a meal. Marnie simply shrugged at her efforts and walked on to
school.

"I'm here, you silly beastie," Beth coaxed.
"Come on, get your breakfast. Come on out."
She knew exactly where to expect those yellow eyes under the nearby bush, but the cat
refused to advance even a whisker from her
hiding place.

Beth took one small step forward. "I see
you. Don't be shy." Her words were almost
inaudible. Another step. The eyes blinked dark
and then slowly showed again. Beth stooped
to make herself smaller and, hopefully, less
of a threat. "Come on, kitty. Let me pet you,

just a little. I don't bite." She took a scrap of food and held it out as far as she could reach in front of her. "Here, kitty-kitty."

No response. Another step forward, and she tossed the morsel on the ground near Penelope's nose. Still no movement toward her.

Beth turned her body away, crouching low and waiting, just the corner of an eye observing. Nothing. She faced the cat again and held out another choice tidbit. "You can trust me," she whispered.

With no more time to spare, Beth placed the remainder of the scraps on the ground and moved slowly away, one step at a time. Even then Penelope held her ground, though the orange nose quivered. "I'll see you tomorrow, silly kitty. God bless you anyway," she conceded, feeling just a bit sheepish.

"Miss Thatcher," a male voice interrupted, "is something wrong?"

"Pardon me?"

Her teaching rival was standing at the corner of the building, hands thrust in his pockets as if he'd been positioned there for a while. "I noticed you here a few days ago also. Are you looking for something you've lost?"

Beth felt her face grow hot. "It's nothing. I was just . . . I was just feeding . . . It's nothing."

"You're feeding an animal?" He looked at

the morsels on the ground. "Is that wise, Miss Thatcher? I'm afraid it will only encourage more vermin to linger nearby."

Beth shook her head and began to hastily gather her school things from the stairs. "It's just a cat, Mr. Harris . . . uh, Robert. Left by the previous owner. I don't want it to starve."

"Oh, cats are very adept at surviving in the wild. I'm sure that—"

"This one, Robert, has been a household pet and was no more than skin and bones until I began feeding it." Her words sounded more clipped than she intended.

"I see." He took a step closer and reached out a hand. "Well, you seem to be ready for school. May I carry your bag? It appears rather heavy."

"No. Thank you, no." Beth hoisted the strap to her shoulder.

Undeterred, he waited, evidently intending to escort her across the street. There was nothing to do but fall in step beside him.

He finally said, "Miss Thatcher, may I make a request of you?"

"What is it?"

"My name—you see, it's rather important to me that the students maintain the appropriate degree of respect. Would you be so kind as to continue to refer to me by my more formal title, rather than with familiarity? I've worked rather hard to lay a solid foundation of respect in my classroom. I would appreciate very much your consideration on this matter."

Beth raised a hand to her warm cheek. *How can he make such an issue of this—and with not a student in sight? But I suppose I have no grounds to deny him.* "Fine then, I shall respect your wishes and use your full name." *If I say your name at all.*

"Thank you, Miss Thatcher. I consider that a demonstration of goodwill."

Beth forced a smile. He seemed entirely indifferent to her tone and distant attitude. She remembered Jarrick's words and tried to shake away her irritation.

"And one thing more," he dared to add. "I would like to propose another meeting. I'd like an opportunity to explain my methods further. I feel our school would benefit from our being of the same mind."

He has just crossed the line. That I cannot do. Beth could almost envision the smug face of Nick Petrakis, the young man who had beguiled and deceived her family during the previous summer. That face was now super-imposed over Robert's. *Oh no, not again. I am no longer afraid to stand my ground. I refuse to be coerced into allowing harm to come to the students I love.* She stopped short in the center of the street. "Mr. Harris Hughes, I'm afraid I do not agree with your philosophy of education. And I feel quite confident that my students are advancing nicely without your methods."

His face puckered in genuine surprise. "I had no idea you felt thusly. I was certain that, if there were anyone in this town who would comprehend the importance of unity and cooperation in such matters, someone who might be my educational equal, it would have been you, Miss Thatcher."

"That is because you have never asked me what I thought. And neither have you listened to what I've tried to say."

"I see."

"Do you? I'm afraid you don't understand just how far from one another we stand."

"I'm flabbergasted, Miss Thatcher. In what way?"

"In every way. From your long lectures to your fancy clothes, from the way you're perpetually correcting the children's speech to the way you leave God entirely out of the picture."

The man cocked his head, eying Beth with apparent confusion. "I'm afraid I don't know what to say. I had no idea."

"Again, because you haven't *listened*."

There came a long and awkward pause. Beth averted her eyes, hoping no one else was near enough to have overheard her outburst.

She immediately regretted her words. They were far too sharp, critical, and disrespectful. She knew she had gone too far. She turned her face back toward him and held her breath. *What will he say?*

He was staring back, and his eyes had narrowed. His words came smoothly and dispassionately. "I dress as I do in order to instill a proper respect for my position in my classroom. I correct my students' speech because it isn't likely to improve if left unchecked. In fact, I've never understood how you can ignore their obvious errors. What good does it do to teach one set of rules for written language but simultaneously allow everyday speech to go on unaltered? I believe this practice of yours fails the student. I lecture because it is a fundamental aspect of all teaching. I can't see that any of these can be changed." He took a short step forward and faced Beth directly, and she was surprised to read so little emotion in his face. His words were rather matter-of-fact despite her own display of temper. "And as far as God is concerned, I simply don't believe in him, Miss Thatcher. He can't be proven, and I can't think of any reason why a supposed god would hide himself from those he makes great claims to love. Religion appears to me to be a vain attempt to control one's environment with superstition. Therefore I have no intention of including ideals about religion in my lessons."

Instead of anger Beth now felt almost frightened. *How can he say such things?*

"You see, Miss Thatcher, I haven't tried to change your personal convictions with which I don't agree. Of course I believe it would be beneficial for you to amend your ways, but in the end it is I who will have the most influence in this community. At your insistence I teach the older students only. And speaking frankly, it matters very little how many Christian stories and verses from the Bible you have your younger class repeat aloud and often—I will have the lasting influence, you see. I'm afraid that in the end they'll leave behind the nonsense you've taught them as easily as they do all other childish fairy tales when they mature toward properly disciplined thought under my instruction."

Beth could only stare with wide eyes.

He paused. "Yet still, I feel as if, if you could just hear me out, you'd understand that—"

"No, sir. I assure you that I will not." Beth spun on her heel and rushed on to the safety of her own classroom, her face burning with anger.

I will not cry, she repeated, pacing in tight

circles through the room while trying to regain her composure. *I will not cry.* Then under her breath, "But I might just move my chalkboard so it covers your ridiculous door, you unreasonable and arrogant man!"

Chapter 10

"Molly, I have a dilemma," Beth said over her shoulder as she rolled small balls of dough into bun shapes and placed them on a baking sheet.

"Ya do, dearie? Sounds serious." The aroma from a batch of bread already in the oven wafted through the kitchen.

Beth wasn't certain how much she should share, even with Molly. "It's about . . . well, the new teacher. Do you realize that he doesn't believe in God—at all?"

With quick hands Molly began punching down another large pan of dough. "That's a shame. Guess we all got our work cut out fer us to help him along."

"Yes, we do." Molly's response touched at a guilty nerve. "On the other hand, doesn't it concern you that he has so much influence over the children? His position is such a pivotal one for their impressionable minds."

Pulling a clean cloth over the dough and hoisting it over to a place beside the warm stove, Molly returned to the kitchen table, wiped her hands on her apron, and eased herself onto a chair. "He does at that, but it sure don't leave the rest of us silent."

"No, no, I'm not implying that. But I am concerned about the kinds of things he's been teaching them in class. Has Marnie said anything to you?"

"Not about that. She don't seem to enjoy his wordy teachin' style, and she'd like to complain about his quirks, though I don't let her get away with such, but she ain't said nothin' about what he believes."

The report surprised Beth. She tore off another piece of dough and began rolling it thoughtfully. "It may not be that obvious—just comes through in the way he explains things, in how he discusses each lesson. History and science, even mathematics. I'm afraid his way of looking at the world pervades everything else."

"Same with us. It ain't right if what ya believe don't alter everything else. Ya want a cup of tea?"

Her casual response annoyed Beth. "No, thank you. Molly, it's just that if the wrong beliefs are allowed to become integrated into a young person's mind, it's so difficult to remove them later."

"You sure ya don't want tea?" Molly stretched to retrieve two cups and saucers from a nearby shelf and set them on the table.

The happy sound of teacups clattering softly against their saucers made Beth reconsider the offer. "Yes, fine then." Molly went to the stove for hot water and the tea fixings, whisking away the sheet of buns Beth had just finished.

As she wiped her hands on her borrowed apron, Beth worked to collect her thoughts. Nick's face rose again to her mind, and she frowned. "I feel it's our duty to safeguard these children against false teachings while they're young," she finally said. "It's so important that we're careful about who influences them." Molly's head bobbed in agreement, encouraging Beth to go on. "We're answerable for what we allow into their lives, especially while they're so young. And I'm afraid Robert has his own agenda."

"How so?"

Beth leaned closer and confided, "As nearly as I can gather from his conversation with Jarrick and Philip, he places education . . . well, in the position of God. He believes that the ills of our age can be overcome by humanity if we're simply educated well enough."

"Well, dearie, that don't seem too surprisin' comin' from a teacher."

"But it's modern humanism, pure and simple. It makes mankind into gods."

Molly set her cup back in its place, shaking her head. "I'm sorry, Beth, I don't have nigh the education of the pair of ya. But what you're callin' this new, modern *humanism* seems to have been around fer a long, long time, don't it?"

"Of course, Molly. It's as old as the book of Genesis."

"An' as much as we wish it, it don't seem practical to try and remove all those who believe the age-old lies from our kids' world." Beth opened her mouth to reply, but Molly hurried on with a pat on her arm. "On the other hand, we ain't powerless, dearie. The truth is gonna win out. And there's love we got as a weapon too. Ain't never been as mighty a weapon for upholdin' truth and winnin' souls as what love can do. And there ain't nobody gets more of our love and attention as our own children. That counts fer a lot."

"It does, Molly. Of course it does."

"Then you keep on teachin' 'em—and we'll all together keep on lovin' on 'em and prayin' fer 'em. And that includes Mr. What's-his-name. The Spirit of truth won't ever be silenced in speakin' to their hearts or his. I don't think we got too much ta fear from just one man."

Beth lifted her teacup to partially conceal her inner turmoil. Since being so terribly deceived over the summer by three people she had thought were friends, she did not consider herself to be so naïve as she'd once been.

For several days Beth hadn't bothered banking the fire to ensure a hot breakfast, but the cold nights of early November were finally too much to ignore. She shivered as she rose from her snug bed and hurried into her clothing. Now that there was snow on the ground, a dependable fire would be necessary to keep her little home warm enough.

Lunch was easy—sandwiches at school using Molly's homemade bread. Dinner, which Beth usually ate alone while Marnie helped Molly, often consisted of just toast and tea, sometimes followed by a can of fruit if she was particularly hungry. It seemed like too much work to fry up something more substantial just for one when the cast iron skillet was so difficult to clean. In the back of her mind was the nagging worry that soon she'd need to manage meals for two, and Jarrick may not be quite as content with a snack-sized meal in the evenings.

The fact was that Beth's skirts were rather loose now around the waist. *What will Mother say? It won't be long until my family comes for the wedding, and I'd best not look as thin as Penelope.* The thought of family brought a sigh as Beth recalled the cook who'd cared for their nutritional needs during her growing-up years. She didn't suppose one could be retained on a Mountie's salary—even supplemented with her teaching income.

Furthermore, she was very busy with events such as Bible club two evenings a week. At first Beth wondered if the older students might lose interest. However, their mothers apparently supported the effort, and it seemed like even the teenagers weren't bored. She had continued where she left off last in the book of Exodus. The stories were some of her favorites and were easy to dramatize, using each of the children to represent a Bible character during the evening. Most of the youngsters' inhibitions had long ago been abandoned, and even the new members seemed eager to take part in the lively action.

Then at last Beth heard the kind of statement she had feared. "Mr. Harris Hughes says there weren't really no pharaohs like the one the Bible tells about." Daniel Murphy was leaning against her desk while the others organized the evening's skit. "He says men called *arch-ologists* been diggin' in Egypt for over a hundred years, and nobody's found a single word about no Israelite slaves."

Beth could feel the hair on her scalp bristling. She struggled to maintain composure. "That's very interesting, Daniel. Have you been studying Egypt?"

"Naw, he was just saying."

Beth motioned him to a chair along with two boys who'd joined him. "Do you know why there's so much sand covering a country that was once so great?"

"No, ma'am," David Noonan spoke up.

"In the time of Moses, Egypt was a very great nation. One of the greatest on earth. People like Abraham often headed off to Egypt when there wasn't enough food or if another enemy was too strong. Later in the Bible, we learn that God even told Joseph in a dream to flee there with Mary and baby Jesus."

"But hows come it ain't like that no more?" chubby little Henry Ruffinelli asked, his eyes fixed on Beth's.

"Don't interrupt her, Huffy! Let 'er talk."

Beth placed a warning hand on David's arm. "Well, boys, in the Bible God instructed His prophets to announce that Egypt would become a desolate wasteland. And that's exactly what happened. Other nations came marching in and destroyed its cities and temples, stealing the gold and jewels wherever they could find them. In time the beautiful buildings were covered with drifting sand and forgotten. However, the Bible recorded the importance of Egypt. And even when many historical scholars wondered if it was quite so special, those who read the Bible knew better. We're only just now beginning to uncover the evidence of what a wealthy and powerful nation it was." The boys were watching her closely with wide eyes. "Mr. Harris Hughes is correct about that. It wasn't until a hundred years ago that a stone was found which helped archeologists to decipher the picture writing, called hieroglyphics, that covers many of the Egyptian buildings. And once they could read more of the secret writings, they could read words inside the tombs and learn which belonged to each pharaoh—their kings. Eventually, that led to one of the greatest recent discoveries of all in Egypt—the tomb of Pharaoh Tutankhamen, or King Tut. Have you heard of him?"

"No," they answered in unison. Four more children had gathered around.

Beth could feel her pulse quicken at their rapt attention. "Most of the tombs where the wealthy pharaohs were buried had long ago been opened by grave robbers, with all the treasures stolen away. But one man was certain he could find the tomb of a particular pharaoh named Tutankhamen, who was just a boy when he ruled and when he died. This archaeologist searched for a long time, and many people laughed at him, but he went right on digging anyway. And finally, just a few short years ago, Mr. Carter found what he had been looking for—the tomb of this boy pharaoh. It had been hidden safely from thieves for thousands of years. Imagine how exciting that was for him to be the first man to peek through a hole in the wall and to see glittering gold covering tables, a throne, and a massive sarcophagus—that's a big box for a coffin."

"Wow!" Several sighs followed.

"What did they do with all that gold, Miss Thatcher?"

Beth smiled. "Most of what they found there stayed in a museum in Cairo, Egypt. So I've never actually seen anything from that tomb, except in pictures. But once when I was at a museum in Toronto with my father, I did see a golden crown, a staff, and another pharaoh's coffin. It was fascinating." Noticing that all other activity in the room had come to a halt, Beth tried to bring things back to her lesson about Moses. "And do you know, children, that the things I saw in Toronto were even older than our story today."

"They were?"

"But, Miss Thatcher, why?" Henry asked. "Why don't any of them writings tell about Moses and the Israelite slaves?"

Beth smiled confidently. "Well, if you were a great and powerful pharaoh and your slaves all ran away, would you allow anybody to write about it in carvings on *your* buildings or on the pages of history that you hired people to record on fancy papyrus papers? The pharaohs were the ones who dictated what would be written. Sometimes they even told workmen to chisel away the names of the pharaohs who came before them, attempting to erase them from history. Do you think they always told the truth when something they didn't like happened?"

"No, ma'am," the boys agreed.

"I guess not," Henry admitted.

"So, if you want my opinion, I think that's why we don't find a record of the Exodus." They seemed to follow her explanation, but before more could be discussed Beth hurried the students back into positions, feeling rather pleased at neatly counteracting Robert's teaching.

"Mr. Harris Hughes made Daniel and David and Huffy stand in the corner today,"

Teddy announced with a full mouth during Friday's supper at Molly's.

"Oh? Why did'a he do that?" Frank asked.

Marnie was quick to commandeer the story. "Fer their *'disrespectful attitudes.'*"

Beth's eyes darted from Marnie to Teddy, searching for additional clues.

"Sounds like'a they deserved to be punished."

"No," Teddy countered, waving his fork back and forth. "They was just tellin' him what Miss Thatcher said 'bout Egypt and Moses. But he didn't like hearin' it at all."

Beth choked a little, quickly reaching for her water glass.

"David told him the Bible talks about King Tut, but Huffy said that weren't right, that it talks about other pharaohs and how God was gonna punish them. And then Daniel said the pharaohs even lied on their walls 'cause they didn't want to tell the truth about God sendin' Moses to save the people."

Marnie chimed in, "And when Mr. Harris Hughes asked 'em where they heard all that, the boys said you taught 'em last night at Bible club. And then Mr. Harris Hughes sent 'em, all three, to stand in a corner." She giggled. "Not the same corner. Different ones."

Beth dropped her gaze to avoid Molly's questioning eyes. "It's not exactly what I said. You know how children are." She tried to laugh it off as she rolled a cluster of peas around on her plate with a fork.

After dinner Frank and Molly took seats on the sofa on either side of Beth. She felt small and subdued, like a child between her parents.

"We wanted to talk with ya," Molly began.

"Oh, Molly, I didn't explain it to them so they'd *argue* with him. I tried so hard to just give them the truth. I don't know how it ended up sounding so . . . so quarrelsome."

Frank nodded, leaning closer. "We believe'a you. It'sa just we worry—that the kids, they will'a be caught in the middle."

"I know." Beth dropped her face into her hands and whispered, "That's not what I wanted." Her fingers slid down her cheeks, coming together at her lips. "I feel terrible. It wasn't their fault."

"Now hold on a minute, dearie. Let's talk this through. That man taught 'em what he believed was true, and then so did you. I don't feel ya done wrong there, unless yer heart was against him. Do ya think so?"

Beth cringed and dropped her hands to fidget with the buttons of her sweater. "I don't know, Molly." She paused, trying hard to speak honestly. "I don't really like him very much. He irritates me every time I speak with him." She sighed and her shoulders sagged. "And, oh Molly, a little while ago I said some things to him that were critical and unkind."

"I see. Well, did ya apologize?"

"Oh—oh, no, I didn't."

"Think ya should?"

The very idea turned Beth's stomach. *How can I apologize for just standing my ground?* "He was pushing his ideas on me, Molly. And so I told him, emphatically, that I was not going to agree with him." Beth slowly recalled that she had said much more to Robert. "I suppose I should . . . should apologize." At the moment it sounded impossible.

Frank caught her gaze again. "That is'a something you'll have to ask'a the Father. But what do you think can'a be done to keep this, this confusion, from'a happening again?"

"He's not going to change—he's quite resolute. But, on the other hand, if I hear the children talking about things he's taught them that go against God's Word, I feel I must tell them the truth. I suppose in an ordinary school it would be the school board that would deal with such matters. But Coal Valley is too small—"

"No, not so." Frank was shaking his head, his face lighting up. "Look around, *mia cara.* We are a big town now, eh? Maybe it'sa time to learn'a to govern ourselves."

"But we don't even have a mayor any-more. The Ramsays were one of the families who moved away in the summer. We've gone backward instead of forward."

"That'sa not so hard. We need another one, eh?"

Beth stared down at the carpet. Her words came slowly. "An election? But who would run for mayor?"

"Who knows? But if it'sa the right thing, then that'sa what we do."

"And after that we get us a school board," Molly put in. "The mayor would be on it fer one. And a few of the parents, I suppose. So that helps ya already."

Beth was feeling a little heady and breath-less. *Yes, a mayor and a school board. Maybe that's exactly what it will take to keep Robert from leading our children astray.* Her mind was quickly sorting through the townsfolk, won-dering who might be interested in serving.

"But," Molly added pointedly, "still think ya might need to pray on the other matter—on that apology."

Chapter
11

Beth tossed and turned all Sunday night in her chilly bedroom. Three times she dashed across the floor to stir up the embers and add more coal. Not much additional warmth came from her efforts, but in the morning she was able to manage a quick cup of tea and a bowl of oatmeal for her roommate. The tea was a soothing balm to her jittery nerves, and the more substantial breakfast for Marnie appeased her guilt. She knew she would have to face Robert and deliver a sincere apology. Worse, she still wasn't sure if she could actually go through with it. *Lord, help me do the right thing,* she prayed as she walked to school.

At the end of the day she straightened her desk and listened for the last of the footsteps out the door to be sure she would find her colleague alone. She took several deep breaths, squared her shoulders, walked into the entryway, and knocked on the doorframe of his open door.

"Yes?"

"Hello, Mr. Harris Hughes," she began timidly, stepping across the threshold. "Do you have a moment?"

"Yes. Certainly. Please have a seat." He waved his hand, and Beth slipped into a front-row desk.

"It has come to my attention . . ." She paused, began again. "I've learned that three boys in your class got in trouble on Friday for some things we talked about at our Bible club. And I just wanted to say—"

"That's not entirely accurate, Miss Thatcher," he interrupted, moving out from behind his desk and half sitting on its edge. "I corrected the boys for speaking out of turn and in an argumentative tone."

"I see." Beth faltered. "I was under the impression that . . . that you didn't approve of what they said and found their statements contrary and disrespectful."

"Miss Thatcher, I attribute no fault in the boys' expressing an opinion different from my own. I find that interchange perfectly acceptable and even invigorating. The exchange of opposing ideas is an excellent exercise for the mind. My only objection was the manner in which they chose to express themselves. I am attempting to train them to respond like gentlemen in any situation. I believe it is crucial to the betterment of society that we each articulate our opinions effectively and defend them as well—but do so using proper decorum."

"I see." Beth had begun with what she hoped would be the easier topic. She now wrestled with how to transition to the second, more difficult issue. "I'm afraid I too failed to speak to you with the proper decorum when we were out in the street last week. And I want you to know that I'm very sorry, Mr. Harris Hughes. I hope you can forgive me."

"Miss Thatcher." He cleared his throat and leaned far back, pushing his hands deep into his pockets, then rocking forward again. "I was not as offended by what you said . . . as by what you did not."

"Excuse me, sir? I don't—"

"I have expressed my desire to meet with you to discuss our shared responsibilities at this school. And you have denied me the opportunity."

Beth stiffened. "I'm sorry, but I don't feel that would be, well, prudent."

"Why, if I may ask?"

This was not what she had expected. Perhaps even worse. "I don't think we can speak together on a subject about which . . . which we clearly don't agree. And we're unlikely to come to an agreement."

"Even if it might simply help us come to a better understanding of one another?"

Beth thought back to their previous discussion and to his intimidating declaration that he would have the final influence on the children. "I don't think you listen—" She stopped short before adding his name.

"Miss Thatcher, as you are the person refusing a meeting at all, I'm afraid I could more reasonably assert that you are the one who chooses not to listen."

Beth's head was beginning to cloud. This man claimed to promote communication, even to encourage opposing ideas, and yet she felt defensive every time she spoke with him. "No," she insisted. "I don't think a meeting between the two of us would be wise."

"As you wish." He stood to his feet.

Beth rose quickly too, retreating down the aisle and back to her classroom without further comment. Scooping up her evening grading before she hurried away, her mind was still reeling.

I don't understand him. His words seem so rational, but somehow there's a sting to them. Then with a gasp she wondered if the students were feeling the same—stifled and small. *Is that what Teddy and Marnie were trying to express? Is there more to this incident, one that he tried to make sound so calm and reasonable?*

꿇

Beth had decided to enlist Marnie's help in making fabric flowers for the wedding. Even during church services, she'd been distracted by thoughts of what she could do to enhance the sanctuary. After a discussion with Molly about the possibility of fresh flowers in April, Beth knew her options would be severely limited—and rather unpredictable. Instead she'd ordered several yards of white organza, tulle, and satin to arrive with Alberto Giordano's next return from the city. She had seen these fabrics cut into petal shapes, the edges heated over a candle to curl them and finish them nicely, and the pieces sewn in mixed layers to produce rather lovely fabric blooms. Several pearl beads in the center gave an enchanting finish. However, the process took a great deal of time.

Placing the order had reminded Beth of her resolve to buy some fabric for new dresses for Molly—a nice light wool for Sundays and two flowered lengths for housedresses. When they were delivered, Molly was quite overcome by the gift.

"But you're always letting me eat with you,"

Beth argued. "This is just a small way to show my gratitude."

"Family is always welcome," the woman protested. But Molly's eyes glowed warmly.

At last Beth and Marnie were ready to begin work on the flowers. The girl borrowed Molly's good sewing scissors, a vast improvement over Beth's school set, and the two went to work at the small kitchen table tucked into the corner of Beth's main room, trying to use an assembly-line approach. Marnie did the cutting, and Beth held the raw edges over a flame with a steady, quick hand. Soon she was able to do so nimbly without scorching the fabric. And then came the stacking and stitching together, fussing over the curling layers until each was satisfactory.

"How many d'ya think you need, again?" Marnie asked for the tenth time.

Beth's answer had gradually changed to simply, "As many as we can make in time."

They soon had used up all of the materials Beth had ordered. She knew she'd need at least twice as much and that with winter coming there would be fewer trips into town. So she was delighted to hear that Philip would be driving to Lethbridge on Saturday for a meeting with the district leaders of their church. He cheerfully agreed to chauffeur Beth, along with his other passenger. Philip explained that the man was a new worker who'd injured his hand when he tripped and fell into some of the sawmill machinery. His fellow workers had already set the bone and stitched the wound as best they could, but it had become clear that Donato needed surgery in Lethbridge. And, in a rather surprising act of benevolence, the company had agreed to pay for the expense.

On Saturday morning, Beth met Philip at the truck. The other passenger had already climbed over its tailgate and into the bed of the clunky old vehicle Philip had borrowed. There were several blankets ready to create a comfortable ride for the man.

"But I didn't know there were only two seats," Beth whispered to Philip. "I don't want him to have to sit in the back because of me. Please tell him I can—"

"You can what? *You* can sit in the back?" Philip shook his head with a cockeyed grin. "This is the only way. But believe me, he's just grateful to be getting the hand repaired by proper doctors. He doesn't mind."

A whiskered smile and a nod in their direction seemed to confirm Philip's claims. Beth watched from the corner of her eye as the man pulled a blanket around his shoulders and tucked the thickly bandaged hand beneath it. Philip helped her into the front seat, and she took a quick glance at the bundled figure leaning against the cab's window. *I hope he'll be all right, but Philip probably will keep an eye on him during our drive.*

It took several miles before Beth could focus on other things. The thought that distracted her most was the possibility of surprising Jarrick and having a nice meal together. But with no telephone connection, she couldn't be certain he would even be in town.

"We might get snow again soon," Philip noted as the vehicle rumbled along. "And this time more than just a light dusting. I sure hope it doesn't come until after we've gotten back tonight."

"I don't mind the feeling of being snowed in. I find it rather pleasant and cozy, at least once we're home again!"

"Agreed," he said, "and at least we know there's plenty of food stored up with all the gardening last summer."

"Oh yes, and what a relief!"

"Say, Beth, I heard a rumor that you're up to something." Philip's voice had taken on a teasing tone. "I'm tempted to say *again*, but that would be overstating—just a little."

"Why, you flatter me," she joked in turn.

"I was intrigued the other day when Frank mentioned that you and he discussed holding an election for a new mayor. At first I was more than a little surprised. And then it occurred to me to wonder why no one else has suggested it before. It seems rather obvious. How did we miss it?"

"Well . . . yes, that's true. We've been stirring things up a little, but what I really want is a school board. Frank's the one who suggested we get a mayor first. So I made up copies of a flyer calling for a town meeting next Saturday evening, and he posted them around town and in the company building down by the river."

"Why a school board? I would think it's much more fun to just do things your own way." The lines in the corners of his eyes were crinkling with merriment.

Beth ignored his mirth. "I'm sorry, but that's just it. I've been struggling with Robert regarding our conflicting opinions on how we teach." She went on to explain their differences, trying very hard not to stumble into personal judgments and gossip. "I think a school board would settle the issue rather promptly, and for that . . . well, I guess we need a mayor first."

"Would you teachers be on the board?"

"I doubt it. They usually aren't included. Although we have such a small community that it might be necessary for now, especially since so few parents are graduates themselves.

What I want is a group with authority to oversee what is taught and how it's presented." She paused and drew her coat collar tighter against the cold in the drafty vehicle, casting another quick glance over her shoulder toward the passenger in the back. She shuddered at his chilly travel situation before continuing, "I'll admit, I'm not particularly comfortable meeting alone with Robert."

"I can understand that. It might not even be considered appropriate, although Coal Valley doesn't stand much on such social prohibitions."

The engine wheezed as they mounted a steep hill; Beth grasped for a handhold and cast a worried glance at Philip, who merely chuckled. "She's old and she's noisy, but she's entirely dependable."

As the truck rattled down the other side, Beth rallied her courage. "Philip, why don't *you* run for mayor?"

"Me?"

"Sure. You're college educated. You know everyone quite well. And everyone likes you."

"Well, not everyone." He tipped his head and forced a chuckle. "You can't preach too many sermons without stirring up *somebody* who feels that you're wrong."

"Seriously, Philip, I think you'd be the ideal candidate."

"Where would I find the time? And what's more, wouldn't that automatically put me at odds with even *more* of the people in my congregation?"

"I can't think of why that would be." But Beth knew he was probably right.

"Besides, I don't want to be a political figure. I want to be more of a shepherd—a servant. I don't think the two roles are complementary. Can you picture me trying to run for office, handing out buttons after church on Sunday? It would be harder to be salt and light while wheeling and dealing to arrive at policy, pave roads, and fine lawbreakers." He gave another laugh. "Let me put it this way, Beth—I don't want to decide where to build bridges, I just want to be one, if you know what I mean."

"I do," she sighed. "And you're right, of course. I guess it was wishful thinking."

Jarrick was indeed amazed to find Beth standing in the station's reception area. Her rushed explanation tumbled out as soon as their eyes met and they hurried toward one another. "I'm sorry I couldn't let you know I was coming, Jarrick. I didn't have any way to get in touch with you."

He clasped both of her hands in his and

drew her closer. "When Ollie said you were here, I thought he was just ragging on me again. This is the very best surprise."

"Are you terribly busy? Do you have any time at all?"

"I'll make time, Beth. I'm just glad I was in town today. I only came back last night."

Beth felt herself relax. "I was worried you wouldn't be here, or that I'd be in the way."

"You never need worry about that." Jarrick turned toward the desk, Beth's arm pulled through his. "Ollie, can you call a taxicab for us? I'm going to take my lunch break early today. Right now, in fact."

The man winked at Beth. "Can't I just saddle up your horse for you, Jack?"

"That's very clever, Ollie. Never heard that one before. We'll be waiting outside." Jarrick rapped on the desktop with a grin at Ollie, then guided Beth out the door.

Already it seemed that time was standing still. As they waited together on the steps of the building, Beth tucked her shoulder closer to him as if to somehow push away the loneliness she'd felt. "This is dreadfully difficult—to miss you so much," she whispered.

"Believe me, I understand what you mean," he murmured against her hair.

The chill wind stung Beth's face, and she turned it closer to his coat sleeve. "Do you really have a horse, Jarrick?" she asked, her voice muffled by the fabric.

She could feel his chest shake as he chuckled. "You don't already know that? Yes, I do actually. Well, not just one. Those of us who move around often have to share them, but I have a favorite mare that I typically ride when I'm in my main assignment area. The roads get much worse the farther north you go, and cars are often useless. And I'll admit I enjoy a chance to ride. I really do. It's an incredible sense of freedom and serenity—at least when it's not raining, or worse, snowing."

"What's her name, your favorite?"

"Her name is Luna, an Appaloosa, speckled with the colors of the moon."

"She sounds beautiful."

"She is. And spunky—like you."

"Well, I'm glad I know about her now." The image in her mind of him riding his horse through the snow felt oddly romantic.

"You know, sweetheart," he said, putting his free arm around her, "there are probably a great many things we don't know about each other yet."

She turned her face to his, pushing a windblown strand of hair out of her face. "Then we have to find opportunities to talk more, or . . . or we'll have to start writing letters again."

His blue eyes sparkled. "Well, why not?

Just because we live closer to one another doesn't mean we can't write letters anyway. It's not as if we see each other much, or that it's possible to talk by phone."

"And," she added, "we'll also have to be efficient—during the times we're together."

"Well, that won't be easy. I keep getting distracted when I look at your lovely face."

"Oh, Jarrick."

And then their taxi arrived to take them to lunch.

As Beth expected, lunch felt far too short, and she hurried to fit in every topic she had hoped to cover, trying to force aside unsettled feelings from their previous discussion in the church. They agreed that Jarrick's two younger brothers would stand with him. Beth's brides-maids would be Julie and Marnie, if the girl agreed.

Beth was happy to report about her students' progress, and then Jarrick shared what he was free to say about recent Mountie assignments. After they had ordered dessert she mentioned the upcoming Coal Valley election.

"You asked Philip to run?" Jarrick seemed amused. "What did he say?"

Beth mutely shook her head.

"Well, who else do you have in mind?"

"I don't know. Toby Coulter, the man who runs the store, has been there as long as anyone, but he works for the coal company. I wouldn't want them to gain additional control over what happens in town, though it rules out quite a few of the men."

Jarrick nodded.

"I can't think of very many who aren't rather new," she explained. "And I certainly don't know many of them outside of church. Howard McDermott is very quiet. I don't think he'd be at all interested. Bill Shaw, and even his son Parker, are possibilities. He's older than his brother Roark, who died in the mine collapse—probably at least in his midtwenties." The meager group of men from which to find their mayor caused a long sigh from Beth. "And if we go ahead and elect someone who works in the mine or the mill, he's going to be under a great deal of pressure from the company bosses. The only man I can think of who isn't new and doesn't work for them is Fred Green. And I wouldn't want to see him elected. He was a good friend of Davie Grant's, and I'm afraid I just don't trust him."

"You're right. There aren't many good options." Jarrick's sigh matched her own. "It's too bad that Abbie Stanton lost her husband, Noah. He would have made a very good mayor. On the other hand, I suppose there's nothing to keep one of the new men from throwing his hat into the ring. I'm sure some of them must be quite capable."

"We'll see." For a moment Beth wavered, uncertain whether to express her next thought aloud, then gave in. "Don't laugh, but . . . I wish that I could run myself—even though I'm a woman. It's not as if things haven't been changing . . . and I could follow in the footsteps of Queen Victoria, right?"

Jarrick's face grew earnest. "I'm sure you'd do a very good job, Beth. But . . ."

Her mind finished the sentence in a dozen different ways. *But you're not a leader. You're too busy elsewhere. You don't know enough about politics. A woman should stay at home. You're small and won't be forceful enough to hold rowdy coal miners in check.* . . . She dropped her gaze to her dessert plate.

He finished, ". . . but I thought we had agreed to go east at the end of this school year."

This was perhaps the worst possibility of them all. Beth had hoped the issue could still be part of an unfinished discussion. "Did we . . . ? I thought . . . Have you spoken to Father?"

"No, not yet. I told him I wanted to take some time before committing."

Beth knew what her father was hoping. *What do I say? Jarrick is the leader in our marriage—of our family someday. I want to follow his leadership. What can I say without sounding like his mother, or even mine?*

"Have you made up your mind?" she asked cautiously.

"I've tried to think of other options, Beth, but other than continuing as a Mountie and traveling far too often—not what either you or I would want—there doesn't seem to be another practical solution." Jarrick was staring at her intently. "At any rate, no matter what happens, we wouldn't be in Coal Valley anymore. Just until the end of the school year. Even if I stayed on the Force and we remained in the West, we'd have to live wherever I was assigned. There's not even a posting in so small a town—"

"But if I were mayor," she tried to joke but quickly abandoned the attempt. The troubling thoughts of the uncertain future nearly overwhelmed her. *After everything I've set out to accomplish here, I'll end up back in Toronto—no more Coal Valley, no mountains, no freedom, no adventures, only a class of city kids who don't really need or want me, if I'm even allowed to teach again. I'll be left running a home with an ordinary life.* She felt her lip quiver. *And Jarrick won't ever wear his uniform again, won't be able to ride his horse, won't be able to do what he's felt called to do.* She tried stealthily brushing aside a tear before Jarrick could notice, but it was no use.

"Sweetheart, what is it? What do you want?"

Beth cleared her throat and attempted a smile. "It's so hard to think about leaving."

The truth, but not all of the truth.

Chapter 12

"Where is that girl?" Molly fretted as she and Beth put the finishing touches on Sunday dinner. "I seen her hurry out after church, and she ain't here."

"That's not like Marnie," Beth observed, brow wrinkled.

"Well . . ." Molly scooped mashed potatoes into a serving bowl and handed it to Beth. "More so than what you'd think. This ain't the first time in the last weeks."

Beth brought the potatoes to the dining room, then returned for a dish of steaming beets. After a last check that all was in order, she motioned for the guests to come, and the men took their places with lively conversation and laughter.

Back in the kitchen, Beth moved close and

asked quietly, "What did you mean by that, Molly?"

The woman shook her head, wiping her face on her apron and hanging it up. "She keeps disappearin' lately, and I have to send Teddy Boy after her. I know it ain't work she's dodgin'. She truly seems ta enjoy all that— even more lately. I often hear her humming to herself when she's workin'. I'm just puzzled, that's all."

"Where does Teddy find her? Not at my place, I presume."

Molly paused, shrugged. "No, he don't really say. Just walkin', I suppose."

"Well, she does like to walk. I'm the same way."

"Mm-hmm. But it's gettin' too cold fer such."

The family filed into their seats around the kitchen table. Marnie appeared at last, sliding quickly into her chair. "Sorry, Miss Molly," she murmured. "I lost track of time."

"Where ya been, child?"

"Just down ta the river and back." Her face was aimed downward, her expression hidden. Beth watched as Molly and Frank exchanged glances.

"Tell 'em." All eyes instantly turned to Teddy, who was scowling across at his sister. "You tell 'em, or else I will."

"Don't ya dare!"

But there was no holding back the questions now.

"What on earth?" demanded Molly.

"Mia cara," Frank began, laying a hand on Marnie's, "we are'a worried about you. You must'a tell us where you go."

"Oh, Papa," she said, lifting now-tearful eyes, "I don't know how to say it." Everyone waited, now even more concerned.

Marnie's head dropped low again, and her shoulders sagged. "I met a friend—a boy." She sniffed and lifted a hand to her eyes.

Beth's gaze traveled around the table. A parade of schoolboys trooped through her mind. *She never said a word. How did I miss this? But Marnie said she'd "met" him.* "Who?" Beth managed aloud.

"Ya don't know him. None of ya."

Molly's voice came low and clipped. "Then where . . . ?"

"In the woods. I met him in the woods. That ain't so hard to believe, is it?"

"Who is he? How long have ya . . ."

At last the information poured out. "His name is Harold. He's a miner. He's new. He come out to join his uncle and aunt, Mr. and Mrs. Edwards. An' he's not a bad person— he's just . . . he's just the nicest man I ever met."

"A *man*? How old is he? Why ain't we seen him at church?"

"He wants ta come," Marnie said quickly, skipping over the harder question. "He says he plans on it. But they're makin' him do the work nobody else wants, 'cause he's new, I guess. An' he has ta go in at times when the others are off."

"On Sunday?" Beth puzzled over the strange claim.

Molly was unrelenting, and before the girl could answer, she demanded, "Then how's it come to be that you an' him meet up?"

"We don't got long ta talk. We just, we just chat a minute or two, in between times—"

"He could'a lose his job, Marnie," Frank said quietly. "You cannot take'a such chances."

Beth held her breath. Molly pushed back her chair and headed toward the stove. Frank's eyes followed her and then turned back to Marnie. "You know it'sa not right to hide this. It don'ta look good. To us . . . or anyone."

"Yes, Papa Frank."

He wiped a hand across his face. "You don'ta go no more to meet'a him in the woods. He wants to talk'a to you, he comes here, eh?"

"Yes, Papa." Her voice was small. "May I be excused, please?"

Frank cast a glance back toward Molly. "Yes, mia cara."

Sunday dinner continued in silence.

❦

Molly and Beth cleared and washed all of the dishes, and Frank dried them, skillfully pinning each piece against the worktable with the stump of one arm while using the towel with the other hand. The kitchen was back in order before Marnie was mentioned again. There didn't seem to be a rush. At least for now the girl was safe in the parlor, reading. She had no place to retreat. Beth was certain Marnie was missing the privacy of her own room, especially now.

Beth laid a hand on Molly's shoulder and kept her voice low. "Want to step out to the porch with me before I leave?"

"That would be nice—a quiet place to talk."

"If it helps."

"You ladies go," Frank encouraged. "I will'a stand guard." He managed a teasing grin.

The rocking chairs were covered with dust and dried leaves. Molly and Beth leaned against the rail, looking out to the street.

At last Beth said, "What are you thinking?"

"Don't know yet. It's a shock to my heart."

"I understand. I can't believe she's been hiding it. I thought she and I were . . ." Beth shook her head with a little groan.

"Frank'll find out about him. Won't waste a day. But if he's a miner, then he ain't no schoolboy."

"How young do they take them in the mine? Paolo Giordano was fifteen when he started. Is there anyone else his age—or younger?"

"Don't know, dearie. We'll have to wait on Frank."

"Molly, she's only fourteen." Beth could hardly keep the lament out of her voice.

"True. But we don't know nothin' yet. Maybe it's just a childish crush. We gotta let this play itself out. Only she won't be walkin' around alone again fer a long while. That I can say fer sure." Molly shook her head. "Thank the good Lord I got Frank fer these hard days."

"He loves her, Molly."

"Oh, he's got a mighty tender heart fer that girl." Molly's face crumpled.

Beth put an arm around Molly's shoulders, surprised to see the weathered face betraying such deep emotion. She was certain about what her dear friend was unable to voice—that Molly's heart was fracturing with how much love she too felt for Marnie.

Back in her rooms and stretched out on the sofa during the lazy afternoon, Beth's heart was too troubled to read. Her thoughts kept returning to dear Marnie, trying to imagine what would happen next. First she pictured Frank standing atop the porch steps, facing off with a leering miner—a grown man with a rough beard, spitting chewing tobacco into the grass. Then she'd see a boy instead, covered in coal dust, far too young for the mines, wheezing out his affections for Marnie. Every scene she imagined only increased her distress.

If only I could reason with her. But Beth wondered what she would say if she were in charge. *I think I would just forbid her to see the boy again. I would put my foot down, insist that she focus on her schooling until she's completed it. That's what my mother would do.* The last thought stung a little. Beth knew far too well how it felt to be young and for youthful wishes to be contradicted and denied—even with the best of intentions. *How ironic that all I wanted then was to teach, and my mother just wanted to see me properly wed. Now Marnie's chance to get a teaching certificate might be in peril because she's lost her heart to a man. But even so, it's different with Marnie. She's just a child, and she has no idea yet what she wants. It's just that the idea of love sounds so tempting, so exciting. She has no way of knowing how hard it is to be a wife.*

Beth looked across toward that cranky old stove. In not too long she'd be solely responsible for keeping the rooms warm day and night, and for preparing meals on it for her new husband. She wasn't certain she could rise to those challenges. But Jarrick would never make enough money to afford household help.

Then again, she wondered if that luxury might indeed be possible if Jarrick worked for her father. *It doesn't matter.* Beth shook her head firmly. *I would rather struggle to put a meal on our table every day here in the West than watch him leave every morning for an office job in Toronto. He'll hate it. Heavenly Father, if only You would work out some way to keep us here.* The prayer sounded selfish, but she rushed on. *And please, please protect Marnie from shackling herself to a kitchen, and laundry, and cleaning, and . . . well, You know all the things she'd face—while she's so young.*

On Monday Molly appeared at Beth's classroom door as soon as all the students had gone. Beth pulled the door closed behind her, and they wasted no time.

Molly kept her voice low as she said, "He is a miner. Frank talked to Lloyd Edwards, his uncle."

"Oh dear, Frank didn't mention anything about Marnie to the uncle, about the two of them—"

"'Course not. Just bein' friendly."

Beth exhaled her relief.

"They call 'im Harry—he's twenty-one." Molly hurried on. "He's a good boy. Come out here when his uncle made an offer of room an' board. His family's poor, and he sends most his money home. Mr. Edwards said he's steady and smart and was the top of his grade-eight class 'fore he started workin' instead."

"He's twenty-one?"

"Yes, but now, don't miss the bigger picture."

Beth sank into a desk chair, and Molly dropped into a seat across the aisle. "Frank says he's met the boy today too. Invited him to the house fer supper soon. And by the look on Harry's face, seems he's grateful fer the chance. So there's something there between 'em."

"He's twenty-one," Beth said again. "He's not a boy."

"Well, he ain't exactly a man though neither, dearie."

"Molly, he's *seven years older* than Marnie! Seven—half her life. She's far too young . . ." But Beth couldn't continue.

A shadow crossed Molly's face. "I was sixteen when I married Bertram, and he was twenty."

"But . . . but things were different."

"Different how? We still fell in love in the same way, seems ta me."

Beth felt frustration growing but fought to stay calm, reasonable. *What should I say, and how can I say it in a way that helps Molly understand?*

But it was Molly who broke the silence. "I see in that girl more ta offer a marriage than I had at the time. Marnie's been through a lot, forced ta grow up quick-like, Beth. Her momma died when she was just a slip of a thing, an' I know she carried a load long 'fore she was ready. She can cook 'most everything I can, knows all there is ta know about keepin' a house, carin' fer others. She's over-mature fer her age. A real capable young woman. It's—"

"Exactly!" Beth interrupted, unable to hold back longer. "She *is capable,* and I . . . I had such . . . such dreams for her. She'd make such an excellent teacher, Molly. She's got so many of the right qualities. I'm wishing so much more for her than keeping a house, slaving in a kitchen . . ."

At the expression on Molly's face, Beth's words abruptly halted and she felt her face grow hot with shame. *That wasn't really what I meant. Or was it?* Confusion clouded her thinking. *How could I say such a thing—and to Molly of all people? Not to mention that I'm looking forward to marriage myself. How can I explain how different this seems?* For a long, tense interlude there was silence.

Molly pulled a handkerchief from her sleeve and drew it across her brow. Beth heard her sigh. When the woman lifted her face again, Beth thought she saw tears glistening in the corners of her tired-looking eyes. To Beth's surprise Molly reached out and took her hand.

But there was no reprimand in her voice when Molly spoke softly. "I know you love her too, and I know ya want her to have the best that life can offer. But, but have ya considered that to Marnie this—this other path—might just be *her dream*? She wants a home, Beth. Her own home. Fer far too long she ain't really had that. Just a house full up with boarders, men she don't know. Ain't even got her own room no more. She wants love, not things. And Marnie has all the gifts of a homemaker, a good wife. I think that when that times comes she'll be more 'an ready. An' she'll do a fine job of it too. She's capable, that girl o' mine. So I gotta trust her. I gotta trust her heavenly Father to keep her."

Beth wiped away her own tear and nodded. "You're right, Molly. I . . . I know that. I suppose I was imagining a life for her that I had no right to plan. I . . . I saw a wonderful potential teacher, a . . ." She wrung her hands together, sighed, and tried again to put her thoughts into words. "Marnie relates so well to children. She has such gifting and is so patient and organized and meticulous. It's just . . ." Beth stumbled to a stop. She plucked at the lace on her sleeve, wondering where to go to make amends for her thoughtless words. Another apology was the only option.

"Molly, it was presumptuous and selfish of me to assume. I had no right. And my words didn't convey how much respect I have for you—for the role you've had in so many lives, for all the ways you give so much of yourself every day. I'm so sorry, Molly." Beth lowered her head and bit her lip to keep it from trembling.

A slight squeeze of her hand lifted her gaze. Molly was smiling. "I know how ya feel, dearie. And now, you must know I ain't sayin' we're gonna let 'em rush things. At present they both seem ta have interest. I'm smart enough to see that light in her eyes. But nobody says they're headin' to the altar anytime soon. We'll just trust 'em to the Lord and let Him be the one decidin' the if and when of it. We'll talk to her, me an' Frank. I have faith that Marnie will listen, so long's we're speaking truth in love, not forcing our own way."

Beth managed a weak smile as she returned the pressure on her hand. "Of course," she responded. "Of course. And, Molly, I have faith in her too."

Back in her home, Beth took a book from the shelf, but she knew it would be impossible to concentrate on reading. Thoughts about Marnie ran through her mind.

Father, she prayed, *I can't help it. I can't help but believe that if she'd just finish school it would open so many doors for her. But I'm sure Molly's right that we can't force her, that we have to allow her to set her own course and listen to Your voice in her heart.*

A perplexing thought nagged at Beth, and finally she asked herself outright, *Am I that much like Mother? Would I truly impose my will on another, despite knowing she wants something else instead?* Beth let the book slip from her hands and clasped them together. *O Lord, please forgive me for believing I know best. I want*

Your will for Marnie's life, not mine. But, God, please give all of us wisdom to guide her in these important decisions. And close our mouths if we have anything to add beyond what You would have us say. Amen.

Chapter
13

Snow was falling on the Saturday of the town meeting, a perfect late-November morning with not a breath of wind. Large, feathery flakes filled the air, suspended in a breathtaking, slow descent. As Beth made her way to the school building, she saw the children calling to each other in excitement, making snow angels, and opening their mouths wide to catch enormous snowflakes on their tongues.

Beth paused to watch for a moment, delighting in their joy in greeting the snow. *They are exactly what this meeting is about—the children. The school is for them, and the town will be theirs soon enough. Oh, Father, please help me to do whatever I can on their behalf, and help me to honor You with every word and action.*

She entered the building and stamped the snow from her boots, slipping her feet into dry shoes she had carried with her. There was already a small crowd gathered in Robert's classroom, many of them standing. Beth worked her way forward, speaking with several mothers before taking a seat near the front. *More people here than I expected,* she thought, pleased as she looked around.

Toby Coulter was going to lead the meeting from Robert's desk. Soon the sharp whistle through his fingers brought conversations to a close.

"Come to order," Toby said, looking a bit sheepish. "We're gonna give this a go. I ain't led a town meetin' before, but we're all friends, and we'll get through it fine. Henry Gowan here's gonna be our secretary—writin' down the minutes—so we even got a record of what's said, all official like."

A deep voice called out, "Should'a had the teacher do it. Everybody knows old Gowan can't spell." Laughter followed.

"All right, all right. We ain't havin' no foolishness today, Fred. Keep yer comments to yerself."

Beth blushed, glad that she had not been asked to transcribe the meeting notes. Then she noticed Robert stand to his feet on the opposite side of the room and nod his head in acknowledgment as the *teacher*. "I'm happy to serve in any capacity, gentlemen."

"Thank ya kindly, Mr. Harris Hughes. We're glad yer here. Might come back to ya if we have a question 'bout a point of order."

Robert nodded again, his tweed jacket and sculpted hair looking incongruous among the denim overalls and rough beards all around. Yet he seemed to be at least acquainted with these men. Beth squeezed her hands together in her lap. *It was Robert they acknowledged as teacher—not me.* It was a humbling realization, particularly when she had arrived a year before him.

"First, we better give a sum'ry of what's been goin' on till now. The old mayor left the records with Bill Shaw, and he brung 'em so we can go over some things. Bill, ya wanna come up and read what ya got?"

"Won't take long! We ain't got much." More laughter.

"Fred, I'm tellin' ya fer the last time."

Sadie Shaw's father lumbered to the front of the room. What followed was a long reading about boundaries and easements, taxes and annexation, departments and committees. *An inordinate amount of bureaucracy for such a small town,* Beth thought.

She soon noticed the same names appearing often in the reports—Silas Ramsey, Stanley

Murphy, Bill Shaw, and Noah Stanton. These men had made up the town council and had been deeply involved in all previous Coal Valley endeavors. But Mayor Ramsey had moved away, and Stanley Murphy and Abigail's husband, Noah, were among those killed in the mine collapse. Even poor Bill had lost a grown son on that terrible day. Beth winced to think that one bereaved father was all that was left of the town council.

"Now, folks," Toby Coulter continued, "we're gonna get into the council nominations, and from there we'll let ya think on it before we hold an election fer mayor. We don't hafta get a mayor from those we elect today, but seems like if you've got a man who's willin' to serve, best ta speak out now. No sense holdin' back any good candidates. Oh, and we're all agreed that we're gonna hold the election after Christmas, prob'ly mid-January. So we'll start collectin' names fer mayor any time after tonight." He paused. "Alrighty then, don't seem to me to be any reason to talk more 'bout it. Let's just get to it, then. Who ya want on the council?"

"How 'bout you?" a voice from the back called out.

Toby shook his head firmly. "I ain't got the time. You all know that's why I ain't let my name stand before now. Who else?"

The long silence was punctuated only by the occasional shuffling of shoes. At last someone said, "Howard McDermott."

"Ya up fer it, Howard?"

An inaudible response.

"Whad'ya say?"

"He said *nay*," said a strong voice from next to Howard. Several men laughed aloud.

"Write that down," Toby instructed their secretary.

He studied the crowd. "Who else?"

Another extended pause. "I nominate Lloyd Edwards." The shuffling sounds increased.

"Yes er no, Lloyd?"

A confident "Ya, sure" carried through the room.

"Good. That's one, then. Everybody know Lloyd yet? Step forward, will ya?"

Beth turned to see a tall man with straw-colored hair and a full beard raise a hand in greeting from his place against the back wall. He seemed friendly enough, making eye contact around the room. *So this is Harry's uncle—father of four new children in our school.* Beth searched in the vicinity of Lloyd for a young man who might be Marnie's beau, but she could see no one young enough.

"Who else?" Toby prodded. Faces began to turn toward each other, reflecting the same question.

At last Lloyd Edwards stepped forward again and said, "Seems like the teacher should be on our board."

Beth froze. This time she was immediately aware that she was not the teacher in question. The realization that Robert might be elected unveiled itself slowly, painfully. She had failed to even consider him, assuming he wouldn't be eligible. Beth had completely overlooked the risk.

"What'cha say, Mr. Harris Hughes?" Toby asked, a hopeful grin on his face.

"I'd be honored."

No! Beth closed her eyes in shock and held her breath. *This cannot be happening!* Robert on the town council meant his influence would be extended, not constrained. From the nods and murmurs, there was no doubt he was fully accepted by the men in the room.

"Good. That's two. Who else?"

Beth was lost to the remaining proceedings, frantically processing what had just occurred. In a single moment everything had slipped beyond her control. She quickly grasped the fact that her failure to predict this unforeseen twist meant that the school board she had planned to propose in this very meeting would likely report to Robert rather than the other way around. The realization silenced her.

In the end, only two other names were added—Bardo Mussante, who had recently married Esther Blane, and Vern Ruffinelli, whose family also was new to town. The names were unilaterally accepted, making up a council of five together with Bill Shaw. Beth quickly found her way to the door, replaced her shoes with boots, and retreated home in stunned defeat.

***

"Miss Thatcher" came the unwelcome voice. "I wonder if I might have a word with you."

All day Beth had been dreading the conversation she was certain would take place. She had suspected that Robert would make a point of seeking her out. Now he stood in the doorway between their classrooms, hands in his pockets, looking rather smug.

Beth swallowed to give herself time to push away ungracious responses. "Of course. Please come in and have a seat."

"This will only take a minute." Moving into the room, seemingly in no hurry to get to the point, he remained standing and looked over the spelling assignment Beth had been writing on the chalkboard. For one frantic moment her heart beat faster, and she fervently hoped there were no mistakes in the words she had posted.

She could hear the faint sound of loose change jingling in his pocket. *Is he mocking me?* She turned to face him fully. His smile, which seemed almost cocky, did nothing to make her feel less awkward. *Is he coming to gloat? To make me feel even more subdued?*

At last he ventured, "I was hoping to bury the hatchet, so to speak. But I'm afraid I haven't figured you out yet, Miss Thatcher. I'm somewhat at a loss over what to say."

Then why make a point of saying anything at all? She set down the chalk and dusted her hands together. "If you've come to ask for another meeting, I'm afraid my answer hasn't changed."

"Surely you don't mean to suggest that you'll never meet with me at all, about anything?"

"Not about teaching philosophy." Beth lifted a stack of readers off a front desk and stooped to transfer them back into place on the bookshelf. "Is there anything else?"

He hedged. "I guess it's a shame, really. When you think of it, almost ironic. The same progressive thought that you're rejecting out of hand because of your religious bias is the very approach that would lift you from a traditional woman's role into a place where you might increase your effectiveness. You could have gained a seat on the town council, where you would have been able to maintain your traditional ideals and suppress advancement. Don't you think that's rather paradoxical, Miss Thatcher?"

So you do know exactly what's going on! Exactly what I was intending. Beth flushed with embarrassment. "I'm sure I don't know what you're accusing me of."

His voice dropped lower. "Miss Thatcher, I'm not your enemy. I can't understand how you came to consider me thus. And I want to assure you that I believe a public servant is, more than anything else, accountable to hear every voice within his constituency—even most acutely, words from those with whom he disagrees."

Beth stretched to her full height, feeling somewhat like a small child looking up at a parent, and not simply because of the difference in stature. "Accountable to whom?"

"Why, to the citizens, of course."

"No, Mr. Harris Hughes. Every public servant is accountable to God, first and foremost. He is the source from whom *all* power derives."

Robert shook his head. "I'm sorry then, Miss Thatcher. You actually may be correct. We simply have nothing to discuss." Beth could not be certain if it was condescension or genuine regret in his expression.

"Good day, Miss Thatcher."

"Good day."

He exited just as ponderously as he had entered.

Chapter 14

On her way home from school, Beth nearly stumbled over a wrapped package the size and shape of a hatbox on the landing outside her door. Juggling books and her schoolbag, she managed to loop her little finger through the string around it and carry it across the doorstep. "What on earth?" she mumbled when she found no note. *It must be from Jarrick. Maybe he sent it with the company car.*

She quickly untied the string and pulled the paper away. Lifting the lid, she found a lovely red felt cloche with matching satin hatband adorned by a single white feather. Delighted, she pulled the bell-shaped hat snugly over her head, tucking in stray strands of hair as she walked to the mirror for a look. Her eyes peeked out demurely from under the low brim. *But I never wear red. I wonder why he chose it for me.* Still, after having nothing new for months, she was thrilled by the lovely surprise. *Perhaps Jarrick will mention it in his next letter,* she thought as she replaced it in its box.

Beth was almost finished grading papers when she heard Marnie's footsteps on the stairs. Since learning about Harold Edwards, Beth's enjoyment in their daily school preparations had faded, particularly now that it appeared Marnie would not go into teaching.

The door closed softly before Marnie turned to Beth. "I was afraid I'd wake ya," she said with a little smile. "Want me to feed Penelope, or did ya do that already?"

"Oh, yes," Beth answered, "a while ago."

Marnie slipped off her winter coat and hung it on her hook. Stopping to check both the sink and the trash, she sighed. "Well, I guess I'm gonna turn in, then."

"Glad you're home, darling," Beth said. "I hope you and Molly made some progress on that quilt she's helping you with." Not waiting for a response, Beth remembered, "Oh yes, Marnie, would you like to see the surprise that arrived today?"

"Sure," Marnie said. "What is it?"

"Look in that box on the chair."

Marnie lifted the cover slowly. "It's a hat." Her voice sounded strangely restrained.

"It is. The box wasn't marked, but I'm sure Jarrick must have sent it. Want to try it on?"

The girl hesitated, and Beth nodded vigorously. Finally Marnie consented. Very gently she lifted the millinery from its box and placed it on her head, pulling it down and moving to the mirror.

Beth rose from her seat so she could share the reflected image. "It looks beautiful on you. Suits your pixie face and your lovely hair color nicely." Beth had a sudden inspiration. "Want to wear it Sunday?"

Marnie let out a gasp. "I—but you . . . it's just, Miss Thatcher, I—"

"I don't mind, really," Beth swiftly assured her. "I'd enjoy seeing you in it even more than wearing it myself. And Jarrick would agree. I know he would."

Confusion clouded Marnie's face, and she turned away from the mirror. "I don't know, Miss Thatcher. I'll . . . I'll have ta think on it."

"It's a small thing, Marnie." Beth placed a hand on the girl's shoulder. "You're the real beauty, Marnie, not the hat. But it does look lovely on you, just the same."

Marnie managed a half smile and drew it from her head. Carefully replacing it, she went off to bed without further comment.

Beth settled in to finish the grading, picturing Marnie wearing the stunning hat come Sunday morning.

⁘

"Harry Edwards is comin' to church today," Molly informed Beth as they met at the boarding house gate. Frank, who trailed a few steps behind, managed to lean sideways and wink at Beth over his wife's shoulder.

Beth caught Molly's hands and squeezed them for a brief moment. "I'm so glad to hear it."

"Marnie said he don't have ta work today. They give him the day off—his uncle's been pressin' them on it. So he's comin' ta church. And then he's comin' fer dinner too."

"Oh, Molly, then we all get to meet him."

"That we do."

The trio moved single file up the snowy road to the church, picking their way through the truck tracks. Their *good morning*s to neighbors burst little clouds into the freezing mountain air.

Marnie was already in the entryway as Beth stepped inside, the red felt easily seen among the other women's hats. Beth pushed across the foyer. The girl looked charming, the blush of winter still on her cheeks. Perhaps, Beth supposed, even the slightest hint of red lipstick. "You look beautiful, Marnie dear. Just lovely."

Her brows furrowed as she returned Beth's greeting. "Thank you."

"Is he here yet?"

"No. Not yet."

Beth began unbuttoning her coat. "Well, we're going to get a seat. Would you like us to save a spot for the two of you?"

"Yes, ma'am," Marnie whispered, still looking somewhat perplexed.

Beth slid along the pew after Molly and Frank until they were settled with room to spare on the end. They exchanged knowing looks, and Beth reached for the hymnbook. Rose Shaw at the small organ was already playing chords for "Amazing Grace." Philip took his place behind the pulpit and signaled for all to stand. Marnie and Harold still had not appeared. Beth rose with those around her, then sidled a few steps toward the aisle to venture a glance toward the back.

Sure enough, Marnie and a young man were standing near the potbellied stove, whispering together. Beth moved back to her place and nodded to Molly. During the second verse, Marnie slipped in beside them followed by a thin rail of a young man with short blond hair and rather protruding ears. Beth forced her eyes back to the hymnal, trying to put the couple beside her out of her mind so she could focus on worship, though she found it rather difficult.

❧

"Now, Harry, you can take that seat there, right next ta Frank. We'll all squeeze in somehow. Scooch forward, Teddy Boy. He's gotta get 'round ya." Their chairs scraped over the wood floor and the table was bumped repeatedly, but each managed to maneuver into place.

Marnie hurried in from serving in the company dining room, her face glowing as she met their guest's gaze once again. "They still need carrots, Miss Molly. I'll get 'em." She heaped them into a bowl, topping them with butter before rushing back to the other room. Beth watched covertly as the young man kept an eye on Marnie's every move.

Molly was explaining, "I got lots of ham today, so eat up. An' there's peach pie fer dessert. Frank, move that bread basket so it don't fall, can ya? Thank you, dearie." Molly was the last into her seat. Immediately conversations halted so Frank could bless the food. When he was done, all were instantly talking again, serving themselves and passing food around the full table. The young man seated across from Molly looked on with wide eyes.

"We're so glad ya come today, Harry. To church, an' then to share our meal."

Marnie stirred uncomfortably and whispered out of the side of her mouth, "I told ya, Miss Molly, he likes ta be called Harold."

"Oh, forgive me. Harold, then, we're glad to have ya."

Frank offered the bowl of scalloped potatoes to their guest. "You must'a know what a big family is'a like, eh?"

Harold nodded slowly, large hands holding the dish of potatoes. "Not sure I ever saw so much food at once." He seemed to compose himself quickly. "Smells delicious, ma'am. Thank you for the invitation."

"Well, it's plenty of work ta fix fer so many, but we ain't complainin' none. We know we're mighty blessed."

"Where does'a your family live, Harold?" Frank asked.

"My daddy works a cattle ranch out on the prairie, though it's not his place. Owner lives somewhere back east. When we first moved there I was just fifteen. All we had was an old empty granary to live in—all seven of us. But now we have a little house we rent." He chuckled, seeming to relax a bit more. "I remember before that, Mama used to say it would be a step up from that granary to be campin' in a tent again! But Daddy always answered her the same. *'Better is little with the fear of the LORD than great treasure and trouble therewith.'* He always says that, still."

Harold scanned around the table, seeming to receive enough encouragement to continue. "Anyway, Uncle Lloyd was workin' the ranch too, till they had to start layin' off men. Up till then I thought I'd follow in my daddy's footsteps and be a hand. It didn't take me long to figure I was gonna need to find work someplace else—now I'm old enough to be on my own." His eyes flickered toward Marnie, but he quickly dropped his gaze. Beth was sure Harold hadn't intended to give so much away by the impulsive glance.

He lifted a few slices of ham onto his plate. "I don't have experience minin'," he said, "but my uncle says I'm catchin' on fast. At least, I'm tryin' real hard. It's just so nice to have a Sunday off for a change and to go to a service. Feels like I'm home again somehow." He smiled. "Havin' a nice Sunday dinner like this brings it all back too."

Beth grew more and more pleased as she listened to Harold speak so freely, answering questions and asking his own in return. He was not as she had pictured him in any of her invented scenarios, and Beth found herself easily liking him. He was polite and well-spoken, cordial and transparent. She decided,

I think Marnie has chosen well, even if he's seven years her senior. Beth glanced down at her plate with a little sigh. *And that girl is definitely a bride worth waiting a couple of years for. Guess he's clever enough to know that—staking a claim before any other boy has a chance ... if only the two are willing to be patient.* Another sigh.

Following dinner, Harold suggested a walk and Marnie was quick to accept, snatching her coat up. Frank and Molly exchanged meaningful looks, and Beth hurried forward. "May I come along? I'd love to have a look around now that winter's really set in."

Harold gave a welcoming nod. "Pleased to have you, Miss Thatcher. Mr. and Mrs. Russo, would you care to come too?" He took the coat from Marnie and held it so she could slide her arms into the sleeves. "The ice isn't quite frozen on the river, and I found some beaver tracks down there. Must have his dam close to the bend where the water's open still."

"You go ahead," Molly answered for them both. "We'll likely sit fer a spell."

Harold stopped and looked around. "Where's your hat, Marnie?"

She gave an incoherent answer, but Harold lifted the red cloche from a hook by the door. "Here you are."

Marnie averted her gaze and pulled it down over her dark hair.

The sun, reflecting off unspoiled snow, had already warmed the air. They stood together on the porch for a moment. "Winter always makes me wish I could paint," Beth said pensively.

Marnie explained, "Her sister paints pictures, Harold. She did lots of 'em fer the schoolroom. I can show ya sometime. They're of the ocean and ships an' things."

He stepped aside so Marnie and Beth could precede him down the steps. "I'd like that," he said. "An' I'd like to see your school, Marnie."

Already Beth was feeling like a third wheel. Yet she knew Frank and Molly were expecting her to keep the young couple company. "Where to, Harold? I'll just follow the two of you."

"Sure, I guess I'm the one who knows the way."

Beth faced a difficult balancing act. She wanted to interact but without monopolizing the conversation. Marnie had fallen quiet, almost reticent. Beth hoped the girl wasn't feeling resentful that Beth was intruding.

"This is a great little town," Harold said over his shoulder as he led them toward the river. "An' it feels so clean and new. Shucks, the wood on the buildings still smells like it's newly sawn. Maybe it's mostly the sawmill, but just the same, the whole place feels . . . fresh and newly born."

Beth noted a bit of a poet in this young man. "Do you like to read, Harold?"

"Sure do. Don't get much chance anymore, but I used to, 'specially late at night. Nowadays I keep fallin' asleep when I try."

"How nice." Beth raised the large collar of her coat until it covered her ears. "Marnie has borrowed all of my series of books about the land of Oz. Harold, did you bring any books with you? What do you enjoy reading?"

The young man turned his attention toward Marnie. "You like that story too? My mama used to read to us every night, and *The Wizard of Oz* was one of our favorites. I didn't even know there were any more than that one, Marnie."

Her answer came softly. "*The Patchwork Girl of Oz* was my favorite."

"Perhaps that explains your grammar and diction, Harold," Beth commented, falling in step at his other side as the path through the trees widened. "You're quite articulate, Harold."

He grinned mischievously and looked sideways at her. "You mean to say I talk too much? I get told that a lot."

"Why, no, Harold. It means *well-spoken* or *expressive*."

He laughed. "Yeah, I know. I'm just joshin'. But now you *do* sound like a teacher." He grinned at Beth and then reached out a hand to catch Marnie's as they crossed a patch of deeper snow, releasing it reluctantly. "Actually, I had a real good teacher. Mr. Flemming. We all liked him, even the kids that were having a hard time with their studies."

Just as Beth was about to respond about the value of a good teacher, Harold added, "Fact is, Mr. Harris Hughes reminds me a lot of him."

Beth turned away in pretense of retying her scarf.

"I know, Marnie, that you don't like his airs, but you're learnin'," he told her. "And that's the whole reason for school." His attention returned to Beth. "I keep tellin' her, Miss Thatcher, she's gotta finish all the way. It's not that many more years—not when you compare it with the rest of her life."

Somehow Beth managed to keep from throwing her arms around Marnie's fine young man. If Harold Edwards had said nothing else all afternoon, this statement alone would have won Beth over. She could only smile broadly, not quite trusting her voice.

Together they found fresh beaver tracks but did not catch sight of the creatures that had made them. To Marnie's rapt attention,

Harold provided a wealth of interesting facts, explaining how they live in small colonies and store up enough food for the winter. Beth followed after, remaining quiet as the couple explored together.

They turned back as the sun began its afternoon descent. Beth led the way this time, giving Harold and Marnie a chance to feel almost alone as their pace slowed and they lagged behind. When Beth reached the gate she called back to them, "I'm going in. You can say your good-byes on the porch if you like."

Harold hurried forward with Marnie close behind. "No, we'll come inside with you."

Molly was stitching in the parlor, Frank dozing loudly in a chair next to her. Beth and Marnie removed their outdoor things quietly and hung them on hooks.

Harold, still in his winter coat, addressed Beth softly, with a glance at Frank sleeping in the parlor behind. "Miss Thatcher?"

Beth looked up from the boots she had set aside and saw he was holding the red hat. Marnie hung behind him, twisting a strand of hair nervously. "I'm afraid I owe you an apology. I went and did a silly thing, and I'm afraid it caused some trouble—a misunderstanding—that I never intended."

"What is it, Harold?" Beth whispered back.

She wondered if the new hat had been damaged somehow.

He glanced down at his hands and back up at Beth. "I'm embarrassed to say, but I'm sure—certain, actually—you'd rather know the truth instead of finding out later some other way. I'd never want to put you in that position." He grimaced, one eyebrow raised in a rather endearing fashion. "This week I dropped a box on the doorstep where Marnie lived, but I failed to write her name on it . . . or mine neither. An' so I caused—"

Beth's gasp stopped his explanation, and she clamped a quick hand over her mouth. "Oh, Harold!" She moved to face Marnie, but the girl was still staring at the floor. "I'm so sorry, Marnie! I just assumed. I very rashly assumed that . . . oh, Marnie, I'm awfully sorry," she repeated.

Only then did the girl shyly look up. "It's fine. No harm done."

Beth managed a laugh, then groaned, then laughed again, and the two joined in. "What if I had"—she faltered over how to say it—"I could have, oh, I'm so embarrassed, I can't even . . . Marnie, did you know it was coming?"

Harold grinned, and Marnie started to snicker. "Well, yes. Harold told me to watch fer a surprise. *'Something to keep the snow off.'*

But then I didn't know what ta say when you showed me. I tried, I just couldn't say anything without soundin' . . ." The shifting expressions on Marnie's face were oddly comical, wavering between pathetic and amused.

Beth laughed harder, wiping at a tear from the corner of her eye. "You must have been fit to be tied."

Marnie took a small step nearer to Harold. "We couldn't think of a good way ta tell ya."

"Oh, darling, and I just kept telling you how lovely it looked on you—your very own hat!" Laughter was shaking Beth's shoulders now. "You must have thought I was out of my mind."

"No, ma'am, just awful kind to let me wear it first."

With a touch on Marnie's shoulder and a tip of his hat to Beth, Harold excused himself, closing the door quietly behind him.

Marnie and Beth walked the short hallway into the kitchen in order to muffle their laughter, each spontaneously breaking into giggles again whenever one looked up at the other, triggering more laughter long after they thought they were done.

Chapter
15

"M iss Thatcher, we got an idea." Three teenage girls stood in a row in front of Beth's desk, their expressions serious. It was lunch break, and Beth was just catching up on some grading while eating her sandwich. A few of Robert's students had begun bringing their lunches so they could eat together in the classroom, but all of Beth's younger ones simply walked the short distance home to their mothers.

Beth looked at each face, from Bonnie Murphy to Marnie and then Luela Coolidge.

"What do you have in mind, girls?"

"We want ta write the Christmas play this year," Luela announced.

Beth quickly restrained a frown. Things were far more complicated this year with two teachers, particularly since she was avoiding meetings with Robert. She had been contemplating a quiet evening of recitations for her own class, their families invited. Beth struggled to find a proper response. "That sounds like a wonderful idea. But why are you asking me? Have you spoken to Mr. Harris Hughes about this?"

They nodded solemnly, and Bonnie made a little face. "He told us just ta talk to you. Said it was yer department."

"Why mine?" Beth asked.

"He said he'll stick with teachin' us science and mathematics and facts and stuff."

"He don't even go to church, Miss Thatcher!"

"And he doesn't say the prayer before class."

Beth sighed. "Fine, then. If that's how he wants it, then of course we'll plan a Christmas celebration. If Mr. Harris Hughes has no interest in spiritual things, then we won't let that stop us," she said as she set her pen in its stand. "What do you have in mind?"

They all talked at once. "We want all the kids to do the show, like last year. . . . We can have it in the church. . . . We'll tell Bertie Benedict to ask her mama if we can use her little baby brother to be Jesus. 'Cause Charlie, we used him last year, he's already one and he don't sit still no more—I mean *anymore*."

"Those are wonderful ideas. I'll speak to Pastor Davidson about holding it at the church. Why don't we get together after school tonight, if you have time after homework and chores, and we can start to work on the details. Shall we start with the script?"

Her suggestion was met with silence. Marnie, the youngest of the three, drew in a breath. "We'd like ta write it ourselves, please, Miss Thatcher. And do all the work fer it too. We can get the kids together on Saturday and give 'em their parts to practice and such."

"You want to do it all?"

"Yes, ma'am." Luela took charge again. "Teddy Boy and Addie said they would help build a set, and Sadie's gonna ask her mama to play the organ fer the songs. We hoped you and Grandpa Frank could do a duet on yer violins again like last year. Maybe even the same song."

Beth thought about her neglected violin. It would require practice if she would be ready for a public event. Frank kept up much better than she did—even with the contraption he had rigged to keep the bow strapped to his wrist after he had lost his right hand. She leaned back in her chair and surveyed the girls. "It sounds like you've given this a great deal of thought and planning already. I'm proud of you all. And it's wonderful to see you take initiative. May I make just one request?"

"'Course!"

"Will you show me your ideas as you're working them through? I think it would be good to have an adult involved and at least aware of what all will be taking place. After all, this will be a school event."

"Yes, ma'am!" They hurried from the room to join their co-conspirators eating lunch next door.

Beth put away her tiny bit of disappointment, smiled, and sent up a quick prayer that the evening would turn out the way the girls envisioned it—and that Robert would not put any stumbling blocks in their way.

❦

"Heard the news, Beth?" Molly asked over a quilt block she and Marnie were piecing together on the sofa. Half of the top was already assembled, an intricate Bear's Paw design set against a light green twill. They had gathered in the parlor, each in favorite places.

Beth, in an armchair, looked up from her book. "What news? I don't suppose I have."

"The apartments in the old company building are ready. So some of the men are movin' there this weekend, an' Marnie can have her own room back. Frank and Teddy

Boy can pick up all her things on Saturday. If that works for ya."

"They finished in *this* weather?"

"Just had the rooms inside left—the outside they got done 'fore the snow."

"Oh, that's good. I'm sure the men will appreciate being able to spread out a little. You must be glad too, Molly."

"Yes, an' no. The money's been real good ta have. Maybe come spring we can put a coat of paint on this old house. But I'm plumb wore out with all the extra washin'. Most of 'em will still come fer dinner, so that's good income yet. Means we're doin' fine still."

"Well, you deserve a break—or at least a little less labor. I'm so happy it's all worked out for you."

Beth could tell Marnie was watching for her reaction, and with an easy approval of it all, the girl seemed relieved. "Miss Thatcher, it's been so nice stayin' with ya. But I do think I'd like my own bedroom back."

"Of course you would, darling. Who could blame you? But, Marnie, you've been the best roommate I could have wanted, and I hope you know how much I'll miss you. You've even taught me many important things, like keeping that silly fire going."

The three chuckled, and Molly said, "Best part is, Marnie dear, next time yer Harry sends a hat, I get to be the one can call dibs. Hope it's a blue one this time to match my new dress."

"Oh, Molly," Beth groaned with a soft smile, shaking her head in response to the woman's mischievous, twinkling eyes.

Marnie muttered quietly, "It's Harold." Yet as she rose to leave, she stooped to press a kiss against Molly's hair and added, "Thanks for yer help on the quilt."

Molly folded up the project for the night and gathered the other supplies to put back in her sewing kit just as Frank returned from the time-consuming job of toting buckets of hot water to fill the bathtub and took his spot in the corner chair.

He seemed pleasantly surprised to find Beth in the parlor. "*Buona sera*, Miss Beth. I thought'a you'd be busy at home."

"Good evening to you too, Frank. I finished grading at school today. So I had a free evening."

"That'sa nice."

Almost to the doorway, Marnie turned to Molly. "Can I use the dining table now, fer homework?"

"'Course, dearie. Just don't leave nothin' behind when yer done."

Beth set her book aside, slipped her feet from her shoes to tuck under her, and settled in for a nice long visit. Having Frank and Molly all to herself was a rare pleasure. "It's so quiet tonight, and it's never quiet here."

Molly laid an afghan over her lap. "There's a meeting fer the company in the new buildin'. Some high mucky-mucks are in town, so they want all their people to gather."

"Where's Teddy this evening?"

Molly leaned back into the sofa with a contented sigh. "At school."

"At school? This late? Whatever for?"

"Mr. Harris Hughes has got 'em workin' on some project. Somethin' about 'lectricity."

"Is that so?" Beth dropped her gaze to the area rug, following the vine all the way around its edge as she mulled over thoughts about Robert. "Do you think he's going to be elected as mayor, Frank?" Turning in the older man's direction, Beth watched him stir and hoped she hadn't awakened him.

"Maybe so. I know you don'ta like him, but the townsfolk, they seem'a to trust his knowledge. An' I think they like'a too that he don't work'a for the mine."

"I suppose." *I'm just as well educated. Well, almost,* she mused. *If I weren't a woman, perhaps I'd be the one.* . . . And then always that second thought, *Except I'll be leaving this summer.*

Frank's eyes had closed again.

"I spoke with Philip about him the other

day." Her voice was so low she didn't think she'd been heard. "He doesn't seem to take issue with Robert either."

Molly answered, "That right?"

"Philip asked me how club was going, and I told him about the kerfuffle with Robert a while back. I was truly surprised that Philip wasn't more concerned." Frustrated, Beth pushed back her hair with both hands. "I'll be blunt, Molly. I don't understand what everyone else seems to see in him. Maybe it's just that I'm closer to the situation—that I cross paths with him daily instead of just socially." Beth shrugged. "Sure, he's a rather nice person out of the classroom. Very polite. Well-spoken."

Molly lifted one eyebrow and cocked her head. "What exactly ya have against him? Exactly," she asked, leaning forward and watching Beth carefully.

Beth bristled at the reproof in her question. "You haven't heard him, Molly. Sometimes when he talks to me he's so . . . he's so condescending and, well, smug."

"Ya mean when he disagrees with ya?"

"Yes, but, it's more than that. It's as if he fully *intends* to disagree with me. And that even when he knows how I feel about something, he's going to do it his way regardless."

Molly settled against the sofa again and repeated, "Ya mean, he disagrees with ya."

"No, it's not just that." Beth's irritation with the man was making it very difficult for her to express her feelings. "He's fully aware of it all, Molly. I don't think people understand the motives behind his actions, behind his words. He realizes that we're a Christian community and he's the outsider. And he intends to *fix* us, I think."

"Why?"

"I'm sorry?"

"Why is it ya think he wants ta fix us?"

"Because I believe he feels he knows better."

"And you don't agree?"

Beth's eyes narrowed. "No, Molly. I don't. I think he's an elitist. I think his first-class, expensive education has made him feel superior. I think because of it he hasn't just put himself above us all, above this whole town, but he's put himself above God too. And I'm afraid for those children who sit in his class every day and hear him spout his noxious ideologies." Beth tried to make herself smaller in her chair. Even she wasn't comfortable with the rancor she heard in that last phrase.

"I see." Molly lifted her head and slowly adjusted her position to face Beth, draping an arm across the back of the sofa. She patted the cushion beside her. "Will ya come sit here, dearie?"

Beth obliged, but her movements were

rather stiff and formal. She sat straight, her fingers laced together in her lap.

Molly leaned closer, reaching across and taking one of Beth's hands in her own, softened with age. "There's a battle—I ain't denying. But ya gotta remember who the enemy is."

Beth's gaze darted toward Molly. The woman's eyes held great concern.

"I'm not sayin' ya can't make a fuss when ya need to. I ain't sayin' that at all. Goodness knows, I done my own share of fussin' in my day. But what I am sayin' is that ya gotta do it right—the Bible way."

"And you don't think I am?" Beth swallowed hard, already knowing the answer in her heart.

"I don't think ya swung a fist out at nobody. Yet." She gave Beth's hand a playful shake. "Ya ain't killed nor stolen nor perjured. It's just yer words are showin' what yer heart is feelin', and I'm afraid you're settin' yerself up pretty hard against him." She added guardedly, "And ya even might'a done some gossippin', don't ya think?"

Beth squeezed her eyes closed. *Molly is right.* "Yes, I've done those things . . . all of them," she whispered through trembling lips, and tears filled her eyes. "But what can I do, Molly? I can't just sit back and watch it happen, can I?"

"Well, I guess that brings to mind a couple Bible verses. I know 'em well 'cause I've needed to recall 'em so many times. The first one's from the Sermon on the Mount. The very words of Jesus. 'Love yer enemies, bless them that curse ya, do good to them that hate ya, and pray for them which despitefully use ya, and persecute ya.'" Molly shook her head sorrowfully. "It's a hard one—powerful hard sometimes. I know that well. But it don't change the fact that it's the Lord's way. And He knew a thing or two about enemies, didn't He?" Beth slowly nodded, wiping her damp eyes.

Molly pressed Beth's hand tenderly. "And the second is from 1 Peter. 'Be ready always to give an answer to every man that asketh ya a reason of the hope that is in ya with meekness and fear.' Now, that fear, it ain't fear of man. It's fear of God only. And no one else. Ya see, the Bible way of fussin' don't mean you can't speak. It just tells ya the right way to do it. And did ya notice those words 'to every man that asketh'? Sometimes our best course is ta wait till we're asked."

Beth blew her nose. "I'm not very good at that—at waiting. And then when I do speak up, I'm usually good and angry and don't do it right at all."

"That's the fleshly way that got passed down to ya from every generation that come before. So that means we *all* got room fer growin'." Molly drew Beth close in a strong embrace. "We're all just pilgrims makin' our way along, tryin' to follow in the footsteps of Him who was the only One who took every single step just right."

Frank crossed the room, taking a seat on the other side of Beth. "Can'a we pray with you, mia cara?"

Beth melted, at last allowing tears to trickle from her eyes. "I'd like that," she whispered.

Molly spoke again softly. "Do ya love him, Beth?"

"Who . . . ?"

"Yer enemy—Mr. Harris Hughes."

Beth wanted to answer *Of course*, but she wasn't certain it would be honest. "I'm not sure."

"Don't be too quick to give up on him yet, to think he's beyond the love of God, beyond hearing the voice of the Spirit."

Frank began to pray, his hand on Beth's shoulder as they asked the Father for wisdom, courage, and love on her behalf. Beth silently wiped at her tears, adding, *And for forgiveness, Father. Again.*

Chapter 16

Beth trudged through drifts that came above her boots. The sharp, cold ice crystals felt as if they were tearing at her stockings, biting at her legs, and freezing any skin they touched. Though the night was still and calm, lit by a cheerful full moon, Beth was not enjoying this particular walk. She had been asked to come to Bonnie Murphy's house to help the girls with the Christmas program. She'd been told there was a problem. And so she struggled along the road in the darkness between the rows of cookie-cutter homes, each identically hung with icicles and framed with snow, like two rows of gingerbread houses.

Beth searched the brightly lit windows for the pink curtains signifying the Murphy home, where Abigail also roomed. *There it is.*

She hurried up the steps and stood shivering on the stoop.

"Miss Thatcher, come in, come in," she heard as the door opened before she had even knocked. "Ya look froze through." Ruth helped Beth over the tumbled boots in the doorway and took her coat. "Daniel, toss another log on. Bonnie, clear a space fer your teacher and give her the throw fer her lap."

The children hurried to comply while Beth accepted a seat on the only padded chair in the small home. Close to the fire, she was grateful for the warmth as she held out her hands toward the stove. Bonnie joined Marnie and Luela at the kitchen table.

Abigail came over with the pot, poured a cup of coffee, and placed it in Beth's hands. It was marvelously hot—still too hot to drink, but it smelled delicious.

The expressions she saw facing her around the table were rather grim. "I'm so sorry ya had to come out in this cold, Miss Thatcher," Bonnie said. "We feel real bad about that."

"What's the matter, girls? How can I help?"

They exchanged looks and Luela blurted, "The boys ain't gonna help with our sets. Said they're too busy now."

"Why is that? What are they doing instead?"

"That project with Mr. Harris Hughes."

"Project? Who all is involved?"

"Addie and Teddy Boy. An' Kenny Edwards an' James an' Peter. All of 'em, leastwise all the boys old enough."

Daniel's mutter carried across the small room. "I'm eleven. I can help ya."

Bonnie rolled her eyes and shook her head at her younger brother. "They had the stable half done already for *our* project. They was, I mean, they *were* buildin' it at the Coolidges' cabin. Now it's too heavy for us girls ta move, but Luela can't do the rest of it herself just 'cause it's at her house."

"What are the boys doing for this . . . this other project?"

"It's a radio," Marnie explained quickly. "It'll play music and tell the news and all sorts of things. But it has ta have a crank on it to make it work—to give it the electricity. We don't got any plugs out here to plug it in. And I guess it's harder ta get done than they thought it would be," she finished in a rush, betraying her own interest in the endeavor.

Beth blew on the coffee in her cup and ventured a sip. "Why can't they finish it after the Christmas break?"

"Mr. Harris Hughes says it's fer a contest an' it has ta be done 'fore he leaves at the end of the quarter. 'Cause he's gonna enter it in a show in Calgary."

The project sounded rather exciting to Beth also. "And they don't have any time to spare at all?"

"Nope," declared Bonnie with a vigorous shake of her head.

Beth sipped again and began thinking out loud. "What if . . . you didn't build a stable this year?" She hurried on before the girls' consternation could be expressed. "No, listen, what if you painted a backdrop of the stable instead? The platform is rather small, you know. We could use rolls of paper from the store taped together, and I have some paint. Then even some of the younger ones could help."

They were unconvinced. "But how do we put the manger in it then?"

"It would go on the floor out front."

"Then how do we—?"

"Wait," Luela interrupted, holding up a palm toward her friends. "If we painted it, then we could have all them other things we weren't gonna be able ta build, like a cow, and a lamb . . ."

"And a camel," Marnie finished, grasping her hands together in delight.

From across the kitchen, Ruth nodded at Abigail, who was arranging cookies on a plate. "That might work. It would be much less trouble. And I think it would be even more creative—prettier and more colorful."

Daniel was hanging an arm around his mother now. "Mama, can I paint the camel?"

The older girls hovered over the table, talking all at once as they planned the next move.

Beth sipped again at her coffee, relieved that the crisis had been resolved. *And without having to involve Robert . . . this time.* She wondered though if there might be more to come. *Oh, Father, help me meet each difficulty with Your grace . . . and love.*

❖

"Boys, sit down!" Beth called over the hubbub. "If I have to tell you again I will be sending notes home to your mothers. I'm very serious." It was the last day of classes before Christmas and, to make matters more chaotic, only a half day of school since the play was to be held in the evening. The whole town was abuzz with anticipation, and the children were wild with excitement.

Beth inwardly wrestled with her own impatience, trying to ignore the clock ticking away the minutes until Jarrick would arrive in the afternoon. The two of them planned to attend the performance and then to leave in the morning for Lethbridge. Jarrick had several days off in a row, and Beth was nearly beside herself at the thought of their first Christmas together.

"Georgie, I told you, no writing on the board. I've already washed it, and I want it left clean. Now, children, all of you sit down and finish your work so you don't have to take it home. You don't want homework over Christmas, do you?"

At last the mine whistle blew, signaling lunch for the workers and, on this day, announcing the end of school till next year. Beth scrambled for her coat, hurrying the last little one out the door and pulling it shut behind. She carefully picked her way across the rutted, icy road and hurried to the stairs for some practice time on her part of the violin duet before Jarrick arrived.

On the first step Beth almost tripped over Penelope. The cat's sides had filled out, and she was far less wild, now frequently underfoot, her bright eyes begging for more to eat. "Not now, Miss Kitty. You'll have to wait for supper." Nudging the animal out of the way with the side of one boot, Beth scrambled up to the landing and unlocked the door.

There was so much to do. She changed into her best dress, hung a matching hat on the hook beside her coat, restyled her hair, and tidied the apartment. It was unlikely that Jarrick would step inside her accommodations unless they were chaperoned, but she wanted everything to be perfect just in case more guests arrived. Taking her violin from the trunk, she brought it into tune and played through the melody. It was not a difficult piece, but she feared she was still dreadfully out of practice.

At last there was a knock at the door, and Beth hurried over, hoping to find Jarrick on the landing. However, Bonnie Murphy stood there with Marnie, both girls on the verge of tears.

"What on earth? What's wrong?" She quickly pulled them into the warmth of her room.

"Oh, Miss Thatcher, the boys ain't here!"

"What? What do you mean?"

"They drove up the mountain this afternoon to get a better radio signal and nobody's seen 'em since."

"The boys drove?"

"No," Bonnie said, almost shouting, pumping her fists in frustration. "Mr. Harris Hughes drove. But the boys went along."

Beth's heart lurched; she quickly reached for her coat and slid her feet into boots. "Who exactly went?"

"Teddy Boy and Addie, Peter and James and Kenny. All the oldest boys who were doing that project."

"How long have they been gone?"

"Hours—*hours*!"

"Oh dear. Yes, come, let's find out . . ." But she didn't finish as they rushed downstairs.

"Everybody's at the school. That's where they're meetin' up now."

Beth attempted to draw on any words of comfort and encouragement that came to mind for the girls. Her private thoughts, though, were frantic. *What if something has happened to them? What if they're stuck in the snow? What if their car went off the road and over a cliff? It'll be dark soon!* She glanced toward the west, the sun a low blur against the dull gray sky. *Oh, Father, please don't let it snow now.*

Abigail met them at the door to the school and reached out to catch the worried girls' hands. "The boys are fine. Mr. McDermott and Mr. Shaw went lookin' for them in the truck. Mr. Shaw just come back on foot to tell us the news. Seems the teacher's car got stuck in a drift, and Peter's daddy is usin' chains to try an' pull it out. Mr. Shaw thought they might even beat him back, but it must be stuck worse'n he thought. He's roundin' up more men in a second truck to go help."

Beth looked back up at the sky. "They'll need blankets. I'll go—"

"Molly already went. Her and Heidi Coolidge are gatherin' as many as they can find. Come on in. No sense catchin' yer death of cold."

Abigail's words only underscored Beth's concern about the boys' safety. It looked like most of the little town had already been mobilized. She took a position by the entry-room window facing out on the street, watching for signs of the boys returning or Jarrick's car. Soon a cluster of the younger ones had gathered around her, more children than she had long-enough arms to draw close.

A truck rumbled past, Philip driving, along with Toby Coulter in the cab. In the back were several men hunkered down to ward off the cold. Beth recognized Marnie's beau, Harold, next to his uncle Lloyd.

"Miss Thatcher, how long's it gonna take 'em to find the boys?" Marian Edwards sniffed. "Mama says Kenny left his scarf and mittens at home." More sniffles followed.

Beth stroked a hand against the blond hair and offered her own handkerchief. "They know where the boys are, darling. And they can sit inside their car to wait, so they're out of the wind."

Wilton Coolidge shook his head slowly. "Uh-uh, my daddy used ta say a car is the coldest place you could be in a blizzard. He said you'd be better off diggin' down inta a snow drift than waitin' in a metal car."

Beth's eyes glanced back out the window. *Where is Jarrick? Why doesn't he come?*

The darkening clouds seemed ready to soon let loose the next snowfall. She tried not to allow her fears to be seen by the children. Taking a deep breath and asking God for calm, she suggested, "Why don't we pray? That's something we can do to help." She turned her back on the window. "Let's sit here together and ask God to protect the boys and the men who are rescuing them. We don't need chairs. We can just sit right here on the floor. It's clean enough. I swept it out near the end of class, remember? Let's make a circle and hold hands. Who wants to start?"

One by one the brothers and sisters, with childlike innocence, began to talk about the frightening situation with their heavenly Father.

"Help 'em get the car out, God. Help 'em be okay."

"God, Kenny don't even got his scarf and mittens on. Can ya keep his hands warm, please?"

"An' don't let nobody get hurt."

"Please, God, keep it from snowin' before they get back. That would just make it all so worse!"

"An' help my daddy not to yell too much at James, least till they get home safe."

Whose fault is this, anyway? Beth pondered. It was the first time she had even considered blame. *Certainly not the boys. Indeed, there's only one adult involved.*

Soon it became too dark to stay put by the front door. So the small group rose and joined their mothers waiting in Beth's classroom, where lamps were already lit and placed strategically around. It was an eerie wavering light, making the large familiar space feel like a great void, casting hulking shadows against the walls whenever a pacing mother would pass near a lamp. The little potbellied stove was crackling with heat and still Beth's hands were cold. She rubbed them together and continued to pray silently.

"There's a car," Henry Ruffinelli hollered. "I hear a car." They rushed for the entryway window, the smaller ones there before their mothers could rise from the seats.

"No ya didn't hear it, Huffy! There ain't nothin' out there." Breathless silence.

"Yes there is! I heard it too." More silence.

Then came the unmistakable sound of a car, and long patches of headlight beams shot across the snow and ice. The watchers streamed outside, calling, "Who's there? Who is it?"

A car door creaked open, and some young passengers scrambled out.

Abigail had brought a lamp and lifted it high above the crowd to reflect off the side of Jarrick's police vehicle and the five teenagers.

They scattered through the crowd looking for their families, not reluctant to accept the long hugs and cries of thanksgiving. "You're safe! Oh, thank God!"

Thank You, Father. Thank You for hearing the children's prayers . . . and mine. Beth pushed forward toward the driver's side and fell into Jarrick's arms.

"I'm sorry I'm late," he whispered, making her laugh shakily. "I was on my way into town when I was flagged down by a couple of fathers."

"I'm so glad you were able to help. I'm so grateful everyone is safe at last."

Beth slept surprisingly late. There was no reason to hurry. The boys were home, the snow had not come, and the Christmas play had simply been postponed until the next evening, though that meant she and Jarrick would be off to Lethbridge and wouldn't be able to see the event. Frank cheerfully agreed to play his violin on his own. *"I have lots'a songs to choose'a from,"* he'd assured Beth.

Beth also recalled the mutters about Robert's ill-advised trip up the mountain during inclement weather as mothers had helped set the school desks back in order and snuffed out the lamps.

"*What did he think he was doing?*"

"*Shows ya all that fancy education don't turn into common sense!*"

"*Just a city boy, after all.*"

"*Can't even figure out it ain't wise to try ta plow through a three-foot snowdrift, with our boys in his car. Who on earth does that?*"

The town's sentiment seemed to have turned against him.

By the time Beth hurried over to Molly's for breakfast, the sun was shining brightly. She could see signs in the snow of the previous night's excitement—tire tracks at odd angles and footprints trampling broad areas. She arrived just as breakfast was being cleared away and was given a plate of eggs and bacon. Frank and Jarrick were still seated with their cups of coffee while Molly and Marnie washed the dishes. Beth couldn't resist a whispered *good morning* in Jarrick's ear as she passed behind him and found a place at the kitchen table.

The news had already circulated that Mr. Harris Hughes had headed out for Calgary before sunrise. Beth asked no questions about the boys' adventure last night and the fate of the project. She did hope for Teddy's sake, as well as the others, that it might still be entered in the contest.

Late in the morning she and Jarrick

packed up the car and said their good-byes, with *Merry Christmas* greetings exchanged by all. Molly insisted they take an extra blanket, *"just in case,"* and propped a towel-wrapped Mason jar filled with piping hot coffee among the bags at Beth's feet.

"One whole week," Beth said as she nestled beside Jarrick. "One whole week of rest and bliss. And you . . ." she added, looking at him.

"I'm ready for that," he answered, looking sideways at her with a tender smile. "Let's hope this trip isn't as eventful as my arrival last night."

"To be sure!"

⁓✦⁓

"Beth, you remember Dillard and Eliza Smith, of course. And that they work in the same ministry organization as Philip."

"Of course." Beth nodded to the young couple standing in the doorway, welcoming Beth as their guest for a second time. "It's lovely to be here with you—and this time not worried about a little boy in the hospital. We'll have a chance for a more relaxed visit."

Beth's hostess smiled, her eyes twinkling as she quickly ushered Beth into the comfortable home, through the foyer, and past a narrow wood stair. "I'd like a chance to get to know you better, dear, if you and I can find the time." Eliza gave Beth's elbow a squeeze, a teasing tone to her voice.

"I don't think that will be a problem, Eliza. I don't actually know anyone else in Lethbridge."

They continued through a doorway and into a sitting room. "Are you certain of that?"

A squeal of delight followed, and Julie rushed across the room, catching Beth in a tight embrace before she could utter a word.

"Surprise!" Julie exclaimed. "Did we surprise you, Bethie?"

"What on earth—*Julie?* What . . . how did you get here?"

Beth's sister laughed and said, "It was your Jack's idea, Jack's and Father's. They were in cahoots, working it out so I could come on the train for your Christmas break. Isn't it wonderful?"

Beth buried herself in Julie's hug. "It is! It's wonderful, darling. I can't think of what to say."

Soon they were seated on the sofa, and Julie was bubbling over with news. Margret was mostly staying at home, awaiting the birth of her second child. Mother was fussing over Margret and supervising Christmas decorations and buying gifts. "I brought yours with me," Julie assured Beth. Little JW was now talking up a storm, climbing on the stair rail, and anxiously awaiting *"Ch'ismas."* Julie promised pictures of him, now packed away in the suitcase upstairs. She also said Father had just returned from a short business trip and would be leaving again after Christmas.

"How generous of him to let you come, Julie, in light of the little time he has—"

"Oh, I won't see Father again for quite some time," her animated sister told Beth. "I'm not going back until the wedding, so I can help."

"Julie, dearest, do you mean it? Can you really stay?"

Julie giggled. "Well, it would be rather nasty to say so if I couldn't. Yes, of course. If you'll have me, that is. I'd have to stay with you, and you've said your place is rather tiny."

"Tiny it is, but nothing could be better!"

As much as Beth appreciated her sister's surprise appearance, she felt a little like a woman divided. For weeks she had been eagerly looking forward to this time with Jarrick, and now she felt torn between these two dear ones in her life. After only a day and a half, she was wondering, *Is there any way to speak to Julie gently and ask for some private moments? Will her feelings be terribly hurt?*

The trouble was that Julie was Julie. She did not gravitate toward reading quietly in the sitting room, she would certainly never choose to turn in early for bed, and she wasn't one to offer to help with something so mundane as decorating a Christmas tree. Julie wanted action and excitement and would create it herself should she find it lacking. And though what Beth wanted most was some quiet time alone with Jarrick, Julie was alarmingly persistent in her need for attention.

By Monday morning the girl seemed desperate for amusement. "Bethie, want to have lunch at that little restaurant again, the one by the train station? We can ride over on the trolley if no one can take us. I like that they play radio music while you eat. You probably don't know this, but lately I've taken quite a shine to Broadway hits. And they're hot on the radio just now. We can go, can't we? You're not doing anything else, are you—nothing that can't wait?"

Beth slid the popcorn she was stringing down the long thread and stifled a sigh. "I'll speak with Jarrick about it in a little while. But please try to understand, Julie dear, that we need to be careful with our funds. We're saving for the wedding—and—and everything that comes after." From her place on the couch, Beth reached in the bowl for another piece of popcorn, needle at the ready.

Julie chuckled breezily. "Oh, that's no trouble. Father gave me enough pocket money to share, and I'll hardly need any of it once we get to your little village. There's nothing good to spend it on there anyway."

Beth started to respond that Coal Valley had grown and changed since Julie had visited but realized immediately it would be useless. Her sister would acknowledge none of the advancements and would laugh at her descriptions of its growth and "civilization." So Beth let the matter drop, giving a weak smile and lift of a shoulder to Jarrick.

He was busy working with Dillard, fastening the fragrant Christmas tree into its stand. Catching Beth's eye, Jarrick cleared his throat, and Dillard peered out from behind the evergreen. Beth noticed Jarrick and the Smiths exchange glances.

"Say, Eliza," Dillard said, his tone nonchalant, "did you hear back from your sister yet?"

"I did," his wife answered as she lifted a box from the floor to the table. "She said she's going to drop in later this morning. Did I tell you, Beth?"

Beth wondered if something was afoot. Her words came slowly. "No, I don't think you mentioned it. How nice—"

"Yes, I think you'll enjoy Mary. She and her friends are very busy, especially this time of year. We can never keep up with them." Eliza opened a box of ornaments and began unwrapping them from their papers. "I believe they're going skiing later today, in fact. Have you and your sister ever been cross-country skiing, Beth?"

Julie sat bolt upright in her seat. "We

haven't been. But I've always thought it sounds like fun."

"Maybe you should ask Mary about it then, when she arrives. She's quite an enthusiast. And there are some lovely coulees in the area—deep valleys just so picturesque, especially in the winter. But they're quite challenging, even for practiced skiers."

At last Beth caught on to the underlying scheme. She shook her head a little. "Well, with Julie not having any experience, it might be best for her not to attempt it. Plus, it's so cold outside. Mind you, not as cold as it frequently is here, but chilly just the same. Julie wouldn't like to be so uncomfortable or to struggle to keep up."

"Don't be a sourpuss, Bethie!" Julie was on her feet. "You know I catch on to new things quickly. And my new coat keeps me plenty warm." Julie's attention turned to Eliza. "Honestly, I'm actually kind of an athlete, in spite of my family's humdrum ways."

"Then you'll really have to get to know my younger sister, Mary. She's only seventeen, and she and her friends are a delightful bunch of kids. I think you'd like them."

"Well . . ." Julie hesitated a moment, looked at Beth. "I'm not sure my sister is up for it. She's more of a homebody. You wouldn't be interested, would you, Bethie?"

Beth hid her face so her amusement wouldn't show. "Oh, don't worry about me. I'll be just fine here. It would be nice to have your help finishing the tree—it might take us all afternoon without you. But after that we'll probably just talk for a bit here by the fire." Beth didn't dare look at Jarrick.

"I suppose I'll go anyway," Julie decided. "Yes, I'd be very happy to join them." She waited impatiently for Eliza's sister and her friends to make an appearance. When Mary arrived at last in the front entryway, Julie was delighted to find the girl was an equally spirited soul mate, sharing a sense of adventure and a similar impatience with sitting by the fire.

"The others are waiting in the car," she said. "Come on. Let's go."

As they departed together, Beth waved good-bye to Julie through the small window in the front door, sighing with relief. She felt Jarrick draw near, looking over her head and placing a hand on each of her shoulders. She leaned back against him contentedly. Everyone was happy. "Thank you," she whispered, watching as Julie stood beside the waiting car being introduced to Mary's many friends.

""Thank you?"" he repeated with a laugh. "I was worried you'd think I was just being selfish."

Beth turned to face him. "Oh no, Jarrick, not at all. I came here to be with *you*. I mean, I'm thrilled to be taking Julie back to the mountains, but I came to be with you for Christmas."

After the tree was decorated, Jarrick suggested that the two of them take a walk. They set out into the gray day, bundled and braced for the cold. Beth's quick short steps, attempting to keep up with Jarrick's long strides, soon had her feeling comfortably warmed. She squeezed her thick wool mitten around Jarrick's arm to help keep his pace.

He looked down at her and covered her hand with his. "Your cheeks are nice and rosy. Warm enough?" At her nod, he asked, "What else is happening out in the wilds? Have they chosen a mayor yet?" His eyes twinkled mischievously. "I don't suppose Philip relented and let his name be added to the hat."

"No, that would have been nice. But you were right. He still insists he isn't interested. And I can't argue with his reasons."

"When is the election? And who's on the list?"

"Oh, it won't be until mid-January," she said, her words coming in breathless bursts. "The town doesn't even have a list of candidates yet. The city council was chosen. You probably don't know half of them. Bill Shaw is back again. And you might still remember Bardo Mussante—he married Esther Blane. But all the others are new. Except that you've met Robert."

"Oh, yes, I should have guessed they'd put him on the council."

"What's so special about him?" Beth knew her prejudices were showing again. She tried hard to remember Molly's admonitions.

"I think he's a fine choice, Beth."

"Yes," she reluctantly agreed, "he is, in a way. He's clever and poised. But he's so . . . so secular, so full of humanistic philosophy."

Jarrick paused, looking far down the road, face silhouetted against the clouds. "I'm not sure you can choose a council based solely on their religious beliefs, can you, Beth?"

"But, you can't say he's demonstrated much wisdom lately."

"You mean . . . getting stuck in the snow?"

"Yes." Beth could feel her chest tighten. She knew even as she spoke that her words were an attempt to turn Jarrick against Robert a little.

"I don't know, Beth. I think he meant well, even if it became something totally different than he intended. I wish you had seen him. By the time I arrived, the other men were practically forcing him to sit in the truck to warm up. He was covered with snow from trying to dig the car out himself, so cold he was pale. And he was utterly remorseful and humiliated. I hate to see any man look so defeated."

The image pricked at Beth's tender heart. "Were they harsh with him? The fathers? The other men?"

"No," Jarrick answered quietly, picking up the pace again. "But with men, especially in a situation like that, nobody really has to say very much."

They walked on in silence as Beth struggled with conflicting thoughts. *I'm sorry, Father. I'll try harder. I will.*

Yet she stubbornly reiterated the question that remained unanswered. *But what about the children? After all, it was Robert who put the boys in jeopardy. And he's the one who maintains so much influence over them all with his teaching that leaves out God. What about them? Aren't they, together, more important than just one man?*

Julie had brought the two bridesmaid dresses from Toronto, and Beth was able to show them to Jarrick. They were exactly what Beth had hoped them to be, though somewhat more luxurious and modern in a mixture of silky satin and soft lace. But the shade of blue was perfect, a lovely cornflower, somehow both soft and bright. To accessorize the dress

Julie had brought beaded headpieces with a wisp of tulle on one side, long strands of faux pearls, elbow-length white gloves and low-heeled shoes that matched the blue almost perfectly. Beth was thrilled to picture Marnie wearing such finery. Jarrick smiled and nodded as the two women explained it all to him, but they eventually collapsed in merriment as his expression gradually changed from interest to bewilderment to teasing.

But better still, Julie had also brought the cherished wedding dress worn by Grandmama, then Mother, then Margret. It was hidden away in the bedroom closet of the room Beth and Julie shared. Beth tried it on and was rather lost in it. But Eliza was certain she knew a dressmaker who could make it fit nicely—with enough tucks to shorten the skirt and a seam or two moved on the bodice, done carefully so that it could be taken out again for Julie. *That is,* Beth thought, *if Julie is willing to wear a second-hand gown, one she'd consider rather old-fashioned.*

Looking at her reflection in the full-length mirror, Beth was alarmed at how thin she looked. Mother, she knew, would be horrified. It was time to put on some of the weight she had lost with her toast-and-tea suppers. She would need to begin cooking regularly, not just for herself but now for her sister as well.

If only Julie would be interested in helping prepare meals while she was visiting. Unfortunately, that seemed unlikely.

The evening following Boxing Day, Beth and Jarrick planned to share a meal alone at their restaurant. Julie helped Beth choose a dress and then worked to put up her hair with extra flourish, adding accessories to the outfit until Beth was certain she'd be a spectacle among the less pretentious diners.

"It won't matter," Julie insisted. "If people here can't understand high fashion, you should just ignore them. And you never know, there might be someone among them who appreciates your *ensemble*."

Beth laughed at Julie's attempt at French pronunciation. It was easier not to argue. In point of fact, she did feel well dressed. And, anyway, almost everything Julie had accomplished would be covered by a hat and long coat until Beth was ready to be seated, and then again almost as soon as she stood to leave. *Little harm can be done in one evening, indulging my sister's more extravagant fashion sense*, she told herself.

Jarrick had arranged for the same table where he had proposed. The candlelit dining room felt comfortable and familiar now, like their own private retreat. Beth settled herself into the chair and smoothed the napkin onto her lap.

"This feels like a dream, Jarrick. I'm sorry we'll have to wake up soon. I'll be back in the Rockies, and you'll be, well, who knows where."

"But not tonight," he said, leaning forward, arms crossed on the edge of the table. "For tonight there's no one else but the two of us shamelessly making eyes at one another in the candlelight."

Beth leaned closer, her head to one side. "How scandalous. Yet how delightful."

They talked for a while about the wedding. Jarrick shrugged while she described the fabric flowers and tulle pew bows. "You know, of course, I can't really picture any of that. I'm sorry, but that's the way it is."

Beth sighed. "I hope it turns out to be what you'll like then."

"It's *you* I'll be looking at," he said. "I'm sure the decorations will be fine." He reached for her hand. "I hope you'll like the plans I've been making without *your* input."

His grin showed off the dimple she loved to see. "What do you mean, Jarrick?" she asked, wondering at the pleasure in his eyes.

"Wedding plans—the part I'm responsible for deciding and arranging."

Beth was perplexed. He hadn't seemed all that interested in the details back in the church.

"You know it's the groom's responsibility to plan an appropriate honeymoon." He watched her face closely.

Her eyes softened in delight. "A honeymoon, Jarrick? Can we . . . are we going to have time for that?"

"Of course."

"But, Jarrick, I'm not sure I'll be able to get away—"

"You will," he assured her. "I've worked it out with the town council."

"What on earth?"

He laughed and quickly explained, "I sent a letter to Bill Shaw, asking that you be given the week off following our nuptials. He said they could bring in a substitute teacher, and you can easily have those five days off. That means we'll have a week plus a weekend of privacy and leisure before we're both expected back at our jobs."

"Oh, that's wonderful! It's so unexpected. I hadn't even hoped for such a thing." But then she was puzzled again. "Will we stay in Coal Valley?"

"Not in town, no. We're going away— someplace special."

"Where?"

"I can't tell you. I won't even let you guess. It's a secret, and I don't want it to be spoiled."

Beth shook her head and smiled. "I never even suspected you were scheming like this. What a wonderful surprise, darling."

By the time dessert arrived, Beth was feeling wistful, knowing their precious time together was coming to a close. "Do you know yet where you'll be posted next?"

"Probably in Calgary for a while. After that, I'm not sure."

"Oh, what a shame. It must be so hard for you, to never know."

"Well, it comes with the territory. You know that, sweetheart."

Beth looked away. "I know. But it doesn't stop me from feeling sad."

He reached across the table and folded his hands around hers. "It won't be for much longer. Once I'm working for your father, you can rest easy. And, well, we can dine in style whenever you like."

Beth pulled her hands away before she realized it. Her face flushed immediately with embarrassment. *Am I acting like his mother? Like my own? But this is Jarrick, and I could never endeavor to turn his head toward what I prefer. Or override his decision on the matter of his work.*

"What is it, my love?" He looked puzzled and somewhat hurt.

She was devastated by his expression. "I don't want . . . I just can't think about that now."

"Why not?"

I don't want you to leave your job, she wanted to insist. But she silenced the thought for fear of being manipulative.

"I don't understand, Beth. I'm trying to do the right thing. But you're obviously not pleased. I need to know what's wrong."

Beth could feel tears beginning to collect in her eyes. She blinked hard. As much as she wanted to explain her reaction to Jarrick, she couldn't allow herself to influence his choice, to be responsible for it. She knew how gracious and how tender his heart was toward her. She was certain he would give in to whatever she asked. So she was determined to remain silent. "I understand all the reasons. But I don't have to *want* it to happen. I'm not going to find it easy. Of course I'll do whatever you think is best, Jarrick."

They drove back to the Smiths' home in agonizing silence.

The next morning the tension between Jarrick and Beth had not dissolved, and it broke her heart to ride away, leaving him standing in the driveway rather forlornly. She wished she could have said everything in her heart, but once they were spoken, words could never be taken back. She hoped she was doing the right thing—the loving thing—with her silence on the matter. Julie's bubbly conversation helped to cover Beth's misery, or at least distract her from it.

Chapter
18

"You've been living *here*?" Julie swung in a circle, eyes wide, arms akimbo. "In this . . . well, I don't want to call it a hovel, but I'm afraid that's exactly what it is, darling." Julie's reaction to Beth's accommodations was rather blunt.

"It's clean and dry and, well, it's kind of warm, if I remember how to bank the fire properly. So I can't complain."

"And you'll be living here *with Jack* after the wedding?" Julie moved into the bedroom and back again, lifting the little patchwork curtain over the kitchen window to peer outside, opening and closing doors and drawers.

Beth sighed. "That's the plan. It's enough for two, and more importantly, it's what we can afford."

"Well, won't the two of us be cozy while

I'm here, sharing a bed like we did when we were little."

"Julie," Beth said, shaking her head, "I never shared a bed with you."

"Yes, I remember you did." Julie squared her shoulders.

"No, I always shared with Margret. You were on your own in that little trundle beside ours until we moved to the stone house, and then we all got our own rooms."

"Are you sure?"

"Very." Beth nudged Julie's arm. "You just *think* you shared with me because you were in my bed so often. You were scared to sleep alone, especially at first. Remember?"

"I doubt it," Julie maintained stubbornly. "I've never been scared of anything. I . . ." Instantly her face fell and she corrected herself. "Well, except . . ." Her brows drew tightly together as the memory of their difficult summer crowded into the room with them.

Beth put her arms around her sister and repeated the verse they had memorized together when they were young, recited often in the weeks that had followed Julie's abduction. "'Behold, God is my salvation; I will trust, and not be afraid: for the LORD Jehovah is my strength and my song; he also is become my salvation.'"

"Amen," Julie whispered. "He alone is my

salvation." For several moments they stood in silence, drawing reassurance from its truth and from each other.

"And anyway, Julie," Beth said as she moved toward her sister's trunk, "you should have seen me when I first got here. I heard noises in the night! I was terrified, I assure you. I hardly slept at all for about a week. You would have found it terribly entertaining and would have enjoyed a good laugh at my expense. And even so, I have to admit that I wanted you here."

"Noises?"

Beth dropped her voice dramatically. "Scratches, and footsteps, and thumps in the night . . ."

"You heard sounds at night?" Julie was looking around, eyes wide. "Did you ever figure out what they were? Have they stopped?"

"I *did* find the culprit. It was a varmint."

"A what?"

"A local pest. Would you like to meet her?"

"What on earth are you talking about?" Julie finally laughed, then looked around suspiciously.

Without explaining further, Beth took a small piece of fish from the icebox and moved toward the door. Julie followed, and they descended the stairs. Beth walked several paces closer to the woods. "Penelope," she sang out. "Come on. Come here, little one. Penelope."

Two bright eyes appeared on cue under the favorite bush. Beth stooped low, holding out her hand so Penelope could reach the food. The cat sauntered forward, lifting her kitty paws gingerly over the crusted snow, her striped winter fur grown thick and full.

Meow. She froze in place and stared up at Julie, quivering ears alert for any threat.

"This is Penelope the cat," Beth said with a laugh. "She sort of came with the place."

"And she lives outdoors?" Julie hunched down next to Beth, trying to coax the creature closer.

"Do you really think for a minute I would let her live in the house? What would Mother say? Here, give her the fish. It's her favorite."

"But where does she sleep at night?" Julie held out the scrap.

Beth motioned toward the stairs. "There's a little woodshed hidden away to store my wood for the stove. Teddy keeps it full. I think she's found a hiding place somewhere behind it all. I suppose it's dry there and warm. It can't be very big."

But her sister was busy luring Penelope close enough to scratch her head and back while the cat slid up against Julie's legs.

"She likes you." Beth felt a tiny bit jealous.

She had been working so hard, had been faithfully feeding the cat, and yet was rarely allowed to place a hand on her back.

"Just so long as she doesn't turn on me and bite."

Beth chuckled. It was unlikely, but not impossible. "Let's go back in. I'm freezing."

As expected, Julie was rather unimpressed with the burgeoning town. Apart from the new church building, she found little to compliment. On Monday morning she accompanied Beth to school, ready to meet the new teacher. Seeing this as an opportunity to possibly view Robert through a fresh set of eyes, Beth told her sister very little about the man prior to the introduction.

"Excuse me, Mr. Harris Hughes?"

He turned from the chalkboard. "Ah, Miss Thatcher, please come in. I trust you had a pleasant holiday."

"I did. Thank you." Beth drew her sister forward. "I was hoping to introduce my sister, Miss Julie Thatcher. She'll be staying with me for a while and helping sometimes in my classroom. Julie, this is Mr. Robert Harris Hughes."

Robert crossed the room, a half smile on his face, moving the tie he had loosened into proper position. "It's nice to make your acquaintance, Miss Thatcher."

"Oh, please, just call me Julie." She extended her hand to Robert demurely. He took it lightly with a nod.

Beth felt herself stiffen and looked from the corner of her eye at her sister. *Was that a familiar tone in Julie's voice?* Beth quickly said, "My sister is visiting from Toronto and will be leaving with my parents after the wedding."

"I hope you enjoy your stay in our little town. Which is to say, I hope you enjoy snow and quiet and isolation."

"Oh, I do enjoy snow," Julie said, ignoring the man's gloomy description. "I just learned to ski, and I'm so looking forward to getting out and trying it here. I bought a pair of secondhand skis in Lethbridge and managed to have them loaded on the roof of the car." She rocked forward slightly, twisting a short dark curl that hung next to her cheek. "Do you ski, Robert?"

He cleared his throat. "I do, Miss Thatcher. But I'm afraid I've left my equipment in Calgary, where my fiancée currently resides."

Beth was relieved by his open response, grateful that Julie now had no reason for further interest. She was, however, dismayed by Julie's immediate attraction to the new acquaintance.

"Also, Miss Thatcher, if I may be frank, I've rather insisted upon being referred to by my full name while in the classroom. If you'd be so kind, I would greatly appreciate your amenability on that count."

Julie grinned impishly. "Of course. As you wish. What is your name again—Mr. Harris?"

"Harris Hughes, miss."

Beth led a hasty retreat to her own classroom.

"Oh, Bethie, what a stuffed shirt!"

"Shhh! He'll hear you."

"How . . . ?"

Beth motioned toward the door in the center of the shared wall.

"Then why did we . . . ?" Julie pointed out to the entryway and the long way around they had taken.

"I don't ever use it." Beth rubbed a hand across the back of her neck and whispered, "That's all I can say. I didn't want it in the first place. I'd just as soon have someone nail it shut."

Julie's eyes narrowed, her expression rather smug. "So I gather we don't like him, then? Why didn't you just tell me so in the first place?" She winked at Beth. "He's awfully cute, in a studious, professorial sort of way. And he certainly dresses marvelously. And way out here!" She gestured expansively.

Beth squirmed. "It's not that I don't *like* him. It's just . . . it's complicated."

"You're not going to tell me?"

"Please, Julie, we'll talk about it later. What little there is to tell. Now, I've got to get ready. My students will be here in minutes. Write these arithmetic problems on the board, will you? That would be very helpful. And once class begins you can sit in the last seat of this row. No one is assigned that desk right now."

"My, how exciting. I've never sat in a classroom like this before. I was secretly jealous of the other girls who didn't have a tutor come to their home. Do I need to raise my hand if I'd like to speak?"

"Oh, darling, just please don't speak at all." Later Beth found a reading session for Julie to lead with the littlest ones and chuckled to herself as her sister, of course, incorporated extra expression into the story.

At lunch Julie requested the key to Beth's door, assuring her that she would find some appropriate pastime elsewhere and that perhaps she would try out the new skis. Beth breathed a sigh of relief, followed quickly by a prayer that God would keep Julie safe and give her wisdom in her choice of activity on her own.

"Did you happen to see the notification in the window of the store? It gave a date for your little upcoming election." Julie was stretched out on the sofa, flipping through the pages of a fashion magazine.

Choosing to ignore the condescension, Beth answered, "No, I rarely have reason to go into the store."

"Well, I guess you should, then. Didn't you insist that this particular event is rather important to you?"

Beth looked up from a lesson she was outlining. "All right, what did the notice say?"

"Well, among other things, it listed the candidates for mayor."

"It did?" Now Beth was listening fully. "Whose names?"

Julie smiled, enjoying the upper hand. "Just two. Want to guess?"

"No. Emphatically, *no*."

"You're no fun at all."

"Who?"

"Fine, then," Julie relented. "Your silly Mr. Harris Hughes was first, and then a Mr. Fred Green."

"Fred Green? What on earth? Whoever would have nominated Fred for mayor?" Beth stared in bewilderment.

"I'm sure I don't know."

"He was a friend of Davie Grant's, the bootlegger arrested last spring."

Julie made a face of mock empathy. "You mean, the bootlegger in whose home you now live?"

"Not any longer." Beth shook her head in frustration. "This is Abigail's now. And anyway, he's long gone."

"But someone in your town is suggesting that his co-conspirator be elected mayor? Well, that's rich."

Beth rested her cheek on one hand, considering the significance. Thinking out loud, she murmured, "That would mean if Robert loses the election . . . Fred would be mayor instead. Well, that's no better. In fact, that's much worse!"

"And if the choice is between those two, one can only guess who'll be unanimously elected."

Beth muttered, "Robert probably nominated Fred, just to be sure of his own win."

Julie rose from the sofa and dropped onto the chair next to Beth. "Would he do that? Is he that conniving?"

Beth shook her head, this time more vigorously. "No, no, I've never seen him do anything of the sort. I can say that much for him. I believe he is *exactly* what he appears. And he has the audacity to say exactly what he's thinking too, rightly or wrongly." She set her pen in its stand and closed the book. "What are we going to do, Julie?"

"*We?* Well, now, that's interesting. You're including me suddenly. And imagine that, I've just been looking for something to do—something to fill the hours. I hear that politics can be rather intriguing."

"No, I don't mean you should involve yourself. I just want you to help me think of something."

"Fine, then. Have it your way. Who else lives in this town? Who could be a potential candidate?"

Beth dropped her head back and stared at the ceiling. She went through the possibilities again for Julie's benefit, listing one name after another and quickly dismissing each.

"That's it? That's everyone?"

"Yes, pretty much."

"And you don't even know many of them, because they're new to town?"

"Unless the workmen go to church, which about half of them do, I'm certainly not likely to have crossed paths with them, even in a town this small."

"Hmmm." The familiar sound of Julie's mental wheels turning. "We can't entice even that delightful Philip. He would have been ideal. Say, Bethie, how young can they be? Could it be a student?"

"I doubt it. Besides, Teddy and Addison are the oldest, and they're only seventeen. I doubt Frank and Molly would allow Teddy to try, and Heidi Coolidge would—"

"What did you say?"

"I said that Heidi—"

"No, silly! You said Frank and Molly."

"Yes."

Julie thumped a hand on the table. "But don't you see it, darling? You haven't considered the most obvious choice of all!"

"Molly? But she's—"

"No, Bethie. *Frank.* Don't you think he's perfect?"

Beth felt her mouth drop open, and her eyes grew large as she processed the idea. *Why didn't I think of Frank? He's surely a Canadian citizen by now. I suppose that's why I inadvertently left him out. He's perfect, and now that he's retired he has the time.* She faced her sister. "What have I been thinking? You're brilliant."

Julie's smile was sprightly, and she tipped her head. "I know. Thank you."

<hr />

Beth and Julie planned to spring their idea on an unsuspecting Frank following dinner in Molly's kitchen on Wednesday. Not long after settling in the parlor, Beth turned the conversation toward the election.

"Frank, you must hear talk around town about the election. Do you think Fred Green has a chance?"

"Oh, I don'ta know," he pondered. "That'a teacher, he said he was'a sorry plenty of times for getting the boys in'a such a fix. But I think'a the mothers wonder if they fully can'a trust him again, eh? On another hand, I cannot see the town'a choosing Fred over Mr. Harris Hughes either."

"You're right. Each of those men is problematic." Julie exhaled slowly. "If only there were someone else."

Beth winced, suddenly uncomfortable with their ruse. She frowned and declared candidly, "Frank, I think *you* should run for mayor."

Molly's face lifted quickly from her mending. "What? What did you say?"

Frank smiled slowly. "Some of the men, they asked me to let'a my name stand."

Beth drew a quick breath. "Well? What did you say?"

"I said, '*I'ma too old now.*'" He shrugged. "That's what I said." He pushed to his feet to refuel the woodstove.

"But that's not true," Beth argued to his back. "Laurier was prime minister until he was almost seventy, and that's a full-time position. This is mayor, and it would be only part-time.

And everyone trusts you, Frank. Both of you." Beth turned to Molly, her fervent expression betraying her deep concern. "The two of you are almost, well, the *founders* of this town."

"Pshaw."

"It's true, Molly. You've lived here almost from the start. Certainly you've both been here much longer than most. And you *know* everyone, an important thing. Goodness, between the two of you there's probably not a soul you don't know well, from the mothers to the miners and also the company men. Don't you see, he's perfect." Her gaze circled the room and stopped at Frank, back in his chair.

Frank shook his head with a chuckle. "What do you think, Mollina?"

"I don't know," she said, staring at her needle without moving it. "I s'pose I'm game fer whatever you say, Frank. I'm sure it's more work than ya been figurin' on for this time in yer life, but if that's what ya want, I wouldn't discourage it."

Beth and Julie exchanged silent congratulations with one another. It seemed that they had their man.

Chapter 19

Julie's considerable energies were now focused on winning the election for Frank. Though Beth felt victory was assured by simply penciling his name under Fred Green's on the list of candidates at the store, Julie seemed determined to complicate matters. As she walked Beth home after school the next day, she was full of ideas.

"We'll have a party. That's what we'll do."

"A party? Where?"

"At the church. And—"

"Oh no. We can't put the church in the center of the election. That's exactly what Philip was trying to avoid."

Julie spun around, gesturing at the school building. "Then we'll have it here."

"Sure, with Frank's opponent on the other side of the door. You can't be serious." One glance at her sister and Beth knew Julie's new election campaign would not easily be diverted.

"Then we can make buttons and give them out. They do it in all the big cities."

"Oh, darling, we can't. It would look ridiculous. And Frank would never allow us to promote him in such a . . . such a blatant way. It wouldn't be proper in this setting."

Julie waved her arms, her frown the same as the one she wore as a thwarted child. "What *will* you let me do? You shoot down my ideas as quickly as Mother."

Beth flinched at the comparison and forced her words to come more slowly. "Julie, anything we do must fit with the community here." She blew out a breath. "How can I explain it? You see, Julie, *small things* matter in Coal Valley. We don't have to create a lot of hoopla. We can be gentle and sincere—you know, dignified."

"Sounds boring."

Beth reached for the stair rail, stepping around Penelope, who was purring and slinking around underfoot even more now that Julie had arrived. "It's not boring, really. Believe it or not, it actually scares me. Any of this. I don't know how you manage the spotlight so well. I'd rather be neither seen nor heard most of the time."

Julie pulled Beth to a stop, motioning that they take a seat on the step, their breath a thin white mist in the air. "I know how you see things, Bethie. I don't understand it, but I realize that's how you feel. So then the question is, how can we make a difference *your way*? I suppose we'd . . . we'd . . . I don't know, *write* something."

"Hmmm, write something? What would that be?"

The sisters watched in silence as the cat wove its way between Julie's ankles. Slowly she lowered a hand and scratched at the tabby's back. Penelope wriggled in delight, moved forward out of reach, then circled back into position again.

Julie smiled. "She likes me."

Beth sighed and watched her sister bond with the persnickety feline. Stretching her hand carefully, she managed to rub a little under its whiskered chin. "What would I write? I can't be seen as working against Robert."

"Here, kitty" was Julie's only response as Penelope played hard to get.

Suddenly Beth pushed herself upright. "*That's it.* We'll write up a summary of what the position requires, and we'll simply state each person's qualifications. It'll be obvious immediately that Frank is the best choice—to everyone. Oh, Julie, what a wonderful idea."

Already Beth was hurrying up toward her door.

Julie trailed behind as Penelope scurried away. "If that's all you're going to do, why not get your students to do it instead? Call it a civics lesson and let them do the work."

Beth had the key into the lock, but she turned to look at her sister. "Another excellent idea! This will keep it from looking like I'm just pushing for Frank."

"But . . . aren't you?"

The project quickly became a school assignment. Beth took some time the following day to discuss the election with her students and to format a list of questions related to their town. What should the mayor do first? What did Coal Valley need most? What problems did its citizens observe? They narrowed it down to only six questions. Beth had every student copy them on a sheet of paper which could be taken home. They were instructed to discuss the list with their families, including older siblings, and would be given extra points if they could find a non–family member to interview as well. Lastly, they were to write down the answers to each of the questions, and Beth would summarize all their findings into a pamphlet that would be circulated as good information for the community, put together as a community effort and a school project, both.

Little Dorothy Noonan whispered to her friend, prompting Pearl Ruffinelli to raise a hand. Beth anticipated the question from her first-grade students. "Miss Thatcher, what if we don't write so good? Can Henry help me? An' can Dotty get David, her big brother, ta help her?"

"Yes, darling. So long as no one else does the interviewing for you. If you're second grade or younger you may have a family member write out the answers for you. But I'd like you to be the ones asking the questions. That's good reading practice too. So I want each of you to be leading the conversations at home, and let's have your papers back by next Monday. Do you all understand?"

"Yes, Miss Thatcher," the class answered in unison, most of them looking rather intrigued at this different kind of assignment.

⁂

Beth and Julie sorted through the results Monday evening. Nothing was particularly surprising to Beth, except for more attention given to town expansion than she had expected. The requests were that the store should be bigger, the roads wider, and there should be more homes built within the next year. Beth was personally enthused about the requested telephone service. This would meet a pressing need, particularly in emergency situations. Though she knew stringing lines so deep into the mountains was unlikely for many years yet.

Some students tucked in their own requests—a carousel, an ice cream parlor, and a runway for airplanes. Beth was disappointed, though, to see no outcry against those ugly stumps abandoned all around town. Apparently no one else felt as Beth did about a removal program.

"What you need now," Julie grumbled when the sorting was complete, "is a printing press."

Beth laughed. "We only need to copy out thirty of the pamphlets. That should cover each family as well as the single men too."

"Why don't you just make it another assignment—in penmanship?"

"I could, but that would put all of the burden on poor Ida Edwards. She's really the only one whose penmanship is up to the task. The others haven't mastered an inkwell enough to avoid blots all over the page." And with that, the two sisters set to work.

***

With only two more days until the election, Beth distributed copies of the pamphlets to the students to deliver to family and friends. It felt a little awkward to place one in the hands of Thomas Green. She wondered what his father would think. His son had written the short description of Fred Green's qualifications— all about fishing—and Beth was sure Thomas would let the man know who had written it.

Ida Edwards had talked with Mr. Harris Hughes for his short biography, and Wilton Coolidge had spoken with Frank. They also were brief. Robert's listed his education, and Frank's covered his many years working and living in Coal Valley.

As Beth watched her class scurry out that afternoon with the pamphlets clutched in mittened hands, she was certain the choice of mayor was obvious. She closed the door behind the last one and prayed, "God, may this do some good for Coal Valley." Then she remembered to add, "And may Your will be done."

Beth woke early on Saturday morning and, shivering in the darkness, stirred up a fire so the rooms might be warm by the time her sister got up. She lit the oil lamp beside the sofa and, covered from toe to chin by a thick afghan, drew out her Bible. Her prayers focused mostly on the election, on the children's well-being, and on the fast-approaching moment when she must leave Coal Valley. And she whispered once again, "Help Jarrick to know what is best. For him and . . . and for our marriage to come."

"What time is it?" Julie asked with a yawn and a long stretch, standing in the bedroom doorway.

"Oh, I was hoping you'd be able to sleep longer, dear. I'm not sure of the time. I didn't check."

Julie pulled up a corner of the afghan and snuggled beneath it with Beth. "I'll pray with you, if you like."

"That would be wonderful." Their heads close together, the sisters broadened the prayer time to include family and friends back in Toronto.

After a breakfast of pancakes and bacon, Beth and Julie prepared to walk over to Coulter's store, where the ballot box had been set up. A considerable number of people were also making their way to the wooden sidewalk in front of the store. Beth was astonished at the sight of a cluster of horses tied to trees at the end of the building.

"Who in the world could that be?" she wondered aloud.

"Isn't that common?" Julie laughed. "A good old-fashioned western automobile, right?"

Beth was in no mood for joking. "Nobody

here owns a horse or could afford the upkeep. Bringing in enough grain and hay over the winter would be impossible. The company car and two trucks serve us well." She didn't tell Julie that she had once suggested introducing a cow, for its milk, to their little town. She felt her face grow warm as she remembered how quickly she was informed of the impracticalities.

They smiled greetings to Betty McDermott and Charlotte Noonan as the ladies approached from the opposite direction. Holding her youngest on her hip, Charlotte thanked Beth for the homework assignment now clutched firmly in hand, adding, "My Dotty was so excited about doin' it. She had me sittin' down while she read the questions all serious like." They laughed and moved inside.

Groups, gathered in various corners, held whispered discussions. A table at the window held the ballot box, waiting for each resident's vote. Beth's eyes swept the room, noting who was present.

Fred Green, in a narrow aisle among the dry goods, was surrounded by a few strangers in long, heavy coats and cowboy hats. Beth presumed it was his friends whose horses were tied outside. She frowned, wondering if he was bringing them from elsewhere to boost his chances. *Surely there are rules about who can vote.*

Toby Coulter leaned his back against the counter, arms crossed above the apron tied around his ample belly. Beth was sure he had never had a crowd of customers this large in the store. He smiled and called greetings to all who entered. "Mornin', ladies," he said above the din. "Glad ya come. We have some fine new yard goods, if you're interested today." And, "Hey, Parker, I seen that the new pair'a work gloves ya ordered is here. You can pick 'em up today if ya want."

At the back of the store, Beth noticed a second, larger cluster of men. These were familiar faces, mostly bearded, of workers and husbands who attended church. Beth was relieved to see Frank among them. She waved hesitantly, but he didn't look up.

Her sister had walked to the counter, browsing the small selection of women's items—simple jewelry and handkerchiefs and such. Since Julie would not be voting, it seemed she had decided to shop a bit while Beth involved herself in conversations with the townsfolk.

Beth chatted for a few moments with some of the mothers, always mindful of the waiting ballot box standing almost forlorn on the table. As she moved on toward another group, she passed a tower of crates and found herself face-to-face with Robert. No doubt he'd been biding his time, watching the proceedings from a safe distance. "Good morning," she offered, catching a quick breath and squaring her shoulders.

"Good morning, Miss Thatcher. And how are you today?"

"I'm fine, thank you." Beth brushed at some dust on her sleeve from the crates, casting a glance around in hopes she'd find a reason to cut the conversation short.

"I see you've come early to cast your vote."

"Yes, there's no reason to delay. My sister and I have been up—" She hadn't finished when he raised his eyebrows and cocked his head.

"You and your sister have been rather busy I see."

"I suppose we usually are. And you are referring to . . . ?"

"To this, Miss Thatcher." He held out a copy of the pamphlet.

Beth was surprised he had received one of their rather scant number of copies. *There's no reason for concern,* she told herself, *there's nothing in the pamphlet but truth.* "Yes," she said, looking directly at him. "I felt Ida did a good job with your biography. Thank you for allowing her to speak with you about it.

In fact, all of the children worked very hard on this project."

"I must admit, I didn't think you were particularly political. I suppose that I've mis-judged you."

Beth cleared her throat, trying to maintain composure. "I really am not, but it seemed like an opportunity to introduce the students to the importance of civic responsibility and public service."

"I see." He smiled slowly, and Beth held her breath. "So it was not a thinly veiled attempt at manipulating the election results?"

"Mr. Harris Hughes, I must say—"

"Don't bother denying it, Miss Thatcher. Your intentions, while not transparent to all, are not especially difficult to ascertain. Mind you," he said hurriedly before Beth could respond, "I'm not disappointed by your efforts. I respect your desire to bring all to light. I just find it a shame that you chose to hide your true motives behind a classroom full of schoolchildren."

"And of what are you accusing me, sir?"

"Miss Thatcher." He clucked his tongue as if he were talking to a child. "You only brought another candidate forward when it became evident there was a possibility I might win. And then you promoted him—rather effec-tively, I confess—with this flier. Why not take full credit for your idea? It was quite well conceived."

Beth could feel her legs beginning to tremble. But she wanted to end the conversation fearlessly. She straightened and said as quietly as possible while still being heard, "You aren't a part of this community, Robert. And you clearly have no serious intention of becoming so. The mayor should be someone devoted to these people and working for their good, not trying to prove ideals that sound good in a lecture hall far from here."

He smiled triumphantly. "Now, then, was that so hard? To tell the truth about your goals?"

Beth pushed past him. "Good day, sir."

"Good day, Miss Thatcher." She could hear the haughtiness in his words. *And was there some mirth too?*

By the time Beth reached the table to cast her vote, her hands were unsteady. She scrawled Frank's name on a slip of paper and stuffed it in the box, forcing a smile at Bill Shaw, who was standing watch a short distance away. She motioned to Julie and hurried out the door.

Julie caught up to her. "What is it, Bethie? What's upset you?"

"I just want to get home," she whispered.

The cold air felt awfully good on her flushed face.

❧

Beth's agitation lasted into the afternoon, even while she and Julie had their usual Saturday visit with Molly. Seated in the parlor, Molly and Marnie stitching on the quilt, no one spoke about the fact that the votes were now being tallied. But a heavy silence hovered over the room, if only in Beth's mind. At last she noticed her sister speaking with Frank privately, who nodded and left the room.

"What did you say to him?" Beth asked.

"It's nothing."

"Julie, what?"

"I just . . . I merely suggested that you might enjoy a nice bath."

"Oh no, it's so much work. I don't want Frank to—"

"He's gonna be busy with baths soon enough, dearie," Molly interjected from across the room. "Ya might as well get yers in now. It'll give ya somethin' soothin' to keep yer mind busy."

Embarrassed that her anxiety was so obvious, Beth accepted the gracious offer and hurried home for a clean set of clothing. When she had returned and settled gratefully into the hot tub of water, she allowed herself to recall Robert's words, and soon her tears were falling. *He knew, Lord. He knew exactly what I intended. Should I be sorry? Was it wrong? Was I wrong?*

Again the faces of the children came to mind. Beth thought too of Molly's advice to "make a fuss in the Bible way." She hoped that's what she had done, and yet the niggling feeling persisted that her motives were somehow askew. Back and forth she argued with herself, first one way and then the other.

"I give up, Lord," she finally surrendered pitifully, whispering into her dripping hands. "I don't know if what I did was right or wrong. I know I prayed about it, and I *thought* You led me, Father. But whatever happens next, I give that up to You. I trust You. God, You've displaced kings and princes, set whomever You desired on thrones. You are powerful and wise and fully capable of caring for this silly little election in a very small town in the middle of nowhere. I surrender my will to Yours. Whatever You want, Your will be done."

The prayer of surrender brought a fresh flow of tears, but Beth's heart at last felt freer and more hopeful.

A knock on the door echoed inside the small room. Julie's voice whispered loudly into the keyhole. "Darling, they've counted the votes. It was very close, but I'm afraid it's Robert who won."

"Thank you," Beth managed before sinking under the water. She knew she couldn't hide away for long. But it was going to take a few moments for her to properly compose herself.

Chapter 20

Beth woke the next day with a sore throat and a fever. Her mind flooded with recollections of last year's Christmas in Coal Valley and how long it had taken to recover from that illness. She groaned aloud in the darkness. She had thought the fragile health of her childhood was a thing of the past, or had at least wished it to be true.

"Julie," she rasped out. "Julie, I'm sick."

Her sister's groggy voice came from beside her, somewhere beneath the heavy covers. "Want me to get you something? An aspirin? A cold cloth?"

Beth realized she was trembling with chills. "Will you . . . could you stir up the fire?"

Julie rose, pulled on a robe, and shuffled into the next room. Soon lamplight flickered through the doorway. At last she returned, sliding back under the covers and shaking a little herself. "Oh my, it's cold even if I'm not sick! I've relit the fire. I think it's catching well. And I hung the afghan over a chair in front of it so it'll warm up for you. I'll bring it to you in a few minutes."

"Thanks," Beth managed. A fit of coughing started her lungs burning. These familiar sensations had all the markings of another awful bout with flu. "Julie," Beth added, "could you also bring the large trash pail, just in case?" Beth felt the covers tossed aside and heard feet scrambling across the floor once more.

The remainder of Sunday was a blur for Beth. She knew Julie was at her side often, that she had been given many sips of tea, and that there was a knock at the door at some point, but she remembered little else. She was most aware of the fingers of cold stealing through gaps in the layers of blankets every time she moved.

Opening her eyes fully at last, she was surprised to see Molly's soft round face peering down at her in the glow of the lamp. "Well hello, dearie. Thought ya was gonna sleep all the way through my visit." A practiced hand felt Beth's forehead and cheeks. "Yup, yer fever's still too high. See if you can sit up ta eat some broth, then we'll give ya another dose of aspirin."

Beth moved to comply, her muscles aching and stiff. "Is it nighttime already?"

"No, it's just past supper."

"But tomorrow . . ." She sat forward, eyes wide. "I have school."

"No ya don't. Already canceled it—your class, that is. Mr. Harris Hughes will still meet with his group. So no doubt yer kids are rubbin' it in to their older kin that they's the ones get to stay home this time."

Beth pushed herself up straighter. "We can't. They have theme papers due, and we're finally caught up with arithmetic and spelling from the fall. I don't want to get behind again."

"What ya don't want's got nothin' to do with it. This is 'bout what ya can't."

Molly placed a mug of soup in Beth's hands and instructed her to do her best. She began to sip it from the spoon dutifully, each swallow bringing pain. Her mind was whirling with solutions for her students. *If I'm out for a day, we can still catch up this week. If I'm out for two, that will take some thought and planning. How many weeks are left? There are thirteen until the wedding, so twenty to the end of school. Yes, we should be able to manage. But what if there's another snowstorm?*

Molly placed a letter on the night table. "And here's yer mail. Ya might like to read this from yer mother."

Beth swallowed a little more soup. "From Mother? Will you read it to me, please?" Just as Beth had hoped, it contained the announcement that Beth and Julie were aunties once more. Margret had given birth to a second son, Josiah Matthew Bryce. Beth breathed a prayer of gratitude for her new baby nephew. Once Molly had departed, Beth pulled out the letter to read again, savoring every word.

Julie opted to sleep on the couch so Beth could have the bed to herself, but Beth still had trouble resting. Her mind seemed to be working to solve difficulties even as her body needed sleep. She woke several times, thinking of her troubles with Robert, of having to move east, of Marnie and Harold who were so young, of her students without a teacher . . .

Monday afternoon Beth woke with a jolt from a bad dream. She had been standing on a mountain cliff, shivering in her nightgown. Far below, her beloved students were being chased by a bear. And then the animal had transformed into a man whose face she could not see. Now awake, she wiped the edge of the sheet across her forehead and under her hairline, trying to dab away the cold sweat. "Julie, are you there?" she croaked out.

Her sister appeared in the doorway. "Where else would I be?"

"Would you do me a favor? Even if it might be a great deal to ask?"

The dark eyes squinted at her. "What now?"

"Oh, darling, I'm sorry for being such a problem. Please, come sit on the bed." She moved aside to make room.

Julie approached reluctantly and stood nearby, but she did not sit down.

"I was thinking, if I kept things very simple—maybe even just doing half a day's work—could you, *would* you be willing to teach my class?"

Julie made a face, laughed, swiped the back of her hand across her eyes, and laughed again. "You must be desperate if you would *trust me* to do that."

Beth met her sister's gaze, refusing to allow any expression of concern on her face. "Of course I would."

"What do you have in mind?" She eased down onto the bed.

"I'd give you the new assignments to distribute, and you could collect the homework that should be done. I'll help you, and we can grade them here. I'm feeling better than I was." Beth blew out a long, wheezing sigh. "You will have to do some actual teaching, but it won't be difficult. You'll have to demonstrate on the chalkboard how to do the new arithmetic problems for each grade. And, Julie, you'll have to go step by step, slowly, so they can keep up with you."

Julie shrugged. "Well, I suppose that's better than sitting around here for another day. Will you be all right on your own?"

Beth propped herself up higher on the pillow, encouraged. "Yes, I'll be fine. Please go to Molly's and ask her to get the word out. The children should come in the morning, and they'll only have to stay until lunch. I'll write out everything you need to cover. You'll need to be patient with them. Very patient."

Another laugh. "And you're worried that I'm not? I can't imagine."

Julie disappeared for much longer than Beth had expected. It seemed forever as she lay in the bed staring up at the same slanting ceiling, the same lines in the wallpaper. At last she pushed her feet out into the frigid air and pulled on long wool socks. Adding two sweaters over her nightgown, she forced unsteady feet to the kitchen. Her head was swimming, but it felt good to be walking around.

Dishes in the sink, articles of clothing draped here and there, and bedding on the sofa indicated Julie's unfettered ways. Several white tulle bows Beth had asked Julie to work on were on the table along with a half-empty coffee cup. Beth felt her way across the room to push the kettle to the center of the stove. *Poor Julie. She must be miserable here, stuck inside playing nurse.* Soon the kettle began to whistle.

She poured her water for tea, filled the basin with the rest of the water to do the dishes, then heard footsteps running up the stairs.

Julie burst through the door. "Oh good, you're awake. Well, you're not going to believe it!"

"What on earth—?"

"Bethie, you're just not going to believe what I heard."

"What is it? Is it bad?"

Julie stuttered out, "No . . . but . . . well, it is surprising, to say the least. Shocking even. I don't know if you'll think it's bad. But probably."

Beth stared impatiently.

"It's Marnie. She's engaged—to Harry!"

Beth reached a hand to the counter to steady herself.

"I went to Molly's like you asked." Julie was already leading Beth to the sofa as she explained the situation further, pushing aside the pillow and pulling the covers over Beth's legs. "She wasn't there, but I talked to Frank, and he said Sunday was Marnie's birthday. She's fifteen now—"

"Oh dear, and I missed it," Beth moaned. She pictured the wrapped gift waiting in her cupboard.

"Just listen, Beth! Harry came over for cake late in the evening, after Molly stopped by here, and he had a small box with him. It turned out to be an engagement ring! He made it for Marnie in the blacksmith shop at the mine, using the silver from four dimes. Can you believe it?"

Beth could not. The idea seemed out of her grasp, especially with her foggy mind. "Where is Marnie now?"

"Still in school. They'll be dismissed soon."

"And Molly?"

"I think she went to speak with some of the other ladies—to get advice, I suppose."

Beth felt her mouth go dry. *Oh, Marnie!* Then, *Oh, Molly . . .*

After only an hour had passed, Beth was unable to bear her questions any longer. She sent Julie back to Molly for more information before Marnie got home from school. It was more than frustrating for Beth to feel this isolated with so much happening.

When Julie returned, Beth was dozing on the sofa. "Bethie? Bethie, wake up."

Beth stirred, twisting her head in one direction, then the other to loosen a painful neck muscle. She pushed disheveled hair away from her face and squinted up at Julie. "What did you find out?"

"Frank already went and spoke with Harry's uncle. Apparently his relatives aren't taking issue with the engagement, though of course they want them to wait to marry. And it seems that Molly and Frank tend to agree. I'm rather baffled. Can you just imagine what our mother would have said? But, as I said, that seems to be the consensus."

Beth closed her eyes and clenched her jaw tightly. *What are they thinking?* "She's so young," she almost wailed. "How can they allow this when she's so young?"

"I don't know. But they all seemed to be saying the same thing. She's ready. She knows the sorts of things that a wife needs to know. It all sounded very old-fashioned to me, but what do I know about marriage or about life here? Maybe she actually *is* ready after all."

Tears were gathering in Beth's eyes. She didn't want to speak her deepest fears aloud, but in her weakened condition they were more than she could hold to herself. "Julie, may I tell you something—something I haven't told anyone?"

"Of course, darling, what is it?" Julie dropped down onto the jumble of covers on the sofa.

Beth's voice was barely audible. "I don't even know if *I'm* ready . . . to be a wife." She buried her face in her hands and felt a comforting arm slide around her shoulder.

"What do you mean, Bethie? Why?"

The tears were now slipping through Beth's fingers. "She's better prepared than me," she sobbed. Then she dropped her hands and looked at Julie. "Do you realize that? She can do *everything*—she can cook, and sew, and clean. I've seen her. There's nothing Molly hasn't taught her already."

"But you can too."

"Oh no." Beth shook her head. "You know that isn't true. You've lived here long enough to know I can hardly cook anything at all. My goodness, I can hardly even keep the stove lit. If I tried to bake bread, how on earth would I hold the fire at the right temperature? If it wasn't for Molly . . ."

Julie handed her a clean handkerchief.

"But it's even worse than that," Beth went on, her voice shaking. "I haven't had much time to learn, but to be painfully honest, I haven't wanted to work at it very hard either.

No, the truth is that Marnie, even at fifteen, will make a much better wife than me!"

The sisters sat in silence for several long minutes as Beth worked to get her emotions under control. At last Julie spoke, uncharacteristically weighing each word. "Aren't you coming back to Toronto anyway? So Jack can work for Father?" Now hurrying, she said, "I'm sure I'm not supposed to know about that, but I overheard Mother and Father talking after dinner one night. I'm sorry if it upsets you that I brought it up," she said quickly when Beth started crying again. "But I just assumed you wouldn't be cooking much longer. That you'd have a housekeeper in the city, and it wouldn't matter."

It was impossible for Beth to form an answer. Her lips began to move, but no words followed. Instead she wiped at her eyes with the handkerchief, feeling pathetic and childish. So Julie continued, "Would you really *want* to live here, Bethie? Here where everything is so primitive and, well, so much harder? Because I need to say it, I just don't know *why* you would."

Wiping her nose once more, Beth managed to respond, "It's not the *place* that I want. It's the people. It's what I feel I can offer the children, and their parents too. And . . ." Her words failed, her throat tightening painfully.

She labored to finish. "And I want Jarrick to do what he has felt called to do. To be on the Force—to be a Mountie."

Julie sighed and patted her back. "I had no idea you were struggling with this. I'm so sorry, Bethie. So what did he say when you told him?"

Beth stared at her sister pitifully. "I haven't."

"What?" Julie stared back with wide eyes.

"I haven't told Jarrick."

"Whyever not?"

Beth twisted the handkerchief as her words tumbled out. "I don't want to be the one who chooses this. It's such a big decision, Julie. I want to be an obedient wife, allow him to be the leader. I keep thinking, what if my views of this are the sole reason that we begin life together . . . in the *wrong place*? I know he's praying about it all too. Surely God will move him to choose wisely." She tried a smile, but then said, "What if . . . what if I'm just being selfish about it, after all?" Again, mental images of her mother's control and Jarrick's description of his own assertive mother filled Beth's mind. She would not voice such thoughts to Julie.

The arm around Beth's shoulder tightened. "I think you could be honest with him. Not demanding—simply honest."

Beth shook her head, tears beginning again. "I'm afraid I can't. Because Jarrick loves me so much, I think he'd feel obliged to do whatever I wanted. And then if things go wrong, I'll know I'm the one to blame."

"Well, that's not so bad, Bethie, to be loved so much." Julie lifted Beth's chin and smiled into her face. "What a good problem to have."

Beth's face tightened. "Oh, Julie, I know that, but it's also such a terrible weight to carry—to know I could alter his whole life, everything he planned and hoped for. How could I forgive myself if I took him away from where he was supposed to be? How could I feel my *own* love was true to him, for his own sake?"

"But then aren't you rather convinced he's really *meant* to be out here as a Mountie?"

"I just don't know." Beth dropped her head into her sister's lap. Her shoulders shook with the force of her sobs, pent-up emotion bursting out. "How can I ever be *sure*?" she wailed.

Julie's hand brushed Beth's tangled hair back from her face, whispering comforting words. With gentle reasoning, Julie finally said, "But you can't ever *really* know, Beth, can you, if he's supposed to be here or if God wants you to come home so that he can work for Father. So if you do talk with him, you're as likely to be urging him to make the right decision as the wrong one. And if you don't speak up, maybe your silence on the matter will push him toward a wrong choice." Julie went quiet, continuing to stroke Beth's hair in sympathy.

At last Beth whispered, "But as soon as I give my opinion, I can't take it back. So I've been waiting and praying." She coughed again and wiped her sore nose with Julie's handkerchief. "And I'm afraid I don't trust my own feelings as much as I used to. I realize more clearly all the time that I'm far more self-centered than I once imagined. This thing with Robert, I can't even express it to you, Julie. And even over our summer trip, I'm afraid I was rather prone to mistake my own emotional responses for decency and honesty. I don't know how to tell the difference sometimes."

Beth was mastering her composure once more. She pushed herself up on the sofa and gave a final wipe at the tears and her nose. The emotions had compounded her congestion. She chose to change the subject. "Well, what about tomorrow? Did you tell Molly about our plan for you to teach?"

Julie looked away, then back at Beth. "Well, not exactly," she answered.

"What do you mean?"

"Oh, darling, don't be angry. Robert—Mr. Harris Hughes—has already made arrangements."

"What . . . what do you mean?"

"He's going to teach in both classrooms with that door between open. He approached me in the street on my way over, actually. He was asking for your lesson plans."

"Didn't you tell him that you were going to teach as my substitute?"

"I did, but he said if I didn't have a college degree I would not be allowed."

"Allowed? Based upon what?"

Julie cleared her throat. "Based on the meeting he had last night with the town council, I suppose."

"They already met?"

"They did. And it was decided how to handle your absence. He wants me to deliver your lesson plans to him yet tonight."

Beth felt her heart squeezed by a tangle of emotions, none of which seemed worthy after her recent prayer.

Two more days were lost to Beth's recovery. She knew Thursday morning that she should not return to school so quickly yet felt compelled. Her fever was gone, and so she told herself that the other symptoms were

inconsequential. Tucking several handkerchiefs and the little bottle of aspirin in with
her materials and wrapping herself up in coat
and scarf, she made her way across the street
in the darkness.

As soon as she dismissed her class for
lunch she sought out Marnie. "Could I have
a word with you?"

"Yes, Miss Thatcher. What is it?"

Beth drew her to one corner and lowered
her voice. "I'm hoping I could talk to Harold
today. Do you think that would be possible?
After his work, perhaps?"

Marnie's eyes darted across Beth's face
nervously. "He's coming here for lunch. Do
ya want to talk to him when he gets here?"

"Oh, yes, that would be fine. Please tell
him that I'll be at my desk."

"Yes, ma'am."

Harold arrived shortly after Beth had
settled herself. "You wanted to see me, Miss
Thatcher?"

"Yes, please. Come in."

He took a seat on the top of the nearest
desk, apparently not the least bit puzzled by
the request for a conference. *He's probably
growing familiar with these same questions,* Beth
mused.

"Harold," she began, "I heard that you
and Marnie have become engaged."

"That's right."

"I know your uncle and Marnie's folks have spoken to you already. But I simply want to remind you of one thing, if you'd allow me."

"Yes, ma'am."

Beth lifted a hand to her forehead against the remaining pressure from her illness. "Do you recall what you told me a while ago on our walk? That you wanted Marnie to finish school."

"Oh yes, ma'am, I surely do."

"And you're still committed to that goal?"

"Absolutely, Miss Thatcher. Why, I wouldn't wanna *let* her quit before she's done. That's very important to me, ma'am, to Marnie and me both."

Beth smiled and breathed a sigh. "I'm so glad to hear that, Harold. She's so precious to us all. We want the best for her—for the two of you."

"Yes, ma'am. Thank you. Is that all you wanted to know?"

"It is."

"All right then, Miss Thatcher. You have a good lunch." He stood and sauntered away, no doubt to find Marnie and report the conversation.

Beth's hand covered her heart as she watched him depart. "Lord, please help them," she whispered.

Chapter
21

Beth crossed another week off the calendar hanging beside the washbasin in her bedroom. She tried to picture little Josiah, her newborn nephew. *Is he already smiling? Sleeping well?* She shook her head as she remembered being right there when JW was a newborn. This would be a very different experience, even for Mother and Margret. *Without both Julie and me, the care will be shared by fewer arms.* Beth set the pencil aside, frowning at a new thought. *And where does Julie spend her time these days? She's often gone. Maybe she's skiing, but so frequently? I hate to question her about it. She's an adult, after all. And there aren't many possibilities for activities around here, but still, I'd like to know.*

Beth sighed and looked again at the calendar, comparing the weeks left till the wedding with her lists. She knew it would be difficult to be ready.

She called through the doorway, "Julie, I think we need to plan a trip into the city soon."

"In this weather? Don't you think it looks like snow again? Don't get me wrong, darling. I would love to go along. I've been wishing for just that for quite some time."

"If we want to be included the next time Alberto drives out, we need to make our wishes known now."

Julie appeared in the bedroom doorway, anticipation in her smile. "What do you need—?" She stopped before finishing and crossed her arms firmly. "Not more tulle. I am not making any more bows." Her dramatic expression said more than her words as she gestured around the two rooms. "You can't possibly want more than this. Besides, where on earth would you store them? It looks like we're living in a wedding chapel already." Indeed, white bows hung from hooks and strings in every corner of the room, and rows of fabric flowers lined the tops of the dresser and rested against the baseboards along each wall.

Beth laughed. "No, not more fabric. I do have a list of other things though. It isn't very long, but I need to have time to prepare everything. Perhaps we could go this weekend."

Julie nodded vigorously. "Goodness knows I'd like to get out of this place for a while."

"Poor Julie. Will you ski again today?" Beth ventured.

"I'm not sure." An elusive look in her sister's eye caught Beth's attention, but then Julie added, "I'll tidy up around here a bit, then maybe I'll go for a walk or sit with a book in Abigail's. Can you imagine how many books I've read since I've come to visit? Father's eyes would pop right out of his head to see my tall stack. I only wish I actually enjoyed it as much as the two of you. I suppose it'll be years after I get home before I'm interested in picking up another."

Beth felt a little pang of guilt that Julie hadn't found more to fill her time. "Well, drop in the classroom if you'd like. I can always find some ways for you to help the students." And she added silently, *Whatever Robert might think of your qualifications.*

"You offer that as if it might appeal to me. I prefer to find my own amusements, thank you very much. And I believe I've thought of a delightful endeavor."

Beth allowed the cryptic comment to pass. Julie swung away to get her coat and was out the door without any of the tidying up she'd offered.

Shortly after Julie's departure, as Beth

picked her way across the ice to school, she noticed a small group of men leaving the building. Robert must have had another early morning meeting. That would be the second just this week. What could he possibly find to discuss so often with the council members?

Bill Shaw tipped his hat toward Beth as they passed on the sidewalk. The others merely murmured, "Good morning," one after another.

Beth greeted them in return and made her way into her classroom. She sighed. There was so much for her students to accomplish before the end of the school year. With wedding plans and evening Bible club, Julie and the others Beth wanted to spend time with, she was feeling stretched. *And then what? After I'm married, after the school year is done? Oh, Father, You're the One who knows . . . the One I can trust with it all.*

⟡

"Miss Thatcher, may I have a word with you?" Robert stood in the entry, holding a notebook.

"Of course. What is it?"

"I've been asked by the council to address a situation with the schoolchildren."

"Oh?"

"They've been playing in the woods on land that belongs to the mining company."

"Yes?" Beth wondered what influence he expected her to exert. It seemed an issue that would be more appropriately discussed with the parents.

"They seem to be collecting a considerable amount of scrap materials there—timber, cast-off boards, even scrap metal." He paused. "Is it possible that you know, or have heard, what their intentions are?"

Beth smiled a little, then said, "No, it simply sounds like curious, energetic youngsters looking for something interesting to do."

"They haven't mentioned if they might be *building* something?"

"No, I haven't heard anything like that." She looked at him quizzically. "Are you asking about students in this classroom? The younger ones? I can't see how they would be able to create very much disorder in the woods."

"No, I believe it's those who are older and in my class, Miss Thatcher. But"—he hesitated, his gaze straying off toward the window—"you seem to know them all rather well, to be included in their confidence, more so than I. They'd trust you more easily with their secrets."

Beth was rather stunned at the admission. "Well, James and Kenny and Peter are a formidable trio. The Coolidge boys might also be with them, though I don't see why they wouldn't just carry out any project of their own at Frank's cabin. I can ask their mothers though, if you like."

"I'm afraid that hasn't been effective to date."

Beth wondered if the issue was more serious than he had expressed. "Are they damaging property?"

Robert stepped closer and lowered his voice. "The concern is that items may have been taken from company grounds. Tools and such."

"Oh my, that *is* cause for concern." Beth hurried on, "But Mr. Harris Hughes, I have absolutely no reason to believe any of the boys I mentioned would be involved in any kind of theft. Please don't rush to judgment. I'll speak with them myself if you like, but we can't presume they're guilty without *some* evidence."

"Of course, Miss Thatcher. However, the company is placing a great deal of pressure on me as mayor to arrive at a solution. And I'm rather perplexed as to how to proceed."

Is he admitting he needs help? My help? Beth felt some unexpected empathy for this difficult man. "I'll do what I can. And if I think of anything else, I'll let you know."

"Thank you, Miss Thatcher. I appreciate

your assistance in any way you can provide." He turned, then swung back again. "Oh, and Miss Thatcher, I have a second request."

"Yes?"

"You see, Ivy, my fiancée, will be paying a visit next week. I was hoping you would be willing to dine with her at Abigail's—you and your sister, if you like—to welcome her and answer any questions she may have regarding the community. I, of course, would cover the cost of the meal for all of you. I feel you would be the most suitable companions as women of similar station and deportment. She arrives in the afternoon on Tuesday next, weather permitting. Perhaps after school that Wednesday would be convenient for you, Miss Thatcher?"

Oh yes, his fiancée . . . Beth tried to picture what this woman might be like while she accepted his offer. "I'd like that, and I'm sure my sister would be thrilled to meet someone new. Will your fiancée be staying long?"

"Just a few days."

"I'll confirm this meal tomorrow, for both Julie and me."

"Thank you, Miss Thatcher." And he disappeared through the entryway.

Beth decided to begin her inquiry with the oldest boys. She approached Teddy while he was chopping wood in Molly's backyard. "Hello. Do you have a minute for a question?"

"Yes, ma'am." The teenager rested the axhead on the ground, handle leaning against his leg.

Beth came right to the point. "Teddy, I've been told that an issue is developing just west of town. Someone has been collecting logs and metal and wood on company property. Have you heard of any project there?"

He shrugged carelessly. "I ain't, I mean, *haven't* been out that way fer a while. But I can ask around. Do ya think it's kids?"

"I'm not sure anyone knows. But it would be odd for an adult to be interested in that kind of scrap material." Beth chose not to mention the allegation of theft. No need to make that link yet.

"Sure, Miss Thatcher, I'll check around."

"Thank you. I'll walk over to Mrs. Coolidge's today and speak with Luela and Addison."

Teddy's face wrinkled in a frown. "Why don't ya just ask 'em at school and save yerself a walk?"

"Well, I don't want to alarm anyone. I'm trying to do this quietly, with discretion. Do you understand?"

"Sure," he answered. "You don't want the guilty kids to find out yer on the prowl."

She covered a smile. "Something like that. But it's not that anyone is really *guilty*. We don't even know what's going on. So there's no sense stirring up trouble."

"I get it, Miss Thatcher. Ask around, but keep it quiet." The young man swung his ax up to rest on his shoulder.

"Thank you, Teddy." She struck out through the woods to Frank's former home. Addison and Luela gave no more insight, though.

~⁂~

After two days of queries, Beth was no closer to finding any useful information. It seemed that none of the mothers or their off-spring knew of any project that would fit the description, and she was convinced that they were speaking honestly. She would have to tell Robert she was unable to help him.

Council members continued to enter and exit the school early in the mornings. *They seem quite concerned about this nuisance. And somehow Robert's been thrust into the center of it all.* Her eyebrows rose as she wondered if he would have let his name stand for mayor had he known of this Coal Valley crisis.

Beth made arrangements for a ride into town on Saturday morning, but she was disap-pointed after school on Friday to see a bank of fierce, dark clouds rolling over the mountains and down into the valley. There would be more snow, the mountain roads would be treacherous, and there wouldn't likely be a trip anywhere.

Poor Julie, she had been looking forward to another visit with Eliza Smith's sister, Mary. And there was something else. Something she seemed only to hint at. Beth knew, though, that probing would get no place with her sister. When and where she would be forthcoming, only Julie would decide in her own time and way.

Speculation about what was happening in the woods had become an open conversation at lunch among the students gathered in Robert's classroom. All of them were adamant that they were not involved. By Monday afternoon even Beth's side of the school was full of speculations, much of the talk beginning with, "My mama says . . ." Beth insisted to the children that they were not going to be drawn into those discussions during school hours.

Frank mentioned on Monday evening that their road had been spared the brunt of the last snowfall and that it was clear again and seemed likely to remain open at least through the weekend. Particularly for Julie's sake, Beth was glad they would make their trip to Lethbridge. And she was also pleased for Robert,

hoping his fiancée would have a pleasant journey on the morrow.

"Miss Thatcher, I can't tell you how
thrilled I am to meet you. Robert has said so
many complimentary things about you."

Beth was speechless for a moment, then
managed, "Why, thank you. That's very kind
of him, I'm sure."

Ivy greeted Julie, then slipped an arm
through Beth's and led the two toward a corner table in Abigail's teahouse. It appeared Ivy
had arrived early and made arrangements for
their meal. "We're sitting here, girls. I already
ordered a platter of sandwiches, a little tray of
sweets, and some tea, if that's all right. But, oh,
do you prefer coffee? Robert tells me that's
more common out here."

Julie slid into her chair, her delight in
the visitor clearly visible on her face. "We're
tea drinkers mostly. That sounds very nice,
Miss . . ."

"Oh, I don't stand on ceremony. Just call
me Ivy. Everybody does."

As Beth took her seat, she was still rework-
ing her imagined idea of Robert's fiancée. Ivy
was outgoing and exuberant with an easy,
confident presence. She was also very striking,
though not what many would label a classic

beauty, with rather sharp and angular features softened with blond curls ringing her face. Her polished nails were a deep red. Everything about Ivy was thoroughly modern and stylish.

Julie was mesmerized. "May I ask where you found your dress, Ivy? It's stunning."

"It's silly, I know. I shouldn't have worn it today, but it's Robert's favorite and I wanted to make him smile. I'll tone it down once I move here—serviceable frocks and such." She winked at Julie.

Beth actually couldn't remember ever having seen Robert smile, since she didn't feel his typical smirks quite counted.

She looked down at her own simple skirt and blouse, her nails badly in need of care, and couldn't stop a small sigh. "I hope you had a pleasant drive and that the roads weren't too slippery."

"Oh, gracious, aren't they a mess? I thought we'd veer off the side of a cliff half a dozen times. I remember thinking it was such a lovely drive in late summer. The lofty vistas are so very different at this time of year."

Julie leaned forward, enthusiasm over this new friend clear in her face and voice. "When do you plan on being married? And where will you live?"

The woman's laugh was infectious. "It's

all very up in the air right now. Robert wants to pin me down. You know, make a plan. He's very much an organizer. But I'm afraid I'm having rather a good time of it in Calgary. I sing at a nightclub there. It's loads of fun. And so I'm not sure when I want to take the plunge. But that won't slow *him* down. He's already negotiating to purchase the lot next to this, so I suppose he'll be ready to build first thing in the spring. My dears," she said, lashes batting demurely, "he writes me often saying he's just lost without me. The sweetest romantic letters—like a lovestruck schoolboy." She laughed. "I've known lots of men, but Robert is . . . well, he's positively unique among them all. So stalwart, predictable. I can always tell what he'll do next. He's never surprised me yet—hardly even tried—and I guess I must like him that way." She giggled again.

Beth chose to ignore Ivy's description of her beau. *She means the lot between Abigail's place and Molly's. That's the community garden and provides food for many of the families— much-needed food.* "Who owns the property?" Immediately Beth wished her words had sounded less direct.

"I believe it belongs to the same couple who used to own this building." Ivy gestured around Abigail's teahouse. "Name of Grant, I believe. The Davie Grants."

Beth cleared her throat, pushing aside the emotions that the name provoked. "Were they *planning* to sell?"

"I'm not sure. I know they don't live here in town anymore. Robert hasn't told me much else. But he usually finds a way to get what he wants."

Julie drew closer to Ivy and lowered her voice. "Well, you wouldn't believe their story if I told you."

Ivy leaned in with a grin. "Do tell."

"You see, Mr. Grant—"

"Julie," Beth put in quietly, nudging her sister. "That's not appropriate for us to tell."

Both pairs of eyes studied Beth, seeming to debate whether or not to ignore her rebuke.

"Well, anyway," Ivy said, breaking the tension, "almost everyone sells if you offer enough, and Robert comes from money. So . . ." Her confident wave of the hand said more than the words.

"What kind of house will you build?" Julie prompted.

Ivy shrugged. "It won't be big, but it's to be brick so that it's snug and warm in this dreadful cold. And it'll have a proper oil furnace for heat, not just a wood stove."

"Electricity?"

"Sadly, not out here. But we'll make do somehow, just like pioneers of old. Imagine me, a frontierswoman! Who would have guessed?"

"Oh, Bethie, won't that be nice for them?"

"Yes, I'm sure that will be delightful." Beth sank back in her chair, her thoughts distracting her from much of the remaining conversation. *Is it possible, then, that they might live next door—and that Jarrick and I would be forced to see them regularly as neighbors? But we won't be staying long anyway. Just to the end of the school year.* She couldn't hold back the sigh that followed.

Chapter
22

Snow was falling softly early Thursday morning as Beth hurried to school. She passed by as Robert bid farewell to Ivy in the moonlit darkness before the students arrived. Later, during lunch, Beth watched through the classroom window as the storm gathered strength. She feared the new snowfall would delay the excursion with Julie to Lethbridge once more. *It's good Ivy was able to make it out in time,* she mused as she turned back to her desk.

The calendar page had been turned to March, but it looked like spring had no intention of making its appearance anytime soon.

At Bible club, Beth was surprised to notice some of the students' mothers gathering in the back of the room while she finished directing the cast for the day's story. Beth closed the meeting with prayer and went to greet the unexpected guests.

The women were all smiles. "We thought it would be just as nice to catch you here as anywhere," Abigail explained, looking a bit mysterious. "Your sister said you were feeling much better now and wouldn't mind staying out a little later."

"Thank you, yes, I am back to normal now." Beth glanced around as cookies, pies, and hot coffee were produced from the next room. They had begun to move desk chairs into a circle. *Is it a prayer meeting? A game night?* "I'm confused, Abigail. What exactly am I staying up for?"

Her question was greeted with a mysterious smile and a squeeze of her hand. Abigail looked around, and at her nod those gathered called out, "Your wedding shower!"

Beth gasped, and her hand rose quickly to cover her surprise. "Oh, that's so kind . . . so kind of you all." *And so generous. So very humbling!* Beth could picture the scantily equipped homes, the patched hand-me-downs on their children. In truth, she had been able to purchase everything she'd needed to set up housekeeping when she arrived. Tears filled her eyes, and she blinked them away.

Julie slipped in to join them, and the circle of chairs filled with Beth's friends, including the older girls. They laughed together and enjoyed their desserts while Beth opened each brown-paper-wrapped package. One after another, Beth held up embroidered tea towels crafted from flour sacks and starched hand-made doilies, a delicate teacup and a set of pillowcases, a colorful kitchen rug crocheted from strips of rags, a feather duster and a tea cozy, and a wall hanging cross-stitched with a Scripture verse. Beth was overwhelmed by their love and kindness. She gazed at the beautifully simple treasures laid out before her, and her heart broke with its familiar sorrow. *I'll never forget all of you. You're such dear people. How I wish I could stay.*

"And now from us, Marnie and me." Molly winked as Marnie carried over a large package and placed it on Beth's lap, standing close while Beth untied the string and lifted a corner of the paper. It was the quilt, the Bear's Paw design they had been laboring to finish. Beth looked up at Marnie, then over at Molly, and whispered a tremulous *thank you*. "Ya needed something warmer fer the two of ya, and it might as well be pretty too," Molly told Beth.

"Oh, it is, Molly. And Marnie, I know you've been working so hard on this." Beth stood and put her arms around the young woman, drawing her close and whispering, "I love it, darling. It's just too beautiful for words." She drew back and mouthed, "But you'll need a quilt too—"

"I can make another," Marnie said quickly, beaming. "Miss Molly an' me already got it started. But that isn't all, Miss Thatcher. Ya gotta look in the folds."

Beth sat again, slipped a hand inside the quilt, and pulled out a book. She held it up—a journal.

"It's not a blank one," Marnie explained quickly. "Miss Molly and I wrote out all the things we thought you'd need to know about keepin' house. We hoped it would be a help for ya."

Beth laid the book in her lap, put her face in her hands, and laughed through her tears.

Julie said, "Just what you need, right, Bethie?"

Her words prompted more laughter, more tears. Beth opened at random and read aloud, "Johnny Cake," in the girl's careful penman-ship, then noted the recipe that followed. She paged through and found "Removing stains" across the top with categories listed down the side and instructions for each, and another, "How and when to make a poultice."

"Oh, Marnie, I can't even tell you . . ."

The girl was giggling, obviously delighted with Beth's response. "I couldn't have written any of it if ya hadn't taught me so well. So I like that I can teach you too." She added quickly, "And, of course, Miss Molly helped too with all the recipes and advice."

Beth hugged both Molly and Marnie once more, then each of the gracious participants by turn, trying over and over again to express how deeply their thoughtful generosity had touched her.

After the group had departed and Beth had sent the gifts home with Julie and Marnie, Molly lingered. She straightened a row of desks while Beth set out items for the next day's lessons. Finally Molly took a seat and spoke quietly. "I want ya to know that yer book's been such a blessing already—ta Marnie and me."

"How so?" Beth sat down next to her, this woman who had turned out to be a second mother.

Molly rubbed at her knee for a moment. "It gave us so much to talk about, both practical and deep. All the traits of what it is ta be a godly married woman. She wrote a verse from Proverbs 31 in the front cover, but we read the whole chapter and studied all of it. She's determined to be a wife like that someday. I'm proud'a that girl."

"You should be, Molly," Beth answered with deep emotion. "She's turning out to be very much like you. And that would be the very best our Marnie could be. You've been a wonderful guide, a teacher to her, and she's going to be the same kind of teacher to another generation."

~~~※~~~

News that Alberto *would* depart with a car after school on Friday meant Beth and Julie could finally ride along—and there would be additional passengers, Harold and Marnie. In spite of some tight quarters, Beth was happy to share the ride and spend more time with the two young people. Harold was taking Marnie to introduce her to his family, who would join them for the overnight visit with relatives in Lethbridge. The girl's excitement was in full view as her beau deposited their bags in the trunk.

To Beth this trip would accomplish the final shopping, but more than that, she would have one more opportunity to spend time with Jarrick. And Julie would have a chance to visit Mary and her friends, to feel the bustle of the city. They planned to spend the night with Dillard and Eliza again, and that evening Jarrick brought in dinner from one of the local restaurants.

"Oh yes," Eliza said at a lull in the conversation, "won't you come with me, Beth? I have something for you." The two slipped away to the bedroom closet, and Eliza produced Beth's grandmama's wedding gown, altered to fit just right. Beth's stomach fluttered, and tears filled her eyes as she stared at the beautiful gown, picturing all the memories it represented.

"I have a box ready so you can take it home with you. If we fold it carefully with paper in between the layers, I think any wrinkles will hang out before the wedding."

"Eliza, I can't thank you enough," Beth whispered as she touched the satin and lace. "It is so wonderful to have it ready."

"It won't be long now."

Beth smiled but didn't say, *It feels as if these last few weeks will drag on forever.*

The impatience only heightened as she walked with Jarrick to the front door for a reluctant good-night farewell.

"I don't feel we've had nearly enough time together, Jarrick. I know I'll think of a million things as soon as my head hits the pillow," she murmured from the security of his hug.

"And tomorrow I head north to Athabasca. I doubt if I'll be back until a couple weeks before the wedding. But I'll send regular letters, I promise. Do you need anything else from me for now?"

Beth smiled. "Well, there *is* one thing. A question I'd like answered."

"What's that, sweetheart?"

"Where are we going on our honeymoon? I need to know how to pack. I don't think you understand that a woman needs to prepare for these things."

"I can't tell you," he said, grinning. "I've been having too much fun keeping it a surprise. But I will tell you a little. You won't need to dress up—maybe one evening. You should be ready to dress comfortably and casually. Perhaps throw in a good pair of walking shoes. Does that help?"

"Hmm." The words only called up more questions. "I suppose that will have to do, then."

He smiled again, kissing her nose lightly. "But the good news is, we won't have to worry about keeping up appearances."

Beth's eyebrows rose. "Then we won't be at someone's home. That can only mean a hotel. But I don't know of a hotel except in Lethbridge. But that would be in the city, and we'd need to dress for it." She frowned. "You'd tell me the truth, right? You're not going to take me someplace without the proper attire?"

He laughed. "I assure you, you'll be fine. However," he added, "that's the last question I'm going to answer on the subject. You'll have to trust me, Beth."

She shook her head at him, hugged him tightly once more, and closed the door behind him. She was determined not to complain further about his secret. As difficult as it was to wait, she did enjoy his look of satisfaction at keeping it from her.

The following morning was busy with shopping. Soon into the excursion, Julie announced she could get much more done alone, and Beth was rather in agreement. However, her sister showed up at lunch with more bags than Beth had expected. "There isn't much room in the car, darling," Beth reminded her. "Especially with five of us, our luggage, and with my wedding dress. We don't want to have to tie things on the top. Do you really need so much when you don't have all that much longer—"

"Trust me," Julie said with her usual confidence.

Harold and Marnie were holding hands when they arrived at the Smiths' home that afternoon for their return. Marnie's eyes sparkled.

Harold's family must have received her with open arms, Beth concluded.

Alberto turned the car back toward the western mountains while Beth, seated in the front with Julie's packages piled around her feet, laid her head against the frame of the door and closed her eyes.

She awoke to find the car back in Coal Valley in front of the boarding house, with several people standing outside engaged in a rather loud conversation.

She leaned forward for a better view through the window, and there was Molly, arms crossed, demanding, "Was that yer plan all along?"

"Yes, ma'am. It was. I'll own to it. But it doesn't change anything." Harold was twisting his hat brim around, knuckles white.

"Oh, yes, it does, Harry Edwards. It changes everything."

Marnie pleaded, "Miss Molly, I—"

"Now you just come home, Marnie. Ya best come in right now without another word."

Beth quickly reached for the door handle and stepped out to see Molly ushering Marnie into the house while Harold stood alone beside the car, looking downward.

"What happened?" Beth whispered to Julie.

Her sister's eyes were round. She swallowed, then said, "They eloped—like Frank and Molly. That's why they came along with us."

"But, he told me, he promised . . . oh my!"

~❧~

Beth, reluctant to enter the boarding house that evening, hesitated on the front porch until Julie pushed past. She gingerly followed, afraid there would be uncomfortable tension. But all seemed tranquil as they found Frank in the parlor, fiddling with a wobbly doorknob. "Come in, come in," he invited. "We were afraid'a you weren't comin' to visit tonight."

"Good evening, Frank," Beth answered, her gaze sweeping around cautiously.

"They aren't home. All of 'em went'a to talk to the pastor."

Beth was filled with relief. Philip would offer excellent advice. She breathed out a prayer for him and took a seat on the sofa. "You didn't go?"

He shook his head. "My Mollina, she's a strong woman, but that'a don't mean she's always calm. I stay out'a the way in this, eh? I give'a my help when it's needed."

"But what happened? What were they thinking?"

Frank set aside his repair project. "Somebody told 'em if they married that'a the company would give'a them a home, a place of their own, because the young man, he works here."

"But they know there aren't enough houses already."

"They heard that'a there was to be an opening, that the McDermotts, they're moving away. And that if they hurried, it might'a be theirs."

"And are they, the McDermotts, moving away?"

"Yes, soon. Howard got'a himself a managing job in the mines near Lethbridge. But their home, it'sa been assigned to your teacher friend."

"To Robert?"

"To him an' his'a wife."

"But Ivy, his fiancée," Beth burst out, "said they wouldn't even be married very soon, and that they're planning to *build* a house."

"Yes, he bought the land from'a the Grants, but the house won'ta be started till the ground thaws an' it won'ta be done till the end of summer. So they will'a rent from the company till the other is finished."

Beth shook her head in bewilderment.

Frank shrugged. "He spoke as if'a she

would come soon. He seems'a so anxious to bring her out from the city. I think he'sa lonely here. Don't you?"

Beth didn't answer, forcing her thoughts back to Marnie and Harold. "What do you think will come of this meeting with Philip? Will they try to have the marriage annulled? Or will the two be given a place together somewhere?"

Frank allowed a faint smile to flicker across his stubbled face. "I'ma gonna wait to hear with the rest'a you." He shook his head. "But I'ma gonna hope these folks will'a be kind to my sweet girl. She'sa not bad, and he'sa not either. They're just too much in love to think clearly, eh?"

Beth remembered Frank's first wife, his Colette—how they had been told they were too young. She supposed he was thinking about her too. "I'll pray with you, Frank, that they'll be treated gently, kindly."

Molly returned soon with Marnie. The girl disappeared upstairs, and Molly moved heavily across the parlor floor, sitting herself down on the other end of the sofa.

Beth reached across to rest a hand on her arm. "I hope Philip was able to give some sound advice."

"Ain't much to be done," she said with

a sigh. "Seems those young'uns already set their own minds. Now they gotta abide by the consequences of that choice."

Beth's face twisted in concern. "What about Marnie's education?"

"Oh, he had an answer fer that one too," Molly said glumly. "She's gonna finish, he claims. In his mind, there ain't no reason she can't be a wife and a student too."

Beth wondered about Robert's opinion on that score but simply offered quietly, "They can have my place, Molly."

"Oh no," Molly said, shaking her head firmly, "they ain't gettin' more 'an they deserve just 'cause they forced things. They'll stay in Marnie's room till somethin' better comes along. And only the Good Lord knows how long that'll be."

Beth nodded, feeling for Marnie and Molly both.

The woman sadly shook her head again. "Harry claims she looked real pretty in that dress you give her."

"What dress?"

"The one fer yer weddin'."

"The bridesmaid dress—the blue one?"

Molly nodded, and Beth sighed again, picturing Marnie standing beside Harold in the cornflower blue. It was a conflicting image for Beth, a confusing mixture of romance and pathos. "I'm so sorry, Molly."

Molly's eyes had already closed. "Don't be sorry, dearie. At least she had somethin' nice to wear. We'd of never been able to give her better."

Chapter 23

The startling news traveled through Coal Valley in record speed. Beth followed Molly, Frank, Harold, and Marnie into their regular pew on Sunday morning, and she watched the various members of the congregation size up the situation. She saw simple curiosity and interest, along with varying degrees of sympathy and support, while a few faces showed condescension.

Following Sunday dinner, Frank went for his usual visit with friends, and Beth retreated to the kitchen with Julie to help clean up. Harold and Marnie had quietly slipped away for a walk, and Beth caught sight of Robert leaving through the front door in his dapper hiking clothes and boots, as was his Sunday custom.

When Frank returned he pulled out the

checkerboard and challenged Beth to a game. She was quick to accept, and they were soon matching hop for hop, piece for piece.

"I'm afraid your mind is elsewhere today, Frank. I'm keeping up with you for a change," she teased.

He looked startled for a moment and then admitted, rubbing at his chin, "Yes, I am'a thinking of other things'a right now."

Of Marnie and Harold, Beth assumed.

He hunched over the table and studied Beth for a moment, then must have decided to bring her into his confidence. "I was walking back from'a the river, where I meet'a my friends, and I saw many hoofprints in the woods where the kids were said'a to be playing with the company's castoffs."

"Was it deer, or maybe elk?"

"It was'a horse hooves. But who was'a the rider, that I don't know. It'sa strange, eh?"

"Yes. Yes, it is."

Frank moved his hand to lift one of his checker pieces and stopped again. "Such a silly thing, and yet the town, they are'a blaming your teacher friend. It'sa causing him many problems."

"But why? Surely they don't think he's involved."

"They think he should'a know what the children are about."

"Even when their parents can't explain it?"

"Yes, some of 'em, even then. I think he'sa fallen from grace and is'a not so trusted anymore."

Beth's imagination fastened on the mysterious hoofprints. *What if it isn't the children at all?*

Monday morning, Julie was finally ready to admit the reason for her many purchases in town. "I've arranged for a shelf in Coulter's store. It's for Coal Valley ladies. Creams and makeup and lotions. Ivy was the one who encouraged me. After all, those things really are needed here, out where the weather is so hard on a woman's complexion. So why not make available my considerable experience to help these women discover cosmetics?"

"Julie, these women struggle just to put food on the table."

"Pish-posh. What I have isn't very expensive. I took that into consideration and only have brought in the most basic and economical."

Beth wanted to object further, but she was simply too weary after worrying about Marnie and fretting about the future for herself and Jarrick. *What could possibly go wrong if Julie tries to sell a few beauty products? At least this will keep her busy.*

That afternoon, upon arriving home from school, Beth was not surprised to find Julie placing labels on small jars spread across the kitchen table and piled into a small crate on the second chair. Beth shrugged out of her coat, her cheeks feeling frosty with cold. A blizzard was descending over their little town, and she had released the students early so they could make it safely home before it hit.

"Well, since it's almost spring, now what do you think of our weather, Julie?"

"If it leaves lots of fresh snow for skiing, I'm happy. There's been far too much crusty, icy mess for my taste. That's what I think."

"You know this means the store will be closed and we'll probably be stuck inside for a day or two."

"My darling, I've felt mostly stuck inside since I got here. And anyway, we can finish those wedding programs you've been pestering me about."

"I haven't pestered you at all. Why I—"

"You have mail, Bethie." Julie smiled sweetly and gestured toward the top of the small pantry cupboard.

"A letter from Mother," Beth said as she sorted quickly through the envelopes. "I'm glad. I haven't heard from her in a while. It's probably some stories about baby Josiah and more questions about the wedding. Perhaps by now they'll know when they'll arrive." She set it aside. "And one from Margret. Oh, I hope she included pictures." And then, "Julie, what's this?"

Another item was stuck to the back of Margret's envelope. "It's a telegram," Beth commented, looking for the name of the recipient. "It must have been sent out from the city along with the mail."

"Who's it for, you or me?"

"Neither, it's for . . . it's for Robert! It must have come to us by accident. We'll need to get it to him as soon as possible."

Julie reached for the telegram, but Beth immediately tucked it away in her coat pocket. "I said it's for Robert. We can't *read* it."

"He'll never know. He—"

"Julie! We're not going to read someone else's telegram. We'll take it to him at Molly's."

"Fiddlesticks! Then you might as well just read it. If he knows you had it he'll assume you know what it says."

Beth paced away from the table and returned again. "Then we'll just take it back to the store," Beth said firmly. "Now, what shall we make for dinner? We might as well get started. I'll get the fire going while you figure out what it will be."

Julie was correct about the further preparations required before the wedding. Mother's letter reenergized Beth to finish the things already begun, including the tedious copying and folding of the programs, while Julie put her artistic skills to work, adding a vine of roses all around the script.

Beth hadn't yet solved the problem of an archway for the center of the platform, but she hoped an idea would come shortly. One that was simple to erect yet would please her own mother—and maybe even satisfy her mother-in-law-to-be.

On the following afternoon, the sisters wrapped themselves in layers, left some scraps for Penelope at the bottom of the stairs, and struck out for Molly's, squinting against the icy crystals flung by the wind.

Teddy answered their knock, hurrying them inside and shutting the door firmly behind them. "We thought ya might find your way over, now that the worst has died down."

Julie stamped her feet on the mat and unwound the scarf from her neck. "Doesn't seem like the worst has died down to me!" she joked. "Have you all been busy? What exciting things have you found for entertainment?"

"Not much," he grumbled. "Unless you wanna watch Marnie and Harry moonin' over

each other in the dining room. The rest of us
are in the kitchen."

Beth and Julie followed him into the warm
room, where Frank and Molly were sipping
coffee.

"Look at you two," Molly teased, "just a
couple'a mountain women headin' out in a
storm like pioneers."

Beth dropped into the nearest chair, rubbing her hands together. "Oh, Molly, it's less
than four weeks until the wedding. What if the
roads aren't passable and my parents can't
come? Oh, goodness, what if even *Jarrick*
can't get through?"

"A Mountie? Not able to travel through
a little snow? Nonsense, dearie. And a good,
sunny day can bring some startlin' changes.
You just wait an' see."

"I hope so."

They were ready to head home when Beth
discovered the telegram still in her pocket.
Still determined not to leave it at Molly's for
Mr. Harris Hughes and have him find out it
had come into her possession, she was sure
that returning it to the store would be best.

"Say, Teddy, do you know if the store is
open today?"

He shook his head. "Nope. Molly sent

me to check. Maybe tomorrow. What do ya need?"

"Oh, nothing, really. But I got somebody's mail by mistake."

"I'm goin' out first thing if the wind dies down by then. Meeting Addie to do some ice fishin'. Want me to take it over for ya?"

Beth, relieved, said, "Yes, please. It's a telegram for Mr. Harris Hughes." She handed it to the boy. "I have no idea what it says, but if it was worth paying to send it, it's probably important. Now, you won't lose it, Teddy, or forget?" she warned as she turned away.

"Hey, says here Mr. Harris Hughes is leavin' soon."

Beth froze. She wanted badly to ask for clarification but knew the boy had already said too much. "That doesn't belong to you. Close it up, Teddy."

"All right." He shrugged. "But it seems pretty strange, him bein' mayor now and all. Guess that didn't stop Mr. Ramsey from movin' away though."

Beth stood for a moment, trying to decide how to proceed. If she left the telegram in Teddy's possession, the information likely would be spread around. "You'd better give it to me," she finally said. "I'll take it over in the morning. And Teddy, you need to promise you won't tell *anyone* what you read here. You were wrong to read it. It's private information," she told him as she returned it to her pocket.

"Yes, ma'am. If you say so."

Beth knew he could be trusted, but the questions prompted by his discovery tumbled through her mind as she followed Julie across the snowy street. *Is Robert truly planning to leave? But Ivy said they were building a house soon. Would they do so if not intending to remain for at least a while? Perhaps they're only making short-term plans. Or perhaps Ivy is incorrect in her assessment of Robert's intentions. After all, she spoke in terms of* supposing *what he would do next.* Then Beth recalled that Frank had mentioned the land purchase had already transpired.

Once home she banked the fire carefully, dawdling over the last chores for the night. Julie retired first, and still Beth lingered, fighting the urge to pull out the telegram. At last she went to change for bed, moving slowly in the dark so as not to disturb Julie's even breathing. She was glad she had been victorious as she slid under the covers.

At first light Beth prepared hastily for her errand. Standing at the door, she asked Julie if there was anything she'd like from the store.

"Something sweet, please? Hard candy or a package of cookies?"

"I'll see what they have." Beth stepped out onto the landing, shielding her eyes from the blowing snow, and picked her way carefully down the stairs. The familiar ring of the bell over the store's door announced Beth's arrival.

Toby appeared almost instantly from the back, smiling cheerfully. "I wondered who'd arrive here first today. You must be out of coffee—or maybe tea, in the case of you and yer sister."

"No, nothing like that. I'd like to buy a ream of white paper, and Julie would like something sweet. I'll go look at your packaged cookies." Beth pulled a mitten off one hand and dug inside her pocket. "I also want to bring this telegram back. It must have inadvertently gotten in with some of my mail."

Toby scratched his head, taking the telegram with the other hand. "That's odd. My fault, I guess. Must be the one for Mr. Harris Hughes. I wondered where it went. Thanks fer bringin' it back. He don't seem like the type could easily overlook such an error."

Beth smiled, glad to be rid of the temptation. "I'll look for Julie's cookies and be back in a moment."

"Take yer time. I ain't got nobody else ta help." He lifted a corner of the account book in the center of the counter and shoved the telegram underneath.

Beth noticed a cloth-covered table near the front window and took a step closer, studying the rows of products forming Julie's display. On a whim she lifted a small jar of lotion. *I might as well give her a little encouragement.* She carried it with her to the display of baked goods.

The front bell jangled again, and Toby called out, "Well, speak o' the devil. Good morning, Mr. Harris Hughes. How'd ya fare in this here blizzard? Ya get out fer your hike yet this morning?"

Beth ducked down a bit as Robert strode forward to the counter. "Good morning, Mr. Coulter," he said, his tone hearty. "How are you? I have just a short list today."

"Ya know we don't always have what ya want in stock, an' we didn't get the last shipment 'cause of the storm. But I'll do what I can."

"Of course," Robert answered. "Of course."

Toby drew a small box from beneath the counter and began gathering the items on Robert's list. Beth kept her head low, hoping to be overlooked.

"Say, a telegram came fer ya, Mr. Harris Hughes. From yer hometown. It got stuck in with some mail fer Miss Thatcher. But she brung it back. Fella who wrote it says somethin' about a bet he made with ya. And that he'll meet ya at the train station to collect on it when ya get back home in June. Ya goin' back east soon?"

Beth felt like she had turned to stone. *Toby as much as announced the contents aloud. And he told Robert I received the message first by mistake!* All her efforts were for naught.

Robert cleared his throat. "I'm afraid that's my own personal business, Mr. Coulter. And I'd ask that you respect my privacy on the matter."

"Sure, sure," the storekeeper answered with a grin, seeming rather pleased with himself. He cast a glance toward the aisle where Beth was trying to hide. "Anyhow, here it is." He passed the folded page to Robert.

Beth breathed out a prayer that Robert's list would be filled promptly, and she looked desperately for a second exit from the room.

Suddenly Toby called, "Ya find those cookies ya wanting yet, Miss Thatcher?"

Beth felt her cheeks warm, but there was nothing left to do but step forward and place the package of Oreos she was holding on the counter. "These will be fine, Mr. Coulter. Would you add them to my account, please? And this jar of cream from my sister's table."

"Sure, miss. And here's yer white paper. Would you like a box?"

Beth kept her eyes directly on Toby's face and managed, "No, thank you. I can carry them just fine without." She accepted the items and stepped toward the door, her gaze on the floor to avoid interacting with Robert.

"Miss Thatcher," he spoke sternly. "Good morning."

She glanced at him, said a quick, "Good morning," and slipped out the door.

⁂

Beth was able to avoid Robert for the remainder of the day, but she dreaded what might happen on Thursday before school. She had absolutely no doubt that he would mention the betrayed confidence and the contents of the message. *Will he deny it? Will he try to explain it away? Or will he simply acknowledge his intention to resign at the end of the school year?*

Though Beth fully anticipated a knock at that shared door, she was nonetheless on edge and startled when it finally came. "Miss Thatcher, might I have a moment of your time?"

"Of course." She laid the chalk on its ledge and drew back her shoulders to foster confidence. *There's no sense waiting for him to speak first,* she told herself. "I presume you've come regarding the telegram. I want to assure you, Mr. Harris Hughes, that I did not at any point read it myself. That I, in fact, was very guarded about the confidentiality of your message. Even so, I'm truly sorry that Mr. Coulter . . . that its contents were divulged. You must be rather perturbed."

Robert lifted his eyebrows and tilted his head in a half nod of acknowledgment. "I appreciate your candor, Miss Thatcher. In most situations I would merely let bygones be bygones, but I felt it was necessary to offer something of an explanation in this case, most especially because your good opinion has come to matter to me."

"I'm sure it's not necessary." Beth's words sounded feeble in her ears, and her mind was whirling. *What? It matters to him what I think? What I think?*

"Nevertheless," he said, clearing his throat, "it's true that I do intend to return east, Miss Thatcher. And when I do I hope to have sufficient data to demonstrate that my educational techniques are effective. I hope to publish and thereby broaden my influence."

"I see."

"However, one year's success would be entirely inadequate for such an endeavor, as I've many times explained to my friend who sent the telegram. My intention is to remain in this town for ten years—for one entire decade. My friend, who has chosen to ridicule my resolve, was *teasing* in his message. But I assure you that once I make up my mind, as I have on this, I see no reason why I should leave any time before the full ten years has passed. During which period I hope to produce measurable improvements in the students who are shaped by this small school."

Ten whole years? Beth felt a strange sensation rising from the pit of her stomach. Not anger or even frustration. It was jealousy, strong and hungry. *Most of my children will have graduated by then. He's going to instruct them all, virtually single-handedly. What will they become under those years of his influence?*

"I see," Beth murmured again.

"I would expect to have a second teacher assigned upon your departure—perhaps one who will share my philosophy. But . . ." He hesitated, glancing back toward the entry door. "I would have preferred to have continued with you, Miss Thatcher. You have been respectful and honest and trustworthy, even though our beliefs could scarcely have been further apart."

"You're generous to say so, Mr. Harris Hughes."

He inclined his head and turned back to the other classroom. Beth sank into a chair and struggled to regain her composure. Her children would arrive shortly. But they were not hers for much longer—they would be his.

Chapter 24

Beth stepped out onto the sidewalk after school on Friday and looked up into the blue sky with a line of soft white clouds sweeping across it. The warmth of the sunshine was already melting snow from the sidewalk and road, one little trickle at a time. *The official first day of spring,* she exulted, then reminded herself that another blizzard could come even tomorrow. But she was determined to enjoy this day while it lasted.

On impulse she stacked her books on the steps to her apartment and struck out for a walk in celebration of the change of seasons and to spend some moments in prayer. Patches of sunshine streaming through the trees led her onto the main road toward Lethbridge. *Toward Jarrick,* she thought, missing him once more.

As she walked she thought again about Robert's disclosure and the children she had come to care about so much. But she said quietly to herself, *I have prayed for God's will, whatever that might be. I will not take back my submission to Him, no matter how much I believe I know what should occur.*

She thought of Marnie and Harold next, so much in love and thrilled to be together. And yet their impulsive decision had created a strained living arrangement, suspending Molly's family in uneasy tension until some kind of resolution was found. *For how long, Father? I can't imagine how they'll be able to afford a home. Will they move into my place after I've gone?* That question reminded her that though the end of the school year was still weeks away, it felt as if she were on the very threshold of leaving Coal Valley.

Beth stood in the center of the road, breathing in deeply with her face tipped upward toward the sun. She lifted her hands toward its warmth. *You know everything about what's going to happen, Lord God. You have a perfect solution. I'll wait for You.* And she said aloud those eternal words, "'But they that wait upon the LORD shall renew their strength; they shall mount up with wings as eagles.'" She wanted that—to have strength while waiting, her hope for the future finding wings to rise above her worries. It wasn't ever easy, this waiting—she knew that full well. But God had always been with her, even in her darkest hours.

At last she turned back toward home, rejuvenated by the freshness of this day full of spring's hope. Her mind focused now on last plans for the wedding. There was little left to do, and she trusted it wouldn't prove too difficult.

Just as Beth approached the stairs leading to her home, she heard a rustling in the bushes where Penelope often lingered.

Beth stepped toward the familiar area and drew back the thick branches, but instead of the small tabby cat, she saw black fur. Lots of it. She let out a cry as the branches snapped back into place. A deep answering growl confirmed it was a bear.

Beth staggered backward, her legs weak with fear and her feet refusing to function. One shoe caught against the other, and she tumbled onto her back on the damp ground. More growling, and a brown snout appeared, sniffing the air. Beth let loose a piercing scream, and she scrambled backward toward the stairs, scraping hands and legs against the rough ground. Now a broad black head, lolling back and forth, emerged, and the gaping mouth spewed another prolonged guttural sound.

"Get away," she shouted, still facing the beast. "Go on!" Desperately clutching at the stair rail to keep from collapsing, Beth inched up the stairs. "Help!"

A fierce hiss from somewhere beneath her feet preceded a gray streak bolting toward the animal. Penelope stood on her hind legs, her front paws spread wide above her head, claws raking the air, as if to appear much larger than she was. The yowling cat lunged and batted at the snout, and it disappeared, retreating back into the foliage.

Beth heard fast footsteps from around the side of the building.

"What's wrong?" Abigail called.

Beth pointed. "A bear! In the bushes!"

Abigail clapped her hands to further ward off the animal, at the same time calling the alarm over her shoulder. "Bear!" She clapped and shouted even more loudly, flapping her apron. "Go on! Get out! Go away!"

Penelope disappeared into the bushes, and terrible growls and yowls, snarls and roars ensued. Tears rolled down Beth's cheeks. The sounds were absolutely dreadful, and she fought the urge to rush forward to save the cat.

Next came an explosion of gunshot from somewhere on the road, and the awful noises faded into the woods. At last there was silence.

"Who saw it?"

"How big was it?" A crowd had gathered already.

"Beth saw it," Abigail answered, pressing her hands against the side of her face. "But the cat took it on, so it can't of been very large."

"A cub?" asked a man.

"Probably a yearling out explorin' on its own, still too young ta know to stay away from the sounds of machinery."

"Then the mother's bound to be near."

More men arrived. From her position on the stairs, Beth was startled at the number of guns that had so quickly assembled.

"Bethie! Are you hurt?" Julie rushed forward, wrapping her arms tightly around Beth.

"It was a bear, Julie." Beth tried to keep the tremble from her voice.

"Did you see it?"

"See it?" Beth choked out. "I was so close I could have slapped it!"

A search party was hastily assembled to look for the cub and its mother. They tramped into the forest, hollering out instructions to one another as they went. Beth was certain she'd never look at the nearby trees in quite the same way. "Julie," she almost wailed, "Penelope fought it. But I haven't seen her since. We must check the bushes."

Both faces white, hands clasped tightly, they warily drew aside the branches. There were clumps of fur, but not a sign of their feline friend.

"What do you think happened, Bethie? Did it *eat* her?"

"I don't think so. I don't think there was time."

"Oh, Bethie! This is dreadful!"

Beth turned wide eyes to Julie. "It could have been you, out in the woods when you've been skiing. You mustn't go anywhere alone anymore, darling. Whatever would you have done if you'd met a bear out there?"

Julie stared back. "I haven't the foggiest notion."

Beth and Julie hurried to their pantry and back again with a dish of scraps. "Here, kitty! Penelope! Please come home."

At last the familiar eyes blinked in the bushes, and their cat trotted forward, looking none the worse for wear except for some patches of missing fur.

"Oh, you dear kitty, you're here. You're alive." They scooped her up and seated themselves on a low step. Penelope moved between their laps, soaking up their affection as they hand-fed her choice bits of dinner.

"You're so brave," Beth fussed over her. "You chased away a bear!"

"Well, darling, to be accurate," Julie corrected, "the gunshot chased it away. I saw

Toby Coulter fire a shot into the air. But she's a brave kitty just the same." Julie stroked the fur for a moment. "Shouldn't we take her indoors, Bethie? Can she be a house cat now? Please."

"Yes, of course—oh, but we can't," Beth lamented, remembering her wedding gown, the rows of fabric flowers and bows, plus the other decorations laid out carefully for the ceremony. "She'd ruin everything. I want to, Julie, but we just can't let her in."

"You're right, of course. But we'll have to fix a place for her outside. Nice and soft and warm."

"We will," Beth promised. "Let's use the woodshed."

True to their word, the sisters stitched up a satin pillow stuffed with leftover tulle. They carefully lifted the layers of logs from inside the woodshed until they found the gap that appeared to belong to Penelope. Beth lined the bottom with more of the satin and Julie plumped the pillow to create a soft bed. Then they restacked logs around and over it until they were certain it was sound and provided an adequate entrance. Finally, Beth draped a small tarp that she bought from Toby to protect it all from the elements.

"That's good," Julie pronounced. "She'll be warm and safe and dry."

Beth had a sudden thought. "But how will we get more wood when we need it?"

After a pause, Julie said, "We'll go to Molly's. We'll carry them over from her pile. After all, they come from there anyway. It'll just save Teddy the trouble of restocking here."

It was silly, Beth knew, but she quickly agreed.

⁂

A knock sounded on the door just as Beth began dishing up bowls of vegetable stew for herself and Julie. Her sister jumped up and pulled the door halfway open, then fell back a step. "What on earth?"

"Surprise!" Beth heard. "I hope I haven't caught you at a bad time."

Julie laughed gleefully and reached for their visitor. Beth set the bowls on the table and hurried closer. "Jarrick! Oh, Jarrick, it's you!"

He caught Beth up in a strong embrace, lifting her off her feet and spinning her around. "I couldn't wait anymore. I had to see you, and with the break in the weather, I thought I'd make a quick trip."

Beth felt the floor under her feet once more, though she would just as soon have stayed in his arms. "This is a wonderful surprise!"

His eyes twinkled as he took in the rest of the room. "Guess you've been doing a little work for the wedding."

Julie laughed, rolling her eyes. "An understatement, Jack. Bethie's had us doing enough for *three* weddings."

Jarrick looked carefully at Beth. "I heard about Marnie's elopement. How did that go over?"

Beth sighed. "It was awfully difficult for Frank and Molly at first—especially Molly. But I think they're getting used to the idea. And Marnie is still attending school, though no one has said anything about next year yet."

Julie waved Jarrick to a chair. "Take your coat off, stay awhile. I think we can scrape up another bowl out of the pot."

Soon they were eating, and Jarrick complimented them on the simple meal. Beth wished she had taken time to add meat to the stew. She had not considered it necessary for Julie and herself.

They chatted for some time about the weather, about Jarrick's most recent assignments, of school news and projects that still needed doing for the wedding. Julie insisted on telling the bear story herself, and Jarrick looked back and forth between them in both consternation and amusement at her dramatic and slightly exaggerated account.

"But, Beth," he said, turning to her with brow furrowed, "that could have been so much worse if the mother—"

"Yes, I know that, Jarrick," she said, seeing his deep concern. "I am very grateful it was not, and thank the Lord for His protection." She paused, then added playfully, "He enlisted our dear little Penelope to save me!"

They laughed again.

"Oh, and I've had a letter from Mother," Beth told him, happy to move to another subject. "They've booked their train tickets and are planning to arrive the weekend before the wedding—on Sunday, just over two weeks from now."

"My folks sent a letter too." His voice sounded strangely forced. "I brought it along with me so you can read it, Beth. I'm sure there'll be time later."

She studied his face, looking for clues to the obvious significance. Julie stirred and said, "Say, you two. I can go over to Molly's . . . or to the store. I don't mind."

"No, no," Jarrick said, motioning with his hand for her to stay. Beth knew he would never overstep propriety, alone with her in her home before they were married.

Beth stood. "Let's all go. Frank and Molly will want to see you—everyone will. There's still time for a visit with them this evening if we hurry."

"Let's stop first at the store," Julie insisted. "I'll show you what I've been doing with some of my free time, Jack."

꧁꧂

Jarrick's arrival at Molly's brought family from all directions. Teddy took the stairs down two at a time, Marnie and Harold hastened from the parlor, and Frank followed Molly out from the kitchen. Their unexpected visitor was ushered to a seat at the kitchen table almost before he had removed his coat. Molly set to work fixing a dessert and coffee.

Jarrick half stood and reached across the table to shake Harold's hand. "I hear congratulations are in order, Harry. As you have discovered, Marnie is a fine young lady."

"Thanks, Mr. Thornton," Harold returned. "I feel very blessed to call her my wife now." The young man's eyes glanced toward Molly, and he added solemnly, "Maybe we kind of jumped the gun a little, but—"

"What's done is done, Harry," Molly said from the stove. "Ya don't need to keep repeatin' that."

A pounding on the door turned their faces in unison.

"Teddy Boy, can ya get it, please?" Molly asked.

Then a husky voice demanded, "Frank in?"

"Yes, sir. He's in the kitchen. I'll get him."

"No need." Heavy boots approached, and a face unfamiliar to Beth appeared in the kitchen doorway. "I got news, Frank."

"What did'a you find, Morgan?"

The grave man hesitated, casting a glance toward Jarrick.

"This is'a Constable Jack Thornton," Frank clarified. "He's a Mountie. You can'a say what's needed to be said."

Morgan grunted acknowledgment. "I did what you asked, Frank. I followed the trail of prints, far as the bend in the river. There was a camp—a fire pit and some trees felled to make a small corral. Weren't nobody there, at least for the last day or two."

"That'sa too bad. I had hoped you would'a find them."

The man swiped at his long gray beard. "Found more prints too. Some of 'em round the mill in the shadows, where the snow ain't melted yet. Gone for sure after tomorrow. You'd best come early if you wanna see 'em for yourself."

"I will. And if he'sa willing, I'll bring my guest, eh?"

"Suit yourself." Morgan retreated out the front door, and all was quiet.

Jarrick broke the silence. "A little trouble here, Frank?"

Frank traced the grain lines on the wood table with his fingers as he explained to Jarrick about the strange heap of scrap materials in the woods. Beth had almost forgotten about it. "Some men, they thought it was'a the work of our students and pushed hard at the new mayor to find out more. But I never thought it was'a the kids. Was too much weight for them—too much'a to carry, or even to drag." He paused and frowned. "An' then we found prints made by horses. We don'ta have no horses 'round here, Jack."

"I understand. But who—?"

"That I don'ta know. But if we can find 'em, we can ask, eh?"

Jarrick set his empty cup on the table. "Be careful, Frank. There's no way to know what you're getting into."

Frank rubbed at the stump of his right hand with the left. "You wanna know what I think?"

"Of course."

"There'sa no reason for it, Jack. It don'ta make sense." He pursed his lips. "Nothing of any great'a value is taken. An' there'sa much else that could'a been swiped within easy reach. Nothing broken. I think it's a trick. A prank."

"But why?"

"A few of the folk here, they don'ta like the new man," Frank said and shrugged. "They don'ta like that he's our mayor, that he seems to think he'sa better than everyone else. So how do they make'a him look foolish?" He lifted his hand. "Simple, eh? They give him a problem that'a he can't fix. It don'ta hurt nobody, but it make'a the teacher look foolish, useless. Maybe they hope'a to send him on his way. Maybe a man who wanted to be mayor instead, he gets his way. That'sa what I think."

Beth dropped her gaze to her lap. *Is it possible? Could Fred be this crafty?* He certainly was associated with the men on horseback—the only horses she could remember seeing in town. She searched Frank's face. In his guarded way, Frank had as much as accused him. *Surely he's not the only one around to wonder if Fred Green is the instigator.*

❈

7   The moon shone brightly as Jarrick followed Beth and Julie through the front gate and out onto the main road. Julie hurried ahead while Beth dawdled beside Jarrick, hoping for a few stolen moments alone. They had visited

at Frank and Molly's until almost midnight, and Molly insisted Jarrick sleep on their sofa so as not to waken Philip so late.

"I'm so glad you drove out," Beth murmured.

He captured her hand with his and slowed their progress. "I've missed you so much. There are a million things I wanted to say to you, and now I can't think of any of them."

Beth leaned closer. "How long can you stay?"

"I have to leave tomorrow, early afternoon at the latest."

"That isn't very much time."

"I know, but at least it's something."

They passed his car parked in front of Abigail's. "Oh, say, I could read that letter to you now. I don't want to forget."

Beth looked around. The moon wasn't quite bright enough to illuminate a printed page.

"Come sit in the car," he suggested. "It'll be warmer, and I have a flashlight. It won't take long, but I want you to hear it."

He opened the passenger door for Beth and closed it quietly, then walked around and climbed in next to her, flashlight in hand. He said soberly, "Do you remember the story I told you about when I was young—the incident with the neighbor's tractor?"

"Yes. It was damaged on purpose, but no one knew who was to blame."

"And my father ended up paying for it, since I had been accused."

Beth could still hear the pain in his voice from the memory. "I remember. You said that sometimes people in town, even in your own family, still bring it up, some joking about it."

He nodded. "Well, I just got this in the mail from my mother. She wrote that when that neighbor passed away, his wife found something in his desk and thought I might like to have it. His wife told my mother that she never believed it had been my doing— that it simply didn't fit the boy she knew. The letter is from my father to the neighbor, Ernest Adler, and was sent along with the payment."

Beth accepted the yellowed piece of paper, positioning it in the light of the flashlight.

Dear Mr. Adler,

I am submitting payment to you for the damage done to your machinery. I want you to know that it is in no way an indication of my belief that my son is guilty. However, you have stated that your intention is to pursue the matter in court, and in God's Word we are admonished as Christians that brother should not take brother to the courts of the world. So I am paying the sum you've requested, even though I still have faith in my son's honesty concerning the matter. I trust that the Judge of all will set things to right someday.

Humbly yours,
Graeme Thornton

Beth could feel the tears filling her eyes. "He believed you all along, Jarrick," she said in a shaky voice. "I'm so glad for you." Resting her head on his shoulder she asked softly, "Will you go back now and try to clear your name? I know how much that mattered to you."

"There's no need." Jarrick refolded the page. "My father trusted me, even though he never found words to tell me himself. That's all I need to know. And it's such a burden lifted from my shoulders. I feel free—washed inside and out, in a way. Both my earthly father and my heavenly Father have pronounced me guiltless. So it doesn't really matter what others say."

"It's so strange," she mused. "He could have so easily spoken with you about it at any time. I wonder why he didn't."

"I'm not sure. Maybe he never thought it was important. Maybe he didn't want to embarrass me, or just wasn't sure how to bring it up. My father isn't a man of many words."

"But you've carried the hurt for so long."

"I know. Then again, I could have asked him about it. And I didn't. Sometimes what goes unsaid is painful. I'm not sure why we don't share more freely." He tucked the letter back into his pocket. "Let's not be foolish like that, Beth. Let's be open and honest with one another. Always."

Beth snuggled against his arm, grateful he had been given the affirmation he had yearned for over the years.

Early the next morning Beth hurried to Molly's in order to have as much time with Jarrick as possible. She learned that he had already gone out with Frank to check the snow beside the mill for tracks.

"Marnie, do you know when they'll be back?" she asked, disappointed.

"They didn't say."

Beth sat at the parlor window with a cup of coffee. She waited two long hours before the men appeared on the road, Robert with them. She moved away from the window and let the lace curtain fall back into place, wishing she could avoid having to interact with the man. But she did want to be with Jarrick for as long as he was available. Reluctantly, Beth moved toward the entry.

Jarrick's face lit as soon as she appeared. "Good morning."

"Did you find anything?"

One by one he pulled the boots from his feet, exposing thick gray wool socks. "No, they were gone, but I've no doubt that Frank's friend saw what he claims. And he took us to the camp at the river's bend too. If it were an official investigation I'd record his statement, but no one seems interested in taking a strong stand in this case."

Robert had draped his jacket over his arm, carrying his boots in the other hand, and prepared to retreat to his bedroom. "I don't expect to hear about this matter again once the council is apprised of recent events. And for that I am grateful, Constable. Mr. Russo." He tipped his hat toward the two men.

"Frank did most of the work on this. Frank and Morgan," Jarrick said. "But I'm glad to know this nonsense will soon be behind you. We still don't know exactly who and why, but it seems likely the motive was to create trouble for you, Robert."

"I'm in your debt, at any rate." Robert began to climb the stairs and then turned back. "Oh yes, and addressing a second matter, if I may. I have received a . . . well, a rather clear indication from my fiancée that we shall not be requiring a home as early as I had first anticipated. The house we are building here should be completed in an adequate time frame. Therefore, I shall recommend that the house we intended to rent from the company be allocated instead to Mr. and Mrs. Harold Edwards, if that seems suitable."

Beth raised a hand to her mouth. *The McDermotts are moving out in less than a week!* Molly hurried in from the kitchen, face alight, and Frank was smiling broadly. "It'sa very kind of you, Mr. Harris Hughes. Very kind."

"Not at all. I'd be living there myself in wedded bliss if I could just get my Ivy to settle down with me. But that's Ivy—she makes up her own mind." He turned rather abruptly to continue on up the stairs.

Chapter 25

Waving good-bye to Jarrick after so little time with him was almost more painful than not having seen him at all. Beth's feet refused to move from the porch, her eyes fixed on the spot where Jarrick's car had disappeared.

Bring him back safely, Father. She turned back toward the house with the firm resolve to help Harold and Marnie move into a home of their own. *What will they need?* She mentally sorted, thinking of several items she never used and could easily do without—a second cast-iron skillet, a padded footstool, a spare oil lamp, a set of sheets, and some dishes. She would gather them up for the newlyweds.

Julie too had decided to contribute a house-warming gift for Marnie, settling on a small collection of creams and some fancy-smelling soaps from the store display. She urged Beth to come with her as she made up her gift.

The bell above the door announced their presence, and they joined a rather large number of shoppers inside. Nodding in one direction and then another, they slipped toward Julie's small table. To their surprise they found Robert standing with an open jar of lotion in his hand, sniffing it carefully. He replaced its lid and exchanged it for another. Beth was amazed, but Julie went right over with a smile.

"May I help you, Mr. Harris Hughes?"

He looked up quickly, obviously uncomfortable. "Oh, yes, I thought I might . . . might purchase a lotion. Can you tell me what . . . which one Ivy might like?"

"Of course. This is one she recommended to me." Julie handed it to him. "Is she in town? Is she planning a visit? I'd love to see her again."

"No. No, I was just thinking about her." He cleared his throat and backed away. "Uh, thank you, but I think I'll wait until I have something else to buy also." He hurried out the door.

"What on earth?" Beth gazed after him. "He was actually flustered."

Julie caught Beth's arm. "You know what

he was doing? He wasn't planning to buy it for her at all. He just misses her that much."

"I don't understand."

"He wanted to catch a bit of her fragrance, to feel as if she were near again."

Beth shook her head in wonder as Julie gathered the items she had planned for Marnie. Then her sister laughed and held up one of the remaining lotions. "I'm giving this to Robert. I'll put it on his desk," she announced with a wink. "I like that he misses her so much. It's romantic!"

How can such a logical man like Robert be so thoroughly in love? It seems such a contradiction of terms.

~❖~

On Wednesday the McDermotts bid farewell before heading out toward the prairie. Every inch of their borrowed truck was crammed full with their worldly possessions. Beth stood among the crowd sending them off after giving notes of encouragement to Peter and Alice, two growing teenagers that Beth knew she would miss. She felt sorry that Sadie Shaw was losing her best friend, and that James and Kenny would no longer be part of a trio.

Soon she stood with Marnie, Molly, and Julie in the empty house, assessing what should be done first. A knock announced Abigail and Ruth with buckets and rags, ready to help with cleaning. Their help was not really necessary since the house was small, but their cheerful chatter and enthusiasm were appreciated even more than their share in the work.

Marnie hung a worn sheet over the window in the bedroom, effusively describing the curtains she'd soon make to replace it. "A field of dark blue speckled with appliquéd stars, so it will always look like night," she explained. She fussed over all aspects of the home, her shining eyes unable to conceal her excitement as each piece of furniture was arranged and re-arranged. It was a dreamland for Marnie, her own bit of heaven on earth. Beth wanted so badly to be thrilled for the girl's sake. And yet she couldn't help but wonder if there would ever be more in her future, or if this would be the whole of Marnie's designated lot in life.

Lingering after the others had left, Beth perched precariously on top of the small dining table to dust the last of the rafters for cobwebs. "I think that's all, Marnie."

"Oh, Miss Thatcher, thank you so much. Everything feels so fresh an' clean. I can't believe we got one of the new houses. Hardly feels like anyone else lived here at all."

Beth forced a smile and offered one last

hug before reaching for her coat. "When does Harold come home?"

"His shift is almost over. The whistle'll blow 'most anytime now. And the soup Molly brought is already heatin'. I think I'll fix some biscuits ta go with. I don't have a bakin' pan for 'em, but I can just use that skillet ya brought. It'll work in the oven if I grease it well."

Beth squeezed Marnie's shoulder. "God bless you, darling."

Marnie blushed. "He has. Oh, He truly has."

Stepping out onto the stoop, Beth pushed her hands deep into her pockets to ward off the chill. *She's so happy. And that's something—an important something.* Then she thought about babies and how impatient Marnie seemed with everything. *Please, Father, can You please help them wait? At least until after she's finished school.*

Slowly she descended Marnie's steps to the ground now frozen once more, her thoughts still on the very young wife she'd just left. *If only she can just finish school.*

The sky was filled with clouds, and with so little light, Beth found it difficult to pick her way across the small yard and through the shortcut between the houses. Her shoe caught on a slender stump, and she started to stumble. With her hands pinned deep inside her coat pockets, Beth fell forward onto her shoulder, banging the side of her head against the hard ground. For a moment she lay still, stunned, tears filling her eyes from the pain.

She managed to extract her hands from the jacket pockets and push up off the frigid ground. Already her churning emotion had turned to anger, which grew with every limping step toward home. *Those horrid stumps! I knew they'd cause accidents. And I'm sure I'm not the first.* The tears dried quickly as she neared Molly's gate, her anger now full boil. *I'm going to get Teddy's ax from the woodshed.* She would chop the irksome thing out herself. The stump wasn't very large. It would be only a small victory, but she might feel a little better.

Returning to the scene, she poked her foot around in the shadowy area until she was certain she was aligned with the correct stump. She clutched the long handle of the ax and raised the heavy blade above her head. It came down almost sideways, striking the ground with a dull thud. She lifted it again and positioned the head more precisely. This time it merely bounced off the narrow top.

She muttered with each succeeding attempt. "It should've been the men doing this job! Why haven't the fathers taken care of these long ago?" Beth chopped away, covering the narrow stump with wounds. "Am I the only one in town who worries about the children? What if one of them falls and lands on it? There's no doctor for miles!" The work was frustrating, and new tears and sweat rolled down her face and neck. Still she had not managed to detach the stubborn trunk from its roots.

"Hello?"

Beth froze, the ax high above her head. She waited, hoping the female voice was speaking to someone else.

"Who's there?" the woman asked again.

Beth lowered the ax. "It's just me—Beth Thatcher."

"What on earth are ya doin', Miss Thatcher?"

"Well, I . . . I'm trying to chop out this stump."

"Yer what?"

"There's a stump. I tripped over it. So I thought I would just . . . would remove it so that no one else tripped here."

The woman was merely a silhouette in the darkness. "Honey, there's jus' too many ta dig out. Might as well leave it where it is. 'Sides, it's too much work, 'specially in the dark. These stumps got a big ol' tap root goes a long ways down. Hard enough fer a man. You're likely to wear yerself out tryin'."

Beth felt her face grow even warmer as she recognized Sadie's mother, Rose Shaw, who played the organ. She hoped her voice would hold true. "I might try a little longer. It's ... it's kind of satisfying just now." But Beth gave up trying to make someone else understand when she really couldn't herself.

Rose pulled her wrap closer. "You can suit yerself, honey, but just don't catch yer death of cold."

"Thank you. Yes, thank you." As soon as Rose disappeared around the corner, Beth fled. It was a purely childish, vain attempt to achieve a small victory. *For whom? For the children? For Marnie? Or for myself?*

As she returned the ax and slipped quietly away to her stairway, Beth wondered how many children would be laughing tomorrow as they retold Rose's tale of their teacher's nighttime encounter and showed off the battered, yet still intact, stump as evidence.

Though on edge most of the morning, Beth was surprised and relieved no one mentioned the incident. She would be ever grateful to Rose if the story remained untold. But when the woman's husband appeared in the entryway as the students departed for home, Beth wondered if something would come to light after all.

"Miss Thatcher." Bill Shaw tipped his hat but simply passed by her door, knocking instead at Robert's classroom.

"Robert, something else has turned up." His voice was alarmingly loud. Beth noticed the door between the classrooms was ajar. She crept toward it, intending to close it quickly without being noticed.

"Good heavens. What is it now?"

"More serious this time, I'm afraid. It's regarding a student. Well, a recent student from this classroom."

A thump, as if Robert had closed a book hard. "Who might that be?"

"Alice McDermott."

Beth halted, her breath catching in alarm.

"And of what am I accused?" A chair scraped the floor, and his throat cleared.

"I've been told you met with her privately on more than one occasion. That you behaved in a less than gentlemanly manner, and that possibly it was for this reason her parents moved away."

Beth felt herself begin to tremble, and she sank against the bookshelf, closing her eyes against the awful words.

"That's ridiculous!" he spat out. "She's

a child. And I'm engaged." Beth could hear the jangle of coins in Robert's pocket, could picture how he was standing just now. "I suppose I did meet with her twice, or thrice perhaps, to tutor her in mathematics. But there were always others nearby. It was at lunch, I believe."

"Now, Robert, you know it's my job to take these things seriously."

More footsteps, louder this time. "Mr. Shaw, I implore you. What you're saying is preposterous. There's not a shred of truth to it—and no proof either."

"We've already begun the investigation."

"How so?"

"I'll be driving out tomorrow with Lloyd Edwards to speak with the McDermotts. If there's anything to it at all, there'll be a formal hearing. At that point it will be out of my hands, Robert. The district will take over."

A long silence then. "I understand." A heavy sigh. "Do as you see fit. I submit to your authority."

Beth backed away, quietly lifting her jacket from its hook and abandoning further grading. She slipped through the entry and hurried home, arriving pale with shock.

Seeing Beth's face, Julie rose to meet her. "What's wrong, Bethie?"

"Oh, everything. Just everything."

Seated outside on the lowest step, Beth idly watched murky clouds gathering. *Snow again, and Mother and Father arrive soon.* Penelope slid her fat body in and out between Beth's legs, begging for another treat, of which there had been many since the incident with the bear.

"Come here, kitty dear," Beth murmured, reaching down to rub Penelope's chin, the tabby's favorite spot. Purring loudly, the animal dropped to her back and wriggled gratefully.

Is there any truth to the charge? Could Robert have taken advantage of his position? As low as Beth's opinion had been of him, there was really no question as to what she believed in her heart. *It can't be true. Unless I hear it from Alice herself, or from her parents, I can't believe such a dreadful thing of him.* Beth recalled Ivy's description. *She's right. He's too predictable and . . . what was her word? Yes, stalwart. That's who he is. As well as honest. Candid to a fault.* She recalled how generous he was to Harold and Marnie, and how the young bride had glowed when hearing of his offer.

Beth picked up the cat and settled it on her lap, stroking Penelope's back and listening to her purr. A sudden realization turned her absolutely still. *I have spent more effort befriending this stray than extending any care or hand of friendship to Robert. Created in God's image, he's a person for whom Jesus died, whether acknowledged by him or not.*

The whole idea was appalling to consider. She slid the cat down to the ground and leaned over, face in her hands. *I'm sorry, Lord. So sorry for my unkindness, for my ungodly attitude, for the ways I've nurtured my prejudices against him.*

After a time of further prayer in deep penitence, she felt a peace begin to steal into her heart, and she knew she was forgiven. *Now, Lord, what do You want me to do about Robert? Please give me wisdom and grace during this very difficult time.*

Frank turned out to be the source of Beth's updates on Robert's situation. Her fellow teacher said nothing to Beth during school and had even become rather reclusive. Frank explained that the ride out to the prairie where the McDermotts now lived had proved rather fruitless. Though Alice had denounced every one of the charges as false, someone else had already contacted the district on their own. A hearing had been set. Beth was shocked to hear that it would be held in Coal Valley on the very day of her wedding.

Poor Robert! Poor Ivy! Dear God, help us all.

"Molly, do you have a moment to talk?"

"'Course, dearie. What is it ya need?"

Beth blew out a long breath. *How to begin?* "It's about Robert. I'm afraid, well, that I've been rather unfair to him, whatever turns out to be the truth in the hearing."

"I believe I did warn ya."

Beth propped her elbows on the table, where Molly was making a pie, and sighed. "Yes. Yes, you did."

"And now?"

"Now I feel like I'm between a rock and a hard place. I believe he's being falsely accused. Likely the same troublemakers who stacked the pile of rubbish in the woods have stepped up their efforts to drive him from town. But I'm ashamed to admit I've been about as good a friend to him as they are."

Molly didn't argue, merely suggesting, "Ain't too late to amend yer ways."

Again Beth sighed. Molly slid a paring knife over to Beth, who reached into the bowl of apples, slowly removing a long strand of peel. Molly set to work with a second blade.

"I really tried to keep my heart pure, especially after you and Frank prayed with me about it."

"Oh, a heart's a poor choice to follow. It's so easily hoodwinked."

"I know that now. And I regret how long it's taken me to recognize my misjudgment."

Molly set down her own knife rather abruptly and rested her arms on the table. "I'm gonna tell ya something I ain't talked about fer a very long time, dearie—leastwise with any other than Frank."

Beth continued to peel, wondering what was coming next.

"I told ya it took some time fer me to learn my lessons too."

"I remember."

"But I s'pose I shoulda been more clear. Shoulda confessed how *far* amiss I've been." Molly shook her head slowly. "Long ago, when my Bertram and me first come to Coal Valley an' bought this big ol' house, it made me feel all head and shoulders above everybody. Ya see, I'd never lived so grand before. So I got myself a mite filled up with pride, I guess. There were them miners all about, not many of 'em settled enough to bring along their wives. An' they was comin' to our door fer meals an' fer a room. So I felt a little like their queen."

Beth raised her eyebrows, trying to picture Molly putting on airs.

"And then this young man I never even

met had set his cap fer a girl—a little young, to be sure. But she was eligible just the same. And there was talk. Oh, lots of talk. That he weren't good enough fer her, being a humble immigrant, an' the like. I let myself join in." She paused. "I should'a known better even then, but I fell right in with it."

Beth froze and held her breath. "Frank."

Molly was already dabbing at an eye. She swallowed hard before she said, "Yes, my Frank—an' his sweet Colette."

"Oh, Molly!"

"Ya see, dearie. Ya see how wrong a heart can be. I up and convinced myself that I knew best, that it shouldn't be tolerated. An' I stood with the ones who tried ta keep 'em apart. Thank the Good Lord He knew better."

There was silence as Molly gathered her thoughts and Beth took in all the implications. "But he forgave you, Molly."

"That he did. He's a good ol' soul. He'd worked out his part long 'fore I come to terms with mine. Ya see, I was there when she delivered her daughter. There weren't nobody else ta speak of, an' I worked the best I could ta save 'em. Both of 'em. But they died despite all I knew to try." The words were strained, her chin quivering. "An' my Bertram helped to dig their graves. Bertram and some'a the other men. We all were sorry by then, but ya can't go back an' fix a mistake sometimes."

Beth reached her hand to Molly's arm. "It wasn't your fault they died, Molly. I'm sure they knew you did your best."

"That I did. But them two should'a been allowed their chance to be together sooner. Their time was so short as it was, but they could'a had another year of joy."

Molly pulled a handkerchief from her sleeve and blew her nose. "Like I said, I did talk with Frank. We made our peace with the past. But I don't wanna see ya do the same. It ain't worth it, dearie. Ya gotta let God be God, and ya gotta remember that you ain't Him."

Beth leaned her head against Molly's shoulder. "I understand what you mean, but how? How do I know—"

"Best as I can say, ya follow the two rules. Ya love the Lord yer God with all yer heart an' all yer soul, and ya love the rest like ya would yerself."

Beth choked a little. "I thought . . . I was trying to protect the children—the way I didn't protect Julie from Nick in the kidnapping."

"But, Beth, you ain't the Almighty. You can't ever entirely protect no one. Ya do what you know to do, an' He does the rest."

The thought began to resonate at last. She had never been assigned responsibility over such sweeping matters. She did not have the power to *ensure* anyone's safety. She could do what she knew was right, and the rest was in God's hands.

Molly went on. "When ya take control, yer rollin' the dice that ya understand it all. That yer able to see the end from the beginning. But none of us can. All we can do is go right back to number one and number two. We gotta love—and love some more. An' we gotta pray that God will do His part and do the safekeeping we ain't able to do. I know I ain't got college learnin', but I been through all the levels in the school of hard knocks, believe me. An' I finally got that much sense in my head."

"Oh, Molly. Sometimes I think I'll never grow up."

"Miss Thatcher, a word please?"

Beth had been expecting it, had been certain that eventually Robert would address the issue. If her "*good opinion*" mattered to him as he had claimed, she knew he would feel the need to speak to her.

Her voice held sympathy. "Of course, Mr. Harris Hughes. Please come in."

He took half a step forward, hands in his pockets, and paused again. He was looking beyond her, as if contemplating the picture of the king hanging on the wall above Beth's head. "Miss Thatcher, no doubt you're aware of the predicament in which I now find myself. There's no point in my denying to you the assertions that have been made. You must by now have already drawn your own conclusions on the matter."

Beth's brows drew together, and she finally managed, "I was told that Alice herself said you did nothing wrong, Mr. Harris Hughes."

He released a long sigh. "But Alice isn't here, Miss Thatcher. And hence the matter is compounded."

"Yes, I do understand. What can I do?"

There was a weighty silence, as if he were trying to gather courage. "I was hoping . . . wondering if you might speak on my behalf as a character reference during the hearing on Saturday after next."

"I'm so sorry." Beth shook her head slowly. His doleful expression was almost unbearable. "I'm afraid that's impossible. It's to be held on the same day as my wedding. There's no way to postpone the ceremony. All of my family will be here—and Jarrick's. There's no way I can be available on that day. I'm truly very sorry."

He cleared his throat. "I understand.

Thank you, just the same," he said, his voice strained.

For the first time, Beth wished she could have offered a hug. A kind word seemed vastly insufficient. "I'll pray for you, Robert. I'll pray for justice."

He smiled feebly and sighed. "At this point, Miss Thatcher, I will accept help from wherever it may come."

Chapter
26

Beth paced impatiently with Julie on the wooden sidewalk in front of Coulter's store, their sight fastened on the road to the east. The recent days, like a line of dominoes, had toppled forward one after another at breakneck speed, and now it was the Sunday afternoon before the long-awaited finale on Saturday.

As thrilled as she was at the upcoming event, Beth was already conscious of the fact that she would miss her fun-loving, unpredictable sister very much. All of Julie's possessions had been packed up, even her skis carefully wrapped for shipment east. The little upstairs dwelling would soon be home to Beth and Jarrick, at least until the end of the school year. Beth gave her head a little shake at the uncertainties to follow. *Thank You, Lord, that I can trust it all to You.*

Even Julie's little display of lotions inside the store had been dismantled, and after a box for Ivy had been set aside, the remaining items were distributed among the women of town. *It was never about making money,* Beth thought, looking with love at this dear sister. *She's not disappointed in her little enterprise, only satisfied that it was something to do and maybe a way to leave her mark on our little town.*

There'd been no ride into Lethbridge available to meet their parents at the train station. The sisters were relieved to hear that Jarrick had taken care of those arrangements, hiring a car to bring their parents to Coal Valley. They should arrive any moment.

The upcoming week would be full—with school and final wedding preparations, as well as relishing the short time together. On Friday morning Jarrick would drive out with his family.

There was a low rumble in the distance, and a black car emerged around the last curve, slowing as it approached the boardwalk.

Beth and Julie rushed toward the vehicle, calling out and pulling open the passenger doors before it had come to a complete stop. Beth threw her arms around Father. "I've dreamed of this for so long, I can't believe you're really here!"

"Gracious," he answered, stepping out onto the dirt street and chuckling as he returned her enthusiastic embrace. "With such a vigorous welcome, I wondered if the two of you were accosting us."

"Oh, Father." Beth fell into his arms again. They all exchanged a round of hugs, though Mother was somewhat distracted by her attempts to view the surroundings.

"It is very small, darling. You told us as much, but I had pictured something a bit more."

"Well, there are more houses farther down the hill," Beth assured her. "You can't really see them all from here—some are behind those trees. But you'll stay over there, in the boarding house. That's Molly's, and I think you'll be very comfortable. And"—Beth threw her arms wide and turned in place, thrilled to share her love for the surroundings—"what do you think of this view?"

"It's magnificent," Father answered for them both. "I've heard these mountains described on occasion, but words have not done them justice, nor even photographs. They're absolutely majestic, Beth. And rather frightening by car." They all laughed, except for Mother, who was still gazing about.

Beth hugged her mother again as Father moved to the trunk and the luggage.

"Now, darling," Mother said, "I thought we would be staying with you. I was looking forward to your hosting us."

"That almost happened," Beth said with a laugh. "And you have no idea what a blessing it is that you won't be staying in my tiny place. Molly's daughter, Marnie, just got married and moved out. It's a long story. But you'll stay in the bedroom that was Marnie's at the boarding house."

"Beth's home is right there"—Julie pointed—"above the teahouse. On the second floor." She grinned impishly as she waited for their reaction.

"The second floor? There *is* a second floor?"

"Why, yes, Mother," Julie answered. "But it's, shall we say, rather petite, hidden away under the roof. An attic, really. However, it's very snug and comfy—at least it has been for the two of us. Four . . . well, that would have meant you and Father on the bed, and Beth and I sharing a borrowed mattress tucked under the eaves!"

Beth didn't know whether to laugh at her sister's delight in adding to their mother's consternation or to send her a stern look. She decided on neither when she looked at the poor woman's uncertainties. She stepped over to guide her. "This way, Mother, not far at all."

Father tucked a smaller case under his arm and lifted two more by the handles. "Well, you'll have to show us where you live later. For now, lead on."

Beth escorted her parents to Molly's, filling the short walk with brief information about the town and its residents. The door opened at their first footfall, and Frank welcomed them heartily.

"Come in, please," he said, warmth beaming out from his whiskered face. "We're so glad'a to see you arrive safely."

"Father, this is Frank Russo. Frank, these are my parents, William and Priscilla Thatcher. And this is Frank's wife, my dear friend Molly Russo—and their son, Teddy."

"We're so pleased ya could stay with us," Molly told them, sincerity in every wrinkle and expression as she shook their hands.

They were shown to their room, given a chance to freshen up, and soon settled comfortably in the parlor, enjoying the modest hospitality Molly offered. Beth was nearly beside herself when her mother produced a small album of Josiah's baby pictures, and she and Julie huddled over it, exclaiming over every milestone in the baby's three-month history.

It seemed almost unbelievable to Beth that so many of the people she loved could be in one place. She stole quick glances at her mother, who seemed to have come to terms with the rather austere surroundings and was making a point of joining in the conversations, particularly with stories about young JW, who had proclaimed himself chief caregiver for his *"litto brudder."* After supper her father persuaded Frank and Beth to play several duets on their violins, ending the evening with tranquility. For the first time since her parents' arrival, Beth could see that her mother was truly impressed.

Monday morning came, and school had its own demands, regardless of the visitors. As Beth carted home the daily grading, she was glad to see Julie, but also a bit envious her sister was able to be with their parents so much. In addition to normal tasks, Beth now had extra preparations for her upcoming week-long absence for the honeymoon. Jarrick still had not even hinted at any more details in his last letter, but it was a pleasant secret to anticipate.

"Bethie? I asked you a question."

Beth turned toward her sister. "Sorry. What?"

"I asked if you were going to have Bible club tomorrow night."

"No. No, we've decided we're done for the year. The mothers suggested it, actually. They felt I'd be too busy with wedding responsibilities—and a new marriage."

"Well, I predict you'll have trouble focusing on anything else for a while," Julie teased, "if tonight is any sign of what's to come."

Beth looked down at the blank lesson-book page. Robert would be overseeing her class on Friday, and the new school board had located a substitute for the week of the honeymoon. Her completed lesson plans for those days were essential. *I have to concentrate,* she told herself as she bent over the page. *I've got to get this finished.*

"Is there any more news about Robert?"

In truth, there had been much talk about Robert's predicament. Residents gathered in small clusters wherever their paths crossed to share their dismay and their opinions at what was transpiring. Beth found herself frequently coming to his defense. Alice held no accusation against her teacher. But the community was largely against Robert. *If only there was a way to bring the girl, and maybe her mother, back to Coal Valley to testify at the hearing. Surely it would put an end to any further questions.* Beth tapped her pen against the inkwell thoughtfully. *I wonder if Ivy will make an appearance too, a show of support.*

"Bethie," Julie said in her best teacher voice, shaking her finger, "you'll never finish if you can't keep your mind on the lesson."

Laughing, Beth shot back, "Then you'll have to stop asking me questions, my dear."

By Thursday Beth's nerves were beginning to fray. At least school duties were behind her. The plan was to decorate the church that evening. The grand parade of carrying all the things Beth, Marnie, and Julie had fashioned for the event to the church began just after supper and took advantage of all available assistance. A car was offered, but Beth was afraid the delicate fabrics would be crushed if stacked atop one another. She felt a bit demanding to insist on her own way, but she gave instructions anyway. The finery was carried to the church by hand.

Beth's father and Frank sorted and hung the decor as instructed, leaving the ladies to fuss over the pieces, fluffing and repositioning the layers. As each bow was carefully inspected and discussed among the women—Priscilla and Julie, Beth and Molly—the men stood back and listened silently, occasionally offering a sideways grin and murmuring comments they didn't want to be heard. Whenever asked, they would shrug and reposition anything not quite right.

Soon the sanctuary began to look like a snowy fairyland, just as Beth had envisioned it. Dark-stained pews held soft white bows, the windows held clusters of white fabric flowers, and the stage was draped in white tulle. It was lovely—all, that is, except for the arch Beth had hoped could be crafted for the platform.

"What about draping something from the ceiling, darling, on wires perhaps?" Mother wondered.

"Too high," Molly countered, tapping her lip as she gazed upward. "Them wires would sag and look all droopy. Something out of wood?"

Priscilla shook her head doubtfully. "It couldn't be finished properly in time."

"You're right, Mother." Beth shook her head. "It's fine as it is. In fact, it's very beautiful. No one else will be expecting an arch, so they won't miss it."

"But *you'll* miss it," Julie objected. "And you do have some fabric left over. It's in the back room now. Do you want me to get it?"

"No, thanks. I don't need to have *everything* I might want. This is elegant as it is. I'm so grateful—so very blessed."

As Beth pulled the door closed behind them she reminded herself that it was, indeed, very lovely. She could focus on what was incomplete, or she could appreciate the beauty—and the blessing of having so many family members present.

⁂

"Mama, I'd like to introduce you to William and Priscilla Thatcher," Jarrick announced over the commotion in the crowded entryway to Molly's home. "Mother Thatcher, this is Sigrid Thornton. And my father, Graeme," he said, motioning, "is hanging up the coats." He pointed above the heads. "And in the doorway are my brothers Wilfred and Roland, and my little sister, Laura."

"So pleased to meet you all." Beth's mother extended a hand to Jarrick's mother. "I'm glad you arrived safely. You must be rather weary from your trip."

"It was a pretty tight squeeze for so many of us in one car, but Jarrick followed in a borrowed truck with our luggage, along with his own possessions for relocating to Coal Valley once they've returned from the honeymoon. At any rate, we're here at last. And we've been so excited to meet all of you. Jarrick has shared so many nice things."

The woman was petite, and Jarrick had

clearly inherited his height from his lanky father. But there was little doubt as to who had passed on his ginger-colored hair. The slip of a woman was still wearing a black-brimmed hat, but thick red braids curled out from beneath it. "Now, where is your Beth?" she queried, looking around.

"I'm here." Beth quickly pushed herself forward, her stomach fluttering. "I'm so glad you've come so far, Mrs. Thornton. Welcome." She reached out to shake hands and could feel the eyes of her future mother-in-law assessing her.

"We haven't ventured nearly as far as your own folks have. Goodness, all the way from Ontario! It must have been quite a ride by train."

Mother said, "It was long, but not unpleasant. We felt we got a good sense of Manitoba's landscape as we went through—it's a very *broad* country, quite flat, I thought. However, I'm sure it must be a farmer's dream."

"Not so wide open as Saskatchewan, I think."

Beth could feel the fluttering gain intensity. She cast a glance to Jarrick in hopes he'd find a way to deflect the conversation.

"Have they unloaded yet, Mama? Should we do that now?"

"There's no need just yet. We'll send you

boys out after a bit. For now, I'm sure we'd all like to get to know one another better. And, Mrs. Russo, if it's not too much trouble, something hot would be very welcome just now."

"I've the kettle on already, Mrs. Thornton. Soon as it starts ta singin' there'll be tea and coffee both—or ice water, if ya like. Why don't ya all take a seat in the dinin' room? I'll bring some sweets to start with."

Beth filed in along with the others, each hesitant to take one of the few chairs. Already Teddy was hustling more chairs from the kitchen. Soon they were all settled snugly around the large table, Beth and Jarrick seated between the two mothers.

"Your home is very nice, Mrs. Russo," Mrs. Thornton told her. "No wonder Jarrick described it as the center of town."

Molly shrugged and answered easily, "Nobody else's got a home big enough fer so many. I'm grateful fer what God provided, but fer my family most of all."

Jarrick's mother only raised her eyebrows in response.

Beth could feel her fingers clenched together on her lap. *Is it just my nerves, or is there already tension? I can't imagine why. Is this what Jarrick means?*

Teatime proceeded with casual conversation, but Beth continued to feel that people were being too rigidly congenial. She worried that it didn't bode well for the pressures of their time together.

For their stay in Coal Valley, Jarrick's family had elected to sleep at the schoolhouse in Beth's classroom. They would lay bedding on the floor, use the privy behind the building, and carry in buckets of water for washing. It was primitive but not altogether different from how the rest of the townspeople lived.

Molly had invited the out-of-town guests to eat in shifts at her place. Father insisted on paying for her hospitality, and the two were still trapped in an amiable contest of wills over the matter. Beth was rather certain Father would be victorious, one way or another. *Though, I believe he's met his match.*

As soon as Jarrick's mother had sent her three sons off to move their family's luggage into the schoolrooms—almost as quickly as the door closed behind them—she turned to Beth. "I've heard that you've already decorated the church. We would have helped, you know. Laura and I have a good eye for detail."

"It was no trouble, Mrs. Thornton. Just one less thing to do."

"May we see it, dear?"

Beth wished there was some way to suggest

they wait for Jarrick, but her mind faltered. "Of course." She tried a smile.

Leading the way, Beth walked with the five women to the church, her heart beating with apprehension. She was certain her own mother would not take well to anything that sounded like criticism. She slowly opened the door, relieved that it really did look beautiful. *I just hope . . .*

"Why, it's lovely. And you made all of these flowers, dear, by hand?" Mrs. Thornton complimented. "How clever. But weren't there any roses to be found? I'm sure you could have had some shipped in. Perhaps we could have brought them with us. What will you do for a bouquet?"

Mother cleared her throat as if to answer, but Beth hurried to reply, "We're making that too, Julie and I, but . . . uh, it's going to be a surprise." Biting a fingernail, she followed the group, trying to avoid commenting and refusing to meet Julie's eye. She knew without looking that her sister was already in danger of rolling her eyes in frustration.

"Your pew bows are charming. Wouldn't a nice red rose or two have just set them off? Or pink lilies from a greenhouse? Yes, that's what I would have done. What do you think, Laura? Oh well, what's done is done." She walked to the front and looked at the platform for a moment. "Oh, there's something missing. Don't you think so? It needs a central focal point. Something to draw the eye."

Julie's voice from behind Beth echoed confidently through the large room. "Oh, it won't be lacking a thing tomorrow, Mrs. Thornton. You see, Bethie will be the focal point. All eyes will be on her and on Jarrick. We wouldn't want anything to take away from that, would we?" Passing nearby, Julie reached out to squeeze Beth's hand and moved on.

Beth's mind hummed, trying to sort through the difficulties. *Love God. Oh yes. Love people—well, that's more difficult. This is her son's wedding too, though. Something she's been wanting for some time. I'll treat her respectfully, lovingly—not just for Jarrick's sake, but for her own.*

"I'm sorry it's not what you envisioned, Mother Thornton," Beth began. "It's the best we have to offer so far from . . . well, so far from almost everything." She gestured toward the windows. "But please remember the wonderful view. God's creation is breathtaking— so much more than anything we can try to duplicate. I'm so blessed to be married in such grand surroundings."

Beth quickly moved to another subject. "Did you find everything you needed at the school? Perhaps we can make you more

comfortable there. Do you have enough blankets?"

The little group was soon finished with
their inspection, and Beth breathed a sigh of
relief as she shut the church door.

Chapter
27

Although Beth regretted leaving Mother alone with Mrs. Thornton and Molly, there was still her bridal bouquet to assemble. Her fingers trembled a little as she drew the box from its place in the wardrobe and laid out the final wedding project on the table. There was little doubt as to what her mother-in-law-to-be would think. *Homemade, no fresh flowers.* The woman would find it inadequate. *But I love it, and I'm certain Jarrick will too. So I won't let her steal away my joy.*

Working carefully with the delicate materials, Julie and Beth gathered the white rosettes they had fashioned out of folded lace handkerchiefs and attached to long wires for stems. Beth assembled them carefully into a tight rounded bunch. One after another she added a variety of glittering silver brooches on wires of the same length so that they stood even with the tops of the lace flowers, a scattering of sparkle and elegance. Finally, she took Molly's best embroidered handkerchief—Beth's *something borrowed* from a very special person—and carefully wrapped it tightly around the mock stems.

When Beth held up the finished bouquet, Julie pronounced it worthy of any high society wedding. She took it from Beth and held it against the wedding gown, now hanging on the outside of the wardrobe, and they both gasped in awe at how the two wedding pieces enhanced one another.

Next came simple boutonnieres fashioned out of various-sized white buttons, stacked two or three high and then clustered over a crisply folded, cornflower-blue man's handkerchief.

Just as the sisters were packing away the last of their work, they heard a knock at the door.

Beth rose to open it, somewhat fearful of whom she would find on the other side, and was relieved to discover Jarrick.

"Can we go someplace?" he said against her ear.

"Of course. Julie, I'll be back soon." Reaching for her wrap, she stepped out onto the landing and followed him down the steps.

"I know it's almost suppertime," he said softly, taking her arm and guiding her behind the building toward the clearing where Beth had once hosted a picnic. "I want some time with you—alone."

"I'd like that too."

Beth lowered herself onto a stump, and Jarrick pulled a log closer for himself.

"How did it go with my mother at the church? I was so afraid she'd criticize."

Beth shrugged. "She did. But she also said affirming things too. I'm sorry it isn't up to her vision—truly I am. But I have to say that I'm very pleased, even proud of what Julie and I accomplished, and Marnie too. It's a labor of love for us, Jarrick, and as long as we're satisfied, I think it's enough."

"I'm sure it's more than anything I had imagined."

"No doubt it is." Beth laughed and reached for his hand. "Since you didn't really bother imagining all that much."

He laughed too, looking a little embarrassed. Then his expression turned serious. "I'm sorry I didn't prepare you better to meet Mama. I thought about what else I might tell you so many times, but I was afraid of how it would sound—to effectively criticize my mother before you even met her. I didn't want to turn you against her. And in truth, what I want even now is to help you *understand* her."

Beth nodded guardedly, and he continued, "You see, she's from a large family, and her own mother, my grandmother, is quite blunt and outspoken. The daughters naturally picked up her manner. I promise you, Beth, I don't think they even know how they sound to other people. They all love each other, but they don't realize what others might think, beyond the family circle." Jarrick put his arm around her shoulders.

"But Laura told me how outspoken she was, and I want you to know that I'm sure she didn't mean to be hurtful. It's just the way she is. It's the only way she knows how to participate, to attempt some involvement with you in the wedding."

Is that what I'm to expect? Years of these awfully direct opinions? "You're asking that I simply ignore her?"

He rubbed a hand across his face, drew her closer. "No, not to ignore her. I'm asking you to love her. But in a way even more difficult than merely overlooking her words. I'm asking you to join me in respectfully, lovingly confronting her from time to time, communicating to her some lines we won't let her cross, in standing united about how we manage our own home. This was one of the things I spent extra time discussing with Lester Carothers, the man who counseled me." He turned to face Beth, his face full of his care for her, his concern. "I know it's a lot to ask, my Beth. But I promise to stand with you—to be a gate for you, ready to come between and close her off when it's too much. And I only ask that you be ready to allow her in as often as you're able." His hand rose to his cheek, and Beth realized with a jolt that he was wiping away a tear. His voice constricted with emotion. "I love her, Beth. She's my mother, after all. And loving someone isn't always easy."

Reaching to embrace him, Beth turned her face close to his. "I will. I'll love her with you."

"I was certain you would." Both arms folded around her. "I've watched you love all kinds of people, give yourself freely and sacrificially to them. It's one of the many things I treasure about you. I've been convinced you could handle Mama too—that we could manage together, that we'll form a bond close enough to weather any storm. It's not really what a bride wants to hear, I suppose. But if it serves to make our marriage stronger in the end, won't that be blessing enough?"

Her head on his shoulder, she silently nodded her agreement.

He started chuckling, and she lifted her head to look at him. "You know, I remember a long time ago when we first met," Jarrick explained. "You asked what my mother called me, and I told you '*Jarrick*'—and that's what you've always called me, instead of Jack like everyone else. I didn't say anything at the time, but it took a while for me to come to terms with that decision of yours. Because I haven't always liked my name. Or, maybe more accurately, the way I've heard it spoken." He kissed her gently. "It sounds so different coming from you though. It made me think about how I even like *who I am* more when I'm with you—the way you challenge me, expect the best from me. I believe we're better people when we're together. At least, I hope I make you feel the same way."

Beth's arms tightened around his neck. "I know I want more than anything to be your wife. I know you're the one God brought into my life to be my husband. So I'll accept whatever comes with you also."

His cheek brushed against her hair, and then he drew away to look into her face. "There's something else we need to discuss. Your father cornered me this afternoon, Beth. He wants to move forward with plans for our relocation east this summer."

Beth stared back at him, holding herself quiet.

"I wasn't sure how to answer him."

"You weren't?" she whispered.

Jarrick faltered. "I want you to have everything, sweetheart. But I don't have peace about that decision yet. Every time I pray, it doesn't feel quite right."

Beth closed her eyes, praying for courage to speak her mind honestly as she had promised him and leave the rest to the Lord. "I'm relieved to hear that."

"What . . . what do you mean?"

"I've tried not to direct you, to let you make the decision, but I fear that maybe it wouldn't be for the best."

"But, Beth, I thought you'd *want* to be near family, to have the comforts of the city. I just assumed it would be what you—"

"Oh, Jarrick," Beth whispered anxiously, "when have I ever said such a thing? But it's my fault, really. I should have talked honestly with you long before this. I just didn't want to . . . to sound like either *your* mother or mine. I wanted to let you be the leader of our new family. But what I really did was leave you to carry this burden alone. And now I don't think that's what God intended for a wife to do either."

He shook his head and breathed in deeply. "Oh, Beth, I'm so relieved—so glad you did speak up."

"Well, I promised to be honest. And I

guess I understand a little more now about what that means."

He put both arms around her shoulders and laughed. "Wait till I tell Philip about this. It's what he's been saying all along."

Beth smiled and relaxed against him. *What a waste of worry we've both been through.* "And now it's your turn, Jarrick."

"For what?"

"To be honest."

He frowned. "But I have been—"

"I'm afraid not," she said, eyebrows arched.

"I'm sorry, Beth. I don't know what you mean."

"Where are we going, Jarrick? I think it's high time you let me in on your little secret."

A smile played slowly across his face. "You want to know about the honeymoon destination."

"I think it's best."

He laughed. "I really thought you would have guessed. We're going to Banff. Now mind you, not to that big, fancy chateau. I couldn't afford that. But we'll have a cabin, very comfortable and snug. And there's a dining room in the lodge. So you won't have to worry about a thing."

Beth chuckled. "That's a relief. We'll have a blissful first week together before you're introduced to my cooking." She looked up into his smiling eyes. "That's lovely. It's perfect."

She paused a moment, looking into the distance. "You know what, Jarrick, I do believe Banff is where my aunt, the first Elizabeth Thatcher, went on her honeymoon." She turned back to look into his face. "I love that you chose it for us too."

It was silly, perhaps, for a ride to be waiting at the bottom of the stairs to carry Beth the short distance to the church, but dear, thoughtful Frank had arranged to borrow the company car and for Alberto to drive it. He had insisted that she shouldn't have to worry about the hem of her wedding gown on the dirt road.

With Julie behind her, Beth adjusted the layers of the full skirt and stepped out onto the stairs for the last time as Miss Elizabeth Thatcher. But her eye was drawn instantly to two vehicles parked in front of the school building. *Robert's hearing. Oh dear, it's going on now.* Beth had somehow forgotten that Robert was facing his accusers today. In all of the last-minute scurrying, she had even forgotten to pray for him as promised.

Heavenly Father, she hurried, *please help the truth to come out for Robert today. Please give him people to speak on his behalf so that justice is done—so that Fred Green, or whoever started this vicious lie, doesn't all but destroy his life.*

But who could stand with Robert? Almost everyone who might speak for him was already waiting at the church. *And the wedding ceremony is about to begin,* she thought in a panic.

Beth turned helplessly back to her doorway and Julie, who was looking puzzled, then peeved. Their father was at the bottom of the stairs waiting to help her into the car. She smiled weakly at him. Even at this distance she could tell his eyes were misted with emotion at seeing his daughter wearing the same dress in which he'd married Mother.

But just at that moment Beth recalled the look on Jarrick's face as he described being unjustly accused by his own townsfolk and the many years of hurt a false accusation could cause. *And Robert's accusation is much worse. What if he's convicted, sent away wrongly?*

An image of the church now crowded with family and friends flashed in her mind. *Maybe Jarrick is already standing at the front, or is he still waiting in Philip's office?* She swept a finger across the handle of her bouquet, tracing the lines of Molly's handkerchief. *What would Molly do? Would she fail to speak up for someone in need just because it came at such an*

*inopportune moment, even a very difficult time?
Would that break that important second rule?*

Beth moved slowly down the steps, Julie
guarding the gown in the back. Father met her
at the bottom, reaching out to offer his hand,
guiding her to the open car door. Beth slid
onto the seat and bunched the dress around
her while Julie entered on the other side. *What
if I just stop at the school?* She looked down at
her attire, so obviously out of place. *But can
I live with myself if I just ignore this moment?
After all, it's only a dress. But what will everybody think? What will Jarrick's mother say?*

Her ashen face turned toward Father. "I
have to make a stop first," she whispered.

"What . . . what do you mean, my dear?"

"There's something I have to do right
now."

Father was speechless, and Julie stared as
if she'd lost her mind.

"Alberto," Beth pleaded, "can you just
stop first across the street? Please let me out
right on the sidewalk so I don't get any mud
on the dress, but I've got to stop at the school
for just a moment."

"Yes, miss," he answered evenly.

Father's face was full of consternation.
"Oh, Beth, you can't!"

Beth passed the bouquet to Julie. "I have
to, Father. I'll never have another chance.

And it might be enough to change the out-
come of a man's hearing, of his life. There's
no one else to speak up for Robert today.
I can't explain it all just now. You'll have to
trust me."

He shook his head from the front seat.
"Do what you have to do."

The car edged forward at a sharp angle,
making a three-point turn in the street and
drawing to a stop so Beth's door opened
directly next to the wooden walk. Gathering up the folds of lace again, she accepted
Father's help out of the car. She stepped gingerly toward the familiar door, her hand trembling as she opened it.

The sound of conversation came from
Robert's room, and she knocked timidly. A
terse voice said, "Come in."

Beth stepped into the room, and the looks
on the circle of faces could not have been
more flabbergasted. All debate stopped midsentence to take in this bride who had obviously lost her way. Beth's eye caught Robert's,
and she smiled faintly, apologetically. Next to
him sat Ivy, gaping in disbelief.

"I'm so sorry to interrupt, gentlemen,"
Beth began. "I guess it's clear that I have
somewhere else to be just now." She tried a
little laugh, but her mouth was too dry. "I
simply couldn't ignore the fact of this hearing,

and I want to speak on behalf of Mr. Harris Hughes, if I could do so very quickly."

Still without words, the chairman motioned Beth to the front, and she moved forward, willing her body to remain steady. Looking at the stern faces of three strangers, as well as those of the town council, Beth breathed a prayer for courage.

"My name is Elizabeth Thatcher. I'm the second teacher here at our school. I want to state for the record that I have never seen Mr. Harris Hughes engage in any activity that was inappropriate. He has always shown proper decorum and respect in every situation in which I've observed him. I have also been assured by several of his students—those who were nearby as he was tutoring Alice McDermott—that they have never felt he crossed any threshold of impropriety." She cleared her throat, hoping her next words would be effectual. "And although I didn't hear her say this myself, I was told by a very reliable source that Alice McDermott has denied any validity to the charges brought today."

"Is that all, Miss Thatcher?" the chairman asked calmly.

Her mouth opened, then closed again. "I suppose it is. . . . Is there anything you want to ask me?"

"No, I think what you've said is quite sufficient."

Beth nodded.

"Miss Thatcher?" Bill Shaw queried, a lopsided grin on his face.

"Yes?"

"Might it be more appropriate for you to hurry on to the church? No doubt there's a young man very anxious to see you appear."

"Yes, thank you." Beth turned once more to look at Robert and Ivy.

Tears were rolling down the woman's cheeks. *Thank you,* Ivy mouthed silently.

Father was pacing anxiously when Beth emerged, and they hurried into the waiting automobile. The short drive up the hill toward the church was accomplished before she was able to fully answer his questions, to tell him that things had gone well.

"I'm proud of you, darling. I truly am." Then he shook his head again in disbelief. Julie had finally found her tongue, and she put an arm around her sister. "Bethie, I can't believe you did this! You are so *brave!*"

Beth laughed. "That means so much coming from *you,* darling."

At the church, Beth took Father's offered arm, and Julie again lifted the skirt as they moved across the grass. Beth stepped into the foyer and allowed Julie to quickly adjust the folds. She could hear Rose Shaw beginning Wagner's Bridal Chorus on the organ. *It's time. This is it.*

Soon Julie was moving forward with Will Thornton. Then Marnie followed on Roland's arm. Beth glanced up at Father, and he patted her hand.

She took her first steps into the doorway of the sanctuary and gasped. There, centered on the platform, Beth saw a lovely white arbor made of silver birch boughs. At the base on either side was a cluster of small birch stumps bound together, anchoring the archway. "Father?"

He lingered in place for a moment longer, allowing Beth to take it in. "Frank got us all involved in making it. He was sure you'd think it was just right," he murmured.

"Oh, Father, it is. It truly is."

Chapter 28

Beth's eyes focused on Jarrick throughout the ceremony, as if there were no one else in the sanctuary. She listened breathlessly as he pledged his love to her and then repeated her own promise back to him. It seemed that in no time they were walking down the aisle, this time together. *Together. For the rest of our lives,* her heart sang, as she smiled at her family and friends on each side who were celebrating with them.

Since there was no other place to hold such a large reception—not even the school classrooms—the church women carried in coffee and cake and laid it all out on tables in the back for folks to serve themselves. A second table was set up on the platform, where Jarrick, Beth, and their wedding attendants were seated in front of the lovely silver-birch arch. Beth kept a hand around her new husband's elbow, not willing to let him go even for a moment. *We're married now!* she thought every time their gazes met.

Looking out at the assembly of well-wishers seated in the pews, she noticed Robert and Ivy slip in among them. Discreetly raising a hand to them, Beth caught Ivy's eye and smiled. Ivy waved back, nodding her message that all had gone well. *Oh, thank You, God.* Beth sighed with relief.

Marnie walked past on Harold's arm, wearing the bridesmaid's dress that also had served her as a wedding gown, clearly flourishing in her new role.

Face after familiar face emerged from the crowd as Beth considered the women here whom she had grown to cherish. Eliza sitting next to Dillard at the front—actively working in ministry alongside her husband in Lethbridge and opening her home graciously to strangers. And in the same row, Esther with her husband, Bardo, their three children beside their new papa. Esther, who had found a new life after the heartrending loss of the first man she loved. Esther, who had once thanked Beth for being used by God to renew her own faith through acting out stories with the children during Bible club.

Seated in the row behind, Beth noticed

that Kate had come with Edward. Kate, the quiet china doll so enraptured by her boisterous fiancé, would clearly follow him anywhere. And Beth noticed Ruth and Abigail standing at the food table, serving once again. Beth contemplated the teahouse, which no doubt had not been Abigail's first choice of occupation, and yet the resolute woman was bearing up well in her entrepreneurial endeavor, continuing to serve and to love in her community.

The thought brought Beth's attention to Molly, who had lived through the death of her beloved Bertram and then moved forward with strength to become the stand-in mother for Teddy and Marnie, as well as a wide-eyed young teacher new to the West. Molly's marriage to Frank would have seemed unbelievable just two short years ago, and yet they had each seen past cultural differences and become a tender couple, caring for one another in these later years.

Beth whispered to Jarrick that she would return very soon, a promise with a smile. She rose and went first to her mother, offering a long embrace with words of thanks for all she and Father had done in raising her to know God. Then Beth approached Jarrick's mother. "Mother Thornton," she said, "I wanted to thank you for your wonderful son—for all you've done to train him up in the way he should go." Surprised, the woman accepted Beth's warm embrace.

Wending her way farther through the crowd, Beth spoke words of gratitude to various others for sharing this ceremony with Jarrick and her.

Soon she and Molly were hugging, crying a little, then laughing because they were crying. Beth told her again how much her friendship meant to "an entirely inexperienced young woman with a call to teach in the West."

Joining Jarrick at the table on the stage again, Beth was thrilled to take his hand once more. She brushed away a tear, casting another look around the room. These women—so varied in personality but similar in the difficult lives they shared—would continue to nurture and care for their families and, each in her own way, their community.

And now, with unrestrained joy, Beth would remain in the West, able to consider herself a woman of the Canadian frontier. She knew it would not be a glamorous role, sometimes stretching her beyond what she thought she was capable of, and yet she was honored to take up the mantle, following her new husband, who was following their heavenly Father—wherever He would lead them.

About the Authors

Bestselling author **Janette Oke** is celebrated for her significant contribution to the Christian book industry. Her novels have sold more than thirty million copies, and she's the recipient of the ECPA President's Award, the CBA Life Impact Award, the Gold Medallion, and the Christy Award. Her novel *When Calls the Heart*, which introduces the elder Elizabeth Thatcher and Wynn Delaney, was the basis for a Hallmark Channel film and television series of the same name. The RETURN TO THE CANADIAN WEST series tells even more of the Thatcher family's story. Janette and her husband, Edward, live in Alberta, Canada.

Laurel Oke Logan, daughter of Edward and Janette Oke, is the author of *Janette Oke: A Heart for the Prairie*, as well as the novels *Dana's Valley*, *Where Courage Calls*, and *Where Trust Lies*, which she co-wrote with her mom. Laurel's growing family includes six children, their spouses, and three grandsons.

More From Janette Oke and Laurel Oke Logan

When new schoolteacher Beth Thatcher is assigned a post in a remote mining community, her courage—and her heart—will be tested in ways she never expected.

Where Courage Calls
RETURN TO THE CANADIAN WEST #1

After a year of teaching in the Canadian West, Beth Thatcher no longer feels at home among her Eastern family. Torn between two worlds, will she find the place where her heart belongs?

Where Trust Lies
RETURN TO THE CANADIAN WEST #2

You May Also Enjoy . . .